continued . . .

"Woven with magic, handsome heroes, lovely heroines, oodles of fun, and plenty of romance . . . a typical Lynn Kurland book—beautifully written with an enchanting, entertaining, and just plain wonderful story line."
—*Romance Reviews Today*

Till There Was You

"Expertly mixes past with present to prove that love endures all things and outlasts almost everything, including time itself. With an eye to detail and deliciously vivid imagery, this paranormal tale of matchmaking comes fully to life . . . Spellbinding and lovely, this is one story readers won't want to miss."
—*Romance Reader at Heart*

"A fantastic story that will delight both readers who are familiar with the families and those who aren't."
—*Romance Reviews Today* (Perfect 10 Award)

"An amusing time-travel romance starring a terrific, fully developed hero whose good intentions present and past are devastated by love . . . fast-paced."
—*Midwest Book Review*

With Every Breath

"As always, [Kurland] delivers a delightful read!"
—*RT Book Reviews* (4 stars)

"Kurland is a skilled enchantress . . . *With Every Breath* is breathtaking in its magnificent scope, a true invitation to the delights of romance."
—*Night Owl Reviews*

When I Fall in Love

"Kurland infuses her polished writing with a deliciously dry wit, and her latest time-travel love story is sweetly romantic and thoroughly satisfying."
—*Booklist*

"The continuation of a wonderful series, this story can also be read alone. It's an extremely good book."
—*Affaire de Coeur*

Much Ado in the Moonlight

"A pure delight."

—*Huntress Book Reviews*

"A consummate storyteller . . . [Kurland] will keep the reader on the edge of their seat, unable to put the book down until the very last word."

—*ParaNormal Romance*

Dreams of Stardust

"Kurland weaves another fabulous read with just the right amounts of laughter, romance, and fantasy."

—*Affaire de Coeur*

"Kurland crafts some of the most ingenious time-travel romances readers can find . . . wonderfully clever and completely enchanting."

—*RT Book Reviews*

A Garden in the Rain

"Kurland laces her exquisitely romantic, utterly bewitching blend of contemporary romance and time travel with a delectable touch of tart wit, leaving readers savoring every word of this superbly written romance."

—*Booklist*

"Kurland is clearly one of romance's finest writers—she consistently delivers the kind of stories readers dream about. Don't miss this one."

—*The Oakland Press*

From This Moment On

"A disarming blend of romance, suspense, and heartwarming humor, this book is romantic comedy at its best."

—*Publishers Weekly*

"A deftly plotted delight, seasoned with a wonderfully wry sense of humor and graced with endearing, unforgettable characters."

—*Booklist*

continued . . .

ROSES IN MOONLIGHT

LYNN KURLAND

JOVE BOOKS, NEW YORK

THE BERKLEY PUBLISHING GROUP
Published by the Penguin Group
Penguin Group (USA) Inc.
375 Hudson Street, New York, New York 10014, USA

USA | Canada | UK | Ireland | Australia | New Zealand | India | South Africa | China

Penguin Books Ltd., Registered Offices: 80 Strand, London WC2R 0RL, England
For more information about the Penguin Group, visit penguin.com.

ROSES IN MOONLIGHT

A Jove Book / published by arrangement with Kurland Book Productions, Inc.

Jove Books are published by The Berkley Publishing Group.
JOVE® is a registered trademark of Penguin Group (USA) Inc.
The "J" design is a trademark of Penguin Group (USA) Inc.

For information, address: The Berkley Publishing Group,
a division of Penguin Group (USA) Inc.,
375 Hudson Street, New York, New York 10014.

ISBN: 978-0-515-15346-0

PUBLISHING HISTORY
Jove mass-market edition / May 2013

PRINTED IN THE UNITED STATES OF AMERICA

10 9 8 7 6 5 4 3 2 1

Cover art by Jim Griffin.
Cover design by George Long.

To my cousin-in-law Claire B.,
who answers all my questions about Britishisms
with such unflinching courage and patience

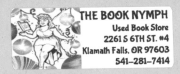
Prologue

A tall, distinguished-looking man of a certain age walked along the back streets of London, his kilt snapping briskly thanks to his haste, his dress sword avoiding the same only because he kept his hand on the hilt. No sense in terrifying the locals prematurely, was his thinking. He had business down the way and suspected he would need every ounce of Scottish canniness to see that task accomplished.

He dodged native and tourist alike who were apparently enjoying leisurely strolls before retiring. He, however, had all his attentions bent on reaching his destination whilst his victim—er, his prey—er . . . well, whilst who was loitering within the building in question hadn't managed to pry himself off the stage and scamper out the nearest exit. Given that getting the man off the stage would be the biggest obstacle they faced, he supposed perhaps his concern for haste was unfounded. But he hurried just the same.

He leapt up the stairs leading to the theater like a hart, then walked through the gates until he entered the darkened building itself. There was no audience there, no lads manning the lights, no actors waiting in the wings, for there was no play being performed that night.

At least no play that any mortal would have seen.

The boards were indeed being trodden, but he temporarily ignored the man standing on that stage in favor of a bekilted lad standing in the shadows, shifting purposefully. He frowned thoughtfully as he considered the sight. The shifting was less purposeful than it was nervous, but that was unsurprising. Hugh McKinnon, laird of the clan McKinnon in days long past, was a fine swordsman and a canny warrior, but when it came to their current business, he always tended to become a little uneasy.

But he, Ambrose MacLeod, laird of the clan MacLeod during the glorious flowering of the sixteenth century, did not shift unless it was to simply avoid the thrust of an Englishman's blade whilst saving himself the trouble of drawing his own. He strode purposefully across a floor that was much cleaner than it would have been in his day to stand next to his compatriot. Hugh looked at him, his ruddy complexion rather more pale than Ambrose would have cared to see it.

"I've no liking for this locale," Hugh whispered. "Too many Englishmen loitering about for my taste."

Ambrose shared Hugh's distaste, but it couldn't be helped. "We'll see to our business quickly, then hie ourselves back to the proper side of Hadrian's Wall."

"It pains me to admit as much," Hugh admitted, looking pained indeed, "but I do wish we had Fulbert de Piaget along for this. At least he might have given that blighter up there a proper bit of trouble."

"Fulbert is, as you know, offering his services to the newly made Earl of Artane," Ambrose said, "even though I imagine young Stephen can manage well enough on his own."

"Ha," Hugh said derisively. "Fulbert is likely spending less time offering aid than he is sitting in front of a hot fire with a hefty mug of ale. I suspect he simply didn't want to burden his delicate ears with the bleating of that prancing fool yonder."

Ambrose studied the man striding about on the stage, pausing frequently to trot out various soliloquies, trying them on to apparently see which one suited him best. It was true that the man was absolutely riveting on stage, but equally apparent that he would be perfectly foul on the ground.

"Should we have looked harder for an appropriate ancestor?" Hugh asked doubtfully. "That one's a bit full of himself, wouldn't you say?"

"It carries him confidently on the stage," Ambrose said.

"But it isn't as if we lack for Scottish players," Hugh countered.

"We do of that vintage. And as you well know, we need an Englishman for this part."

"An Englishman?" Hugh echoed pointedly.

Ambrose sighed heavily. "Very well, I'll admit he isn't technically an Englishman."

Hugh stuck his fingers in his ears briefly and sang part of a heroic battle anthem. Then he scowled at Ambrose. "That was to cleanse the palate. I don't want to think about where he was born."

"I can't blame you, my friend." Ambrose glanced at the man on the stage. "Nay, Hugh, this is what's required. Unfortunately, no matter from whence he hails, I fear this one will be hard to manage."

"I suppose that's one way to put it," Hugh muttered.

Ambrose turned his full attentions to the spectacle. He was impressed in spite of himself by the lighting the shade had created for himself. That was a lad who knew which side of his profile was the best and wasn't afraid to display it.

"Did you tell him we wanted to speak to him?" Ambrose murmured, so as not to disturb the show.

Hugh nodded. "I caught him at the stage door and said we wanted to meet him in the pub at midnight."

"Was he amenable to the suggestion?"

"Nay, but I told him I'd stick him if he didn't come."

"And?"

Hugh lifted his eyebrows briefly. "He might be carrying a sword up there, Ambrose, but it isn't sharp, if you know what I mean."

Ambrose did. "Very well, then, let's go await him down the street."

The crowds outside the Globe had thinned to a mere handful of the braver sort, which made it easier to wend their way to the nearest pub, The Bard's Board and Keg. Ambrose settled himself in a secluded corner with Hugh, then plucked a mug of ale out of the air to his right. He indulged in a sip or two, then sat back and looked at his compatriot.

"Aye?"

"This is a tricky one, isn't it?" Hugh ventured. "Complicated."

Ambrose had to concede that point. There were times, he had to admit, that endeavoring to keep the strands of time woven in their proper order was a dodgy business indeed. And if orchestrating events in their proper order wasn't delicate enough, trying to add in the choices of two headstrong mortals . . .

It was enough to lead a shade to thinking perhaps 'twas time to hang up Cupid's arrows.

If the shade in question had been made of lesser stuff, of course, which he was not. He was already sitting up straight, naturally, but he mentally threw back his shoulders and steeled his resolve. The souls in question were difficult and stubborn, but when pointed in the right direction they would no doubt do what needed to be done.

There was honor at stake, after all.

"I don't like it here, Ambrose," Hugh said suddenly, clutching his own mug of ale in his hands. "Still too many bloody Brits cluttering up the place."

"It can't be helped," Ambrose said, though he had to admit he shared the other's unease. If he'd had a back in which a dagger might have successfully rested, he might have been somewhat tempted to take the odd glance over his shoulder. But since he was leaning back against a sturdy pub bench, he felt very confident in ignoring any unusual and unaccustomed unease.

Hugh gulped.

Ambrose looked up to see a man swathed in Elizabethan finery sweeping in through the front door. *Through* being, of course, exactly what he was doing. Apparently he hadn't been willing to wait for someone of a more corporeal nature to open up for him.

"Perhaps we should have looked harder," Hugh whispered.

"We did," Ambrose murmured into his cup. "That one is the necessary lad."

Hugh sighed as the man flung his cape back over his shoulders and glanced disdainfully over the crowd as if he searched for someone in particular. Or two someones, rather.

He pursed his lips with the vigor of a man who had sucked on a particularly tart lemon, then strode across the floor as if he were performing in a particularly passionate scene. He came to an abrupt halt next to the table and looked down his long, pointed nose at them.

"I am Sir Richard Drummond," he said, the crispness of his consonants slicing through the air like a finely sharpened blade. "I was told I must meet you here." He looked around, then lifted an eyebrow as he reached out to swipe a finger across the table. "In this *place*."

"I can't believe this," Hugh muttered under his breath. "I could have found someone more suitable at Euro Disney."

Ambrose looked at Hugh in surprise, then had to stifle a laugh. He was inclined to agree, but decided discretion dictated that he refrain. He looked up at their guest. "How kind of you to join us."

Sir Richard sniffed. "Threats were issued, threats I didn't have the time or the desire to address properly."

Ambrose ignored Hugh's snort and gestured to a chair he conjured up for their guest. "Please sit and take your ease."

Sir Richard examined the chair for dust, took off his gloves and brushed at it a time or two, then sat down and spread out as if he'd been Henry VIII himself sitting on his throne. "Well," he drawled, reaching up and drawing a heavy pewter mug from a spot to his right and imbibing heartily, "what did you need me for?" He looked over the rim of his mug. "Costuming ideas? You both look as if you could use a fair bit of aid."

Ambrose's hand shot out and grasped Hugh by the forearm almost before the thought to do so occurred to him. Hugh glared at him, then deliberately folded his arms over his chest. Ambrose chose to ignore the fact that his left hand was tucked under his right arm where it might most readily grasp the dagger tucked into his belt. Hugh, as many a foe had found out too late, was ambidextrous. Ambrose turned back to Sir Richard.

"I believe, friend, that our concerns might turn out to rest a little closer to home than you know."

Sir Richard pursed his lips. "I have no idea what you're talking about."

"Don't you?"

"I most certainly do not."

Ambrose set his cup aside and placed his hands on the table in plain sight. "Then allow me to enlighten you. We've a task for you to accomplish—"

"What!" Sir Richard said, drawing himself up haughtily. "Give me a task, you say? You, sir, have overstepped your bounds."

Ambrose continued without hesitation. "There are two who must be brought together."

"Who? Are we interbreeding again with McKinnons and MacLeods?" Richard asked, lacing his tone with a heavy layer of disdain. "Oh, yes, that's right. That's what you two are, isn't it?"

Ambrose stopped Hugh before he had even begun to lunge. That gave him something to do besides fling his own sweet self forward. He looked at Richard coolly.

"There is a goodly work for you to do."

"Unless it requires my presence in Drury Lane, my good man, it is not goodly."

"Something even more interesting than that," Ambrose assured him.

"I can't imagine what."

"Then allow me to tell you," Ambrose said pleasantly. "There is a particular lad who needs to meet a certain lassie at a distinct point in time. There will be things that try to get in the way of that."

"Good sense?" Sir Richard asked politely.

"Your big nose," Hugh shot back, "poking itself in places it don't belong whilst ignoring the places it should be poking itself!"

Sir Richard shot him a look of undisguised antipathy, then turned back to Ambrose. "Do tell."

Ambrose slid a carefully cut piece of parchment across the table and waited until Sir Richard had read it before he spoke.

"There are the particulars for the young woman. On the reverse is a description of the young man. Try not to mistake him for anyone else."

Sir Richard curled his lip. "I doubt that's possible, unless he's up to his usual tricks of disguise."

"One never knows," Ambrose conceded. He looked at Sir Richard pointedly. "Fail, and you know what the reward will be."

Sir Richard looked for the briefest of moments slightly pale, but that passed quickly enough. He tossed both the parchment and his mug into oblivion, then rose. He wrapped his cape around himself and looked down at them coldly.

"I will do what you have requested because it suits me," he said. "No other reason."

And with that, he swept out of the pub. Ambrose watched him go and considered the encounter. It hadn't gone as well as he'd hoped nor as poorly as he'd feared. He sat back and reached for his ale. He would, of course, oversee the entire affair as best he could, but there were things he simply wouldn't be able to control, places he perhaps could have gone but dared not go.

"Does he know?" Hugh asked, his face scrunched up thoughtfully. "What will happen if he fails?"

"Of course he knows."

"He isn't happy about it."

Ambrose looked at him. "He's an Englishman." He paused. "Well, at least he's playing an Englishman as a permanent role."

"He's good at it."

Ambrose smiled. "He certainly would like to be, I imagine. We might have to make certain he's about his business properly at first, but I daresay with what he has at stake, he won't shirk his duties."

Hugh shook his head. "Ambrose, I'll tell ye plain. I'm happier when things are a bit more removed from where we stand."

"And speaking of that," Ambrose said brightly, "shall we return to the Globe and see how our current Drummond is taking these recent tidings we've given him?"

"Only if I can fling things at him from the floor."

"Why not?"

Ten minutes later, Ambrose was standing again in the shadows watching Richard Drummond chew the scenery. He was no longer even attempting to restrain his ego. He was absolutely furious.

Ambrose smiled.

All was as it should be.

Of course, there were the usual things that still concerned him, namely trying to bring together two rather stubborn souls who might not particularly want to be brought together. But in this case, there were things that hung in the balance: lives that depended on the cooperation and, aye, it had to be said, the affection of those two sterling souls. And Richard Drummond knew it as well as anyone else.

Ambrose conjured himself up a comfortable chair. He had the feeling it was going to be a long night.

Chapter 1

Samantha Josephine Drummond set her suitcase upright, lifted her face to the sky, and took a deep breath of freedom.

Well, she was actually only looking at a ceiling and sampling nothing more rarified than the air inside King's Cross station, but she wasn't going to complain. She was standing alone in the midst of a crowd and life was very good.

She looked around herself to get her bearings, then glanced reluctantly at the small booklet of instructions in her hand. She supposed the fact that she was holding on to that sort of thing was her own fault. She had a smartphone and knew how to use it, and she was perfectly capable of keeping track of a plane ticket and money for a cab. Unfortunately her parents were stuck in a time warp where she was still twelve and they were eternally in their late thirties and she allowed them to keep on with it because it was easier that way.

Or at least she had until her plane had touched down on British soil. Things were going to be different from now on. As soon as she figured out where she was going.

She had another look at the little album in her hands. It had obviously been made by someone with a predilection for grunge-style scrapbooking paper and rubber stamps. At least this one had taken pleasure in her work. Samantha had, over the course of her twenty-six years, been gifted with an appalling number of similar books, though she couldn't remember any in the past that had been fashioned with such care. She could only imagine the comments that had been made during the crafting of those life aids by the graduate assistants gang-pressed into doing so.

She checked her map, had another look around to make sure she was pointing in the right direction, then took hold of the handle of her suitcase and dragged it along behind her. She wasn't unused to the number of people she had to weave her way through, but it was a little disconcerting to hear so many other tongues than English. She had to admit she was rather relieved to find her train and get herself into a seat on it with a minimum of fuss.

The train pulled away from the station and she had the oddest sensation of leaving her known life behind. It was even stronger than what she'd felt as her plane had taken off from the States. She'd been to London several times with her parents for various reasons, but this was something else entirely. This was just her on her own. She supposed Newcastle upon Tyne wasn't the most glamorous spot in England, but it was easy to get to other places from it and it boasted a couple who had been willing to have her come house-sit for them for the summer.

And it was close to Scotland.

It was probably better not to think about that at the moment on the off chance some do-gooder thought she was about to start hyperventilating.

She looked out the window and happily watched the scenery rush by as she contemplated the miracles that had happened to get her where she was at present.

It had been her brother, of all people, to plant the first seed of subversiveness in her head. That was surprising given that she couldn't say that she and Gavin were particularly close. He had left home when she'd been eight, scampering off to England to study art in London, then fall effortlessly into the cushy job of gallery manager for a woman who had subsequently retired and left him for all intents and purposes as the owner. He was almost as bad as their parents in treating her as if she were a perpetual child, though it wasn't as though they spent enough time together for him to have any other opinion. Until his last visit home, of course, when he had apparently decided it was time for her to make a few changes to her life.

They had been suffering through yet another miserable Thanksgiving family gathering when he had casually pulled a book out of his stylish leather portfolio. Samantha didn't really believe in paranormal happenings, but she couldn't deny that a hush had fallen over the room, as if something monumental was about to happen.

Gavin had started to hand her a book, but her mother had intercepted it before Samantha could touch it. Gavin had frowned, but there was nothing to be done about it. When Louise McKinnon Drummond wanted something, she always got it. Samantha had watched her mother examine the cover of that rather musty old tome on Victorian ivory buttons, then toss it Samantha's way with an uninterested sniff.

"Already read it," she had said.

Samantha had thanked Gavin for something new to read, managed to get through the rest of the evening, then carried the book up to her room—on the top floor, of course. She'd shut the door, then sat on her bed for a few minutes, trying to still her rapidly beating heart. She'd finally opened the book and read the note hidden inside the front cover, taped carefully under the dust jacket.

Have clients in Newcastle who need a house sitter every summer. Interested?

She'd felt faint. Gavin was a boor and a cad, true, but he wasn't an idiot. He had managed to escape their stuffy little East Coast college town, after all, and get himself out of the country. Of course, he'd known full well that he was leaving behind two sisters who would never have his freedom. Well, Sophronia had managed to escape as well, but she was another story entirely. Gavin had known that she, Samantha, had always been and would always be her parents' last, best hope for the perfect child. Rapunzel had been a world traveler compared to how locked down she'd been her entire life.

Interested?

No, she hadn't been interested, she'd been breathless. A desperate hope had bloomed inside her that she might finally manage to get out from under her parents' collective thumbs.

She hadn't managed it that first summer; she'd been working like a slave for her mother's latest exhibition of fine Victorian antiquities. But she'd gotten a message to her brother that next Thanksgiving, a note taped to the bottom of the plate sporting canned cranberry sauce their mother wouldn't have touched if it had been the last thing in the house left to eat. Gavin had sent an email to the appropriate party, winked at her, then helped himself to the rest of the cranberry sauce.

All of which had led her to where she was, watching the train pull into a station she'd never seen before and wondering if she shouldn't just rip up the pages in her current journal that spelled out every step she was supposed to take during every day of the three months she was to spend in England so she could just do what she wanted to do instead.

She considered, then slipped the book back into her bag. She would rip later, when she could take a penknife to the book and do a proper job of it. It was a pretty journal, so she thought she actually might like to use the rest of it.

She slung her backpack over her shoulder, pulled her suitcase down from overhead, then got off the train and looked around her.

Unfortunately, the first thing that caught her eye was a grinning idiot holding a bouquet of flowers in one hand—cheap ones, she could see that from where she stood—and a sign in the other that read, *Samantha Josephine Drummond, your carriage awaits!*

She almost turned around and got back onto the train.

She could hardly believe her eyes, though she supposed she shouldn't have been surprised. Theodore Alexander Mollineux IV, the fly in her ointment, the suspicious substance in her soup, the annoying insect that kept buzzing around her loudly without really making the commitment to land. She'd heard he planned a summer internship in England and she'd been told it would be in Newcastle, but she had clung to the hope that he would forget she was going to be within shouting distance.

She supposed, looking at it with a jaundiced eye, that he hadn't come to England merely to intern. Given what she knew of his family and hers, he had likely been assigned the task of not only keeping an eye on her but convincing her to marry him. Her father thought he was just the sort of young man to take her in hand and show her who was boss, and his father thought she was just the sort of young woman who needed a bit of bossing.

Not if she had anything to say about it.

Never mind that she'd only managed to dredge up the courage to decide that in the spring. She'd been plotting for weeks how her life would change once she was on her own. Planes and trains had only been the beginning of what she was sure would be an adventure she would never forget.

And with any luck, she would be telling her parents all about it via email while she lived happily in a very small house in a coastal fishing village where access to the Internet was limited to satellite cards.

But first she had to get past the test that was awaiting her there on the platform. She closed her eyes briefly, then stepped away from the train and walked over to the man she would ditch as soon as humanly possible. More difficult was to avoid Dory's questing lips, but she managed that as well.

"Let's not," she demurred.

"Oh, you may have a point there," he said, in an affected British accent that she was sure he thought displayed his blue blood to its best advantage. "When in Jolly Olde England, do as the natives do, eh?"

"Oh, yes," she agreed quickly. She traded him her suitcase for the sign—which she murmured appreciatively over before rolling it up and stuffing it in the first garbage can she saw—and the flowers, which she didn't bother to smell. They were carnations, which made her sneeze. She'd been actively avoiding dating Dory Mollineux and his carnations for almost a year. She would be, she had to admit, damned if she was going to find herself saddled with him now that she was so close to freedom.

"We'll take a taxi," he announced. "We could have walked if you were a bit less fragile, but your parents made me promise not to let you overtax yourself."

"My parents?" she echoed.

"The Cookes are wonderful people," he continued, as if he hadn't heard her. "I'm sure you'll get along famously."

Samantha managed to keep from gritting her teeth because

she had a lifetime of practice. She was not fragile; she was frustrated by her current life situation. She was also hardly able to believe that she was listening to Dory talk about her employers. The only way he would have known anything about them was if he had visited them to relate heaven only knew what sort of personal details about her. She imagined he had a list and that her parents had been the authors of it. The only thing she could hope for was that her brother had taken the trouble to tell the Cookes to reserve judgment until they met her. They had been willing to hire her, so perhaps that told her everything she needed to know.

She let Dory carry on the conversation because it was easier that way. Besides, he was very fond of the sound of his own voice, and since he was an expert on every subject and not shy about discussing those subjects, there was much to be fond of.

It was unfortunate, actually. He was extremely handsome, in a Top-Sider, khaki-trousered, blond-highlighted-hair sort of way. She was half surprised he didn't wear a knitted V-neck vest and carry an old-fashioned cheerleader megaphone. His under-grad degree was in international relations, he had a law degree from Georgetown, and never used either of them. She wasn't quite sure what he did except attend symposiums on various topics ranging from politics to musicology. He was the youngest son of the dean of the college of humanities at the small, exclusive university where her parents both taught, which she supposed was enough for them.

She had managed to avoid him for most of her life because he'd been sent to boarding school at five and had, she was sure, never looked back. In that, she couldn't blame his parents. If she'd been his mother, she would have packed his little suitcase for him herself.

She had wondered more than once over the past year if there was perhaps something wrong with her that she wasn't left giddy by his interest. She was fairly sure that anyone else would have taken one look at Theodore Mollineux and immediately tripped daintily in front of him so he would have had to not only notice her but leap to rescue her from potential injuries. He was rich, handsome, and heavily degreed. Maybe if she'd been able to just convince him to keep his mouth shut so he didn't speak and ruin the illusion, she might have been able to do something more with him than look around for the nearest exit. How she was going to survive an entire summer with him in the same town, she couldn't say.

She was obviously going to have to invent a few disguises in order to elude notice.

The taxi stopped sooner rather than later, which gave her hope for a Dory-free afternoon. She scooted out the door, reached in for her suitcase, then extricated her belongings before Dory had even stopped talking about whatever it was he'd been talking about.

"Thanks," she said with her best smile. "Sure appreciate the rescue. I'm not sure how much we'll get to see of each other . . . here . . ."

She stopped talking partly because he wasn't listening to her and partly because he'd gotten out of the taxi himself.

"I'll be fine from here," she said. "I really appreciate the ride. I'll treat you for scones with clotted cream the very first chance I have."

"Sooner rather than later, because the old man hasn't put my allowance in the bank yet," Dory said. He looked at her with a frown. "Have any cash?"

And there in a nutshell was the reason she had only gone on one date with him. Never mind that her father had handed her a cool hundred on the way out the door to that movie. She was not interested in dating a guy who wasn't prepared to at least fork out cab fare.

She knew she should have simply turned around and walked away, but something stopped her. She wanted to say it was good breeding, but it was probably just her inability to stand up for herself. She muttered uncomplimentary things about herself and Dory both under her breath, set her suitcase on the ground, then pulled her notebook out of her pocket.

There was money there, of course, in almost precisely the right amount for the taxi. Her mother would have determined that ahead of time, of course. Samantha paid the cab driver, then started to put her notebook away. Dory stopped her with his hand on her arm.

"Got to get back to my flat, you know."

She gritted her teeth because she knew she was going to hand him money in the end anyway so there was no point in not handing him money from the start. She dug around in her bag for her secret stash of pound coins her brother had sent her inside a box full of ratty Victorian period costumes their mother wouldn't have touched on pain of death, counted out what she'd handed over the first time, plus a little extra, then put it all into Dory's hand without delay.

"So appreciate the escort," she said waving vaguely in his direction, "but I've got to go. There's no time like the present to make a good impression on the employers."

"Already done that," he said, taking her by the elbow and pulling her toward the door. "Introductions first, then we'll go have lunch."

Not if she could help it. She would bide her time, then make her escape, which would hopefully include being on opposite sides of a sturdy door from him. She didn't argue with Dory as he took her suitcase and gallantly led the way up the two steps to the stoop just outside a dark brown doorway that seemed to blend into the stone of the building it found itself in.

The door opened and a neat, elegant woman in her forties stood there. Samantha was wearing her best work clothes, but she had to admit she had a ways to go if she were ever to stand next to that stylish woman and not feel a little frumpy. Maybe she could spent a little of her carefully hoarded money on something not insisted on by her mother. Nothing said serious scholar, apparently, like dark trousers, a polyester long-sleeved shirt, and sensible walking shoes.

Before Samantha got her mouth open to introduce herself, Dory was doing the honors for her.

"Lydia Cooke, this is Samantha Drummond. Samantha, allow me to present Mrs. Lydia Cooke. Her husband is off in Stratford, making certain their situation is what was promised."

Could the taking of a rolling suitcase and using the heavy, wheeled part to knock a New England blue blood in the face be blamed on jet lag, or would she have to come up with a more drastic malady to excuse her bad behavior? It was excruciating in the extreme to have to listen to Dory continue to tell her details about the Cookes that she was quite certain Mrs. Cooke would have preferred to reveal herself—quite possibly somewhere besides the sidewalk.

"You know, Mr. Mollineux, Miss Drummond looks suddenly quite tired," Mrs. Cooke said, reaching for Samantha's suitcase. "Perhaps she could use a bit of a lie-down, yes?"

"Well," Dory began doubtfully.

Samantha found herself and her suitcase drawn inside the house and Dory forced to step back down onto the sidewalk by the apparently unintimidatable Lydia Cooke.

"It is a long journey from the States," she said easily. "I think she would enjoy a lunch date much more tomorrow." She looked over her shoulder. "Wouldn't you, Samantha?"

Samantha wasn't about to spurn the rescue. "Definitely."

"And so it's settled," Mrs. Cooke said brightly.

"But I have an agenda already planned out," Dory complained. "I don't like to get off track."

"Then perhaps today's schedule could be set aside as a fall-back plan should something else fall through in the future. Do you need to have a taxi called—no, there's one right there waiting for you, Mr. Mollineux. *À bientôt!*"

And with that, she shut the door, paused, then turned and smiled.

"You didn't mind that, did you?"

Samantha tried not to look as pathetically grateful as she felt. "Not a bit."

"Well, some lads working to impress a girl tend to become a little trying," Mrs. Cooke said. "I doubt I dampened his spirits for long. I'll show you to your room, then you can either have that promised lie-down or a tour of the house."

"Thank you, Mrs. Cooke."

She laughed. "It's Lydia, of course. There's no call for formality. And I'll call you Samantha, if you don't mind. A lovely name. Very substantial and powerful."

Samantha felt neither at the moment, but she wasn't going to argue. She picked up her suitcase and followed Lydia up two flights of stairs to a room that resembled every artist's garret she had ever seen depicted in any romantic movie. It wasn't luxurious, but it was charming and comfortingly free of either her parents or any preppy interlopers.

"The bath is across the hall," Lydia said. "Once you've freshened up, come downstairs and I'll show you around."

Samantha thanked her, then waited until she'd shut the door before collapsing on the bed with a happy sigh. She had made it. Against all odds, she had escaped. It was a miracle.

She allowed herself approximately five minutes to simply sit and breathe before she looked around to see what her summer was going to include. She was sitting on a bed that ran north and south in a room where the window was east and the door west. There was no closet or armoire, but she didn't have all that many clothes so she would make do with the pegs on the wall and the very tall, thin dresser tucked into a corner. There was a useful lamp on a table next to the bed and a rug under her feet. She couldn't ask for anything more.

She put her suitcase on the bed, dug around for her tooth-brush, then considered her bag. She never went anywhere without it, ever, but that was simply because she'd grown accustomed to having her life tucked inside it. At the moment, it contained all her money, her passport, and her personal notebook. She didn't suppose anyone would care about it, but she slid it under the bed all the same, used the bathroom, then descended the creaking sets of stairs to the ground floor.

Lydia was in the kitchen, making tea. Samantha joined her at the table and indulged with hardly a pucker. She wasn't much for tea, but when in England . . .

"Your brother says your degrees are in textiles," Lydia said without preamble. "Interesting choice."

"I wasn't given much choice," Samantha admitted. "My mother is—"

"Louise Theodosia McKinnon," Lydia said with a smile. "Yes, I know—and not just from your brother. She has an amazing reputation here in England. The Victorian era is her specialty, isn't it?"

"It is," Samantha admitted. "I came this close to being called Fanny."

Lydia laughed, a sound that was so kind and gentle, Samantha had to smile as well. "No doubt. So, you were lured into the fascinating world of antiques but chose Renaissance England for your master's. Any reason for it?"

"Rebellion," Samantha said before she could stop herself.

And if her mother had any idea just how far she intended to rebel during the summer, she would have collapsed in a professional-looking swoon onto an original, perfectly restored fainting couch.

"I like you already," Lydia said promptly. "We don't have anything very interesting upstairs, but my husband *is* fond of antiques. Let me show you his treasure room and you can tell me all the appalling comments your mother would make about his poor collection. I can guarantee there is nothing there to offend your Elizabethan sensibilities."

Samantha nodded, then left her tea behind and followed her employer up the stairs.

The treasure room was actually much more impressive than advertised. Both her mother and her brother would have been quite happy to poke through things and argue over their value. For herself, she was satisfied to limit herself to identifying the most valuable pieces immediately and heaping praise on her host for their acquisition and the lengths gone to in order to house and display them properly.

Lydia shot her a look of amusement. "It isn't your era, is it?"

None of it's my era was almost out of her mouth before she managed to bite her tongue. No, the Victorian era wasn't her favorite, but that was probably because she'd spent so many hours helping her mother catalogue its remains when she could have been babysitting and making some money. She actually got chills down her spine when she contemplated how many years of indentured servitude she would have been engaging in if she'd actually had to pay for her education instead of getting scholarships and graduate assistantships.

"Gavin would be very impressed, though," Samantha offered. "He loves nineteenth-century silver." That in itself was a surprise given that she'd heard her brother vow as he'd left the house for college that he would never, ever have anything to do with anything that needed to be dusted while wearing gloves.

She understood completely.

"We would like to extend our reach back a bit more in history," Lydia said, "but that would require a better security system, I think. The great houses are very careful about that sort of thing, as you might imagine. Perhaps as time and means allow. And as for you, I think you might want some proper supper before you fall asleep. I'm not sure you'll want to wake up for it later."

"Oh, I think the tea was plenty," Samantha protested. "Or I could go to the grocery—"

"Of course you won't," Lydia said without hesitation. "Room and board is part of our agreement, along with the remuneration. And I think we'll have the odd side job for you now and again. If you can bear to have anything to do with actors or lovers of antiques."

"My brother has a big mouth."

Lydia started to speak, then hesitated. "If I can say this without overstepping my bounds," she said carefully, "I think it's safe to say Gavin simply wants you to be happy and thought he might spare you discomfort if we had some idea of your likes and dislikes before we unintentionally upset you."

Samantha looked at her and tried not to sound defensive. "I'm not really fragile. No matter what they say."

"Oh, I never imagined you were," Lydia said. "But you do look tired. I think rest might be what you need, if I could offer an opinion. Feel free to make yourself at home in the kitchen if you wake in the night."

Samantha parted ways with her at the stairs, thanked her, then trudged up the stairs to her garret with as much spring in her step as she could manage. The thought of bed was almost too irresistible to be ignored.

She walked into her room, then sat down with her gear. She unpacked, because she didn't want her clothes to be too wrinkled, then pulled out a backpack and hung it from a peg. She'd hoped for the occasional opportunity to do a few touristy things and liked to travel light. That would be easier to use than a suitcase.

She took her plane ticket and shoved it in the drawer of the nightstand near her bed. She didn't intend to be using it anytime soon and didn't suppose anyone would want to steal it, even if the Cookes' security system wasn't what it should have been. She pulled her bag from under the bed, unzipped the secret pocket she'd put in behind the regular pocket inside the lining she'd installed herself—there was no sense in not being a decent seamstress if she couldn't revamp things to suit herself—and took out the entirety of her funds.

It wasn't much, just a few hundred pounds Gavin had traded her dollars for at Thanksgiving. He hadn't given her much of an exchange break, she was sure, but she'd been willing to pay for the convenience. She counted it out, considered, then took most of it and looked for someplace to stash it. She finally decided on the underside of the drawer of the nightstand. After securing it there with the small amount of duct tape she never left home without—it was better than a stapler for blown-out seams or unraveled hems—she put her mother's agenda back in her bag along with other necessities and decided it was probably time to sleep while she could.

She got herself ready for bed, then lay there and looked at the ceiling for far longer than she should have. She had made it. She had escaped the confines of her former life and marched boldly into her future life.

She sighed. Perhaps it would turn out to be nothing more interesting than her old life where nothing exciting ever happened to her, but at least that boring life would be happening in a different country and without her parents scrutinizing her every move. She might actually attempt something daring, like leaving the house without checking the weather first, or attending a show with absolutely no educational or career-furthering value whatsoever. It could be very exciting.

She fell asleep smiling.

Chapter 2

There were times a man simply couldn't take any more of the criminal class.

Derrick Cameron stood at the window of a small office overlooking Hyde Park and contemplated the truth of that. He was an ordinary man with ordinary tastes. Good food. A good book. Pleasant company. Of course he wasn't going to argue if someone offered him tickets to Drury Lane or insisted that he shuffle off to supper in the back of a Rolls, but on the whole he preferred dealing with average blokes who worked for what they got and shunned shady dealings. He wasn't at all fond of blighters who took what didn't belong to them, much less tried to sell it to those who should have known better than to buy valuable items from lads with shifty eyes.

He had spent his share of time trying to understand what motivated those who preferred to steal instead of earn, for no other reason than it helped him decide where they might strike next. The unfortunate thing was, in his current business the thugs looked far too much like respectable—even very visible—

citizens of the Commonwealth. That left him shaking his head more often than not.

He supposed it was nothing but his own fault. He had signed on to work for his cousin as part of Cameron Antiquities, Ltd., eight years ago, a year after he'd first clapped eyes on Robert Cameron. There was some history there that he mulled over when he had the leisure to, but thinking about it generally left him shaking his head in disbelief. Today, he didn't particularly feel like making himself dizzy, so he left those contemplations for another time.

He'd spent seven years as part of a very exclusive cadre of six who had formed the nucleus of that particular business. He had always been quite fond of history, but Robert Cameron's passion for it had inspired him to take that fondness to the level of obsession. He had never thought antiques would become his life's work, but they had.

He could identify genuine from fake from ten paces and difficult cases with only a minor examination. His nose twitched when presented with anything pre-Tudor and he could honestly feel his ears begin to perk up when something predated 1400.

Their client list was *very* exclusive and requiring absolute discretion. He had hobnobbed with everyone from the filthy rich to the richly titled, including nobility from several countries. A phone call, a subtle expression of interest, or a discreet note always began the chase and the quarry was always caught and delivered with a minimum of fuss. There wasn't a part of it that he didn't relish, from the research to the schmoozing.

After all, what was there in the world that could possibly be more exciting than finding things that couldn't be found and buying them from souls who didn't want to sell them? Cameron Antiquities's only condition of sale was that the collectors of said unattainable items be thoroughly vetted as to their plans for their acquisitions. He could think of only half a dozen men and women who had failed that test. Their fury had been memorable, but in the end quite futile. Robert Cameron apparently had nerves of steel because in each of those cases, he'd let the rejected applicant breathe out all manner of vile threats without flinching.

Of course, Derrick knew why that was, but that was something else to be thought about later.

Cameron had turned over the business to him the year before. He'd wanted it, of course, badly, for the sheer exhilaration of the chase. What had surprised him, however, was how quickly the role of recoverer of stolen goods had been added to his job description.

Unfortunately, he hadn't been surprised by how much of his time that sort of thing took up. He turned away from the window before he blinded himself with the afternoon summer sunshine. This was absolutely the last case of that nature he would take on. He would solve this bloody problem for the gentleman in question, then turn everything from now on over to Scotland Yard.

He pursed his lips as he walked across the plush carpet of his office, suppressing the urge to curse. Unfortunately, he imagined he wouldn't be calling in any detective inspectors anytime soon. The adrenaline rush he got from undoing the work of bad guys was simply too strong to walk away from.

He opened his door and looked at the collection of souls in the reception area. The offices were stunning, of course, because Cameron Antiquities was only part of the Cameron clan's empire, and he was only a small part of that clan. It was handy, however, to have his office right next door to his cousin's. It made the clients who dared be seen frequenting the place feel pleased to be hobnobbing with Scottish nobility.

Cameron's personal secretary was holding court behind an intimidating antique desk that sported a phone, a dedicated, hack-proof computer, and pictures of her grandchildren. Derrick smiled at her, then looked at the men lounging in the chairs there, flipping through supermarket tabloids and looking like trouble.

The worst sort of trouble, Oliver, looked up from reading apparently about the latest royal intrigues.

"Where're you off to, boss?"

Derrick wondered if he would ever become accustomed to that. Though he had indeed wanted it, that business of Cameron Antiquities, Ltd., and he supposed he'd put enough work into it over the past eight years to accept it almost without flinching, being the owner of it still sat uncomfortably on his shoulders.

Then again, there were no assets in the company to speak of save the power of the Cameron name and the reputation Robert Cameron had built up over the years. Derrick supposed he'd had a hand in that often enough himself not to have it feel like charity.

"I'm not sure yet," he said slowly.

Rufus, their driver extraordinaire, sighed. "I'll consider going to warm up the getaway car."

Derrick smiled briefly, then looked to find his cousin himself, the laird of the clan Cameron, standing at the door to his own office, smirking. Derrick looked at Oliver and Rufus first, because it was simpler.

"I think I'm off on a little explore," he admitted, "but I'm not sure I'll be driving."

Rufus went back to his newspaper, relic that he was. Oliver didn't shift, but he never shifted. He simply watched Derrick with an unblinking stare that had made many a man blurt out his innermost secrets without having to be asked.

"I have my mobile," Oliver said.

"I may be giving you a wee ring on it."

Oliver only lifted one eyebrow, then rose gracefully to his feet. "I'll go recharge the battery then, shall I?"

"You should." He turned and looked at his cousin. "Aye, my laird?"

"Just wondering what you're about," Cameron said with a shrug. "Perhaps you'd like to come inside and tell me about it."

Derrick nodded, then followed Cameron into his office. He shut the door behind himself, then leaned back against it.

"Anything in particular you're curious about?" he asked.

Cameron only sat down on the edge of his desk and smiled pleasantly. "You don't work for me any longer, Derrick, as I believe we've discussed at length."

"Feudal obligation, my laird."

"We're Scots, ye wee fool, not Brits. We call it *fealty* up north."

Derrick would have smiled, but he had little to smile about at the moment. He did nod, though, because he agreed completely. He had certainly spent his share of time south of Hadrian's Wall, but that was years ago, before he'd found it to be a place he didn't want to linger. He was more than happy to cling to national pride.

He shoved his hands into his jeans pockets because that was preferable to wringing them like a fitful alewife.

"You remember that piece of lace that went missing about the time of the troubles with Nathan Ainsworth?"

"Vividly." Cameron studied him for a moment or two in

silence. "It was restored to its proper owner, though, if I'm remembering it aright."

"Briefly," Derrick said grimly. "I had a wee ring from Lord Epworth a few days back, asking if I wouldn't be so good as to track it down for him again."

"And of course you said him nay, because you aren't a private detective and it isn't your affair to help anyone hold on to their priceless treasures," Cameron drawled. "Or do I have that wrong?"

Derrick suppressed the urge to swear. "I said I would think about it."

Cameron laughed. "Of course you did, though I imagine the exact words were, *Of course, Lord Epworth, I would be happy to retrieve it for you.*"

"You know, there are limits to the deference my fealty demands," Derrick said darkly.

"I'm quite sure there are," Cameron agreed. "Very well, so you've turned yourself into a retriever for this poor doddering old Englishman. Why do I have the feeling that isn't the end of the tale?"

"Because that isn't the last thing that's trotted off into the ether as if it had legs."

"Isn't it?"

"You needn't look so nonchalant about this all."

Cameron shrugged. "You'll find it all, I imagine. Not my problem if you don't."

"You know, you would be far less annoying if you could stop exuding that aura of wedded bliss."

"I'm walking the floor with my son every evening as he howls and Geoff Segrave rings to complain because apparently the walls are too thin for his taste," Cameron said mildly. "Is that bliss?"

"I'm sure you're relishing every moment of each."

Cameron hesitated, then smiled. "I can't argue with that, though I think young Breac gives me more pleasure than he does Geoff." He looked at Derrick unflinchingly. "I won't offer aid."

"I wouldn't ask for it."

"But you could."

"And I won't repeat what you would tell me, though I'm sure it would involve foul language."

Cameron tsk-tsked him. "Refuse to aid you after all these

years of faithful service? Never." He folded his arms over his chest and smiled. "Where are you going to start?"

Derrick walked across the floor and collapsed happily in one of the guest chairs in front of the desk. "I've eliminated the usual suspects, leaned on a couple of others, and come up empty-handed." He considered, then looked up at his cousin. "What do you think of actors?"

"Don't ask."

Derrick supposed he deserved that, as well as the smirk that accompanied it, so he refrained from comment. "I have a hunch about something."

"And it involves actors?"

Derrick shrugged. "It might."

"Then if you know where to start, why are you here talking to me?"

"Thought I'd have a bit of train fare from you."

"I imagine you didn't. Are you looking for permission to go make a nuisance of yourself to someone you shouldn't?"

Where to begin? He couldn't believe who he was thinking about investigating. Even voicing the name would leave Cameron looking at him as if he'd lost his wits. He wasn't entirely sure he hadn't, the idea was so daft.

That, and it would lead him back to a place—and to individuals—he most certainly didn't want to encounter again.

He sighed. "I'm not sure about anything."

"You're not a very good liar, you know," Cameron remarked. "I'm surprised James MacLeod hasn't sharpened up that skill on your little jaunts to wherever it is you go."

"And I'm surprised you would want to go anywhere near the topic of where Jamie and I have been going," Derrick said just as mildly.

Cameron smiled. "Touché."

"Touché, indeed," Derrick said, pursing his lips. The occasional trips he made with James MacLeod were adventures, to say the least, but nothing he could talk about with anyone but the man standing in front of him. He scowled at his cousin. "It isn't as if I haven't given you a full report about every trip, just to satisfy your unwholesome curiosity about times and dangers not your own."

Cameron held up his hands in surrender. "I'm far past having the stomach for anything but continuing to woo my stunning wife and corral my rambunctious son. You can jaunt all you like. I'm assuming you haven't found anything on your journeys that will aid you in your current quest to retrieve missing lace."

"Nay, nothing," Derrick said with a sigh.

He had to suppress a yawn as well, but in his defense, he was bone weary from trotting back to a fairly respectable reenactment of sixteenth-century Scotland with James MacLeod the previous weekend, just to pop in on one of the man's ancestors. He wasn't sure how Jamie managed his boundless amounts of energy and enthusiasm. Just tagging along after the man for any length of time at all was exhausting. Crossing swords with him was terrifying and trying to keep up with his peculiarly accented Gaelic headache-inducing. If he hadn't spent the past nine years shadowing Robert Cameron, he never would have managed the latter.

He didn't particularly care to think about where he'd learned the swordplay—he still had the shadows of bruises and hints of scars to show for that—and there were times he heartily regretted ever having set foot on MacLeod soil and coming face-to-face with the laird of the keep there.

Then again, it made chasing down thugs seem like a relaxing afternoon spent lounging in front of the telly.

He looked at Cameron. "I think this could become rather messy."

"Could it?"

"Very bad publicity for someone."

"But you don't intend for that someone to be you."

Derrick took a deep breath. "No, I don't. Wouldn't want to sully the Cameron name."

Cameron only smiled. "Of course not."

"My laird might take me out and hack me to bits otherwise."

"I'm sure you live in fear." He rubbed his hands together purposefully. "So, what do you need on this little adventure of yours?"

Derrick hesitated. He needed backup, true, and the lads that worked for him were at his disposal, equally true, but he didn't want to leave his cousin without any sort of security. And, after all, Cameron had been the one to gather to himself that collection of lads whose loyalty was unquestionable, who would have done anything for him, who had knelt before him in a particularly medieval way and pledged him a very formal sort of fealty.

Derrick considered the list. Ewan was their cousin, his and Cameron's, and could have been mistaken for a lighthearted twit. Derrick knew what he was capable of in a tight spot, though, because he had been the beneficiary of that more than once. Then there was Oliver, whose murky past was an asset rather than a liability, and Rufus, who looked every inch the very skilled rugby player he'd been in a former life, and Peter, who floated through life as if he lived for nothing more than a delicate artist's life but who was Derrick's lad of choice in a good brawl.

"Take Oliver."

Derrick looked at Cameron quickly. "But you—"

"Have a perfectly terrifying security detail," Cameron said with a shrug, "all of whom have seen battle in one form or another and haven't a clue as to who I am in truth. Sunny and I are perfectly safe. Besides, the lads have been working for you for almost a year now. How is this different?"

Derrick sighed. "I don't know. It feels dodgier than usual for some reason."

"Then take Oliver for security and Ewan for his charm. Or spare yourself the annoyance and leave Ewan in Scotland. Either way, call on the lads as you need to, of course." He studied Derrick for a moment or two in silence. "What exactly is it that bothers you about this?"

Derrick dragged his hand through his hair, then looked at his cousin. "Have you ever felt like Fate was breathing down your neck?"

Cameron looked at him for a moment or two with absolutely no expression on his face, then he laughed. He was still laughing as Derrick cursed him and left his office. He pulled the door shut quietly behind him instead of slamming it because it was his laird inside, after all, and he was nothing if not a deferent vassal. He looked at Oliver, who had apparently found a plug next to a comfortable chair.

"Let's go."

Oliver unplugged his phone and got smoothly to his feet, his expression utterly impassive. Oliver at his most enthusiastic, as it happened. Derrick said good-byes all around and walked with Oliver from the building. He waited until they were outside before he looked at his partner in anti-crime.

"We're going after the lace."

"I suspected as much. North?"

"North."

"Taking the Vanquish, are we?"

"No," Derrick said, with feeling. "I don't want some random thug dinging it."

"Very well, I'll meet you at the station, what?"

"That'd be lovely."

"Destination?"

"Newcastle, but we'd best buy tickets for Edinburgh."

"Throw 'em off the scent, eh?"

Derrick grunted. "Somehow, I doubt anyone's going to be following us."

"Best to be sure."

"Care to see to that?"

Oliver smiled. "I imagine I would."

Derrick checked his watch. "It's three."

"Train leaves at five, gets us there by eight, if you like."

"You frighten me," Derrick said honestly. He truly didn't like to think about the thoughts that ran through Oliver Phillips's brain. Too terrifying.

"I like to have all possibilities considered," Oliver said easily.

"And you have the train schedules memorized."

"I'm not the one with the photographic memory," Oliver said with a shrug, "but I do the best I can." He walked off with a "cheers, mate" thrown over his shoulder.

Derrick only shook his head and went to find a taxi. He might have had a perfect memory, but Oliver, well, he had a nose for things that had saved Derrick more grief than he wanted to think about at present. There was a lad Jamie MacLeod would have appreciated for his particular skills.

He gave the cabbie his address and sat back to consider his near future. He would pack up a few things he kept at his very small, very discreet flat, then be on his way. There was no need to ring Lord Epworth because as Cameron had already indicated, he had already accepted the charge to find the earl's little piece of lace. How could he not? The lace was spectacular and the earl was one of those who truly valued his collection of antiques. His grief over its loss had been genuine and almost unassuageable. Derrick had agreed to the rescue whilst His Lordship had still been wringing his hands.

Half an hour later he was walking into his flat and up the stairs to his spare room. It looked like a prop room in a very busy theater, but that was only part of what hid behind walls and inside trunks. He owned thousands of pounds' worth of all kinds of technology, though he had to admit his hack-proof phone and small tablet had become his tools of choice lately. And aye, he knew his gear wasn't hackable because part of the way Peter kept himself busy every day was trying to break through Derrick's layers of security. The man would have likely been in prison if anyone with any power had known what he could do. Either that, or Her Majesty's spooks would have gang-pressed him into service for the cause. Derrick was simply happy to know Peter was for them and not against.

He filled a backpack with the usual things he never went without: colored contacts, facial hair, wigs, easily changed clothing that would radically alter his aspect. For the rest, he would rely on skills he had paid dearly for but never used for anything but his business—

He turned away from that thought before it blossomed into anything that would distract him from what he needed to do. The past was dead and buried and he preferred it that way.

He was tempted to do a little snooping online before he left for the station but decided against it. There would be time enough to delve more fully into the lives of his suspects whilst he was waiting for them to make a wrong move. It wasn't his usual modus operandi, to leave things unexamined and uncovered, but, well, Fate was still standing right behind him, blowing her chilly breath down the back of his neck. He shoved his phone in his pocket, his tablet in his pack, then locked up and headed for the station. He would give his suspects a bit of a head start, just to make things more interesting.

He would have shaken his head, but he couldn't bring himself to. He was going to have to figure out something to do with his life at some point besides chase bad guys. Because somehow, with all that chasing and rescuing, he never seemed to manage to rescue a girl. He had teased Cameron about his wedded bliss, but the truth was, he did envy him. Not only did he envy Cameron his happiness, he wanted something very much like it for himself.

One more job, then on to other things.

Chapter 3

Samantha walked to the window of her minuscule garret room, pulled the lace curtain—not handmade, which she had expected—back and looked out over the street that definitely had a medieval sort of feel, which she hadn't expected. She had been fully prepared to live in a shed if it meant she could put an entire ocean between herself and her former life, but this was definitely a step up. She was going to have to write her brother a very nice thank-you note.

She sank down on the little bench set under the window and looked at the people walking along the street below her, going about their business as if they had every right to. She watched them for a moment or two, then leaned her head back against the side of the window and closed her eyes.

She hadn't dared think about it before, on the off chance that her plans went awry, but she was in the middle of perpetrating a strategy. It was almost ridiculous to think that at the ripe old age of twenty-six she was trying to figure out a way to cut the old apron strings, but that's what it boiled down to. It wasn't that her parents were bad people; they were just . . . difficult. Her older siblings had been a disappointment, so the burden of perfection had always rested on her.

She'd had enough of that, actually.

It wasn't that she hadn't tried over the years to assert her independence. It was true that she was still living in the bedroom she'd grown up in, but she had recently begun to refuse to sleep on a sleeper while accompanying her mother to conferences, insisting instead on a bed of her own.

She paused. All right, so it had been an extra bed in her mother's room. She had put her foot down about penny loafers. She had gotten her master's in historical textile preservation with an emphasis on Elizabethan offerings instead of Victorian. And she had begun to insist that her mother pay her for help with exhibitions instead of simply offering her room and board. She knew she should have gotten an apartment long before now, but every time she made noises about moving out, her parents looked as if she'd said she was going to ditch her conservative uniform of tweed and polyester for tie-dye and dreads. What was the last child to do but try to keep the peace?

The truth was, her parents weren't terrible people. They just always both seemed to need an audience. Unfortunately, unlike her older brother and sister, she'd never managed to get out of the front-row seats, much less the theater.

Until two days earlier, that was.

She picked up her bag and slung it over her shoulder. She had cash, a debit card, and a map Lydia had given her earlier that morning with useful places marked in red. Lydia had invited her to take the day and investigate the environs so she would be comfortable when they left her alone in their house for the summer. Life was good.

She jogged down the stairs, feeling remarkably fresh for it still being the middle of the night on the East Coast, and almost ran into Lydia bodily in the entryway.

"Oh," Samantha said in surprise, "I'm sorry—"

Lydia put her finger to her lips quickly. "You have company," she whispered. "I think you might escape—"

Or maybe not. The door to the salon opened with a flourish and there stood Theodore IV, ready to set sail for points she didn't want to know about. She managed to suppress a flinch only because she'd had so much practice.

"Off we go," he said brightly. "Thank you, Mrs. Cooke, for your hospitality."

And that was that. Before she could say anything, Samantha was hustled out the door and herded toward a taxi. She balked at that.

"I can't afford a taxi," she said firmly.

Dory drew himself up. "As if I would ask you to pay," he said huffily. "I'm treating today."

Unless things changed later on, of course. Samantha was half tempted as he got in first to simply jump back, shut the door, and run down the street, but she supposed he would just follow her. She sighed, then climbed into the back of the cab with him. Last time. Honestly.

"Where are we going this morning?" she asked reluctantly.

"The Castle," he said, checking his phone, "then lunch, then the bridge, then the Discovery Museum."

Her feet hurt just thinking about it, but she supposed she wouldn't waste breath saying anything. It would just add to her already unwholesome reputation for fragility.

The thing that surprised her the most as they approached Newcastle's landmark castle was the fact that the taxi dropped them off on a sidewalk that was immediately adjacent to the steps that led up to an enormous wooden set of doors. She stood on that sidewalk and looked around her in amazement. She had seen her share of pictures of castles, but they'd always been on a bluff, or out in the country. Outside of London and Edinburgh, she'd never truly considered that a modern city might sit around a structure that had been more or less intact since the thirteenth century.

She walked up stairs that had no doubt been walked up hundreds of thousands of times over those eight hundred years and felt something slide down her spine—and that wasn't Dory Mollineux's hand. She looked over her shoulder, but there was nothing there.

Weird.

She learned at the entrance that they were going Dutch, which she supposed shouldn't have surprised her. So much for being treated that day. She pulled out enough money for her own entrance fee, then declined to buy a guidebook when invited to do so by her companion. If he wanted one, he could buy it himself.

They started on the ground floor with the chapel, but Dory didn't seem to be particularly eager to stay there. In fact, she realized almost immediately that his idea of touring was to walk into a room of any size, nod, then stride on off to the next thing. She hadn't paid her four pounds to sprint through the entire place, so once they hit the first floor and a room with exhibits, she put her foot down.

"I'm going to read all these," she announced.

He blew his perfectly highlighted blond locks out of his eyes. "Don't be ridiculous."

"I'm not being ridiculous; I'm poor and I'm not going to waste my money on something, then not look it over thoroughly." She pointed to a bench surrounding a pillar. "Go sit on that if you're bored."

He looked at her with a slight frown, as if he couldn't quite understand why she was forming words that didn't include *of course* and *whatever you want*. He studied her for a moment or two longer, then walked off to sit down. She ignored him and decided to start at one corner of the room and work her way around.

Only the corner of the room she had selected was currently occupied. She looked at the man standing three feet from her and felt a sudden and unaccountable increase of temperature in the room.

All right, so she had seen men before, several of them. She had even gone out with a couple, handpicked by her parents, of course, and possessing pedigrees that would have made any blue blood worth his salt green with envy. There had even, in the long progression of males she had admired from a distance, been a few who had been tall, dark, and handsome.

But she had the feeling that just a glance from the man standing next to her would have sent all those guys off into therapy for years.

He was tall, substantially taller than Dory's wishful-thinking not-quite-six feet. He was wearing jeans, boots, and some sort of T-shirt that sported a sentiment in Middle English she would have translated if she'd had the presence of mind to do so. After all, she'd agreed to Latin and Middle English if her mother laid off her about Scottish Gaelic.

She couldn't see the color of his eyes, but his hair was dark and his face was, well, *flawless* was the only word that came to mind. And she knew that his face was flawless because he had turned it toward her and was watching her gape at him.

She quickly turned away and walked toward the nearest case filled with artifacts. She had no idea what she was looking at. She read the words written there but found no meaning in them. She felt as if she'd just come down with a terrible cold, feverish, as if she needed a serious lie-down sooner rather than later.

It made her feel a little silly even thinking that, because she felt as if she were quoting directly from one of those contraband romances her great-aunt Mary had slipped her during high school, buried under balls of tatting thread and musty old patterns included to throw her mother off the scent. But there was no denying that the man standing over there, leaning over a case with his hands clasped behind his back, was absolutely stunning.

"Hurry up, Sammy," Dory said loudly.

The annoyance was plain in his voice. She looked over her shoulder to tell him to keep his voice down—and stop calling her that name she loathed—when for the second time in as many minutes, she felt herself stagger in place.

There was a man standing right there next to Dory, a tall, distinguished-looking man with jet-black hair swept artistically back from his forehead. It wasn't so much that he was wearing full-blown Elizabethan gear, including an enormous ruff, a heavily embroidered doublet, and a velvet cape tossed artistically over one shoulder, or that he was looking at her as if he found her rather lacking. It wasn't even that she suspected that with only a hint of an invitation, he would break forth into a Shakespearean soliloquy right there in front of her.

It was that she had the feeling, crazy as it might have been, that she was looking at someone who just wasn't quite of the corporeal world.

She tore her gaze away from him to look at Dory, who was still complaining that she wasn't going fast enough. She pointed behind him and tried to speak, but realized fairly soon that while her mouth was moving, nothing but garbled babbling was coming out.

And then she watched the Elizabethan type lean over and flick Dory on the ear.

Dory leapt up, looked around him, then frowned fiercely. He looked at her.

"Who did that?" he demanded.

She felt a shiver start at the back of her head and work its way quickly down her back. She had spent her share of time with things of a vintage nature, watched more than her share of ghost-hunter shows, and been sure that the shadows that seemingly moved just out of her line of sight hadn't been just her bangs tricking her, but she'd never imagined she would actually see—in broad daylight, no less—a . . . well, a *ghost*.

"Well?" Dory snapped.

She took a deep breath, then pointed at the reenactment guy standing behind him.

Dory looked over his shoulder, but the only other person within ten feet of him was the dark-haired man who had sent her pulse racing. That man glanced at Dory in a way that sent her escort sitting back down without comment. Samantha wasn't surprised by the dirty look Dory sent her way, but she found herself completely unaffected by it, for a change. She was simply too busy gaping at the Elizabethan ghost standing there, looking down at Dory as if he'd been a bug.

She had to admit that in that, she heartily approved.

"What in the hell are you pointing at?" Dory demanded.

Samantha curled her fingers into her palm and dropped her arm down by her side. "Don't you see him?"

"See what?"

Well, if he couldn't see that guy standing right there in all his Renaissance glory, she wasn't going to waste her breath talking about it.

"Um," she began.

"You're jet-lagged," Dory said briskly, "and I'm done here. Hurry up before I leave you behind."

She turned back to her exhibit, though she supposed now that she was wallowing in her independence, she would have to do something about the jerk behind her. After all, it wasn't as if her parents could send her to her room for being rude to him. She was certainly old enough to run her own life.

She was beginning to regret not having come to that conclusion long before now.

She tried to read the exhibit information but couldn't help surreptitious glances over her shoulder. Those turned out to be not nearly enough. She finally had to turn sideways and watch the spectacle. The man dressed in Elizabethan gear that Dory couldn't see had apparently only just begun his work. He pestered Dory, tugging on his hair, blowing down the back of his neck, then finally rolling his eyes and delivering a smart cuff to the back of Dory's head.

She was surprised to watch Dory fall off his bench and go sprawling, but perhaps there were things about ghosts she just didn't understand. The exertion did seem to affect Mr. Doublet adversely, though. The shade put his hand on the pillar and gasped artistically for breath, but since that wasn't anything she wasn't used to from her own father, she didn't think much of it. Far more interesting was what was left of Master Mollineux.

He crawled to his feet, then whirled around, his face contorted in fury.

"Who did that?"

Samantha opened her mouth to enlighten him, then realized there was nothing to enlighten him about. The man with the ruff flicked the lace at his wrists, sent a thoroughly supercilious look her way, then vanished.

She almost sat down hard enough to break the glass behind her.

Dory stopped turning in circles, no doubt looking for someone to blame, smoothed his hair back from his face, then swept the occupants of the room with a disgusted look and started for the door.

"Ten minutes or I leave you behind," he threw at her as he left.

Well, if he was going to be that way about it, she just might have to linger for a bit longer than she'd intended to.

She leaned to her right to look around the pillar in the middle of the room, on the off chance that she'd missed something, but no one was there. She supposed she shouldn't have expected anything else. Not only was she in England, she was in the bowels of a very old castle.

Along with her endless supply of mysteries and romances, her great-aunt Mary had been a connoisseur of all things paranormal. She had instilled a curiosity in Samantha that Samantha was sure would be her undoing at some point. She had just never thought she would have something of her own to report on.

She turned back to the exhibits, but the truth was, her mind just wasn't on them. She was too tempted to ease over to where she'd seen her spectral rescuer working his magic on her primary tormentor. She glanced over her shoulder again, but there was nothing there to be seen. The only thing left in the room was a gorgeous man who was working his way over to her. She reached for a free brochure to fan herself because she was fairly sure she'd just seen a ghost, not because she was looking at the poster boy for Gorgeous Guys, Inc.

He was a careful reader, that much she could say about him. She was having trouble making sense of what was in front of her, but he didn't seem to be having the same problem. She didn't bother to point out to him that he was starting at the wrong end of the bank of display cases, because obviously he didn't care. She managed to get through two displays—and yes, she was counting—by the time he'd done six and they'd met in the middle. She'd stopped fanning, mostly because the wrinkled piece of paper she held in her hand had simply given out under the strain.

She took a deep breath and looked at the man standing next to her.

He was watching her with a grave expression on his face, as if he waited for something pithy to come out of her mouth.

"Do you believe in ghosts?" was the best she could do.

He seemed to consider. "Why do you ask?"

"Because . . . well, never mind."

The man looked at her from the most amazing pair of green eyes she had ever seen. She wished suddenly that she'd gone ahead and sprung for that guidebook. At least that might have left her with something else to use to keep herself from perspiring.

"Did one frighten off your escort?"

She looked at him in surprise. "How did you know?"

"It's a castle," he said easily. "Nothing should come as a surprise here."

She would have smiled, but he was a stranger and she didn't

want to look like an easy mark—on the off chance he wanted to steal her wallet, of course. Because she couldn't quite understand why a man that good-looking would be in the middle of a castle museum. Even more baffling was why he would be talking to her.

"Are you a tourist?" she blurted out before she thought better of it.

He smiled a very small smile that was so charming, she found herself smiling in return.

"No," he said with consonants so posh he had to have been either very well educated or some sort of upper-crust type, "just a student of history. Had a free day and thought this might be interesting. And you?"

"Ah," she said. "I'm just a tourist."

"And your boyfriend?"

"He isn't my boyfriend," she said quickly. "Just someone I know." She almost added *unfortunately*, but thought that might have been too much information.

He only lifted his eyebrows briefly, then nodded. "Have a lovely visit," he said, then he turned and walked away.

Samantha was slightly surprised by the abruptness of his departure, but since that seemed to be the state of affairs with the men in her life during the past half hour, she supposed she couldn't expect anything else.

She sat down on the bench surrounding the pillar in the middle of the room and tried to regroup. She attempted it until the room filled with foreign-speaking tourists and she realized she wasn't going to get any serious thinking done.

She managed to get out of the castle and catch a bus back to the Cookes' without seeing Dory. She could only assume he'd stomped off in a huff and was intending to punish her by his absence.

Lydia answered the door at her knock. "Have a good morning, love?"

"It was interesting," Samantha said, because there was absolutely no way she was going to talk about what she'd seen. She was almost convinced she'd imagined the whole thing.

Lydia smiled. "You know, Samantha, I was just wondering if you might be up for a little errand tomorrow."

"Will it require my traveling long distances?" Samantha asked hopefully.

Lydia laughed a little. "Actually, I was hoping you wouldn't mind nipping down to London and delivering something to a colleague for me. I'd go myself, of course, but Edmund and I start rehearsals soon." She smiled apologetically. "You know how that goes."

"I do," Samantha said, and boy, did she ever. Her father's stage career had been all consuming for him. Even the university lived in fear of conflicting with his theater schedule.

"There is no hurry, actually, about your arrival," Lydia said. "I'll give you a phone number to ring when you reach the city. I hadn't intended for you to do this, but I thought you might want to—what's that phrase you have?"

"Get the heck out of Dodge?" Samantha supplied.

"That's the one," Lydia agreed. "I can suggest a place or two of interest, or you can just wander without a plan."

"Oh," Samantha said, feeling something akin to unease take hold of her. "No plan? I'm not sure that's wise."

Lydia smiled gently. "Then let me choose for you, just this time. Castles or gardens?"

"Castles."

"Medieval or Renaissance?"

"Medieval," Samantha said reverently. "If it wouldn't be too much trouble."

"Then I'll book you a couple of spots to stay, suggest a well-preserved medieval relic or two, then send you off in the morning to the station. I'll get you a key to the house as well, of course. You'll need to get back in when you return, won't you?"

Samantha nodded. "I'll pay you for the hotels—"

Lydia shook her head. "Of course you won't. You're doing me the favor of running an errand for me. The least I can do is cover your travel expenses. You can see to your meals, if you like."

"You are too generous."

Lydia shrugged, as if she were a little uncomfortable with the thanks. "Not to worry, darling. I'll go make your arrangements."

Samantha thanked her again, then made her way up to her

room to consider what to take. The entire place was comfortingly free of Elizabethan specters and obnoxious New Englanders both, which was a bonus as far as she was concerned.

Now, if she could have perhaps encountered an extremely handsome guy wearing Middle English sayings on his shirt—and no doubt knowing what they meant—she might have considered that things were truly looking up.

Maybe tomorrow, if she was lucky.

She considered what to take, then decided she would pack as light as possible. Money for food and some ID were probably enough. And as far as clothes went, she wouldn't take more than would fit in her rather small backpack. After all, it wasn't as if she would be seeing the same people all the time.

She went to pull her backpack down off the wall and get ready to go.

Chapter 4

Derrick leaned against a handy outcropping in an otherwise quite uninspired bit of brick wall and watched the
door a hundred feet to his left. It was not quite seven, but he'd
had a feeling the excitement would begin quite early in the day.
He glanced to his right as Oliver simply appeared from nowhere,
two cups of something steaming in his hands. He gave one to
Derrick, then joined him in his leaning. He looked alert, which
Derrick could definitely not say about himself, and he had been
the one sleeping through the night whilst Oliver kept watch over
the Cookes' residence.

"You could have slept in this morning," Derrick remarked.

"I slept at the office last week."

There was no denying that. Among Oliver's many gifts was
the uncanny ability to lose himself in slumber in any location
and on any surface. Derrick had avoided him rather well in the
lobby of Cameron's suite of offices, stepped over him several
times in the middle of the rug in his own office, and marveled
at his ability to make himself comfortable on a sofa that just
wasn't quite long enough for him.

"Perhaps I'll sleep on the train," Oliver continued easily, as if he discussed whether to have a scone or a croissant for breakfast. "Or not. No matter. What of you?"

"I slept."

"After you snooped, no doubt."

Derrick conceded that with a slight nod. "Had to have something useful to do."

"What'd you find out?"

"Nothing that makes any sense."

"Criminals are like that."

Derrick sighed, then returned to his study of the Cookes' front stoop. "They're both humanities professors, though they seem to do an appalling amount of acting." He had to take a deep breath because he did indeed know more about Edmund Cooke than he wanted to admit, but it was nothing he would divulge. He would just have to feign a sort of baffled ignorance. "They're not rich," he continued, "but they're comfortable. No points on their licenses, no brushes with the law, current on their council taxes, no illegal telly time."

"How boring."

Derrick almost smiled. "It would look that way, wouldn't it?"

"And what do they have of ours?"

Derrick looked at him then. "A rather large, perfectly preserved piece of sixteenth-century lace."

"The one the Earl of Epworth left behind his utterly inadequate piece of glass?"

Derrick nodded. "That'd be the one."

Oliver shook his head and looked vaguely unsettled, if such a thing were possible. "Don't care much for that thing, if you want the truth. I think it's cursed."

"Or worth a fortune."

"*Cursed* sounds more interesting." He sipped his coffee. "How do you know they stole it?"

Derrick set his cup down at his feet, then folded his arms over his chest. "I watched the security tapes at Epworth's castle. Professional burglar, if you can believe it. The Cookes were also attending a house party at the castle the same night."

"That's a stretch."

"So was watching the thief as he visited our good Mr. Cooke

in his office a week later. I thought perhaps our sticky-fingered lad's backpack seemed a little lighter afterward."

Oliver pursed his lips, but his eyes almost twinkled. "Still on the thin side, don't you think?"

"The subsequent conversation Mr. Cooke had with his wife about their new lacey acquisition wasn't."

"Very well, I'm convinced. What now? Are you telling me these two paragons haven't been squirreling away their ha'pennies, waiting for just enough of them to buy this legally?"

"That's what I'm telling you."

Oliver shook his head. "Not much market for a whacking great piece of lace of that vintage, is there?"

"That's what baffles me," Derrick admitted. "It isn't as if they could dispose of it at a flea market, is it? I didn't pay any calls to seedier suspects, but I did have friendly visits with most every legitimate dealer who would be interested in that sort of thing. I came up empty-handed."

"Most," Oliver repeated, glancing at him briefly. "Who'd you miss?"

"This is what doesn't make sense," Derrick said slowly. He looked at Oliver. "The only reputable bloke I didn't talk to was Gavin Drummond."

Oliver rolled his eyes, which for him was an appalling display of deep emotion. "That pansy-waisted Yank? He can't even overcharge for bad art and you think he's in the market for stolen lace?"

"I'm just wondering about him," Derrick said, shrugging. "I've often wondered if he's using Yolynda's gallery as a stepping-stone to bigger things." He shot Oliver a look. "Do you know who his parents are?"

"His mother is some long-winded harridan with a penchant for cheap Victorian knickknacks and his father is a blowhard who thinks he's the second coming of Sir Laurence Olivier, and both of them hold court in some exclusive little university in the States where their students no doubt live in fear of what'll happen to their marks if they indulge in a very justifiable bit of sleeping to stave off the utter boredom of the classes this narcissistic pair purports to teach." He looked at Derrick blandly. "Is that about right?"

Derrick laughed a little in spite of himself. "Something like that."

"And why do you think Gavin Drummond's trying to better his life?"

Derrick watched the door open and a woman in her twenties step out onto the sidewalk. She was pretty, in a bookish, spinsterish sort of way. All she was missing to complete the picture were librarian-style glasses. He wondered, absently, what she might look like if someone had cut off the thick, nondescript braid that hung down her back. He had certainly considered that a time or two the day before when he'd been putting himself in her way in the Castle's great hall. He nodded toward her.

"Because of that lass there."

"The one who looks like she's been kept in storage for the past thirty years?"

"The very same." Derrick looked at him. "Know who she is?"

"Samantha Drummond," Oliver said. "Gavin's youngest sister." He lifted an eyebrow. "I believe you were shadowing her yesterday."

"My faith is restored."

"I wasn't snoozing."

"You never do."

Oliver shrugged. "I have a reputation to maintain. Pray I don't disappoint when you need me the most."

"I do, laddie, every day."

"And you think she's involved in this?"

"I can hardly credit it," Derrick said, "but the timing of her arrival is suspicious. As is her occupancy here with this particular set of antique collectors." He glanced at Oliver. "Wouldn't you say?"

"It's convenient," Oliver conceded. "Find out anything useful about her yesterday?"

"She believes in paranormal happenings."

Oliver smiled briefly. "How interesting."

"I thought so, too."

Oliver was silent for a moment or two, then pushed off from the wall. "See you at the station. I'll catch her bus. I checked us out of the hotel, by the way. In cash."

Derrick expected nothing else. They'd both spent so many years flying under the radar whilst ferreting out details for

Robert Cameron that remaining as anonymous as possible was simply second nature. Derrick wondered now and again if that had made him paranoid, but he never wondered about it enough to change how he did business. He tossed his coffee in the trash, slung his backpack over his shoulders and walked down the street to catch a taxi on the busier cross street, not looking up as the bus passed him. The next train south left in an hour, which was enough time to make a few alterations to his appearance, have breakfast, then get a seat near his quarry.

It was possible, he supposed, that she might go another direction besides south. It had been all he could do earlier that morning not to hack into Lydia Cooke's bank account as well as paw through her emails to see what sort of travel arrangements she'd booked for Gavin's sister, but that would have made things feel too easy.

The very sad truth was, he was slightly bored.

He wasn't proud of it, but there it was. He wasn't so bored that he'd become sloppy, not truly, but enough that he had left things unknown that he normally would have investigated without hesitation. Perhaps he had spent too many years rubbing shoulders with villains and the criminal class had ceased to hold any fascination for him. Their methods were different, true, but in the end they were all nothing more than a lot of punters with no respect for the law or anyone else's property.

He supposed there were those who might say the same about him for reading their private correspondence, but he supposed he wasn't the only one, so perhaps that made it less unpalatable than it might have been otherwise.

He crawled into the back of the taxi that pulled to a stop in front of him, gave the cabbie his destination, then sat back against the seat with a weary sigh. He was getting old, perhaps. He would be thirty-two in the fall, old enough to have settled down by now. Perhaps he was getting broody, though he couldn't imagine any woman wanting to settle down with him. Instead of nights down at the pub with the lads, he spent his weekends—and some weeks, truth be told—with James MacLeod. Not exactly anything to write home about.

Perhaps he simply had too many irons in the fire. He could give up something, perhaps, and have a bit more peace in his life. Cameron Antiquities, though, was his business and his

source of not only pride but funds to keep petrol in his cars and
food on his table. The other, well, he wasn't sure he was willing
to give up the exhilaration that was traveling to exotic locales
with the madman from the castle down the way. It was no wonder Jamie was addicted to it. It was a damned good time.

And what would he give it up for? If he'd heard one more
London socialite coo, "Ooh, you're Robert Cameron's cousin,
aren't you?" whilst attempting to look discreetly around him for
a Ferrari hiding behind his back, he would have likely cracked
his teeth from grinding them in frustration. If he'd had one more
Scottish lass from the village he'd been a part of for the better
part of his life do the same, well, he would have moved to London permanently.

He paid the cabbie and walked into the station, choosing a
fairly large group to become a part of. He already had the train
times committed to memory, so he kept a casual eye on Samantha Drummond, then noted the track she subsequently walked
toward. He purchased a ticket, then followed her with equal
casualness, passing and ignoring Oliver on his way. He waited
until the train arrived, waited until the others disembarked, then
followed Miss Drummond on board. He slid into a seat across
the aisle and a row or two behind her where he could keep an
eye on her without being overly obvious.

He supposed to be fair he would have to admit that she was
really quite lovely in a New-England-prep-school sort of way.
He wouldn't have been surprised to have watched her break out
a mystery novel and read it whilst dressed in bobby socks and
saddle shoes. If he'd been going on first impressions, he would
have said she was nothing more than a very sheltered though
well-educated youngest daughter of two academics with sterling
reputations who had sent her across the Pond to associate with
other sterling-reputationed academics who would look after her
innocent self with as much care as her parents would have.

Obviously, it was a very well-crafted front.

Determining what lay behind that front caused him to lift a
mental eyebrow, but he firmly resisted the impulse to pull out
his tablet and quickly find those answers. He would pretend to
be just a normal bloke without access to all sorts of things he
shouldn't have had access to and see if he couldn't pry answers
out of her the old-fashioned way. He wasn't quite ready to resort

to a deerstalker hat and pencil and paper, but he was close. He was that desperate to keep himself awake.

He watched her for an hour, wondering where in the world she was going to stop and who, if anyone, would meet her there. Perhaps she was off on a little explore to look for other items of a textile nature to poach.

She started to gather her things together as they approached the station at York. That wasn't where he would have expected her to get off, but then again, what did he know? He was just tracking down a priceless piece of lace for a man who simply wanted a piece of history behind glass and hadn't listened when Derrick had told him to improve his security system.

Derrick supposed he hadn't done himself any favors when he'd paid His Lordship a little visit one evening. He'd listened to a few of the earl's stories, then bid the man a fond farewell, leaving him sitting in his study with a glass of wine. He had then waited half an hour before he had broken back into the man's house, disarmed the security system and lifted that very fine piece of lace in under ten minutes, silently and without detection. He'd walked back in the front door, been escorted to the man's study, and handed him his treasure.

It was, he was absolutely convinced, only the sterling reputation of the Cameron name that had saved him from being dragged off in irons right then. The earl, white-faced and trembling, had taken his lace back and promised to have someone out the very next day. Either that hadn't happened or the abilities of the security firm had been sadly lacking.

Derrick followed his little librarian off the train and out of the station. He continued to trail after her as she wandered along streets, looking down at a journal she held in her hands, completely oblivious to what was going on around her. He raised his eyebrows briefly. Either she was cleverer than she looked, or the Cookes were idiots. He felt something stir in him that wasn't the very vile pasty he'd snagged on his way to the platform. It was something that felt almost a bit like interest. Enthusiasm was overstating it, but a flicker of interest, aye, that was possible.

Who would entrust a piece of lace that valuable to the clueless tourist in front of him who was gawking at everything around her as if she'd never seen anything interesting before in the whole of her life?

His phone chirped at him. He looked down and found a text from Oliver waiting there.

Have scissors?

Derrick smiled to himself, because he'd been thinking the same thing, though as he followed Samantha Drummond, he found himself less tempted to cut her hair than simply unbraid it. She could have done with a bit of, ah, unbuttoning.

The rest of his morning included nothing more interesting than watching her check without fanfare, though rather early, into a modest hotel. He found himself a discreet place to sit and watch the front door, then he sat and watched. No curtains moved, as if she peered out to see who was coming to meet her. No shifty-eyed textile brokers slipped into the lobby for an exchange of goods. Nothing happened at all except for his eventual inability to feel his backside and a slight twinge in his knee that made him look heavenward to see if it was going to rain anytime soon.

Time crawled by.

Oliver texted him a picture of a hotel he'd checked them into. Tourists passed him, chatting in various languages. An old granny on a bicycle almost ran over his toes, then cackled as she pedaled away. He almost fell asleep in the sunshine, then woke to the feel of his pack starting to leave his fingers. He glared at a cheeky yob, who then held up his hands and bolted.

He sat there for at least another hour before he couldn't ignore his stomach any longer. Either Samantha Drummond had snuck out the back, which hacking into the hotel's security camera had assured him she hadn't, or she was the single most boring thief in the history of textile thievery. He'd had more interesting mornings helping Cameron's secretary clean out her spam folder.

Oliver appeared suddenly and sat down next to him on the bench. "Go. I'll shadow her for a bit."

"Shadow," Derrick echoed with a snort. "Shadow her where? She hasn't gone anywhere."

"Wherever else she doesn't go, I'll follow her." He looked at Derrick and frowned. "You need a lie-down."

"Why are you so well rested?"

"I've already had four lattes this morning," Oliver said blandly.

Derrick smiled. "Don't lose her whilst you're in the loo."

"I'll try not to."

He looked down at Oliver's shoes. They were fluorescent green. It was such an appalling sight, he could hardly believe what he was seeing.

"Discreet?"

"Backup plan," Oliver said. "In case the lattes fail."

Well, either those shoes would keep the lad awake or they would give him nightmares. Derrick sighed and picked up his backpack.

"I'll be back in a couple of hours."

"No worries," Oliver said. "I've plenty to do here."

Aye, fight off the boredom of watching for a woman who was probably inside her room either watching the telly or having a long, luxurious nap. He was struck by a feeling that he eventually identified as envy.

Perhaps he needed a holiday.

Derrick rose. "Best of luck."

Oliver waved him off, looking as if he were somehow not quite sitting still as he sat there, still. Derrick headed toward his hotel. Of course Oliver hadn't provided him with an address, but that wasn't surprising. There would have been no sport in having everything laid out for him.

He found the hotel without trouble, accepted a key, then took himself upstairs and decided that perhaps he would succumb to weariness and have himself a decent rest. He took off his boots, then simply stretched out with his hands behind his head. He stared up at the ceiling and wondered about Samantha Drummond.

What in the world was she up to? Admittedly, she was Gavin's sister, which meant she could have been up to almost anything, but even Gavin had spoken kindly of her the one time he'd actually spoken of her. She didn't fit the profile of a high-class thief and her background probably wouldn't allow her to become a low-class thief.

He shook his head. He just couldn't figure her.

But he would.

Just as soon as he woke up, hopefully not after having dreamed about those vile green shoes he'd just been subjected to.

Chapter 5

Samantha put her bag up on the counter and looked at the girl behind the desk. She had unpacked, watched a bit of television, then spent an hour or two looking over the list of interesting sights Lydia had made her. She was a little surprised that nothing had appealed to her, but maybe she had eclectic tastes not shared by her hostess.

She had already seen a bit of what York had to offer on her way from the train station. She had gawked at the York Minster on her way to her hotel—the outside, at least—but she hadn't been at all tempted by any exhibits on torture through the ages. She wanted open spaces, no blood, and no crowds. She wouldn't have expected York to be so busy so early in the day, but maybe lookers at historical artifacts liked to get an early start.

The girl smiled at her. "How can I help you?"

"I'm trying to decide what to do with my day," Samantha said. "Do you have any suggestions on what to see? Maybe something out of the way?"

The girl considered. "If you're keen to get out of the city, you could try Castle Hammond. The earl has very lovely gardens which are open several days a week."

That sounded promising. She couldn't say she was a big garden looker, but maybe that was just because she'd never had the chance. Her forays into tourist-like things had generally been limited to standing in museums and being uncomfortable as she watched her mother bully poor, unsuspecting curators into letting her fondle things not available to the ungloved fingers of the general public. She had also spent her share of time being excruciatingly embarrassed when her determined parent had brought out the long knives for directors of exhibits who showed a bit of spine. Maybe gardens would be a breath of fresh air.

"Does the family still live there?" she asked, wondering how that worked. Letting people walk through her house was something she didn't think she could ever do. Then again, perhaps nobility did whatever it took to keep the lights on.

The girl nodded. "It's unusual these days, but they do." She looked behind her counter, then pulled out a brochure and handed it to Samantha. "This should tell you what you need to know to get there. It looks like the house is open today as well."

Samantha took the brochure, thanked the girl, then walked out of the lobby. The hotel was small but centrally located. She'd already checked room prices and been slightly surprised by how expensive it had been. She supposed she would work it off eventually.

She waited an hour for the bus, having just missed one of them, but that didn't bother her because it gave her a chance to people watch for a bit. It was possible that she had spent too much time locked in various back rooms, looking over textiles, but it seemed to her that the people around her had an appalling amount of freedom.

Which, she supposed, she had at the moment as well.

The journey out to the castle was lovely and she felt extremely adventurous deviating from Lydia's list. That she should find that out of the ordinary probably said more about her than she was comfortable with.

Two hours later, she had finished a tour of the gardens and found herself wishing for at least a hood to pull up over her head to shield herself from the rain. She supposed it should have occurred to her that there was a reason she'd been almost alone in the gardens except for some guy with green hair that matched his green running shoes, but she'd been too busy concentrating on what she was seeing to pay attention to the weather.

And honestly, she'd been a little unnerved by the green-shoed guy. He'd had a notebook and obviously been sketching the various specimens of flora and fauna to be found in the earl's garden, but in spite of the fact that he seemed unobtrusive, she'd been nervous. Again, too much time allowing her imagination to run wild.

She left Mr. Green Twinkletoes seeking shelter near a hedge and ran back along paths and up to the front door. She stood under the shelter of an awning and knocked. A butler-ish-looking sort of man with silver hair opened almost immediately. He didn't step aside to let her in, though, which she found to be slightly unnerving.

"May I come in?" she asked.

"I'm sorry, miss," he intoned. "The house is closed today."

She blinked in surprise. "Is it?" She would have pulled out the brochure to double-check, but she'd made good use of that hour she'd spent waiting for the bus and was fairly confident she had the whole thing memorized. "But you're supposed to be open today."

The butler looked as if he might have liked to say something else, but in the end, apparently discretion won out. He simply shook his head.

"I apologize for the inconvenience," he said, sounding genuinely sorry. He looked over her head. "I see the bus still waiting to take on passengers. I'll send someone out to make sure it's held for you, if you wish to return to town."

Well, there didn't seem to be any arguing to be done. She nodded, then turned and walked out to where the bus was indeed being held apparently thanks to the efforts of the teenager who had sprinted past her to make that happen. She thanked him on his much slower return trip, then got back on the bus. She collapsed into a seat with a sigh, then looked out the window at the rain. She was very grateful she wasn't going to have to either wait out in the rain or walk back. There were just some things she wasn't prepared to do just for the sake of having a look at local culture.

"I heard there was a theft."

Samantha wasn't an eavesdropper by nature. She had learned early in life that when people were talking in whispers, sometimes it was just best not to know what they were discussing. Unfortunately for her, the ladies behind her obviously had a different idea of what constituted a decent whisper than she did.

"Of what?"

"Lace."

Well, now that was a different story. Too many years of being on the hunt or being responsible for the care of delicate and valuable textiles had left her with her ears perking up involuntarily whenever that sort of thing was discussed, no matter how quietly. She put her head down and forced herself to read the bus ticket she was still clutching in her hands, but it was impossible to concentrate when such salacious details were being discussed.

"What sort of lace?"

"Can you keep a secret?"

"Of course!"

So could she, really. She gave up pretending to read and started listening in earnest.

Voices were lowered, sort of.

"I heard," said the first voice, "that it was a piece of Elizabethan lace, stolen right out from under the earl's nose."

"No!"

That had been her reaction, too, because the thought was just so shocking. What sort of person would steal Elizabethan lace? And right out from under the earl's nose? It was appalling.

"'Tis true," the first woman whispered. "Worth a fortune. I suppose the thieves will try to sell it somewhere, but who'll buy it?"

"Someone with a fortune, I imagine," the second woman said in hushed tones of awe. "How'd you hear?"

"My sister's niece's flatmate heard it from the woman at the chemist's who's the sister-in-law of a woman who belongs to the same garden club as the woman who manages the gift shop at the castle. Very hush-hush, though. Don't spread it about."

Samantha frowned slightly. She wasn't sure how reliable that rumor could possibly be, but it was difficult to deny that something had been up at the castle. Maybe there was some safety in assuming the report was true.

But if it was, she seriously doubted the earl would ever see his precious lace again. Her mother was forever complaining about those who made it their business to buy and sell antiquities to anyone but serious scholars. Those who stole the same for profit weren't even fit to breathe the same air as the rest of them.

As for herself, she could honestly say that despite her education and the years spent dusting her mother's antiquities, she would be just as happy to never see another piece of anything to curate. She couldn't even say she was particularly fond of the Elizabethan era. The only reason she'd written her thesis on the glories of late sixteenth- and early seventeenth-century handwork was because it had irked her parents to have her veer from what they'd told her to do. A tiny rebellion, but one she'd engaged in willingly.

If she'd had her choice, she thought she might have liked to have investigated a few medieval things, but that was probably out of reach now. She had the feeling the best she could do was simply ignore the whole subject of history and any expertise she might have had in any facet of it and for a change simply be Sam who liked castles and wanted to hide behind the obscurity of house-sitting for absentee employers for the summer.

She wasn't sure what the alternative was, but she was fairly sure it would require her to do things she wouldn't want to do.

The ladies behind her moved on to other subjects and she moved on to deciding what her evening should look like. She had to admit she was rather uncomfortable being by herself, but when the alternative was hanging out with Dory, she would take solitude every time.

She happily walked back into her hotel an hour later and flopped down on the bed where she could contemplate the rest of her day. She looked up at the ceiling for a minute or two, then reached for her bag and fumbled around in it until she found her notebook. She pulled out Lydia's list on it and glanced reluctantly at the suggestions for the day, most of which she'd already discarded. The list hadn't changed.

She checked her watch. It was only two, which left her more free time than she actually wanted to have to fill up.

That was, she decided, perhaps the oddest sensation she had ever had. She had spent the whole of her life having her days filled for her, her life plan decided for her, every moment of every day already spent for her before she even woke up. No one had ever asked her what she wanted to do, not her professors and certainly not her parents. She was the daughter of Louise Theodosia McKinnon and Richard Olivier Drummond. Of course she would follow in her mother's footsteps. Her father's shoes were, as everyone knew, just too big to fill.

That wasn't to say that anything had been handed to her. She'd done the work to get where she was and she was unfortunately quite good at what she did. She'd been approached by several prestigious museums with substantial offers for her to come ply her trade on their collections. Naturally she hadn't been able to accept. Her mother had needed her. Samantha was convinced her mother had frightened off her potential employers, but she couldn't prove it.

Not that any of it mattered now. She pulled out the decision she'd made as she'd flown over that great big ocean and examined from all sides as if it had been a priceless treasure that only she had access to.

She was going to make a change. A big change. For at least the summer, she was going to try on something else, a new her, a her who didn't know anything about antiquities or textiles or overbearing and controlling parents.

She was now Samantha Drummond, artist and free spirit.

If she'd owned anything made from cotton, she would have put it on. As it was, she would just have to make do with polyester until she'd sold her first painting and could afford something in a natural fiber. She might even buy a pair of Birkenstocks. She was sure that her new wardrobe would not contain anything either brown or gray.

With those happy thoughts to keep her company, she freshened up, then left her room and went downstairs to ask for the nearest art-supply store. Directions in hand, she faced the lobby door and marched boldly into her future, repeating her newly made affirmations.

She was never going to have another thing to do with fabric or lace or actors' costumes. She would take her extensive knowledge of lace patterns and construction details and put them aside for use only in a pinch—or if some actor had paid her a staggering sum to paint his portrait and she felt like recalling them. She was never going to agree to alter a costume on the fly,

repair blown-out trousers, or stand near an outlet with a glue
gun at the ready to reattach anything shiny to any of her father's
more outlandish outfits.

And she was never, ever going to have anything to do with
anything of an Elizabethan nature again.

She opened the door and walked out into the world. She had
an entire afternoon in front of her and lots of beautiful things to
think about sketching. There was no time like the present to get
started on her future.

Seven hours later, she stood on the edge of the group gathered
near the York Minster, hoping she wasn't making an enormous
mistake. Her hotel was only a few minutes from where she stood,
so she supposed she could run all the way back if she had to
without getting mugged in the process. She looked critically over
her fellow ghost walkers, but didn't see anyone who looked suspicious. There were mostly couples of varying ages, a pair of
college-age guys who looked fairly skeptical, and a trio of women
her age who had obviously already enjoyed several after-dinner
drinks and were ogling a tall, very handsome man who had
obviously avoided their bar. He was seemingly impervious to
their overt attempts at flirting with him, which she found rather
attractive. If she'd been interested in a guy, which at the moment
she most definitely was not. Transitory relationships were not
something she was interested in.

She hovered on the edge of the group as the guide, dressed
appropriately in black, introduced the subject and got them
started with the shivers. The trio was already squealing, which
she found particularly annoying. She wished her Elizabethan
ghost from Newcastle would make an appearance and shut them
up, but she supposed she shouldn't hold out any hope for it. She
wasn't altogether certain she hadn't imagined that entire episode. She had been rather jet-lagged, after all.

Ten minutes later, she found herself walking next to the only
unattached male in the group, that attractive man who'd been
unimpressed with his admirers. Two men in two days. It had to
be some sort of record for her. She tried not to gape at him in an
obvious manner. She only caught shadowy impressions of his
face given where they were walking, but that was enough to

leave her rather relieved the night was cool so she didn't have to fan herself.

"Believe in any of this?" he asked.

She considered his accent. Canadian, maybe. She would have to listen a little more. Just to use it as an academic exercise, of course. She smiled politely. "Of course not. Do you?"

He shrugged. "I'll reserve judgment until after the evening's over."

"What made you come to York?" she asked.

"Backpacking through the British Isles," he said easily. "Off on holiday while the exchange rate's tolerable. What about you?"

"I'm house-sitting," she said. "Friends of the family."

"From America, are you?"

She lifted an eyebrow. "From Canada, are you?"

He laughed briefly. "Might be."

Samantha commanded herself to remain unaffected, but that didn't work as well as she would have hoped. What was it with the men in England? It was the second time in as many days that a guy had turned her brain to mush.

She reminded herself that giving a complete stranger any details about herself was idiotic, but she supposed he would have figured out where she was from soon enough anyway.

"Chilly out tonight," he remarked.

She nodded, then pulled her jacket around her, because it did seem a bit chilly all of the sudden. Too much paranormal activity, apparently.

And she was not, she was absolutely *not* seeing an Elizabethan gentleman out of the corner of her eye in every deep shadow she passed.

She looked up at the man walking next to her. "Do you believe in ghosts?"

"Seems like as good a reason as any to take the tour, eh?"

She studied his face by the light of a streetlamp the next time they paused and wondered if she was destined to spend her summer meeting for the briefest of moments men who were just too good-looking for their own good. He reminded her a bit of the man she'd seen before in Newcastle, but she couldn't figure out why. Similar cheekbones, she supposed, though there was an aura about this guy that was much less reserved than the one at the Castle.

She looked around again for her sixteenth-century shade but saw only the group she'd started the tour with along with the three rather inebriated and now very irritated girls who were obviously annoyed at being displaced.

Samantha considered. Samantha Drummond the textile historian would have backed away immediately and let them have at her Canadian friend, but that wasn't who she was any longer. She was Sam Drummond, artist, and she didn't give way to drunks in stilettoes. She lifted her eyebrows archly, then continued on with her companion.

She was just in the process of looking for something pithy to say when her phone beeped at her. She supposed she was going to have to answer eventually, though she'd been ignoring the text messages all day. She excused herself, pulled up the message and read it, then suppressed the urge to roll her eyes. It was a good thing Dory had an unlimited text plan otherwise he would have bankrupted himself already. He was starting to have his messages loaded with more exclamation points than letters, though, which probably should have worried her.

Off on an errand for the Cookes, she typed. Will let you know when return.

She sent it, turned her phone off, then shoved it into her pocket, ignoring how even that made her a little nervous. She had no doubt if she pushed Dory too far, he would call her parents and let them know she was being uncooperative. Then again, he was probably typing up a report on her on a daily basis, so a frantic phone call wouldn't make things any worse. Her mother had a big exhibition coming up and her father was up to his ruff in his summer Shakespeare season. They wouldn't have time to do anything but send her brief and pointed emails warning her to behave. Those she could delete easily enough.

By the time she reconnected with her surroundings, the tour had moved on. She supposed she shouldn't have been surprised that even that small hesitation had cost her the company of that very attractive Canadian man. Those completely sauced girls obviously knew a good thing when they saw it. She honestly couldn't blame them. She looked around her casually, on the off chance there was a stray specter with a rapier loitering around, then, seeing none, carried on.

After being properly chilled and thrilled by all sorts of

things she fully believed were true, the tour wound up and she realized that she was not exactly as close to her hotel as she might have wished to be. She turned her phone on, ignored the dinging indicating half a dozen texts, then wondered if merely beaning a thug with her phone would be enough or if she would have to use her bag as well.

"What about an escort for our friend here?"

Samantha looked up to find the Canadian hunk standing there, not doing much at all to fend off the groping of his person that was being perpetrated by his admirers. But at least he was trying to be as gallant as possible.

"Thank you," she said, feeling rather relieved. "I wasn't looking forward to getting back to the hotel alone."

"No problem," he said, staggering just slightly as one of the girls draped a bit too hard. "Let's go, then, ladies. Lead on, Miss, ah—"

"Samantha."

"Miss Samantha." He nodded away from where the tour had ended. "After you."

She went, grateful that she had at least a decent sense of direction. That came, she supposed, from all the years she had spent in museums without a map. Perhaps she didn't have all that many skills—especially considering how many she intended to ditch instead of carrying into her future—but she could definitely tell east from west in a sixth-sense sort of way.

She found her way unerringly to her hotel, feeling rather less than comfortable at the sensation of being followed by three giggling women who were probably going to mug that Canadian tourist the first chance they had. She couldn't blame them, she supposed. If she'd had the guts to indulge in a fling, she might have been tempted to fling with that man there.

She stopped in front of the doorway, then looked at her escort.

"Thank you so much," she said politely.

"No worries," he said easily.

Samantha started to thank him a bit more but found herself distracted by the man that had walked behind that little group. She wasn't one to let her imagination run away with her, but he looked like someone she wouldn't have wanted to meet in a dark alley. The look he shot her chilled her to the bone.

"Ah," she said faintly. "Um, I think . . ."

The Canadian looked at her, then over his shoulder. "What is it?"

Samantha shook her head. "Nothing." She started to explain, then shook her head. "That bald guy over there just gave me the creeps when he looked over here."

Mr. Canada frowned, then shrugged. "Maybe we're too loud."

That was her thought as well. Maybe that unpleasant man had been looking with disapproval at the bimbos who were making a serious ruckus, not her.

He nodded politely. "Well, if you're safe now, we'll be on our way."

"Yes," Samantha said, "thank you. Very much."

She walked inside the door and was happier than she likely should have been to have it shut behind her. Maybe she had just had one too many paranormal experiences over the past two days and she'd gotten paranoid. There weren't ghosts following her and there weren't random tourists giving her the evil eye.

She was just an understandably cautious woman living for the summer in a country not her own, traveling on her own. It was only prudent to keep a weather eye out for strange things, so she didn't get caught up in them.

She ran up to her room and quickly locked the door behind her. She was actually very relieved to find everything as she'd left it, though she had to laugh a little at the thought of anything else happening. She was a nobody off on an errand that no one could possibly care about. It wasn't as if she'd stolen a piece of Elizabethan lace and had half the countryside out looking for her.

She put herself to bed, then set her alarm for a reasonable hour. She would see what of the sights she could on her way south, then get back to Newcastle and get on with the new her.

Chapter 6

Derrick woke to the sound of a dirge blaring next to his ear. He groped for his phone and looked at the time. It was barely six. He didn't bother with the light. He was fairly sure he'd been having dreams of being chased by either a lad in Elizabethan finery or a garrison of Roman soldiers, but perhaps that was just the aftereffects of thinking about his quarry being herded by a bluestocking Yank in penny loafers.

He would have rolled his eyes if he could have unstuck them from his eyelids. He couldn't imagine Samantha Drummond was seriously involved with that obnoxious snob, but what did he know about women? He just knew that he hadn't wanted to go home with any of the three bints he'd used as cover the night before. Was it at all possible to find a serious girl who preferred staying home to partying?

His phone continued to ring. He sighed and took the call, though he had the feeling he wasn't going to like what he was about to hear.

"What?" he rasped.

"She's on the move."

Derrick sat up so quickly, his head spun. "What?" He fumbled for the light, knocking the hotel clock off the nightstand in the process. "Fully packed?"

"Unless she's off for a wee run with all her gear."

Derrick swung his feet to the floor. "Any idea where she's headed?"

"I would suspect the station, but that's a guess. She's just leaving her hotel now."

Derrick cursed and pushed himself to his feet. "I don't know if I'll make her train."

"If not, I'll keep you apprised."

Derrick didn't doubt it. He hesitated to be anywhere near the wench without some sort of disguise, but time was short. He supposed his fellow passengers would just have to make do with his having limited his toilette to merely brushing his teeth.

He traded his own green eyes for blue, pulled on a very faded T-shirt with a pithy saying about Liszt on the back, and pulled his hair back into a very inadequate ponytail. He briefly considered a moustache, but settled for sunglasses and a bit of scruff. All he could do was keep his fingers crossed that Miss Drummond had been too distracted by paranormal happenings over the past two days to pay attention to either his shoes or his jeans, which he couldn't change. His jacket was nondescript enough that surely she wouldn't notice anything about it.

He tossed his key at the night clerk on his way out the door, then walked swiftly toward the station. He sent Oliver a pointed text as he did.

?

In line, came the succinct message, followed by the equally succinct, run.

Well, he bloody well was, as it happened. He didn't want to draw any attention to himself by stumbling into the station, gasping for breath, so he did slow to a walk before he hit the doors. He told himself not for the first time that he was going to have to splash out at some point in his life for a rail pass whilst chasing miscreants so he didn't have to waste time buying tickets.

London by way of Sudbury.

Sudbury? Derrick bought a ticket to Cambridge, then another

to Sudbury. Aye, he would most definitely get himself and Oliver both bloody passes for the next fortnight.

He shook his head. Sudbury? He considered possible final destinations for his little lace thief, then decided tentatively on Hedingham Castle. It was a bit out of the way for a rendezvous, but if she was trying to discreetly unload the goods she was carrying with her, it made perfect sense.

He slung his backpack over his shoulder and walked through the crowd toward the train. He supposed he would be left buying something to eat on the train, but that was his own fault. He should have anticipated that Samantha would make an early start. He supposed he also should have anticipated that the Cookes wouldn't want to wait too long to deliver that lace to the highest bidder.

He loitered on the platform, watched as Samantha got on the train, then waited a bit longer to make sure she didn't get right back off. It was possible, he supposed, that she might go another direction besides south. It had been all he could do earlier that morning not to hack into all Lydia Cooke's accounts and see what sort of travel arrangements she'd booked for Gavin's sister, but, again, that would have made things feel too easy.

He blew out his breath. He needed a change, and soon, before he ruined his career and his life.

Third car, halfway back. Seats full save next to me.

That would have to do, he supposed. He walked down to the appropriate train car, then hopped on board at the back. He wondered absently what Oliver had done to keep that seat free. Perhaps he'd just given all potential travel companions that look he had. Derrick had known the man for over eight years and that look still brought him up short.

He made his way without haste to the appropriate place, made a production of asking for a spot, then collapsed into his seat with a minimum of fuss. He settled in for a bit of a ride, then checked his phone.

Interesting choice, German.

Very, Derrick replied.

Pair of blokes on board.

Derrick didn't crack so much as a smile. Bald, skinny lad and a dark-haired business type?

Damn ye.

Derrick did smile then, then kept himself awake by silently

conjugating verbs in his rather rusty German, praying that he might not actually have to use it if he encountered the tightly laced Miss Drummond in person.

He had the feeling that he was getting far too casual about things. It was going to come back and bite him, he was sure of that.

He looked at the back of Miss Drummond's head three rows and on the other side of the aisle in front of him and wondered about her. He realized he'd been in the same place the day before, but he seemed to look quite often at the backs of heads as he was following people. It might be nice, he supposed, to look at the front of a head now and again.

Which was an absolutely ridiculous thing to be thinking. Obviously, he hadn't slept enough. He rolled his eyes and sighed, hoping he could stay awake on the way south.

He followed her all the way to Hedingham Castle, making sure she heard him doing his best impression of a slightly baffled tourist. He kept her within sight the entire time, but she made no move to talk to anyone. She simply made her way to the castle as if that were the entirety of her plan. If he hadn't suspected differently, he would have thought her nothing more than a typical tourist, gobsmacked by the sight of a decently maintained castle boasting a perfectly preserved Norman arch. She read all the plaques in the castle, studied her guidebook diligently, kept her hands in her pockets as she looked in the gift shop but purchased nothing.

He frowned to himself. She was without a doubt the most unlikely criminal he'd ever seen.

Then again, perhaps not. He realized at one point that she was very aware of him. She was fairly adept at glancing casually over her shoulder without being too obvious about it, but not perfect at it.

He watched her as she carefully ate what she'd paid for— every last bite, which left him wondering if she were short of funds and didn't anticipate any supper—and suspected that perhaps the Cookes weren't paying her very much. If that was the case, maybe she had no idea what the value was of what she was carrying. If someone had wanted him to courier that piece of lace, he would have named a figure that would have left them gasping.

The day wore on. He began to wonder what else Samantha Drummond could find exciting about a small castle in a remote location, but perhaps she was looking for things to steal.

Or perhaps she was killing time until her contact arrived.

He followed her as she left the keep. He would have expected her to trot right over to the bus, but again, what did he know? He was just the bloke charged with the task of getting property back for a man who trusted him to do the job with absolute discretion. He should have at least been professional enough to have done his research.

He watched Miss Drummond sit on a bench near the castle and pull out a journal she then studied intently, completely oblivious to what was going on around her. He supposed if he'd had any sort of altruism in his soul, he would have rung the Cookes and told them they needed to find better couriers in the future. If that lace wasn't stolen because she wasn't paying attention to it, he would have been very surprised.

Perhaps it was time to do something besides tail her. He sighed, then walked over to make a more direct nuisance of himself. It might be possible to startle her into a confession.

"Might I sit?" he asked, pausing beside her and putting on his best German accent. "A rest would be welcome."

She blinked at him. Then she shut her little journal quickly and put it in her bag.

"Sure."

He sat down and made a production of taking pictures of the castle with his phone. "My English is *nicht so gut. Wie* is your German?"

"Worse than your English, definitely."

He suppressed the urge to wince, because she'd said it in German and her German was much better than his. He considered, then jumped in feetfirst.

"Have you many castles seen?" he asked.

"One or two," she said warily. "You?"

"I come from a land of many castles," he said with a shrug. "They do not hold my attention for long."

She nodded uneasily, then looked at the castle in front of them as if she might like to run inside it and slam the door shut against him.

"What do you do?" he asked.

She looked at him quickly, then seemed to consider the question. "I'm, um, an . . . artist."

Of course she was, just like she was a fabulous liar who could apparently take on a persona and never fall out of character. Either that, or *slightly batty tourist* was the persona she was actually going for and she was making a brilliant job of it.

"Are you?" he asked politely. "What do you art?"

"I . . . paint," she said. Then she took a deep breath. "And draw. Both." She looked at him. "And you?"

"A bit of this and that," he said. "Nothing interesting enough to discuss."

"Well," she said, bouncing up suddenly, "it's been a pleasure. Gotta run."

He watched her rush off back toward the castle and frowned thoughtfully. She was truly a mystery. If her goal was to baffle and confuse everyone in her vicinity, she was succeeding.

He got to his feet and followed her, because that's what he did, then decided, after she'd looked back over her shoulder with an expression of alarm, that it was time for a change of costume. He texted Oliver to let him know Samantha was his for a bit, then strode off toward the castle car park to see what sort of ride he could find. Twenty quid bought him a ride to the station from an obliging gardener type, which left him time to duck into a loo and make a few changes to his appearance.

He made himself a spot in a corner of the station and decided the time had come to use his phone to its best advantage. He knew about Samantha's parents, of course, because he'd done business with Gavin Drummond before—unfortunately—and he liked to know more about his clients than perhaps was polite. But when it came to Miss Drummond herself, it took him quite a bit of time to determine even the most basic details about her. She was the single most inaccessible suspect he'd ever encountered. She had very little social media presence, unlike her parents, who seemed determined to let the world know their every thought.

Odd, though, how they didn't say anything at all about their children. It was as if they didn't have any.

Samantha Drummond's details were sketchy, but telling. Hadn't she said she was an artist? He snorted. She was a rather good liar, actually, given that her degrees were in history and textile curation. He had learned also that she'd spent the past three years tending to her mother's extensive collection of Victorian artifacts. What she was doing being a courier for the Cookes was beyond his ken, but not beyond his ability to discover.

He glanced up to see Bloke One and Bloke Two sauntering through the station behind the future van Gogh, trailed by Oliver, who somehow managed to never look the same even if he happened to be wearing the same clothes. Spooky was the only way to describe him.

Derrick wondered briefly who the first two lads were, but as long as they were limiting themselves to knives and fists instead of guns, he wasn't going to worry too much. He couldn't imagine the Cookes would have sent security after Samantha, but he found himself continually surprised by what crooks were willing to do to accomplish their ends. Surprised, but not surprised, if that made any sense. Why people couldn't just be honest and forthright—

Well, that was an argument for a different day. He had enough to worry about at present without delving into the moral morass that was the mind of the average thug.

He got on the train, walking past Samantha and choosing a seat a few rows in front of her. The only thing he could say for certain was that he was thrilled he would never have to have anything to do with her because she was just the kind of woman he would never, ever want anything to do with. Too excited about ordinary happenings and pedestrian sights.

That was all he needed: an idealistic thief.

He texted Oliver to make sure he had line of sight, then closed his eyes and decided that perhaps the only thing that would make sense was to take a nap.

He tried, really he did, to force himself to sleep, but slumber eluded him. There was something bothering him that he couldn't quite lay his finger on.

It was strange that Samantha had gone out of her way to Castle Hedingham without doing anything more useful than looking around. He had been watching her the entire time save at the end when Oliver had taken over. He hadn't seen her leave anything behind, pick anything up, speak to anyone but the woman selling entrance tickets. She had checked her phone a couple of times, but that could have been just a random thing.

Or it might have been her contact warning her off.

The two men following her left him puzzled as well. He supposed they could have been sent as security for her—heaven knew the lace was worth that kind of care—but he hadn't liked the look of them.

Then again, if he'd been sending someone to watch a priceless piece of lace, he would have sent fairly unfriendly-looking lads as well. He had, as it happened, and more than once. Oliver could vouch for that.

Obviously he was dealing with a strange breed of crook.

He settled more comfortably into his seat and forced himself to relax. He would give Samantha Drummond another couple of hours to make contact with whomever she'd come south to meet, then he would nab her before she managed it. And any twinge of regret he might feel upon watching her and her braid be carted off to jail would be tempered quite nicely by the memory of Lord Epworth's voice when he'd rung to say his lace was missing.

Criminals.

He had had just about enough of them.

Chapter 7

S amantha was in trouble.

She wasn't quite sure when she'd gotten into a great big vat of it, but the truth was hard to deny. She would have been quite happy to be in a Nancy Drew–type level of trouble, where the danger was limited to venturing where she shouldn't have without a flashlight, but she was well past that. This was thriller-movie-level trouble, complete with men following her, strangers sitting next to her on benches, and public transportation as her only means of escape.

Take her current situation, for instance. She was sitting on a train headed toward London. That in itself wasn't noteworthy. What was noteworthy, however, was the fact that she was sitting three rows behind a man she had just realized she'd been seeing over the past three days in several different guises.

She wanted to argue herself out of that conclusion, but she couldn't deny what her eyes were telling her. She supposed she might have been able to ignore the different colors of his eyes, or the changes of hair, or the glasses, or the clothes, or the languages, but there was one thing a man in a T-shirt couldn't hide and that was his build. Even with his jacket on as it was now, he couldn't hide the set of his shoulders.

She supposed she had her father to thank for giving her the skills that had led to that conclusion, a conclusion that had left her with panic that was running through her like a wildfire. She had altered so many costumes over the years for either him or his protégés that she could eye a build and have whatever she was working on fit without having to take measurements. It hadn't been an ability she'd purposely set out to acquire. She had certainly never in her wildest dreams thought it might become something critical to her survival.

She had to force herself to take a deep breath or two to calm her racing heart. She clutched her backpack, her bag tucked underneath it, and hoped she didn't look as terrified as she felt. She tried to convince herself that maybe she'd just read too many of her great-aunt Mary's mystery novels when she was growing up—never mind all the other things Mary had slipped her when her parents weren't looking. That helped a little. It was probably just her imagination running away with her.

And besides, what could she possibly have that anyone would want? If the Victorian embroidery had been all that valuable, the Cookes would have hired a professional to take it for them, or taken it south themselves. They certainly wouldn't have entrusted it to her.

She looked at the map in her hands only because it made her feel like she was doing something constructive, not because she needed it. She had already memorized it earlier. She could get off the train, take the Tube, then get herself to her hotel without incident if she stayed in a crowd. Then she would . . . well, she would call . . .

She would call her brother and tell him all about what had happened to her and then have a thorough and well-deserved freak-out—

She took a deep, careful breath. No, she couldn't do that. Gavin would lose any faith he might have had in her good sense and arrange for the Cookes to fire her. Her brother was nothing if not ruthless. And his recent bouts of generosity aside, he still looked at her as if she were approximately twelve years old.

No, she would have to handle this on her own.

She attempted a silent, scornful laugh. Handle what? Getting herself to her hotel? That was so easy, even a hapless tourist could manage that. She might even tempt fate and stop to have something to eat on the way. That might make up for the fact that she hadn't been able to enjoy her meal at Hedingham Castle because of that German guy who had been watching her.

Only that German guy was now a grungy guy sitting in front of her.

Why was he changing his appearance?

She took another deep breath. Getting to her hotel could all be done in a calm, measured fashion. Measured, measuring, not needing to measure . . . that was really the problem, wasn't it?

She looked at the man and wished she wasn't seeing what she was seeing. Unfortunately, as much as she would have liked to deny it, there was no denying that not only was he the German from Hedingham, he was the Brit from the Castle in Newcastle, he was the Canadian with the moustache from York, and he was currently the scruffy-looking guy in plain clothes who had walked past her an hour ago and collapsed into the seat three rows in front of her.

"Are you unwell, miss?"

She looked up to find a conductor standing there. He checked her ticket, then handed it back to her. At least she didn't recognize him, which she found to be rather reassuring somehow.

"I'm fine," she said, her mouth very dry. "Fine."

He didn't look convinced, but she imagined she hadn't been very convincing.

She wondered if she dared turn the tables on the chameleon in front of her and follow him for a change. She was half tempted to do it, but she could hear her great-aunt Mary telling her not to borrow trouble as clearly as if Mary were sitting next to her.

The train ride was interminable, but somehow just not long enough. She spent most of that time forcing herself not to wring her hands. She was very tempted to just get up and scream for help, but for all she knew that would land her in jail. Then again, considering the craziness that seemed to be swirling around her, maybe that wouldn't have been a bad thing.

Before she could really work up a good scream, the train pulled into the station. She had no choice but to get off with the crowd, following after her changeling, who got off in front of her. He was at least six foot two, which made him easy to keep an eye on. He didn't look to see what she was doing, which she found oddly comforting.

Maybe she'd just been imagining things.

She watched him go, then wondered if she could just go another way and lose him. She looked quickly at the signs, made a decision, then pretended nothing was going on in what was left of her fevered mind. And she made sure once they left the tracks that he was headed to the left before she turned quickly and headed to the right.

She decided abruptly that food could perhaps wait. She didn't run, but she didn't amble. The only thing she stopped for was to double-check her directions so she wound up at the right hotel.

No one shouted her name as she'd hurried down the street. No one stepped in front of her to prevent her from walking swiftly with the rest of the foot traffic. Not even the desk clerk looked at her meaningfully, as if he intended to alert every bad guy in the area that yes, indeed, she had arrived and they could come and get her at their leisure. He simply handed her a key, then went back to a conversation with his coworker that seemingly revolved around what they each hoped might be left warming on the stove by the time they got home.

Samantha was fairly certain she didn't breathe until she reached her room. She knew she would have been better off to have just crawled into bed and pulled the covers over her head, but that seemed a little too fragile even for what her family would have expected from her. She took a deep breath, then lifted her curtain and looked out the window. There was no one standing under a streetlight looking up at her. Somehow, though, that just didn't make her feel any better. She felt *watched*. What other reason would there be for that man to have changed himself into three different people to try to hit on her, then a fourth to ignore her?

She paced for a bit, but that didn't make her feel any better, so she sat down on the bed and looked at her backpack. It wasn't large, because the one useful thing she had learned from her mother was how to pack light. It tended to offset the endless suitcases her father required for a trip across town. She dumped everything out and sorted through it.

She found nothing else but the usual necessities of travel: clean underwear, a couple of shirts, a rolled-up skirt, and bathroom stuff. She checked all the pockets and zippered pouches inside the pack itself, but they were empty. It was exactly as she'd packed it herself the morning before.

She shook her head. She couldn't imagine she was being followed because she was so terribly interesting, but she was definitely being followed, so perhaps someone had . . .

Her thoughts ground to a halt.

Had someone planted something on her?

She had the renewed sensation of having fallen into a bad crime drama, made all the more believable by people around her pretending to be who they weren't and an unidentified bald guy chasing her. She looked quickly at her door, but it was locked and bolted. She got up, checked the armoire, the bathroom, and under the bed, just to be safe.

She sank down on the bed and looked at her messenger bag. She'd been using it all the time and certainly hadn't noticed anything extra in it. The only thing she had in it besides her wallet, her passport, and money was what Lydia had given her.

Samantha took the package out of the zipped compartment and turned it over in her hands. Lydia had shown her the embroidery, of course, then taken it away to wrap it up. Samantha had thought nothing of it at the time, but now even that simple act was beginning to seem a little sinister.

She attempted a light laugh, but unfortunately what had seemed ridiculous seconds ago seemed much less ridiculous at present. She very carefully undid the tape, unzipped the zipper closure, then slid the embroidery out. It unfolded to reveal itself to be nothing more than what it was.

She rolled her eyes and took her first good breath of the day. She had let her imagination get the better of her. There was nothing unusual, nothing ominous, nothing out of the ordinary. She started to put the embroidery back into its sack—

And then she realized there was more to the package than there had seemed at first glance.

She had to wipe her hands on her trousers before she was able to unwrap layers she hadn't noticed at first. Then she picked up with a shaking hand something that had her gaping.

It was a very large piece of textile.

She held it carefully under the lamp and identified without thinking that it was Elizabethan and it was in perfect condition.

She started to shake. She could hardly believe that she was entertaining the thought, but she was absolutely sure that what she was holding in her unwashed hands was the piece of lace those ladies had been talking about on the bus back from Castle Hammond. That theft had been what had left the house in an uproar and her outside in the rain.

She almost dropped it—a knee-jerk reaction to not wanting to have anything to do with it—but she wasn't unused to handling valuable things. She forced herself to set the lace down on top of the embroidery, because that seemed the cleanest place to put it, and considered the ramifications of her discovery.

That enormous piece of lace had been hidden in a package containing something entirely different. She had been sent off on an errand to deliver embroidery that hadn't been just embroidery, it had been a Victorian sample plus that large piece of stolen lace. The only time she hadn't had her bag within reach had been in Newcastle when she had trusted that it was safe in her room. And the only person with access to that room had been Lydia Cooke.

Which meant that either Lydia Cooke was absentminded or she was a thief and a liar.

Samantha tried to put the brakes on her imagination, but the ride had already left the station and was rocketing up the tracks at about eighty miles an hour. She was looking at a stolen piece of lace that was worth a small fortune. She supposed she could pull out her phone and try to investigate just how much it might be worth, but it would be just her luck that Scotland Yard would be watching all textile sites and figure out who she was and where she was. She had the feeling it would all end with her in jail.

She held her phone in her trembling hands and rehearsed in her head the most coherent way possible to explain what was going on. She closed her eyes briefly, then dialed her brother. At present, she didn't care what he thought of her. She was in trouble and he was her only hope.

"What do you want?" was the brisk answer to the second ring.

"Gavin, it's Samantha—"

"Obviously. I can't talk now."

"But—"

"I'm in the middle of a deal," Gavin said with exaggerated patience, "which means *I can't talk now*. Call me tomorrow."

"But I'm in trouble now!"

He swore. "How many days did you make it, Sam? Two? Three? That's really pathetic—"

"I'm being followed by thugs," she said quickly. "I'm in London and I need help."

"Look," he said in a low, tight voice, "I've got a lot of money riding on this thing and no time to indulge your stupid fantasies."

"Please," Samantha whispered. "Please, Gavin, I really need you—"

"I'm not your damned babysitter."

"I don't need a babysitter, I need a big brother."

Well, if there was one thing that could be said for Gavin Drummond, it was that he was slightly susceptible to guilt. She could only hope she'd caught him on one of his more susceptible days.

"Unbelievable." More swearing ensued. "All right, damn it. Can you find the gallery?"

"Yes," she said, hoping that was the case. She had the address, because in her own way she was just as compulsive a list maker as her mother. "I can find it."

"Then come now, if you can lose your *thugs* for however long it takes you to get here. Melinda can show you the back room. *Stay there* or when I'm finished, I won't help you."

"Thank you," she managed, feeling terribly grateful.

He made a sound of disgust, then hung up on her.

It was good enough. She could get herself to his place, then get him to help her. He would see how dire her circumstances were and maybe even feel slightly responsible for getting her into the situation in the first place.

Though how in the world he would have known what the Cookes were up to, she couldn't have said.

She folded the lace back up, flinching a little at touching it with her bare hands—old habits died hard—and then put everything back as close to its original wrapping as possible. The only thing she could say for the Cookes was at least Lydia had had the good sense to put the whole thing in a heavy-duty, archival-quality plastic zippered bag. She put it into her bag, then stood up.

She didn't want to look out the window, but she supposed she might as well. She pulled the curtain back and looked around.

There was a bald man standing under a streetlight, looking up at her.

She jumped back, her heart beating in her throat. She took a deep breath, but that didn't help matters any.

It could have been anyone, of course. But speculation about just who he might be was enough to leave her feeling very faint. It could be a cop, which meant that she would get caught with a stolen piece of lace and tossed in jail. It could be a thug, which meant she would be caught with a stolen piece of lace and perhaps thrown into the Thames. There was nothing between those two alternatives that was in the slightest bit comforting. What she needed was a respectable gallery owner with a sterling reputation to get her out of the pickle she hadn't purposely put herself in. She couldn't do anything else.

She stepped out of her hotel and tried to ignore the sight of two men loitering across the street. She looked to her left as if she'd simply been looking for a taxi and thought she saw someone else she recognized, though in her current straits, she really wasn't sure of anything.

She checked her map because it seemed like something a normal tourist would do. Her brother's gallery was down by the new incarnation of the Globe, which wasn't all that far away. She thought about the Tube, but she supposed it might be safer to stay on the street where there were people.

She walked quickly, but hopefully without giving any indication of her distress.

Or at least she did until she realized, fifteen minutes later, that what was standing between her and the Globe was a blasted street fair. It was as if Renaissance England had been reconstituted right there in front of her. She supposed it was great for the tourists, but it wasn't doing anything for her.

She looked over her shoulder on the pretext of seeing where she was and saw that instead of that stranger from across the street, the man who was following hard on her heels was the identity-changing man from the train. And he had given up any pretense of not watching her. She gasped, then turned back forward and ran into the crowd.

That was perhaps what saved her. She found a seller of cos-

tumes and threw money at the woman in return for an Elizabethan servant's dress that she pulled down over her head and an
apron that she had help tying around her. The latter handily
covered her messenger bag, which contained something she
most definitely shouldn't have had in her possession.

"In a hurry, are you?" the woman asked pleasantly. "Are you
one of the players?"

"Sure," Samantha managed. "And I'm lost."

"Just up the way, on the right before the theater," the woman
said with a smile. "Break a leg."

Which was preferable to breaking her neck, or having her
neck broken for her. She rushed through the rest of the stalls.
Her vow to leave the 1600s behind wasn't panning out very well
at present, but that could be fixed, she was sure. She looked over
her shoulder and found that she was still being followed by the
tall, heaven-only-knew-what-color-eyed guy who had been stalk-
ing her for three days now.

Maybe he knew about the lace and thought she had it.

She started to run. That went fairly well until she ran into a
group of young men who had obviously hit the mead several
times already that day. They were happy to accept her into their
little circle, though she wasn't particularly eager to remain
there. She ducked under arms and went sprawling onto a grassy
spot right next to them. She pushed herself up, then saw she was
in the middle of a circle of mushrooms. She crawled to her feet,
brushed her hands off, then looked down and realized the mushrooms were still there, but different. Unless she had gotten completely turned around, the side that had been open was now
closed. As if it hadn't bloomed yet.

And that was very, very weird.

She looked behind her, then realized that the guys she had
recently become quick friends with were gone as well. Maybe
she'd been longer at the task of brushing off her hands than she
thought. She stepped out of the mushroom circle, because, frankly,
it gave her the creeps. She looked at the vendors and frowned.
There were tents enough there, to be sure, but it was as if someone had dumped a very large bucket of authentic over everything. She wondered briefly if maybe she had bumped her head,
but there was no bump there that she could feel.

She looked over her shoulder and there was the Globe,

though it was looking slightly more rustic than what she had
seen five minutes ago.

She looked around for her pursuer. She supposed that was
the only bright spot in the gloom, because he was nowhere to be
found.

Then again, neither were sidewalks or nice, tarmac-covered
streets.

She pulled her phone out of her bag and frowned. She had
power, but no signal. She looked over her shoulder at that ring
of mushrooms in the grass, then at the air shimmering there in
the middle of that ring.

That was odd, wasn't it?

She sniffed. London in the summer was pretty fragrant, but
somehow that had just been kicked up a notch. Well, several
notches, really. She thought she might lose what lunch she had
managed to gag down.

She looked up, then realized there was not a single tall building within her line of vision. Not only that, the buildings that
she could see were something out of a vintage period movie.
And the language was, well, it was rather more authentic than
she would have expected for modern-day London.

She wondered if maybe she had actually suffered a bonk on
the head that had landed her in some sort of self-inflicted hal-
lucination where everyone was living out their lives in her least
favorite time period. Well, perhaps that wasn't completely accurate. She didn't really dislike Elizabethan England. She just
didn't want to be responsible for curating its treasures—or those
of any other vintage, as it happened—any longer.

She frowned. How was it possible that everyone around her
could be sharing in her delusion?

And why were those men over there looking at her as if she
had just walked out of a fairy tale—and not one they had been
happy to listen to?

She decided that there were two things she needed to do:
first, blend into the crowd; and second, get rid of what people
were following her for.

And the sooner she saw to both, the happier she would be.

Chapter 8

D*errick* watched Samantha Drummond disappear in front of him and felt his mouth fall open. He gaped at the ground at his feet, then backed away instinctively. He looked down at the patch of grass, not unheard of in the city, and saw that in it was a ring of mushrooms, half of them opened, half of them closed. The fair attendees seemed to steer clear of the place, a show of good sense for which he would have congratulated them had he been capable of it. As it was all he could do was stand there and swear.

He pulled his phone out of his pocket and texted Oliver.
Where are you?
"Right behind you."
Derrick turned to find that was indeed the case. He looked at him seriously. "I've got to go get her."
Oliver's expression didn't change. "Where did she go?"
"I'll tell you when I get back." He needed clothes, and quickly. He walked over to a likely-looking stall, purchased what he thought might be necessary, then ducked behind a screen and changed jeans for baggy workman's trousers. He simply pulled

a tunic down over his shirt. He had no intention of being wherever Samantha had gone any longer than necessary, but he had to at least attempt to look the part. He could only hope she had perhaps gone to Elizabethan England. It was a random thing to hope for, he supposed, but they were near the Globe and he was standing on the edge of a Renaissance faire. It was a good guess.

Heaven help them both if she'd disappeared into a far different and perhaps much less civilized century.

He could hardly believe he was even thinking any of it with any degree of seriousness, but the unfortunate truth was, he knew better than to doubt.

He shoved his jeans in his pack, then found Oliver and handed his pack over. He put his phone into his pocket only to realize that he didn't have any pockets. After indulging in another choice word or two, he decided he would just have to hold on to it.

He sighed, then went to stand on the edge of the grass. He looked over his shoulder at Oliver. "Push me into that ring of mushrooms."

Oliver looked for the first time faintly startled. "What?"

"Back into me, then make a production of dusting yourself off. Maybe everyone will forget they've seen me disappear."

Oliver shut his mouth with a snap. "Whatever you say, boss."

Derrick would have thanked him, but Oliver had already given him a serious shove. He fell upon his arse, truth be told, but looked up to find himself in a different century. He didn't want to think about how or why he knew that. It was enough to know he'd managed to get through a gate to a century not his own.

He jumped to his feet and stumbled out into what he supposed could reliably be identified as not-modern London. He honestly didn't care what year it was as long as it contained Samantha Drummond and what he was convinced she was carrying in that little messenger bag of hers.

He knew he should have been prepared for the change of venue, as it were, but he wasn't. The first thing that struck him was the smell. Present-day large cities had a particular smell, true, but that was more cement and living than it was simply raw sewage. He dragged his sleeve over his madly watering eyes, then looked around for his missing thief.

He found her standing in the middle of a crowd, gaping. He couldn't say he blamed her. He was accustomed to time periods not his own, of course, but there was nothing quite like the shock of getting off the train, as it were, and finding oneself in the middle of an entirely different country.

He worked his way over to her only to have her look at him, then *look* at him. She squeaked, turned, and bolted.

And he lost her.

Of course that might have come from too much fastidiousness on his part. He needed to stop flinching at the raw sewage he was stomping through, perhaps stop paying so much attention to things being flung periodically from upper windows, and concentrate more on the fact that he was four hundred years out of his own time and so was a priceless piece of lace.

He slowed his pace from frantic to slightly panicked, then looked more carefully for Miss Drummond.

He was unsurprised somehow to find her standing yet again in the middle of a group of yobs who were definitely interested in a woman who, he had to admit, was not all that hard to look at.

He looked around himself quickly, then stepped over to a likely-looking man.

"Borrow your sword, good sir?" he said in his best Renaissance England accent.

The man sized him up quickly, then handed the rapier over hilt first. "Good luck to you, sir."

Or words to that effect. Derrick had a look at the circle of lads—a circle that had enlarged itself quite suddenly, as it happened—and watched one of the company catch a sword tossed his way. That lad flung off the sheath without the slightest hesitation and grinned at Derrick.

Wonderful. Derrick rolled his eyes. Obviously it was going to be a reenactment of every Shakespearean battle scene he'd ever been in, only now the swords were real.

He stepped into the circle and put himself in front of Samantha Drummond.

"Stay behind me," he said. He looked briefly over his shoulder. "Don't move."

"Ah—"

"And take my phone. Do *not* drop it."

"Bu-bu-bu-bu—" Her mouth continued to move, but only garbled noises emerged. She was pointing in front of him, her mouth hanging open.

He managed to save his head from being cleaved in twain, but it was a near thing. He found himself rather more thankful for endless fencing classes at university than he was for anything James MacLeod had taught him. Because the rapier he was holding wasn't exactly a Claymore and the man facing him was very good at his craft.

But then again, so was Jamie, and with every type of blade he put his hand to. Derrick had to give credit where it was due. If things went south, at least he could ditch his polite parrying and engage happily and quite successfully in a street brawl. Jamie would have approved.

Only the fight didn't last nearly as long as he'd expected it would. He had hardly gotten himself warmed up before he heard someone sound the alarm.

"Guards!"

Gasps ensued. He gasped as well, but that might have been at the sting in his shoulder. He didn't think the wound was a bad one, but he had the feeling it would give him grief. At least that blade hadn't gone through his heart. He looked behind him at the liveried men wending their way through the crowd and decided guards were the last thing he needed. It was one thing to get trapped in a time not his own, but another thing entirely to be stuck there when the Tower was a handy place to stash miscreants who might possibly be labeled a serious threat.

He feinted to the right, then very unsportingly punched his opponent full in the face. He tossed the sword to its owner, thanked him politely for the use of it, then was rather relieved to find Samantha Drummond still behind him where he'd left her. He reached for her hand and pulled, actually a little surprised that she didn't fight him. Then again, she looked absolutely stunned, so perhaps he was crediting her with good sense where he shouldn't have.

He threaded his way through the crowds, dodging things being thrown out of windows and trying to ignore the smell. He wasn't unaccustomed to changes of environment thanks to his travels with James MacLeod, but he couldn't say he wouldn't be glad to get back to the London he was accustomed to. Well, that and he fully intended to get things squared away, reacquire his lace, then have something decent to eat. If he'd had to make do with food purchased at train stations much longer, his stomach would have rebelled.

He hustled Samantha back through stalls of vendors selling everything from food to trinkets, then right into the circle of mushrooms that were startlingly similar to what was found four hundred years in the future. He staggered a little at the transition from one century to the next, but was happy to find himself back where he'd begun. Oliver wasn't there, of course, but he hadn't expected him to be. That one wasn't fond of drawing attention to himself. Unfortunately, Samantha Drummond wasn't nearly so reticent. She was wheezing with the enthusiasm of a serious asthmatic.

"Is that blood?" she gasped.

He glanced down at his shoulder, then looked at her. "Ketchup."

"But—"

He ignored her and continued to pull. He made certain he and Samantha were a goodly distance from the gate, checked for thugs and found none, then continued on to the stalls past where he'd bought his gear. He released Samantha's hand briefly, though he honestly wondered about the advisability of that. She was a runner, that girl. He considered returning the clothes but realized abruptly that he had no jeans on under his trousers.

"Is that blood?" the man asked, pointing at a rather large stain on the arm of his shirt.

"Marinara sauce," Derrick said promptly. He stripped the tunic off and handed it back. "Have it cleaned and it'll be good as new."

"Ah—"

Derrick walked away before the man came to any other conclusion. He took his phone from Samantha's unresisting fingers, then pulled her along after him. He texted Oliver with one hand.

We're back.

Got you.

He was more grateful for that than perhaps he should have been. He suppressed the urge to tell Oliver that he loved him, then turned to more pressing matters. He dropped Samantha's hand and spun to face her.

"Where is it?"

She blinked. "Where is what?"

"Don't play stupid," he said briskly.

"I don't know—"

"Of course you do," he said. He realized he was barely keeping his temper in check, which wasn't usually the case for him. In his defense, it had been that kind of day so far. "I don't know why you're involved in this and quite frankly I don't care. Just give me the lace and we'll call it good. I won't see you prosecuted."

"I don't know what you're talk—" she began.

"How stupid do you think I am?" he demanded.

She looked up at him. "I don't know," she said slowly, "how stupid are you?"

Stupid enough to continue to push a woman who looked like she was on the verge of throwing up. He suffered a small feeling of pity but squelched that immediately. She was a thief and a liar. At the very least, she had been willing to take employment with a couple who had caused a very lovely old man a great deal of distress.

"I'm not stupid enough to find *myself* standing in front of a magistrate," he said briskly, "which perhaps makes me just a bit more clever than you. Now, where is the lace?"

She would have made a lousy poker player. "I don't have it."

He started to speak, but his phone rang. He shot her a warning look. "Don't move."

Her mouth worked for several moments, then she drew herself up. "Go to—to—to, um . . ."

"Hell?" he finished for her. "Already there, thank you."

He thought not for the first time that he really had to make a few changes in his life. He needed a girlfriend, one who could tell him to go to hell without sounding as though she'd never considered the thought before. He answered his phone, surprised that Oliver would ring him instead of texting.

"You're surrounded," Oliver said urgently. "You need to move, *now*."

He almost dropped his phone. *"What?"*

"Two behind you and two up the way. Two we know, two we don't. Very unpleasant sorts."

"Perfect," Derrick said. "I'll find a cab—"

"Rufus will be pulling up to the curb if you can last another two minutes," Oliver said. "Though that may be a stretch—"

"I'll manage."

"Thought you might. Must dash."

Derrick supposed he must as well. He hung up, then realized that Samantha was ten feet away from him, engaging in a bit of a dash herself. He caught up with her easily and took her by the arm.

"Let's go."

"Are you insane?" she squeaked. "Let go of me!"

He stopped abruptly and glared at her. "Listen, you silly girl, someone is after you and it isn't me. If you want to die, just stand here and wait. Otherwise, stop acting like an idiot and come with me."

"Are you out of your mind?" she wheezed.

He pointed back over his shoulder. "Would you rather take your chances with those lads back there?"

She looked, then blanched. He thought that was a show of good sense after all, so he continued on until they'd reached the curb, then looked over his shoulder. They were being followed, hard, which might not have alarmed him except that the woman next to him was carrying an enormous piece of priceless lace. He looked to his right, then didn't bother to suppress his sigh of relief. He continued to hold on to Samantha Drummond until Rufus glided to a stop right there where the handle to the back door was within reach. He opened it, urged Samantha inside as gently as possible, then dove in himself.

"Get off me!"

He heaved himself up into the seat, trying not to crush her in the process, and fumbled for the door to pull it shut as Rufus sped off. He sat back, dragged his hands through his hair, and sighed deeply.

"Thank you, Rufus," he said. It seemed a rather feeble display of appreciation, but he supposed he might frighten the good Miss Drummond if he fell upon Rufus's neck and sobbed like a bairn.

"Where to now, Master Derrick?"

"*Away* is enough for the moment," Derrick said. He shifted on his seat and looked at Samantha, who was still fumbling with her seat belt. Safety first, he supposed, which he wasn't going to argue with. Far easier to get his lace back if she wasn't trying to get out of the backseat.

He watched her for another moment or two, then reached over and buckled her seat belt for her. Her hands were shaking too badly to manage it herself. A guilty conscience, no doubt. Add to that her absolutely white features and there he had a criminal caught red-handed.

And on the subject of being red-handed, he looked down at his own hand, covered as it was in blood that had dripped down his arm. He was fairly sure it wasn't anything more than a scratch, so he ignored it in favor of staring down the miscreant sitting next to him.

"Where is the lace?" he demanded.

"I don't know what you're talking about," she said faintly.

"Of course you know what I'm talking about."

He watched her hand creep under her apron. He wasn't altogether sure she didn't have a knife with her, but he supposed being stabbed by that couldn't make his arm hurt any more than it hurt at present. Plus, he wouldn't have any trouble disarming her. He waited until she had started to fumble with whatever she'd found before he lifted the apron of her dress and removed what turned out to be a small notebook from her trembling fingers.

"Give that back," she said, reaching for it.

He held it away, then glared at her. "Give me back the lace first."

"I told you, I don't know what you're talking about!"

"Listen, Miss Drummond—"

"How do you know who I am?"

He shot her what he hoped had come out as a supercilious look. "I know all kinds of things," he said curtly, "including the fact that you have in your possession a piece of lace that does not belong to you, a piece of Edwardian textile—"

"Elizabeth—" She looked at him, the word dying on her lips.

"Elizabethan?" he asked politely. "How interesting that you should know that. Now, where is it?"

She shifted uncomfortably. "I don't know what you're talking about."

He wasn't in the habit of throttling those of the fairer sex, but he was tempted to shout at her at least. He might have wondered if she were actually telling the truth, but she just looked so profoundly guilty. He looked at her sternly.

"I want answers."

She looked absolutely terrified, which began to leave him

slightly unsettled. He wasn't about to credit her with anything of an altruistic or noble nature, but the woman didn't look as if she could have stolen a sweet from a shop with any success.

"I don't have any answers," she said, "so you might as well let me go."

"Straight to Scotland Yard, if I had any sense," he said grimly.

"A dangerous place for you, I'd imagine," she said, looking down her nose at him. Unfortunately, the fact that her teeth were chattering ruined the aura of bravado.

"What does that mean?"

"It means how do I know *you* aren't a textile thief?"

He frowned. Things were not going quite as he'd expected them to, which bothered him. He was accustomed to knowing what would happen before it happened. This business of the unexpected . . . well, he wasn't sure he cared for it.

"Derrick, we have a couple of friends behind us," Rufus interjected suddenly. "What do you want me to do?"

Derrick considered furiously. His arm was about to make him daft with its throbbing, he had a very uncooperative courier sitting next to him, and they were both being followed by unknown quantities. He couldn't imagine that they were friends of the woman sitting next to him. Perhaps some time in a quiet location would cause the answers to bubble to the surface. With the way his companion was wheezing, he didn't suppose that would take very long.

He texted Oliver. Hotel?

Already done.

Where?

Ritz, of course. Cameron's buying.

He'll bill me.

Prob.

Derrick wasn't a fan of big, splashy hotels, but the security and visibility of the Ritz was undeniable. A difficult place in which to find oneself mugged. He sighed. "The Ritz, please, Rufus."

"Very good, Master Derrick."

Samantha Drummond was making noises that sounded remarkably rodent-like. If he hadn't known better, he would have thought Cameron's Mercedes had mice nesting under the seats. He pursed his lips, then looked at his companion. Her face was only occasionally lit by the traffic, but he saw all he needed to. She was absolutely terrified.

"I'll scream," she said, sounding as if she would only scream after she'd lost what lunch she'd managed to ingest.

He shifted so he could look her full in the face. "I have no intention of harming you," he said, though he would most certainly and with a certain amount of cheerfulness turn her over to the authorities once he'd had his lace back from her. "I don't think the others following you are nearly as altruistic."

"Bald guy?"

He nodded.

"Skinny guy?"

He nodded, deciding that perhaps it would be discreet not to mention the other two Oliver had seen in the crowd. For all he knew, there were even more.

"What do they want from me?"

"What do you think they want from you?"

She put her hand over her mouth and turned to look out the window.

Derrick wasn't unused to waiting people out. It had served him very well over the years, that waiting. He could surely outlast a simple scholar from across the Pond, even one who was foolish enough to try to make a little extra from a bit of thievery. Perhaps she'd considered lifting the lace herself. He imagined with enough time and a handful of disappointed looks, she might be dissuaded from a further life of crime. A pity she would spend so long in prison. He didn't imagine she would look quite as lovely after her stint.

But that wasn't his worry.

Why he couldn't have done that at a cheap hotel, he didn't know, but there it was. At least he would get something decent to eat out of the bargain.

He leaned his head back against the seat and closed his eyes. He pressed his free hand against his shoulder and almost lost consciousness. That wasn't good, but it could wait.

He gave Samantha Drummond half an hour before she was singing like a lark. His arm would last that long.

Or so he hoped.

Chapter 9

Samantha stared up at the façade of the Ritz as the very nice car she was sitting in slowed to a stop in front of it. She had spent the ride thinking about how she might best get away from her—well, she couldn't decide if she should call him her rescuer or her captor. He had certainly hoisted a sword in her defense and he had gotten her away from those very unpleasant-looking men who seemed to be wanting to have a little chat with her. Then again, he had also shoved her into the back of a car and driven off with her, which she couldn't say was a point in his favor.

She forced herself to take deep, even breaths, then decided she would make a list of events, because making lists always made her feel more in control of her life. And if there were ever a time in her life she needed some control, it was then.

The first item of interest was the fact that she had just spent an unusual half hour in the midst of some weird, reality-show-like street fair complete with extremely unsettling sewage-like props. Second, she had been rescued by a man who had borrowed a rapier from someone else, then fought with it as if he'd known what he was doing. Third, after a few more thrills and chills that felt far too paranormal for her taste, she was being let out of a very expensive car in front of a hotel that she never would have gotten closer to than gawking at it online.

She was going to have to examine all of those at greater length, but first she had to get herself somewhere safe. And at the moment, if her choice was staying out on the street where she was potentially in the sights of very unpleasant-looking thugs or going inside the hotel where she could maybe go hide in the ladies' room and start screaming in order to be rescued, she would take the inside route.

The door was opened by a bellhop. She might have considered bolting right there, but that Derrick person had suddenly materialized next to her and taken her by the arm. She allowed that and continued on into the lobby, hoping a handy escape route would present itself sooner rather than later.

It was hard not to feel like a country bumpkin when she walked through sheer luxury. She was acutely aware of her dress, which had acquired a few suspicious substances during her trip through the street fair, and her shoes, which had unavoidably encountered an open sewer on the same jaunt. The truth was, she smelled, and not in a good way.

She clutched her bag to her under her apron and didn't protest when Derrick, last name unknown, took her by the arm and led her over to the concierge's desk. He at least didn't seem to be bothered by her outfit. Then again, the sleeve of his shirt was wet with something so dark that either he had run into a glass of burgundy or he was bleeding. That didn't seem to faze him, either.

He looked at the man behind the counter. "I believe we have a reservation."

The concierge looked first at him, then at her, as if he just wasn't quite sure what to make of either of them. He started to speak but was immediately hip-checked out of the way by an older, more distinguished-looking gentleman.

"Her Ladyship phoned ahead," he said. "I am Maurice. It is, of course, a pleasure to serve any guest of the Countess of Assynt."

Samantha suppressed the urge to stick her fingers in her ears. "Who?"

Maurice looked at her and a slight pucker formed between his eyes. "The Countess of Assynt. And you are—"

"Someone very famous," Derrick said smoothly. "She prefers anonymity."

Samantha felt her mouth fall open. "No, I wouldn't—"

"She would," Derrick insisted. He leaned forward slightly. "Method acting and all that, of course. Elizabethan part, as you can see by the costume. We've been rehearsing an abduction scene."

"We're not rehearsing anything," Samantha exclaimed. "He's kidnapping me—"

"For the scene," Derrick interjected. "Of course."

Maurice looked slightly alarmed. "If I might ask—"

"Or perhaps not," Derrick said with a smile. He lowered his voice to a conspiratorial murmur. "I can't mention names and this one is too modest to, but she's a very famous American actress." He nodded. "Yes, *that* one."

"She doesn't look like her—"

"None of them look like themselves without their stylist, do they?" Derrick said dismissively. He straightened and was again all business. "I need to get her out of the range of any photographers. If you wouldn't mind?"

"Of course, Mr. Cameron."

Samantha was starting to get dizzy from looking back and forth between them and trying to get her mouth to form words. Before she could, unfortunately, Maurice had beckoned and an assistant of some kind was instantly there.

"Show them to their suite without delay, Shawn."

"Ever so good of you," Derrick said. "I'll be sure and let Her Ladyship know the sort of service we received."

More compliments were exchanged. Samantha found that she could do nothing besides continue to splutter helplessly, all the way across the lobby and into the elevator. Derrick, whoever he really was, still had hold of her elbow, but she managed to rip her arm away from him and glare at him. He only smiled indulgently, then nodded meaningfully at their escort.

Samantha considered furiously. Things were rapidly going downhill inside the hotel, but she wasn't too dumb to realize they wouldn't be any better *out*side. Her options were limited to either calling her brother again or calling the police. She wasn't sure the police would be a good option given that she was currently in possession of a very expensive piece of lace, but Gavin hadn't seemed all that interested in helping her, either. Given that he likely hadn't found any enthusiasm for the idea of helping her since the last time she'd talked to him, maybe she was just on her own.

She exited the elevator with Derrick the Gripper resuming his hold on her arm and kept her eyes peeled for a way out of her current predicament. It wasn't as if she could bang on a door and hope—

Or maybe she could. She contemplated that as she walked down the hallway. There might not be anyone willing to open up to her, but just that gave her what she was fairly convinced was an idea even Carson Drew would have approved of.

She waited until she was standing in front of what was apparently the end of the line for her, then smiled at their escort. "Thanks so much. I'm being kidnapped, you know."

"Isn't she droll?" Derrick said in accents so posh, she thought they all might cut themselves on them. "Still in character, even here in the hallway." He looked at her lovingly. "I believe we should hurry inside and finish the scene, darling, don't you agree? We wouldn't want Scotland Yard offering an opinion on—"

Samantha pushed past the man sent to accompany them, jumped inside the room, then turned and shoved the door shut. She bolted it for good measure, then leaned her forehead against the wood.

There was silence on the other side for a moment or two, then a very stern voice that came very clearly through the door.

"Open the door, Miss Drummond. It's time to come out of character."

"Go to—" She chewed on the word for a moment or two, then cast caution to the wind. "Go to hell," she said firmly.

She could hear voices outside, discussing the dilemma. She turned, then leaned back against the door.

Then she jumped half a foot.

A woman rose from the couch, someone who could only have been a Bond girl. Samantha was starting to feel as if instead of falling into a bad crime drama, she had become part of some slick British television show. She wished she could have patted her sidearm meaningfully or given her companion a cool look of disdain, but all she could do was gape at her.

The Bond girl crossed the room to her, then held out her hand. "I'm Emily," she said, her accent betraying her as French. "Who are you?"

No wonder she looked so effortlessly chic. Samantha wasn't sure that her Renaissance garb was very stylish, but she was very sure that her normal middle-aged-scholar style would have left Emily wincing involuntarily.

"I'm Samantha," Samantha managed. "And I'm—"

"A thief," Derrick growled from the other side of the door.

Samantha pointed back over her shoulder. "He thinks I'm a thief."

"You *are* a thief!" came the accusation, muffled, through the door.

"Please, sir, the other guests—"

"The other guests be damned!"

Emily pursed her lips, then laughed a little. "I think, *chérie*, that perhaps we had best let him in before he lands himself in trouble."

"He kidnapped me," Samantha said quickly. "I need help."

Emily looked utterly surprised. "Kidnapped?"

"Well, what else would you call it? He's been following me for days, he chased me through a street fair, then he threw me into a car and brought me here."

"That does sound suspicious," Emily agreed, "but maybe he was trying to rescue you."

"I want my lace back!" came the voice very clearly through the door.

"Derrick, be quiet," Emily called.

"Is this part of the scene, Mr. Cameron?" said the concierge's assistant. "Or should I call the police?"

"Yes," Samantha said loudly.

"No," Derrick said firmly. "Emily, open the door!"

"No, don't," Samantha said quickly.

Emily frowned. "What are you afraid he'll do?"

"I'm afraid he'll take me off somewhere and lock me up until he's decided what he'll do with me." She paused. "Which he seems to have already done."

"At least the surroundings are lovely."

Well, there was that. And honestly, she couldn't imagine even a highly paid thug taking his prey to the Ritz. And what sort of guy would have someone as chic as Emily the Bond girl babysitting that room? She considered, then looked at Emily.

"He's not dangerous?"

Emily shook her head.

"But he won't listen to me."

Emily drew her away from the door. "He will listen to me."

Samantha put her hand on the door and kept it shut. "I don't trust him."

Emily paused, then looked at her seriously. "I cannot blame you, of course, but I will tell you that I would trust Derrick Cameron with my life. I *have* trusted him with that life in the past, more than once."

Samantha didn't want to believe that, but Emily looked so reasonable that she was beginning to doubt her doubts. She frowned at Emily. "Who are you?"

"I work for Robert Cameron, the Earl of Assynt," she said. "Doing odd jobs, attending to his wife, things they both need me to take care of." She smiled. "We are trustworthy."

Samantha wasn't entirely sure she could count Derrick in that group, but at least Emily looked trustworthy. If things went south, she could hide behind Emily and call the cops.

And again, she was standing in a gorgeous suite at the Ritz. If Derrick had been a thug, she would have been in a crappy hotel in the wrong part of town. Sort of like where her stuff was currently residing.

She stepped away from the door and allowed Emily to open it. Derrick thanked their escort, then walked into the room and shut the door behind him with exaggerated care.

"Good evening, Emily."

"*Bonsoir, mon cher,*" Emily said, leaning over to exchange kisses on both cheeks with him. "How has your day been?"

"Interesting," Derrick said politely. "I don't suppose Cameron would splash out for supper, would he?"

"I imagine he would, since he's billing you for the room."

"Unsurprising." He leaned back against the door and looked at Samantha. "Good evening, Miss Drummond. I suppose the least I can do is feed you before I throw you back out to the wolves."

"Derrick," Emily chided, "stop it. This sweet girl here told me she had nothing to do with anything of yours."

Derrick snorted. "Don't believe her. She has a habit of prevarication."

Samantha blinked. "What in the world are you talking about?"

"You," he said crisply. "Saying you were an artist. You've a bloody degree in history and textiles, Miss Drummond, not art. I doubt you've ever picked up a paintbrush."

Samantha felt her mouth fall open. "How do you know anything about me?" She looked at Emily. "Who is he? Some sort of private detective?"

Emily smiled. "The second coming of Sherlock Holmes, rather."

Samantha would have burst into tears, if she'd been the type to do so. With her mother, she'd never really had the opportunity to. Her mother was a tsunami of personality and activity, leaving her with no chance to do anything but hold on to something solid and hope she survived. Her father, well, her father was who he was. But tears weren't allowed. Shakes, though, were looking like an appealing option. If they were done artistically, she supposed even her father would have approved.

"This is kidnapping," she managed, trying to keep her teeth from chattering.

"And theft is a felony," Derrick shot back.

"Derrick, don't be difficult," Emily warned.

He looked like he was ramping up for a good bout of it. Samantha decided abruptly that she'd had enough. They could keep her in that room, but they couldn't keep her silent. She dug around in her bag for her phone, fully intending to dial 911 or 999 or HELPME; whatever worked.

But her phone wasn't there.

Obviously she'd dropped it, but she couldn't think of where. She looked at Derrick. "Did I leave my phone in the car?"

"How the hell do I know where you left your phone?" he said, sounding rather angry.

She thought she might want to sit down fairly soon. The next thing she knew, she was sitting down on the couch with Emily peering intently at her.

"What is it?" she asked.

"I've lost my phone," she said slowly. She ignored Derrick's noises of impatience and Emily's concern and ran back through the afternoon and evening's events. She had, she had to admit, suffered a moment of panic and pulled the embroidery out of her purse and . . . well, that was probably when she'd lost her phone.

Emily pulled her phone out of her purse on the coffee table. She started to hand it over, but Derrick reached out and took it before she could. Emily looked at him in surprise.

"What are you doing?"

"I don't want her calling anyone until she's given me the lace."

"I don't have the lace," Samantha managed.

Derrick waved Emily's phone at her. "At least you admit that you know what I'm talking about."

She wondered how someone so good-looking could be so stubborn and unreasonable. "Is it your lace?"

"No," he said shortly. "It belongs to my client."

"Are you a cop?"

He pursed his lips. "No."

"Then how do you know anything about it?"

Derrick looked at Emily. "I'm finding it difficult to believe I'm having a conversation with a thief. Tell me why I just don't rip her bag out of her hands and get back what she's stolen?"

"I didn't steal it," Samantha said.

"No, you were working for other people who stole it," he said, shooting her a dark look, "which I'm sure you knew."

"But I had no idea—"

"Ha," he said triumphantly. "Then you admit you have it."

She started to protest but realized that maybe there was no point. She took a deep breath. "I had it," she said. "But I had no idea that I had it. It was hidden inside a piece of Victorian embroidery that I was asked to bring south to London."

"Unbelievable," he said with a gusty sigh. "And you didn't think to question any of this?"

"Why would I?" she asked. "The Cookes are friends of my brother's—"

"Who has terrible taste in friends," he muttered. He dragged his hands through his hair and looked heavenward. "At least the lace is safe. We can worry about the rest of it later." He held out his hand. "I'll take it and make sure it gets back to the right place."

"And why in the world would I trust you with it?"

"Because I have been charged by its *owner*, Lord Epworth, with getting it back," he said, with exaggerated patience, "and get it back I shall. Now, do the right thing and hand it over before I call Scotland Yard and counter every thing you've said."

"You work for Lord Epworth?" she asked in surprise. "Really?"

"Yes, really," he said in a perfect American accent. "Relinquish it so I can ring up the poor man and ease his mind."

She was on her feet without quite knowing how she'd gotten there. She paced a bit, then turned and looked at the other two in the room. Emily was sitting on the couch, the picture of elegance. Derrick was frowning at her, as if he couldn't decide whether to shout or simply take her bag and get the lace himself. She took a deep breath, but that didn't calm her nerves any.

"I don't have it," she said.

"Of course you do," Derrick said.

"No, I don't."

He folded his arms over his chest. "Prove it."

She supposed since she didn't have a phone, there was nothing in her bag that was really worth saving except her wallet, which was uninteresting, and her notebook, which she was just going to display, not hand over. He'd already flipped through her notebook and handed it back to her in the car, so she supposed there was nothing else she had that would shock him. She pulled the strap over her head, then emptied the bag onto the coffee table. Derrick only looked down, then at her.

"Where is it?"

"Probably with my phone," she said, "which I probably dropped while hiding the lace."

He blinked. "You did what?"

"I hid the lace," she repeated slowly. "You know, as in putting it somewhere out of the way?"

"You *hid* the lace?" he asked incredulously. "Where?"

She gestured behind her, because she had a very good sense of direction. "Back there. In that street fair."

He swayed. "You hid a priceless piece of Elizabethan lace in a *street fair*?"

"Under a planter," she said defensively. "And it was in archival quality plastic, not a paper bag. It'll be fine." She paused.

"Actually, I'll admit that the location worried me, because that seemed to be a rougher part of the fair than I started in—"

"What?"

She looked at him. "Where you and that guy were sword-fighting. I'd hidden it just before I walked into that group of, well, bad guys."

He blanched. She had never seen the color disappear from someone's face like that before. It was, she had to admit, a reaction that seemed a little more than circumstances called for, but then again, it hadn't been her lace she was hiding.

But she would probably be liable for losing it.

She realized she was swaying only because Emily had caught her by the arm and was holding her up.

"I think what you need, *chérie*, is a hot bath. Let's get that started, then I'll order something for you to eat."

Samantha went with her because Emily was an irresistible force of manners and chicness and actually the thought of a hot anything sounded good. She looked back over her shoulder before Emily drew her inside a bedroom. Derrick was sitting on the couch with his head in his hands.

She couldn't blame him for that. She wasn't exactly sure she hadn't assumed that very same position when she'd realized what she had in her bag.

She sank down onto the edge of the bed and watched as Emily opened up a suitcase full of clothes and laid things out. Maybe she intended to put on a fashion show for Derrick.

"You have your bath, Samantha," Emily said, nodding toward the bathroom. "I'll go keep watch in the sitting room."

Samantha could hardly believe she had found any sort of ally in a world gone mad. She simply looked off into nothing for a moment or two before she turned to Emily. "Why should I trust you?"

"Because I don't think you're a thief." Emily zipped up the suitcase and set it on the floor. "You look a little lost to me."

Samantha pointed toward the door. "*He* still thinks I'm a thief."

"Derrick can be intense." She looked at Samantha. "Is that the word I want?"

"I think *jerk* is a better choice," Samantha muttered. "I'd say I would reserve judgment, but I don't plan on being in his august presence for that long." But while she had answers, she supposed she couldn't be blamed for wanting them. "Who is he?"

"Just a man."

She shot Emily a look. "Please."

"He's not nefarious, if that's what concerns you. His cousin is the Earl of Assynt, after all, and he's a very lovely man."

Samantha wondered if things could get any stranger. She was being kidnapped by a man who was related to an earl and she was being taken in hand by that earl's employee. She looked over her shoulder on the off chance there was a ghost there to add a bit more character to the party. She was very relieved to find there wasn't.

"I'll leave you your privacy," Emily said, "and remind our Derrick to find his manners."

"I'm not going to be here long enough for him to manage that."

"That is, of course, your decision," Emily conceded. "I will keep watch, though, if you'd like to change."

Samantha gestured to the clothes on the bed. "Who do those belong to?"

"You, *chérie*," Emily said.

"How . . ."

"I will tell you," Emily promised, "but perhaps not now. You're perfectly safe here. I'll see to it."

Samantha considered that. At least she could maybe exit the place looking so different that no one would recognize her and follow her.

She was definitely starting to feel as if she'd wandered into some sort of Impressionist painting. Everything around her was starting to take on a sort of splotchy, color-driven, shapeless kind of form. She watched Emily walk toward the door, then waited until the door was closed before she locked it, then looked around for something to put in front of it. A chair seemed rather less substantial than she would have liked, but she stacked a very expensive-looking crystal vase on it. At least that way she would hear it when it crashed. What she would do then, she had no idea, but maybe something would come to her in the moment.

She walked over to the window and looked down. Too high to jump and no ledge to crawl out on. She was stuck.

She headed for the bathroom. Maybe water would help her think. It usually did.

Though she had the feeling that not even a shower to be found at the Ritz could possibly manage to inspire her with a solution to her current problem.

Chapter 10

D*errick* looked up as Emily pulled the door shut behind her. He had to admit he was perhaps rather more grateful to see her than he should admit to. There was something about her ability to walk into any situation and take charge that was unaccountably soothing.

She wasn't his cousin by blood, but she might as well have been. They had spent part of their youth together when she hadn't been in France, she as the granddaughter of Madame Gies, the Cameron cook, and he as the grandson of old Alistair Cameron's valet. Never mind that his grandfather had actually been Alistair's cousin. When one threw the current laird Robert's genealogy into the mix, the family tree became very convoluted indeed. But he was grateful, as he always had been, for family, no matter how distant the connections.

"You look as if you've had a difficult day," Emily said, sinking down on the couch gracefully. "I can watch over your charge for a bit if you'd like to go rest before dinner."

"Good," Derrick said shortly. "I'm liable to kill her if I have to have anything else to do with her."

"What you need, *mon cher*, is a lesson in manners."

He rubbed his hands over his face. "I'm sorry, Emily. Thank you very kindly for coming to my rescue tonight. I'm assuming you brought clothes."

"For you both, though *you* don't deserve them."

He would have smiled, but he was too damned tired to. "I daresay I don't."

"Go have a little rest," she said, pointing to the doorway of the other bedroom. "Behave better when you've finished."

He rose, kissed her hand, then thanked her very kindly before he walked into the other bedroom and shut the door. He knew he should have snatched what sleep he could, but all he could do was pace. The things that were currently causing him stress were so many and so varied, there was no possible way he would manage to even close his eyes.

Before he had truly begun to wear a trench into the carpet, a knock sounded on his door. He walked over and opened it to find Oliver there, gear in his hands. He took his own pack that he'd given to Oliver on his way through the time gate as well as Samantha Drummond's that Oliver had obviously collected from her hotel.

"Anything interesting?"

"I just shoved her gear into the pack, mate, I didn't paw through it."

"Leaving that to me?"

"You don't pay me enough for that sort of work," Oliver said, straight-faced. He started to go back out the door, then turned and looked at Derrick. "Several lads outside are showing more interest in your doings than's polite, if you're curious."

"I was. Thank you."

Oliver shrugged. "Happy to be of service. Any news about the item of interest?"

"She stashed it."

"Where?"

"Under a planter."

"Hope no one thinks to water anytime soon."

Derrick decided that it was best not to reply.

Oliver nodded toward his arm. "That doesn't look good."

"It just needs a wash."

Oliver walked over, ripped off the sleeve of Derrick's T-shirt, then sliced the sleeve into a strip with a knife he produced from his pocket. He tied it around the wound. "Shall I ring Lady Sunshine?"

Derrick wasn't sure he would ever get used to calling his sister-in-law that, which was probably for the best. She never would have answered him if he had.

"Nay," he said, through gritted teeth, "the throbbing will subside soon enough. A clean shirt will do the trick for the moment."

"Make it a dark one."

"I thought I would."

Oliver frowned at him. "I'll be around," he said, starting out the door. "Perhaps closer than I intended."

"Be careful."

"I always am. I might sleep for a couple of hours, if you think you'll be doing the same."

Derrick supposed he had no choice, even if it meant sleeping on the floor in front of the doorway so Samantha Drummond didn't escape during the night. He nodded, promised Oliver he'd text him in the morning, then shut the door and locked it. He changed his shirt, wincing at the pull in his arm, then decided that perhaps it wasn't too late to ring someone whose advice he valued.

The phone only rang twice before the call was picked up.

"Ah, Derrick, lad," a male voice said, sounding pleased. "Schedule's freed up for a little adventure, is it?"

"I'm afraid not, Jamie," Derrick said. "I rang you for advice."

James MacLeod purred. If there was anything he loved, it was to immerse himself fully in the role of elder statesman on whatever subject might come up. "I'm prepared to hear about anything."

Derrick had no doubts that was true, or that Jamie had heard just about everything at some point in his life. "I'll be brief," he said. "I don't suppose you've heard any rumors about Lord Epworth having a piece of lace go missing."

"What I heard was he had a fit when you broke into his very secure hall and lifted said piece of lace from practically under his nose in fifteen minutes."

"It was actually eight and a half," Derrick corrected politely. "It would have been eight, but I had to stop and tickle the Pomeranian under the chin and feed him his favorite doggie treats."

"I suppose we can all be relieved you haven't chosen a life of crime," Jamie said dryly. "Very well, so the lace has gone missing in truth this time. I'm assuming you're hunting for it?"

"Aye," Derrick agreed. "It's just where it's gone missing that's presenting a bit of a problem."

"Tell me about it."

Derrick could just imagine Jamie settling comfortably in his expensive leather chair in his thinking room, as he called it, and flexing his fingers purposefully.

"In brief," Derrick said, "it was given to a courier who managed to lose it in Elizabethan England."

"Interesting."

"She put it under a planter."

"Hope it was wrapped well."

Derrick pursed his lips. "That thought has occurred to me as well."

Jamie clucked his tongue. "I don't think I need to tell you how perilous it is to leave two of the same thing in the same place."

"How perilous?"

"The deviation from the natural order of things might not be so noticeable at first," Jamie said slowly, "but I'm not exaggerating when I say that the fabric of time becomes . . . hmmm . . . let's say it becomes *disturbed* when things are added that shouldn't be there." He paused. "In some cases, when it comes to individuals perhaps, I have come to believe that those additions were meant to be. But when it comes to tangible things—"

"Bad?"

"They have a way of turning up where they shouldn't and the result is never pleasant. Do you remember that fellow traveler we acquired during that trip a couple of months ago?"

"Vividly." They had spent a week on board a Victorian frigate with a C. S. Forester nut who had heard a rumor about Jamie's familiarity with time periods not his own and had been determined to test its veracity. He had followed them back in time, then continued to follow them onto the ship. It was only when he succeeded in poaching the captain's sword that they had realized who he was and what he was up to.

And, well, Jamie was right. That sort of thing belonged in its proper time and place. He and Jamie had had a hell of a time getting the sword back where it belonged. They had managed, again just barely, to also get the would-be Horatio Hornblower back to the current day, but the man had eventually had to be institutionalized.

Time travel wasn't for the faint of heart.

"I'd pop back and get it, were I you."

Derrick could see the wisdom in it. "There's just one problem," he said slowly. "I'm not sure that the woman who stashed the lace will come along. And I'm not sure I want her to."

"Can she give you directions?"

"I don't think she will, even if she could," Derrick admitted. "I think I could find it myself. She didn't venture too far afield."

"Then what's the trouble?"

Derrick hardly knew how to voice his thought, but he hadn't called just to chat. "I was thinking," he began slowly, "that perhaps if I used a gate to simply go backward a day, just to yesterday, and managed to get the lace back from her before all this madness . . ."

Jamie made a noise that wasn't quite disapproval, but it was definitely warning.

"Have you ever tried it?" Derrick asked.

"Aye," was all Jamie said.

Derrick waited, but Jamie didn't say anything else. It had to have been terrible, else he would have described the experience in minute detail. Derrick sighed.

"Very well, I'll go back to the proper time myself."

"Want company?"

Derrick smiled. "I think I'll manage, though I'll try to send word if things go awry."

"I'll keep an eye on the Tower inmate list."

Derrick would have laughed, but he didn't suppose he dared. "That would be very kind."

Jamie laughed a little. "You'll be fine, laddie. We'll go have ourselves a goodly adventure somewhere safe after you've restored old Epworth's treasure to him."

Derrick thanked Jamie for his help and rang off. He considered, wished he hadn't ditched his Elizabethan costume, then decided there was nothing to be done about it. He would scrounge something out of a rubbish bin, perhaps, and see if he couldn't find the treasure. He couldn't lay claim to many skills, but he had a very good sense of direction. He would retrace Samantha Drummond's steps, then see what he could find. With any luck, he would run across her phone as well.

He told Emily he was going out, then left the suite.

Two hours later, he was sitting back on the couch, suppressing the urge to indulge in colorful language. He had sent Emily home courtesy of Rufus, who also never seemed to sleep, then settled down to brood. That he hadn't slept very well in a pair of days most likely contributed to his foul mood. The fact that the gate hadn't worked was also adding to his unhappiness.

He turned his mind back to the problem at hand, namely figuring out how to get back in time to rescue Epworth's lace. Perhaps he had to have Samantha with him. Perhaps he would never get back to where he needed to go and the lace would languish back where it had come from, though now there were two copies of it where there should have been just one. The fabric of time would be forever marred and Jamie would frown. Derrick supposed he would have deserved it if Jamie had suggested a wee trip out to his training field where he could show his displeasure by using Derrick's gut as a resting place for his very well-loved Claymore.

The other bedroom door opened, startling him. He looked up to find Samantha Drummond standing there, dressed in clothing he was sure she never would have bought on her own. She had gone from looking about forty to looking like she was scarce sixteen. She was wearing jeans, a trendy shirt, and a sweater that he would have bet good sterling was cashmere. He would get a bill for the entire outfit, he was sure.

She was, he had to admit dispassionately, rather pretty now that she was out of her librarian's gear. Her hair was still behind her—in a braid, no doubt—and she still exuded an air of a woman who had grown up in the relative safety and innocence of the 1950s, but that only added to her charm.

Of course, he wasn't interested in her in more than a purely academic way, but he was a man, after all. It would have been impolite not to at least look.

She looked at him, lifted her chin, then marched over to pull her bag up off the table. She pulled it over her head, then continued her purposeful march to the door. She stopped in surprise at the sight of her backpack sitting there next to it.

"Where did this come from?" she asked suspiciously.

"It was fetched for you."

"I don't suppose I should bother asking how you knew where to go get it."

"I don't suppose you should."

She shouldered her backpack, muttering under her breath what he was certain were very uncomplimentary things.

"They're still out there, you know," he said mildly.

She paused. "Who?"

"Those two lads who were searching for us in the fair today," he said, "as well as another two who have apparently decided to join in the fun."

He heard her quick intake of breath. It wasn't quite a gasp, but it was close.

"You're lying."

"Test it and see, if you like."

She had her hand on the door and was wearing what she no doubt considered to be a look of fierceness. He would have smiled if he hadn't suspected her of nefarious deeds. Then again, she didn't look at all capable of nefarious deeds. She looked like a fresh-scrubbed, wide-eyed Yank who was completely out of her depth.

"You know," he said slowly, "we might both be served by something to eat. I think I could order us dinner that wouldn't be poisoned."

She didn't move. "And if I rip the phone away from you and start screaming?"

"I'll have the concierge ring the bobbies and they'll lock you up in Bedlam."

She turned to look at him. "You're bluffing. You don't have Bedlam anymore over here."

"I think there might be worse things." He looked at her evenly. "I don't think you want to test it."

She pressed herself back against the door. "Where's Emily?"

"I sent her home."

"If you think I'm going to stay in this room for one more minute with you—" She paused for breath. "You're crazy."

"The alternative is, I assure you, much worse."

She glared at him. "I don't know you well enough to dislike you, but I would if I did."

"You were couriering a piece of lace stolen from one of my clients by your employer," he said with a shrug, "and that makes you rather unpopular with me."

"I already told you," she began through gritted teeth. "I had no idea that lace was in the package!"

"But you were willing to carry the package—"

"Well, of course I was," she said, looking at him as if he were the one who was daft. "The Cookes are friends of my brother's and I'm working for them. Lydia asked me to run that embroidery down to London for her, so I said yes. What else was I supposed to say?"

He sat back and studied her for a moment or two. "You could have asked her why she wanted it delivered."

"It's none of my business why she wanted it delivered," she said in frustration. "I'm *working* for them. I'm house-sitting for them all summer. She was giving me a chance to see a few sights before I'm trapped in Newcastle for the next three months."

"And it didn't occur to you that she might be up to something?"

Her mouth fell open. "She and her husband are very reputable academics. They're Shakespearean actors, for heaven's sake. What's more reputable than that?"

Derrick shut his mouth before he answered. His opinion of actors was something he was probably better off not voicing.

He studied her for a bit longer. He didn't like to give any potential thief the benefit of the doubt, but he also could say with a fair amount of certainty that he had a finely attuned BS meter. He could spot a liar from across a ballroom. The woman in front of him might have been a Yank—and she could hardly help that unfortunate circumstance of her birthplace—but he was almost positive she wasn't lying. He wasn't willing to commit to that fully, because that mucked up his neat-and-tidy solution to his lace problem, but he was willing to consider it.

He studied her for a moment or two longer, then leaned forward. She opened the door, but didn't go out into the hallway. She only looked at him as if she fully expected him to jump up and throttle her. He held up his hands.

"I think I've misjudged you," he said slowly.

She looked at him suspiciously. "What's that supposed to mean?"

"It means just that," he said carefully. "Why don't we have supper in this place that's safe and we'll discuss it."

She peeked out into the hallway, then looked back at him.

"The devil you know," he offered.

"I'm not sure you're an improvement."

"I might be when you consider that those lads there haven't bought you supper or offered you a safe place to sleep."

"You threatened to call the cops on me," she said. "Oh, and I forgot about Bedlam."

"We don't have Bedlam anymore."

"You said you have worse."

"I might have lied."

She clutched the doorframe. "I'm finding that quite a few people lie."

He leaned back and tried to look as harmless as possible. After all, he needed her to get where he was going.

"They do," he agreed, "but I don't."

"Ha," she said, though she seemed less eager to bolt than she had been just a moment earlier. "Spoken by one who's been lying about his identity for the past three days."

He blinked. "What?"

"In Newcastle, in York, at Hedingham, on a couple of trains?"

"You're imagining things," he said dismissively. "Many people take trains to London."

"Via Sudbury?" she said pointedly. "First as a Brit, then a Canadian, then a German, then a scruffy-looking nobody?" She looked down her nose at him. "Your German is lousy, by the way."

"And yours is very good," he conceded without hesitation. "My fault, I suppose, for choosing amiss. What else do you speak?"

"You're changing the subject."

He shook his head. "Trying to distract you so you'll shut the door and I can order supper." He leaned forward. "Miss Drummond, I give you my word I will not harm you. If you'll shut the door and come sit, I'll be completely frank with you. Perhaps there is a way out of this mess for the both of us."

She considered. Apparently good sense prevailed because she finally shut the door, though she didn't move away from it. She simply looked at him.

"How do I know I can trust you?"

"Lord Epworth trusts me. What does that tell you?"

"That you might be a criminal who has turned his life around," she said without hesitation. "You might be a very good criminal, which doesn't say much about your character."

He sighed. Perhaps he was getting old, or tired, or jaded, but there was just something about the woman that shouted *innocence*. If she'd cheated on a test and lasted ten minutes without a full confession, he would have been surprised. He stood and gestured toward the sofa.

"Leave your gear, Miss Drummond, and please come sit. Let's see if the kitchen is still willing to prepare something for us to eat. I don't know about you, but I'm starving."

She looked at him for another moment or two in silence, then she set her backpack down by the door. She wrapped her arms around herself. "I haven't eaten very much today."

"Let's remedy that."

She crossed the room, then sat as far on the opposite end of the sofa from him as possible. He fetched the menu, had a look for himself, then handed it to her. She named something very small indeed, which surprised him a little.

He was beginning to think he had seriously misjudged her.

He ordered enough for four people, then sat and shifted to look at her.

"How did you know it was me?" he asked, because that was what interested him the most.

"Set of your shoulders," she answered absently. She had picked up the menu again and was obviously adding things up in her head. "I've fitted my father's costumes for years." She glanced at him. "I'd suggest shoulder pads in your jackets, but maybe you don't want to go that far."

"Most people aren't that observant."

"I'm not most people."

"I'm beginning to suspect that."

She looked at him then, bleakly. "I feel like I've fallen into a bad dream and can't wake up."

"Trust me," he said, with feeling, "I understand."

"I've never been kidnapped before."

"I'm not kidnapping you now."

"I don't hold your driver responsible," she said, as if she hadn't heard him, "because he's probably just doing what he's told to save his wife and dozen children."

"Living in Dickensian squalor," Derrick said wryly. "And he only has four, all grown up and moved on."

"You know, for all I know, *you're* a thug who just wants that lace," she continued. "Maybe you stole it in the first place and this is all an elaborate ruse to get it back from the unsuspecting patsy."

"You read too much."

"Prove me wrong."

He started to tell her he absolutely wouldn't when he realized he had basically said the same thing to her. He rubbed his hands together, not because they ached, but because he was tired and needed something to eat.

"I could tell you what I do for a living."

"How about you show me instead," she said pointedly. "A website for your business. Maybe a business card."

He shook his head slowly. "Don't have either. We're very exclusive."

"Most high-end thieves are."

"And you would know?"

"I can read the news, just like everyone else. And who's *we*?"

He supposed he owed her that at least. He sighed lightly, then attempted a smile. "Let's begin with introductions—"

"After all we've been through?" she asked. "Why bother?"

He considered. "I saw that Elizabethan ghost in the great hall at the Castle."

Her eyes almost bulged. "You didn't," she breathed. "Really?"

"Really," he said. "He did good work on your boyfriend."

"Dory's not my boyfriend."

Then the wench had at least some amount of taste. He looked at her seriously.

"My name is Derrick Cameron," he said, "and I am the, ah, owner of Cameron Antiquities, Ltd."

"The *Ah Owner*? Is that something British I don't understand?"

He was torn between scowling and smiling. "It's a recent thing."

"And you're not comfortable with it yet."

"Actually, no, I'm not," he agreed.

"What sort of business is it you're uncomfortable with?" she asked. "Or should I not be curious?"

He lifted an eyebrow briefly. "We deal in the very rare and hideously expensive. Antiques, mostly."

"Would my brother know you?"

"Well," he said slowly, "I'm afraid he would, but I wouldn't suggest you go to him for a character reference."

"Steal something filigreed from him?"

"Salt cellars," Derrick clarified. "And I didn't steal them. I used my impressive powers of persuasion and vast amounts of charm to convince the owner to give them to me instead of to your brother."

"That couldn't have been too hard," she said with a snort. "Gavin has no charm and a lousy personality."

"But he drives a hard bargain," Derrick said. "He wasn't pleased."

"He rarely is.". She assessed him. "Did you give this Lord Epworth the lace in the first place?"

"I sold it to him, aye," Derrick said. "It came from a private collection."

"How did you know it was in this private collection?"

He shrugged. "I like old things, so I accept any invitation to view antiques people are proud of. I keep those in mind, on the off chance the knowledge becomes useful. When a potential client thinks of something he or she wants, they contact me and I get it for them."

"Always?"

"Almost always."

"Why are you so competitive?"

"I have a brother."

"That answers that, I suppose."

A knock saved him from explaining that further. He rose, swayed, then cursed silently as he made his way across the room. He was going to have to do something about his arm, and sooner rather than later. He opened the door, waited until room service had done its bit, accompanied of course by one of the assigned flunkies whose job it was to see that his every need was catered to, then happily collapsed in a chair in front of food that smelled thoroughly edible.

"Your shoulder is bleeding."

He would have argued with her, but she was right. He sat back and sighed, hoping he wouldn't bleed on the upholstered chair. Samantha frowned, then reached for a plate.

"What do you want?"

What he wanted was a very long night's rest followed by a day where he didn't wake with a headache and didn't know that the bulk of his work was still in front of him, not behind him. But she was talking about food. He sighed.

"I don't care, really. You choose."

She filled his plate, set it down in front of him, then helped herself. Derrick ate, because there was nothing in the world that would stop him from filling his belly. He realized, though, that Samantha was spending more time watching him than she was doing the same.

"What?" he asked.

"Those were real swords."

He considered, then nodded. No sense in not telling her the truth. She'd seen ghosts. Maybe the rest wouldn't come as much of a surprise.

"In a street fair?"

"I don't think that was a street fair."

She put her fork down. That was probably wise, given that her hands were shaking. "I don't think I understand."

"Remember that Elizabethan ghost?"

She nodded uneasily.

"Strange happenings here in England," he said. *And Scotland*, he added silently. He added it silently because he didn't think there was any point in burdening her unduly.

"What kinds of strange happenings?"

"This part might be hard to believe."

She folded her hands in her lap. "How hard to believe?"

"I don't know," he said slowly. "What sorts of things do you consider to be unbelievable?"

She considered. "Well, I managed to get myself to a country where my parents don't live, which seemed pretty unbelievable at the start. Then I took a little job and wound up with a priceless piece of Elizabethan lace in my purse, which also seems pretty unbelievable. Is it worse than that?"

He nodded.

"Worse than ghosts?"

"Maybe on the same level."

She had a sip of water, but it didn't go all that well for her. He imagined the tablecloth would survive and her jeans would dry.

"Go ahead," she said, her voice breaking. "Lay it on me."

He decided there was no sense in not being honest. She would have to find out eventually.

"You left the lace in Elizabethan England."

Chapter 11

Samantha heard the words, but was just sure she'd heard them wrong. Or maybe she'd heard them perfectly well, which led her to a conclusion she didn't want to think about but couldn't avoid any longer.

Her host was bonkers.

It was a pity, really. He was extremely handsome and when he wasn't paying attention he had a bit of a very attractive Scottish burr. Then again, she'd heard him speak with half a dozen accents so far, so who knew which one was the real deal? He was a Cameron, which could have made him Scottish, but then again his family could have migrated south, which could have made him English. Perhaps he'd spent his life trying to temper a Birmingham brogue. Perhaps things had slipped out that he hadn't intended. Perhaps he'd just escaped from the local loony bin and was trying to suck her into his delusions.

Unfortunately, he looked less crazy than she would have liked.

"So," she said slowly, "what you mean to say is I left the lace in an Elizabethan England sort of area."

"No."

Well, he was obviously very attached to his alternate reality. "What you mean is *yes*," she said, nodding encouragingly.

"No," he said, drawing the word out carefully, "what I mean is that the place where we were, where I had that little dance with the sword that did more damage than I intended it to—" He paused. "That was a different place."

"Yes," she agreed, "it was. A very authentic street fair."

He rubbed his fingers over his mouth briefly. "You know, I've never had to try to make this sound believable before—"

"Don't strain yourself on my account."

He smiled, very faintly. "I'll try not to." He watched her for a moment or two, then shook his head slightly. "I'm actually not sure where to begin."

She supposed that was standard fare for most kooks, but the problem was, he didn't look crazy. Then again, sometimes that was hard to judge from looks alone. She had a couple of cousins who were completely unhinged, but that was her father's side of the family. Maybe it had to do with absorbing too much greasepaint over the years. Who knew? She had enough crazy in her own life at the moment without speculating on the level of it in someone else's.

Derrick reached for his water, but stiffened slightly as he did so, which told her he was very good at ignoring things that hurt. He was also going to have to have his arm seen to before long or he was going to be in trouble.

"Why don't you relax," he said with what he probably thought looked like a harmless smile, "and I'll tell you a story or two."

"Will those stories be the truth?"

"The absolute truth." He had another sip of water, then set his glass down and looked at her. "Rumor has it that, near where I was born, there was once a medieval laird who loved his lady so greatly that he escaped death and followed her to a time far different from his own."

"Sounds like a cheesy romance novel."

"I imagine it does," he agreed, "but the thing is, the story is true."

"What part of it?"

"All of it."

She snorted before she could help herself. "Time travel? Is that what you're talking about?"

He nodded solemnly.

"You *are* crazy. I was worried about it before, but I'm convinced now."

The look he gave her was, unfortunately, all too lucid. "I used to think the same myself."

"When?"

He toyed with his water glass, as if he wasn't altogether comfortable telling her anything. She couldn't blame him, actually. She had known him all of about an hour and she wasn't at all sure she either liked him or trusted him.

He did have the most amazing pair of green eyes, though. She wasn't sure if they were dark or light. She imagined it depended some on the light and what he was wearing. Hers were a very boring sort of blue that was just blue. No shades of anything else, just blue.

She pulled herself away from those nonproductive ruminations and held up her hands. "You don't have to give me those details if you don't want to. I probably wouldn't believe them anyway."

"Again, I wouldn't blame you," he said. "Suffice it to say that I have seen a few things over the past year that have convinced me that things I never would have believed ten years ago are indeed quite possible."

"Like Elizabethan ghosts tormenting annoying prep-school dropouts?"

"Is he a dropout?"

"His father has deep pockets and lots of contacts, which is the only way he got into college."

Derrick didn't look terribly surprised. "Money talks. And yes, things like Elizabethan ghosts." He studied his water for a moment or two, then looked at her. "Did you see that circle of mushrooms you stepped into?"

She rolled her eyes. "Yes, and I don't like mushrooms, so it gave me the creeps."

"Dislike might not be the only reason for that reaction."

She would have scoffed, but the expression on Derrick's face stopped her. He was absolutely serious. She set her fork down, because that seemed like the most prudent thing to do. She wasn't managing to eat anything anyway.

"What are you saying? That there was some kind of portal there? To the sixteenth century?"

His expression didn't change. "That's what I'm saying."

She pushed back against her chair. "You are certifiable."

"Am I?"

"Well, of course you are," she said, because that sounded reasonable. "Maybe some of your buddies are trying to pull a fast one on you." She paused and looked at him. "Are you on drugs?"

He shook his head. "Don't like the loss of control."

"Booze?"

"I don't drink."

She suppressed the urge to sigh. "There you are, an uncomfortable head of an antique shop, and you look so normal. How can you be so nuts?"

He had a sip of water, which made him wince again. She frowned thoughtfully. It was curious, that wound. Wasn't it?

"I'll be blunt," he said. "When you ran into that street fair, you ran through a patch of grass that took you back in time to Elizabeth the First's day. You left that lace, quite understandably, under a planter. Unfortunately, that planter is rather out of reach at the moment."

"How out of reach?"

"I'd put the date somewhere around 1600."

She didn't even dignify that with a response. She wondered if she could get herself, her bag, and her backpack out the door and down the hallway before he caught her and tortured her with any more of his nonsense.

"Elizabeth was still queen and the Globe was still standing," he continued. "And they were rehearsing *Hamlet*."

"Lots of people rehearse *Hamlet*."

"Not in the original Globe."

She shook her head, but that didn't clarify anything. "I don't understand what you're saying."

"What I'm saying is, that lovely piece of Elizabethan lace is now languishing under a planter in Renaissance England," he said slowly, "and you and I are going to have to go back and get it."

She pushed away from the table and got up. She walked over to the window and pulled the curtain back. She was slightly surprised to realize that she was overlooking a garden she hadn't noticed before, but maybe she shouldn't have expected anything else. She'd been distracted. It also occurred to her that the room had to have been staggeringly expensive. She wondered how in the world Derrick could possibly afford it.

Unless he was a very exclusive antiques dealer, or knew the mysterious Countess of Assynt and she was spotting him a few thousand to keep up appearances.

She turned and leaned back against the wall. Derrick was sitting where she'd left him, watching her, silent and grave. He didn't look crazy. In fact, when he wasn't being a jerk, he was extremely handsome. If she had met him under different circumstances, she might have been tempted to give him another look. But he had just professed a belief in time travel, which put him firmly in the *nutcase* category as far as she was concerned.

"That's crazy," she said finally.

"What is?"

She gestured vaguely. "This whole thing. Time travel. The Cookes being textile thieves."

"Life is strange."

She frowned at him. "And just what am I supposed to do now? Help you?"

He looked at her carefully. "I don't think I can get the lace without you."

"Have you tried?"

"Whilst you were having a meltdown in the shower."

"I wasn't having a meltdown," she said archly. "I was indulging in a few deep breaths." Then what he'd said registered with her. "You tried this *Somewhere in Time* thing already tonight?"

He nodded. "It didn't work."

"Why not?" she asked. "Not enough faith in your mushrooms?"

"Actually, I think you need to be there with me." He paused, then shrugged. "Maybe it would have worked if I'd had more time, but there were a few unsavory types more interested than they should have been in what I was doing."

She clasped her hands behind her because she didn't want to watch them shake. She didn't want the man sitting at the table to watch them, either. "Why would unsavory types be looking for you?"

He met her gaze steadily. "I don't know, Miss Drummond. Why do you think?"

"Because of me," she managed. "And it's Samantha."

He inclined his head. "Samantha, then. And yes, they were following you and saw you make a run for it with me. I think you are entangled with some very dangerous people."

She wondered if it would frighten him if she had another meltdown, this time right there in front of him. "I had no idea."

"I believe you."

"What am I going to do?" she managed. "There's not a soul in this country I can trust."

He considered, then pulled his phone out of his pocket. "Did you ring anyone when you got to London?"

"Don't you know already, Sherlock?"

He didn't smile. He simply looked at her. "I would imagine you already called Gavin and asked for aid. We'll text him first and tell him you had a change of plans but you're all right."

"Why would you assume I called my brother in the first place?"

"It's an educated guess," he said. "You were unnerved; he's here. Why wouldn't you ring him? Apart from the fact that he's an utter ass."

She laughed a little, because it was either that or start shivering. "He wanted me to come wait in his back room until he was finished with a megadeal."

"He was probably selling fake spoons," Derrick said with a snort. He put his phone near her plate. "There you are."

She sat back down, because it seemed a handy way to ignore how badly her knees were shaking.

"Just start typing," he said. "It's untraceable, so you'd best identify yourself."

"What should I tell him?"

"What did you tell him before?"

She took a deep breath. "That I was being followed."

"Then tell him you were imagining things."

"He already thinks I'm crazy," she said, "so this won't worsen my reputation with him."

She started to type, really she did, but after the third time she dropped the phone, Derrick took it away and finished. He held it toward her.

"Sufficient?"

"You make me sound so composed."

"I'll put more smileys in, if you like."

"More exclamation points. He'll expect that."

Derrick smiled, edited, then sent it. He looked at her and his smile faded. "Now your contact here."

She returned his look. "Don't you know that, too?"

"I can try to guess."

"Go ahead."

He considered for a minute or two, then typed in a number and showed it to her. She was unsettled, that was the only reason she had to go get her notebook and double-check. She looked at him and felt herself go cold.

"That's the guy."

"It's what he does for a living."

"Nice living."

"Very," he agreed. "When were you supposed to contact him?"

"Tomorrow."

He frowned thoughtfully. "Let's do this. Why don't you tell him you were delayed on the journey south and you won't be able to meet him for another couple of days. Then we'll text Lydia Cooke and tell her that you've lost your phone and you're borrowing one from a very nice man who said he's a detective inspector for Scotland Yard. I think I can safely guarantee she won't push the issue."

"That's devious."

"Too much time with the criminal element," he said with a sigh. "I fear it's rubbed off. Now, what shall we say to the broker?"

"You make it up. I'll be thinking about Lydia."

And the things she was thinking weren't at all nice. She could hardly believe that the Cookes could be crooks, but what else was she to believe? She supposed Derrick Cameron could have been the master thief who was just trying to convince her of things that couldn't possibly be true so he could get his hands on that lace himself. That would have explained his rather elaborate actions at present.

But that didn't explain the sword wound in his shoulder.

He finally set his phone aside and looked at her. He blinked in surprise when he apparently realized she'd been watching him.

"What?" he asked.

She shook her head. "Who *are* you?"

"No one of importance," he said.

She didn't believe that, but she wasn't sure how to say as much.

He looked at her seriously. "Your brother found the job for you?"

She nodded. "I was supposed to come over last summer, but I couldn't get away." She paused, because it was too ridiculous to tell him how locked down she'd been. "I came this year instead."

"Did he know what he was getting you into when he sent you to the Cookes, do you think?"

She looked at him in shock, then she laughed. "Gavin? Are you kidding? He couldn't even get himself into Harvard. There is absolutely no conceivable way he could think up something like this."

Derrick smiled, a very small smile that was rather charming, all things considered. She had no reason to like him—in fact, she didn't like him at all—but she had to admit he was just too handsome for his own good. Or for her peace of mind. But that was okay, because she had no intentions of having anything to do with him longer than it took to bid him a swift good night after supper, bar her door, then hopefully check out early in the morning before she got stuck with the bill.

Derrick considered. "It is always surprising how the criminal mind works."

"Gavin's mind is too vapid for criminal activity. His ACT scores were abysmal."

"And yours weren't."

She started to say that no, they absolutely weren't, but she realized he was looking at her with not quite a smirk but definitely the faintest of lights in his eye that said he knew more about her than she would be comfortable with.

"Do you have my grades memorized as well?"

"Haven't had time," he said easily, "and actually I hadn't had time to dig up your test scores, either, if that eases you any. I'm just guessing. And despite your brother's thick head, it is entirely possible that he could be involved in things he shouldn't be. But let's hope not."

She wasn't overly fond of her brother, but she hoped not as well. "What now?"

"We get the lace first, then we figure out whom the Cookes were selling it to, then we put them all in jail."

"I don't think I want to be a part of this."

"I imagine you don't, but I also think you're safer with me than on your own."

"Where'd you learn to fence?"

He opened his mouth, then shut it. "Here and there."

"Most people learn to fence as part of an acting degree."

"Most do."

"Did you?"

He rubbed his hands together. "It's getting late."

"And I'm getting under your skin," she said, feeling rather pleased.

"Yes, you are." He nodded toward the bedroom she'd been using. "I think we should sleep for a couple of hours, at least, but no more. I would like to be at the Globe well before dawn and back home before sunrise."

"And then what?" she asked lightly. "You go to Castle Hammond and I go either to jail or the graveyard?"

He looked at her steadily. "We'll work that out when we get back. But I don't leave women unprotected, if that's what you're thinking."

"How chivalrous."

"Up north, we call it honor."

That was hard to argue with. It was also hard to argue the ridiculous notion of time travel, but since the man across from her was the only thing that seemed even remotely stable in a world that had suddenly gone absolutely insane, she supposed she would just have to take his word for it. She nodded, because that was the best she could do, collected her backpack and bag, then took herself off to her extremely luxurious bedroom and locked the door behind her. She set everything down on the floor, then looked at what Emily had purchased apparently for her. It was, unsurprisingly enough, all effortlessly chic and not a square inch of it was made of rayon or polyester. Her mother would have had a fit if she'd seen it.

She checked the door one more time, then decided to just trust that she would wake up still in one piece.

She left the vase on the dresser.

She woke up in one piece, but still in the dark. She fumbled for the clock and found that it was not quite three A.M. Maybe Derrick had been making noise in the sitting room, determined to hold to his idea of walking along the Thames in the dark. She opted for a robe over her silk pajamas on the off chance he thought it would be better to go looking in the daylight and she might get to go back to bed, then left her room.

The sitting room was as she'd left it, but his bedroom door was open. She picked up a handful of grapes on her way by the table, then walked quietly over to the open doorway.

She frowned. Either he had company, or those were moans of pain. She considered, then flicked on the light.

He was facedown on the floor. She was relieved to find he had at least passed out before he'd had the chance to get his jeans off, though she supposed she shouldn't have been happy that he was only semiconscious. She hastened over to peer down at him.

Wow, was the Ritz going to have to replace some carpet.

She would have panicked completely, but she could see that the blood had come from his shoulder. How that was better, she didn't know, but she supposed it was. She put her hand on his back and winced. He was burning up.

It took her several tries before she managed to get him over onto his back. She patted his face, which only made him groan softly. She considered, then slapped him smartly. He sat partway up, cursing as he did so, then looked at her. It took him several blinks before he managed to focus on her. Then his eyes rolled back in his head and he fell back over.

She knelt down next to his head and suppressed the urge to wring her hands. What in the world was she going to do now? There was no possible way she could call her brother. He would wonder what she was doing in a fancy hotel room with someone she didn't know, which would lead to all kinds of questions she wasn't going to want to answer.

She jumped when she felt Derrick's hand groping her. He

took hold of her arm and looked up at her. His eyes were crossed, but she imagined that in his current condition, it didn't bother him.

"Phone," he rasped. "Sunny."

"Who's Sunny?"

"Cousin."

Well, she had no idea what a cousin could do for him, but since he was trying to get himself into a sitting position she didn't suppose she could argue. She looked around for his phone, found it, then brought it back and knelt down next to him.

"On . . ."

She found the on button, then watched as he fumbled for it and pressed his thumb against the screen. Of course she memorized that. She was a good memorizer, as it happened, and one never knew when a little detail like that would come in handy.

She found his contacts, then scrolled through them until she found an entry for Sunny.

A man's voice answered after only a couple of rings. "I don't know very many private callers who would dare ring me in the middle of the night. Who's this?"

"Um, I'm calling for Derrick Cameron," Samantha said hesitantly. "There's been an accident."

The reply was brisk and businesslike. "What sort?"

"He was, ah, stabbed by a sword in the shoulder. He said for me to call Sunny."

"Where are you?"

"At the Ritz."

"Oh, aye, I knew that. Very well, we'll be there in a few minutes. Is he bleeding heavily?"

Samantha thought that it was entirely possible that she was currently having the weirdest conversation of her life. And given the things she had experienced over the past three days, that was saying something.

"Well, the carpet will need to be cleaned," she said.

"What sort of sword was it?" the man asked.

Samantha closed her eyes briefly. "An Elizabethan rapier."

There was silence on the other end for a moment or two. "Who are you, lass?"

"Samantha Drummond." She paused. "He thought I stole his piece of lace."

"Did you?"

"No, but I was inadvertently carrying it with me." She paused. "It's complicated."

The man made a noise that was a bit like a snort. "It always is. We'll be there as quickly as we can."

"I think he would appreciate it."

She hung up, then simply sat down on the floor next to Derrick and wished she had at least some first-aid skills. She considered putting a pillow under his head but was afraid that might give him a kink in his neck. She settled for a blanket draped over him. No sense in his catching a chill.

It took longer than she feared for a knock to sound on the door. She jumped up and ran into the other room to open it. She wasn't sure what she expected, but a couple in jeans with a baby wasn't it. The man looked her over quickly and efficiently, then held out his hand.

"Robert Cameron. I'm Derrick's cousin. This is my wife Sunshine. Sunny, this is Samantha Drummond."

Samantha tried not to gape. That was the Countess of Assynt and her husband standing there. Well, coming inside the room, really. She shut the door behind them, then followed them over to Derrick's bedroom. Robert Cameron then made noises of disapproval as he pulled away the blood-soaked cloth wrapped around Derrick's arm.

He muttered something half under his breath that sounded remarkably like Gaelic, only spoken with an accent she had never heard before. He looked up at his wife.

"Think you can heal this wee fool here?"

She handed him the baby, then took his place on the floor at Derrick's side. Samantha looked at Lord Robert.

"I didn't realize it was that bad," she said helplessly. "I mean, the whole thing's kind of strange, don't you think? That someone would poke at him with a sword?"

Lord Robert exchanged a brief glance with his wife, then looked at her with a smile.

"Strange happenings in the world sometimes, wouldn't you say?"

Samantha let out a shaky breath. "After this week, I would have to agree." She looked at Sunshine Cameron pulling things out of a backpack she hadn't realized she had been wearing, then turned back to her husband. "Is there anything I can do?"

He shook his head. "Honestly, I think the best thing you could do is just go back to bed. He'll be fine by the morning. Sleep as long as you like. I'll keep watch."

She studied him. "Are you really the Earl of Assynt?"

"To my continued surprise, I find that I am."

"I was just curious," she said slowly. "I'm not sure who to trust. I think I trust him"—she nodded at Derrick—"but he's currently unconscious. But if you're his cousin . . ."

He smiled. She couldn't say he looked exactly like Derrick, but there was obviously a family resemblance. Something about the eyes, maybe.

"Not to worry, Miss Drummond. You can sleep in peace."

She nodded, turned, then turned back slightly. "There's nothing I can do?"

The Earl of Assynt shook his head. "I'll let you know if anything changes."

She nodded, then walked back to her bedroom and shut the door behind her. She wasn't sure she would sleep, but found that it was impossible to stay awake.

A man who had lifted a sword to defend her. Another man who had been completely unsurprised to find the first man had been wounded by an Elizabethan sword.

She wondered just what she'd gotten herself into.

Chapter 12

Derrick had never thought he would die on a frozen tundra, but perhaps he deserved it for all the times he had leaned on hapless collectors of antiquities to inspire them to relinquish their goods.

Or perhaps he was languishing on the burning Sahara. At the moment, he honestly couldn't tell where he was. He was alternately parched and freezing, so perhaps he'd merely been consigned to a circle of hell he'd never read about.

And then the voices began.

"Aren't you going to ask me if we should take him to the hospital?"

"Nay, Sunny, I'll trust the herbs. And you."

Derrick tried to frown, but it was too much effort. He was listening to Gaelic, but the cadence was slightly off. He'd learned the mother tongue, of course, because he was a Scot and because it had irritated his father . . .

He managed a frown. He hadn't thought about either of his parents in years. He missed his mother, occasionally, though he never thought of her without wishing that she had been a little more willing to stand up to his father. His father, that arrogant punter, had looked down on everything that smacked of Scotland as if it were less somehow than what was to be found south of the border. Or at least he had when he hadn't been angling for the job of laird of what was left of the clan Cameron, though that had been merely for the power of it, not for the love of it. Derrick was sure that if he hadn't had his grandfather there to instill a bit of proper Scottish pride into him, he never would have amounted to anything.

He drank something at one point that was so bitter, his eyes watered and his tongue took flight. Someone called him a useless woman. He was certain his retort to that nameless, faceless insulter had been brisk and to the point, but before he could recall the words and examine them for their beauty, they slipped away from him.

Time crawled.

"He thought you were a thief?"

"Yes. I can't really blame him, though. I don't think he knew anything about me except that I was staying with the Cookes."

Derrick pursed his lips, but found they were slightly more numb than he would have liked them to be. That was a Yank speaking there. Her name was there as well, just past where his numb lips resided in a swirling vortex of swords and lace and Roman soldiers stomping through his brain, but it was too much trouble to reach for it. He closed his eyes and sighed.

A woman laughed lightly. "I'm surprised he didn't have your entire life history at his fingertips."

"It isn't a very interesting life, and I'm not sure my degrees would have exonerated me."

"And why is that?"

"Because they are, unfortunately, in antique textiles."

Derrick realized he was listening to Sunny and Samantha. He was rather proud of that feat, actually. He struggled to open his eyes, but that was impossible.

"Oh, look, he's awake," Sunny said cheerfully. "Let's get some more of that tonic down him."

He tried to protest, truly he did. But all opening his mouth earned him was a gallon of Sunny's worst brew poured down his throat. He swallowed, because he had to, then spat out a few choice curses. Unfortunately, that was all he spat, because that

vile liquid was burning its way down his gullet to rest happily
in a spot he might have called his belly at any other time. At the
moment, his tum felt more like an enormous medieval hearth
where there lay roasting half a bloody tree. He gasped out a plea
for aid, but only had cackling laughter as a reward.

He slid into senselessness accompanied by what he was just
sure he wasn't hearing.

Double, double, toil and trouble.

He certainly had enough of both.

He woke. It took him several moments to become accustomed
to that fact, but it was inescapable. He felt as if he'd been run
over, then rolled over by a steamroller, then left there to have
sand sprayed over him to mitigate the effects of a good snowfall.
He was certain that the snow gritter had concentrated on his
eyes alone, because they felt as if they were full of rocks. He
would have rubbed them, but he simply didn't have the strength.
He wasn't a fatalist by nature, but he hoped the next time he was
overcome by an Elizabethan sword wound, someone would just
do the right thing and put him out of his misery.

An indeterminate amount of time later, he managed to turn
his head to see if anyone was by his bedside, worried about his
condition. Well, there was someone sitting by his bedside, but
she seemed to be less worried about him than she was about
checking her email.

Not only was she checking her email, she was doing it on his
tablet. He would have frowned sternly, but he didn't want to
waste any energy on that. He was saving it up to give her a proper
dressing down, but he couldn't quite remember for what. Then it
occurred to him that she was using his tablet.

"Hey," he croaked, "how'd you break into that?"

She didn't even have the decency to look up, the heartless
wench. She only continued to poke at the screen. "Lord Robert
gave me the password," she said absently.

"How'd he know it?" he rasped.

"He said you'd ask that."

He waited, but she was obviously not going to be divulging
anything on her own. "Well?" he demanded.

"He said to tell you, and I quote, that he has a brain, too, you idiot, and what were you thinking not to call Sunny sooner?"

Derrick would have snorted, but he thought that might upset the delicate balance he was maintaining between feeling like death and actually dying. He closed his eyes briefly, concentrated on breathing in and out for a bit longer, then attempted speech again.

"I believe the last bit, but not the first." He opened his eyes and looked at her again. "How did he get my password?"

She was watching him solemnly. He wondered how it was that a certain sort of ambient light coming through diaphanous curtains could take a woman's hair from uninspired brown to a lovely mahogany that sported strands of red here and there. Her face was, he had to admit, less stunning than it was simply lovely, all pale-skinned with a handful of freckles across her nose, as if she hadn't spent much time in the sun. He imagined that was the case, given that she'd no doubt been putting in her time in some museum or other. Or apparently altering costumes for her father.

"Your password?" she said absently. "Well, I'm not sure I should tell you how he got it."

"I don't have it written down anywhere," Derrick said crossly. "What'd he do? Beat it out of me?"

She only shook her head.

He tried to sit up, but that left him almost breathless with the aftereffects of what he supposed had been a colossal fever. He held out his hand. "Give me the tablet."

"I beg your pardon?"

He shook his hand impatiently at her. "I need it now."

She looked at him as if she couldn't decide whether to hand it over or clunk him over the head with it. Good manners apparently won out because she simply laid it on the bed next to him, got up, and walked out of the room. She shut the door softly behind her.

He considered. It was possible that he had been too long in the company of thugs and their bad habits had rubbed off on him. It was also possible that he hadn't dated anyone seriously in several years and that the bad manners of the women he did see casually had, somewhere along the line, begun to seem acceptable.

Or it was possible that he was just an ass who, judging by the date on his watch, had been completely unconscious for almost three days and had just been rude to his nurse?

"Miss Drummond," he croaked loudly.

She didn't return, though he honestly hadn't expected her to. He supposed he was lucky she didn't open the door and throw a bucket of ice water on him. He forced himself into a sitting position, was rather grateful he hadn't eaten to have anything to throw up, then continued to sit until the stars stopped swirling around his head. It took a bit, but enough feeling finally returned in his legs that he could sense he was wearing trousers. It was for damned sure that he couldn't see them at the moment.

He waited until the waves of nausea receded and his head stopped pounding long enough for him to actually open his eyes and peer at what he was wearing.

MacLeod plaid. Sunny's doing, obviously.

He wondered if Samantha realized the insult that had been paid to his unconscious self, then decided he didn't care if she did or not. He had been polite to her, because he'd felt bad about misjudging her. Now, what he needed her to do was get him through the gate, lead him to the place where she'd stashed the lace, then come back with him so he could get the lace back to Lord Epworth and the Cookes to Scotland Yard. He had no other use for her than that, no matter what his cousin and that cousin's wife had dressed him in, no doubt giggling like school-girls whilst they'd been about it.

And then once he was finished with his present business, he was going to get on with his life. He had plans to start dating, big plans, important plans that he would see to, aye, just as soon as he solved his current case.

Never mind that he'd just decided that at the very instant the thought had occurred to him.

There was a T-shirt thrown over the bottom of the bed. He managed to get it over his head without undue distress, but he supposed that would have to do for any and all grooming efforts for the day. His arm ached abominably, which he found slightly disconcerting. He touched the puncture wound gingerly, hardly daring to speculate on what had found its way inside. There was a bandage there, but he didn't imagine Sunny had put in stitches. If she'd done more than just put a plaster on it after packing it with her miracle salve, he would have been very surprised.

He gathered his courage, then got to his feet. He staggered to the door, then leaned against it for several minutes until he thought he could get the door open and continue on.

He tottered into the sitting room and managed to get to the sofa, but no farther. He sat down heavily, then put his hand over his eyes and simply breathed until he thought he could open his eyes and not have the world continue to spin wildly around him. He squinted at the coffee table in front of him and blinked in surprise. Waiting there was tea, broth, and juice. He suspected that wasn't for Samantha's benefit. He wasn't sure any of it looked very appetizing, but he wasn't going to be ungracious. Well, any more than he had been already.

He looked up to find Samantha sitting in a chair at the table, watching him.

"Thank you," he said.

It came out more brusquely than he had intended, but what did she expect? His arm was on fire, his head felt as if it were stuffed with gauze, and there was a piece of Elizabethan lace sitting somewhere under a planter four hundred years in the past and it was that woman sitting over there's fault.

"You're welcome."

He scowled. Why didn't she just stand up to him and give him a right proper ticking off?

He didn't want to think about why that bothered him so much, so he simply didn't. He ate what he thought he could manage, then sat back and tried to ignore how dreadful he felt.

He needed a vacation. In fact he couldn't remember the last time he'd had a vacation. He was beginning to wonder if perhaps he shouldn't take a vacation at a charm school.

His head was pounding, his tum was far from settled, and he thought he might have to soon go have a little lie-down. And still his lace languished in a place where it shouldn't. He looked at Samantha to find her looking off into the distance where he wasn't. He sighed, then set his computer on the table.

"I think I might have to sleep a bit more."

"Sure."

He pushed his tablet toward her. "Surf all you like, if you want."

She nodded but didn't say anything.

"We'll try to go tonight."

She looked at him in surprise. "You're kidding."

He wished he were. "I can't leave that lace behind any longer."

"But you're in no shape—"

"I will be," he interrupted sharply.

She didn't reply and for some reason that irritated the hell out of him.

"How did Cameron get my password?" he demanded.

She looked at him then. "He asked you while you were delirious. He pretended to be the ghost of Christmas future, promised dire retribution if you didn't cough up the goods, and you blurted it out like a man with a secret."

He wasn't sure he'd ever heard her say so many things in one sentence.

He imagined his cousin had greatly enjoyed his role as reproving ghost. Perhaps there was something to be grateful for that it had been Cameron in the role and not some damned ghost in truth. In his delirium, though, he likely wouldn't have been able to tell the difference.

"Unsurprising," was all he could manage to say, though he supposed it was a particularly lame comment on the whole situation, a situation that was absolutely untenable. His arm was killing him, which led him to wonder briefly if he shouldn't have had a proper doctor look at it. His computer had been compromised—with help, apparently—by a woman who was too polite to tell him to get over himself.

And he still had lace where it shouldn't have been, but he was honestly not at all sure he would manage to get to it before someone else did.

He decided that perhaps the best thing he could do was get himself back to bed and rest for the afternoon. He took a deep breath, then pushed himself to his feet.

He supposed, looking at it in hindsight, it was the deep breath that had been unwise. Perhaps he should have fortified himself with several, as well as a lad on either side to keep him upright. Instead, what he had was Samantha Drummond, doing her best to make sure he didn't destroy the coffee table.

She caught him before he fell. He supposed it was just dumb luck that the table was topped with marble instead of glass. As it was, he heard something give under the weight of his knee on it. A porcelain saucer, perhaps.

"Sorry," he gasped.

She put her arms around him and simply held on to him, cleverly avoiding his shoulder. "Breathe," she suggested.

He supposed that was good advice. He didn't want to rest his chin on her shoulder, but in his defense, he was not at his best at present. He patted her back, because his hand was there and it seemed like a friendly thing to do.

"I think I'm going to be ill," he wheezed.

"Please not down the sweater," she said. "It's cashmere."

"Textile snob."

She laughed a little. "If you only knew." She simply stood there for a bit longer, apparently having to brace herself solidly to keep him from pitching forward onto her. "How are you?"

"Still considering ruining your sweater."

"You know, you might feel better if you didn't talk so much."

He would have laughed, but it was simply beyond him at the moment. Instead, he did as she had suggested and simply breathed until he thought he could make it back to his bed.

"Better," he managed.

She put one hand on his good shoulder, then the other on his chest and held him steady until he could right himself. He was afraid he found it quite impossible to stay on his feet without holding on to her, even with the coffee table sitting between them.

It didn't bode well for his evening.

"I feel better," he announced weakly.

"Sure you do. Here, let's get you back to bed."

He found he simply didn't have the strength to argue with her. It was taking all his energy just to keep his gorge where it belonged.

He didn't fight her when she eased around the table, then drew his good arm over her shoulder. He was fairly sure he'd gasped out an apology or two, but it was entirely possible he'd imagined that.

Samantha stopped him just inside his bedroom. "Bathroom?"

"Egads, woman," he gasped, "my dignity."

"Which will be more seriously damaged if I have to rescue you with your trousers down around your ankles."

He wasn't quite sure there was any farther south he could travel when it came to his pride, so he nodded, accepted her as a crutch, then stumbled along with her to the loo.

Five minutes later thanks to sheer determination, he got the door open and managed not to fall into her arms.

"You look green."

"I feel worse."

"Back to bed with you, then."

He wasn't about to argue. He managed to get himself flat without ripping open his shoulder, but he supposed that was more Samantha's doing than his. She peered at his shoulder.

"I think that might be starting to bleed."

"This is my favorite . . . T-shirt," he managed.

"I guess you could pretend it's marinara."

He looked at her and did his best not to see two of her. "Had to tell him something believable."

"Well, the truth wouldn't qualify for that," she said, sounding increasingly far away. "I'm going to call Sunny."

He closed his eyes. "Cameron once thought she was . . . a witch."

"Is she?"

He shook his head, which was a very bad idea. "Herbalist."

"Want a doctor instead?"

"Please, nay," he said. "Just Sunny."

"I think that's wise. I'm not sure how you'd explain this otherwise. I'll go call her."

He made a grab for her arm, which was a failure. She paused at the foot of his bed.

"What?"

"Sorry," he said. "Arse."

"Yes, I believe you are."

He didn't bother to argue. He simply closed his eyes and fought the urge to lean over the side of the bed and vomit. He was fairly certain Sunny could fix that by working on his feet, but he wasn't sure she would be willing to after Samantha got through describing his behavior, which she no doubt would. Damn her.

He realized with a bit of a start that he was angry, but he couldn't decide whom he was angry with. Himself, definitely, because he was being rude and couldn't seem to stop himself.

Samantha Drummond, absolutely, because she wouldn't tell him to go to hell.

He just wanted to have it all over with so he could get her and that damned piece of lace out of his life once and for all. He didn't know her, but he was sure he wouldn't like her if he did. Too mousy.

Of course, another lad might have called that characteristic *gentleness* or *kindness*, but he was who he was. He liked fast cars and brittle women, truly he did.

He knew he was beginning to drool, but he couldn't stop himself. All he could do was cling to the last vestiges of thought and concentrate on a plan. He would brush up on his accent when he had a minute, get himself and Samantha Drummond to the appropriate spot, then get in and out of Elizabethan England with a minimum of fuss.

And then he would be done with everything associated with the ill-advised venture.

Chapter 13

There were odd things going on in the world.

Samantha sat at the table with the afternoon sunlight streaming in the window and contemplated the oddities she had been faced with over the past few days.

First was Derrick Cameron himself. He was a chameleon, apparently possessing a fairly substantial collection of personae and the courage to make use of them. He was CEO of his own company and obviously trusted enough by Lord Epworth to have been given the task of retrieving a matchless piece of lace. He owned a computer that had lots of things on it that she couldn't get into, things that looked very suspicious, which only added to his cloak-and-dagger aura.

But the man also believed in time travel, which in her book cast serious doubts on his sanity.

She rested her elbows on the table and considered a few more things. Take his cousin for instance, and his cousin's wife. Robert Cameron was from all reports the Earl of Assynt and looked absolutely like what she would have thought a Scottish lord dressed in a business suit should look like. His wife, Sunshine, was elegant in a midwifey, herbalisty, I'm-so-happy-with-my-hunk-of-a-Scottish-husband-that-I-can't-stop-smiling sort of way. Their son was adorable, their happiness palpable.

And their utter lack of surprise or disbelief over where Derrick had gotten his wound unnerving.

She had watched them get Derrick into bed three days earlier, then listened to Cameron laugh softly over the pajamas Sunny had brought with her. He had accused his wife genially of keeping extra pairs on hand for emergencies such as the current one, had a kiss on the cheek in response, then the two of them had set to examining Derrick's shoulder.

Sunny had concocted something, packed the wound, then they had sat down to chat as if there wasn't a man lying in that bed with a stab wound that definitely should have been seen to by a doctor.

The one thing she could say for Sunny, the former herbalist and current wife of a Scottish laird, was that she seemed very capable. Her knowledge of herbs, as far as Samantha could tell, was extensive, and her faith in the ability of the body to heal itself with the right help was absolute. By the time she and Lord Robert had dragged themselves off home later that next morning, Samantha had been a believer herself.

The ensuing three days had fallen into a pattern of sorts. She had slept and used Derrick's credit card—the number very thoughtfully provided by Emily who had come once or twice to bring her more clothes—to download several books of dubious scholarly quality to his tablet. She had ordered room service and thoroughly enjoyed getting lost in mysteries and romances she would have had to hide under her bed at home.

Sunny had come to keep watch over Derrick, spelled by Cameron, and neither of them had seemed to think there was anything strange about that. Samantha had spent her share of time with them, chatting about everything from British football to the weather in Scotland.

She had felt a little disconnected, as if she'd been a statue in the middle of a play going on around her. The play had been very normal, but she had been the odd man out, the odd man thinking about a man who was lying in a bed, recovering from a stab wound, whose doctor had been an herbalist and his cousin not at all interested in calling the cops.

Very strange.

She had spent her share of time sitting by Derrick's bedside, wondering if he would ever wake back up. Sunny's brew that she forced down him as often as possible had seemed to have the side effect of leaving him completely out of it, but she supposed that had been a good thing.

The reality of the rest of her existence was perhaps even harder to swallow. She had unlocked Derrick's phone using his unconscious and unresisting thumb and sent another couple of texts, one to Lydia and another to Gavin, assuring them she was all right but that she'd had a little accident and was laid up, conveniently with friends of the original detective inspector from Scotland Yard. She could hardly believe she was using Derrick's ploy of fending off the interest of thugs, but she hadn't known what else to do and she hadn't really been willing to talk to either Sunny or Lord Robert about it.

It was, after all, a little difficult to discuss the fact that she was the reason Derrick had gone back in time to Elizabethan England and gotten that hole in his shoulder.

So she had stayed where she was and done what she could to be useful because the alternative was going outside, empty-handed, to find herself in the care and feeding of men who would probably kill her if she didn't produce what they obviously thought she still had.

All of which left her where she was, sitting in a suite at the Ritz, nursemaiding a man who had gotten up earlier that morning and looked as if he might pass out in her arms. How he thought he was going anywhere that day was beyond her.

A soft knock on the room door had her jumping so abruptly that she almost tipped her chair backward. She put her hand over her heart, got up from the table, and staggered across the floor with the grace of one who had been in bed for three days, suffering from a shoulder wound. She peered out the peephole, then sighed in relief.

She opened the door and let the adorable Countess of Assynt in as if she had known her all her life. Sunny smiled and shut the door behind her.

"How are you?"

"Freaked out."

Sunny laughed a little. "I think you're holding up very well. At least you have a great place to freak out in."

"There is that," Samantha agreed. She nodded toward Derrick's door. "He's in there."

"Surly and unpleasant?"

"Both."

"Then he must be feeling better."

Samantha shook her head. "I don't think he is, but he's determined to be up and about. I think he's crazy." Well, she thought he was crazy about a lot of things, but she wasn't sure quite how to broach the subject with Sunny. "I put him back to bed this morning and he's been there ever since, very quiet."

"He's probably plotting something," Sunny said wisely.

"I wouldn't doubt it," Samantha agreed.

But she couldn't bring herself to even bring up the subject of what Derrick might be plotting, because she was fairly sure Sunny had no idea what that might be. She waved Sunny on to her patient, then took to pacing.

She paused by the window, looked down into the garden, and fortunately for her peace of mind found nothing unusual there. She didn't suppose that said anything, but a girl could hope. She finally sat down at the table because she had nothing else to do. Unfortunately, that gave her too much opportunity to eavesdrop.

"I feel fine!"

There was a pause. Samantha imagined, judging by the tone of the next statement, that a stern look had been delivered.

"Derrick, you're being nasty."

"I feel nasty."

"You just said you feel fine."

Swearing ensued.

"You know, I can call a doctor and then you can answer all kinds of questions you don't want to about what you've been doing over the past few days."

"Sunny, you have no pity."

"None. Apologize, or I won't come back."

Gusty sighing ensued. "I apologize. I was an unmitigated ass."

"*Jerk* would have sufficed."

"People keep using that word when they talk about me."

"There's probably a reason for that."

Samantha snorted before she could stop herself. She turned when she heard Sunny come out of Derrick's room and pull the door shut behind her.

"Well?" Samantha asked.

Sunny walked over to the table and cast herself down into a chair with a gusty sigh. "He's on the mend."

"Painfully."

"Loudly." Sunny looked at her. "Are you married?"

"Heavens no," Samantha said in astonishment. "Not even dating anyone seriously."

"Well, I'll tell you now: When they start to snarl, that means they're on the mend. It's at about that point that my Florence Nightingale impulses have ceased and I'm happy to limit my tending to tossing them the remote and telling them to get their own damned soup."

Samantha looked at her, then laughed. She put her hand over her mouth, because she wasn't sure laughing was an appropriate reaction. Sunny was only looking at her and smiling.

"How in the world did you get mixed up in all this?" she asked, still smiling.

"I have no idea," Samantha said, honestly. "I was just trying to run away from home."

"Overbearing parents?"

"Academics," Samantha clarified. "No offense to academics, of course. Mine are just a little . . . intense."

"Mine are linguists," Sunny said, "so I understand where you're coming from. My sister and I were always foisted off on relatives and Swiss finishing schools when they were busy. What about you?"

"I was locked in a museum."

Sunny smiled. "Poor girl. Well, you're out now. What are you going to do with the rest of your life?"

Now that her employers were revealed to be crooks, her brother had proven to be useless, and she might possibly be facing jail time if Derrick didn't stop being a jerk, she had no idea what she was going to do with the rest of her life. She looked at Sunny and swallowed uncomfortably.

"I'm not sure. I would just like to sort of disappear."

"Cottage on the coast? Small garden? Simple husband?"

Samantha smiled. "How did you know?"

"I think we are a lot alike," Sunny said. "You might be careful what you wish for, though. You never know what you'll really get."

"What did you get?"

"Pantyhose," Sunny said without hesitation. "Well, Scottish rain as well, which I suppose mitigates the horrors of pantyhose."

Samantha considered. "I can see how it might."

"Have you ever been to Scotland?"

Samantha shook her head. "Thought about it now and again, but that's it." That was probably an understatement considering all the time she'd spent over the years looking at pictures of Scotland, or borrowing library books about Scotland, or surfing travel sights about Scotland. But that was more than Sunny needed to know.

"It's a lovely place," Sunny said. "You would probably like it."

"I imagine I would," Samantha agreed, though she very much doubted she would ever make it that far north. At the moment she was mostly worried about making it out of the country without getting arrested.

She looked at Sunny and realized the countess was watching her more closely than Samantha was comfortable with. She searched for something to talk about that didn't have to do with anything serious.

"You're an American?" she asked.

"From Seattle. I came over here to visit my sister. Then a set of fortuitous circumstances put me in the same place as Cam and here we are. It's funny how things work out, isn't it?"

Samantha supposed in her own life it was less funny than strange, but Sunny didn't need to know that, either. But speaking of strange, she had a woman sitting across from her who had looked at a stab wound and thought nothing of it. It was tempting to speculate on what else she might think nothing of. Maybe there was no harm in venturing a casual comment or two. Nothing ventured, nothing gained. She looked at Sunny.

"Have you seen odd things here?"

"What sorts of things?" Sunny asked easily.

"Um," Samantha began, "odd things. Paranormal things."

"Like ghosts?"

"That'd do for a start."

Sunny smiled. "Of course. It is England and Scotland after all. Lots of history hanging around."

"Can you be specific?"

Sunny shrugged. "Our neighbor to the south has a piper who plays whenever his lord is in the mood for a little battle dirge."

"So?"

"Well, that piper is a ghost," Sunny said with a smile. "He's very good."

"Have you heard him?"

"Yes, and I've seen him as well."

"Interesting," Samantha said faintly. "Anything else?"

"What sort of anything elses?"

Samantha could hardly believe she was going to give voice to the words, but she had to know. She was starting to feel a little crazy.

"This seems so silly," she began, finding that the thought sounded less silly than it did absolutely insane, "but what do you think about time travel?"

Sunny's face was absolutely expressionless. Samantha couldn't say she was any sort of investigator, but she thought she might be able to put on her Derrick hat and consider the facts of the case. Sunny had been animated before; now she was very cautious.

Something was up.

"I think," Sunny said slowly, "that there are many things that are possible." She smiled. "Why not this?"

"Because it's crazy."

Sunny shrugged. "Traveling in a plane or talking on a cell phone would have seemed crazy to someone who lived two hundred years ago. Maybe there are just things we don't understand."

Samantha decided there was no point in not being frank. "You didn't seem surprised by Derrick's shoulder wound."

"It's London," Sunny said. "Lots of things happen in London."

"You didn't call the cops."

"There are some things that are better kept to the family."

"But," Samantha blurted out, "he thinks I left the missing lace in Elizabethan England."

Sunny looked at her blandly. "And what do you think?"

"I think he's crazy," Samantha said, but she had to admit she didn't think he was as crazy as she'd thought him before. "Mostly."

"Lots of crazy things in the world."

"He thinks we're going to go look for the lace tonight."

"Now, that *is* crazy," Sunny said with a smile. "He did admit as much to me which is why I gave him my supersecret, frighten-any-bug-left-in-you-out-of-you brew. He'll be fine. He'll also sleep until tomorrow afternoon."

Samantha smiled in spite of herself. "He'll be furious."

"With me?" Sunny scoffed. "I'm not worried. I'm also not going to hang around. Give me a call if he starts hallucinating."

"And just what am I supposed to do until you get here if he does?" Samantha asked, profoundly alarmed.

"Bean him with his laptop would be my suggestion, but he was rude to me and I found his apology somewhat lacking so I'm probably not his biggest fan at the moment." She smiled and rose. "You have our numbers. Call if you need help. And watch as much pay-per-view as you like. Use the personal shopper downstairs if he gets really feisty. He's picking up the tab, after all."

"Oh, I don't think I'll need the shopper," Samantha said faintly. "Emily keeps bringing me things."

"Perfect," Sunny said cheerfully. "I'll check back in later."

Samantha thanked her and saw her to the door, locked it behind her, then looked at her afternoon stretching in front of her and wondered what she should do. She had Derrick's tablet, which she supposed would keep her busy for a while. She could probably have another nap in a very luxurious place, as well as a couple of meals she would probably never match again in her lifetime. She might as well take advantage of it while she could.

She wondered what would happen if she called the airline, dipped heavily into her savings to purchase a hideously expensive same-day ticket, then called a taxi and bolted for the airport. If she'd had the guts, she would have sent the personal shopper downstairs out for a wig so she could have escaped detection.

But that would only have solved one of her problems and that was her current location. There would still be people who thought she had lace she didn't have. She would still be thinking quite seriously that Lydia Cooke was responsible for planting that lace on her. And that lace would still be sitting in

Elizabethan England under a planter she sincerely hoped didn't get watered anytime soon.

She got up and paced, trying to convince herself that none of those things mattered.

She paced for a very long time.

She finally sat down and gave in. She considered a movie, then downloaded another book to Derrick's computer. Maybe it would take her mind off her past, which she couldn't erase, and her present, which she couldn't seem to avoid. It would do nothing for her future, she knew, which left her feeling rather unsettled.

Because she had the feeling that after she went to Elizabethan England with the currently unconscious grouch in the other room, she would be on her own.

Chapter 14

D*errick* leaned his head back against the very lovely leather seat in the back of Cameron's Mercedes sedan and wished he were back in bed. He wasn't sure he was going to manage what he needed to do, but he knew if he went back to bed all he would manage would be to ingest more of Sunny's brew that would knock him out for another day. Damn her anyway.

He glanced beside him to make sure his charge was still there. Perhaps *charge* wasn't the right thing to call her. He had no idea, actually, what to term her. Captive, probably. He supposed any magistrate worth his wig would have called it an open-and-shut case of kidnapping. All the more reason to get to where they needed to go and get home before Samantha Drummond got the bright idea to flag down any bobbies.

He suppressed the urge to scratch the collar seam that was rubbing him raw. Emily had appeared earlier in the day with costumes he hadn't asked for. Then again, considering he'd now been unconscious for a total of four days—against his will, as it happened—his family had had plenty of time to think about where he was going, prepare those who might still find the idea of time travel to be absolute rot, then plan for the worst. He was enormously grateful for all three.

He looked at Samantha. The servant's costume had been a stroke of genius. How Emily had gotten her hair all the way up under that cap, he didn't want to think about, mostly because he didn't want to think about Samantha or her hair. At least the staff at the Ritz had only nodded knowingly at them as they'd left that afternoon, whispering things he could hear about days locked in their room practicing their roles. He had fallen into the Mercedes, trusted Rufus to get them where they needed to be, and hoped fervently that he wouldn't lose consciousness at an inopportune moment.

At least he was dressed in rather substantial Elizabethan gear. People would think he was sweating from too much velvet and lace, not that he was so feverish he was on the verge of passing out. He clambered out of the car with Samantha, then looked around for a handy bench to sit down on for a bit. What he really wanted to do was to look back at the street, find Rufus waiting to ferry them elsewhere, and know that all he had left in front of himself was getting from where he was to the curb. Getting from where he currently stood to Elizabethan England seemed almost as doable as getting himself from London to the moon.

"Are you going to make it?"

He looked at Samantha and had to take a minute to get his eyes to focus on just one of her.

"Fine," he said thickly.

"That wasn't what I asked."

"I'll be fine."

She looked doubtful. He felt doubtful, so in that, at least, they were in agreement.

Oliver appeared out of nowhere, startling him so badly, he almost fell over. Oliver put his hand on Derrick's shoulder and steadied him.

"You look terrible, mate."

"I'm fine."

Oliver looked at Samantha. "Is he fine?"

"I think he needs to go to the hospital."

"I'm fine," Derrick said. Well, he supposed he had growled it, but there was only so much nursemaiding a man could stand.

He looked at Oliver and, feeling rather pleased with himself, only saw one of him. "We need a distraction whilst we step into the gate."

"That's why I'm here."

At least the fair was still in full swing. He could only hope that was the case on the other side of the gate as well. He walked with Oliver and Samantha to the appropriate spot, took her hand, then stepped into the circle of mushrooms. He supposed if he'd been thinking properly, he would have been relieved to find it still in the same place. He was obviously not at his best, but he would be damned if he would go back home and sit until he felt fully himself. He would make do.

He staggered a little at the smell, which told him he was definitely in the right place. Someone behind him—several someones, actually—gasped. He turned around and smiled as pleasantly as possible.

"Blinded by the glory of the sun?" he asked, pointing upward, "or mayhap the passing of Her Majesty's barge?" He pointed toward the Thames and nodded knowingly.

A woman looked at him in alarm but started to nod to apparently keep up with his nodding, which he couldn't keep up for very long at all. Fortunately some enterprising soul thought he'd seen something—Derrick sincerely hoped it wasn't the queen herself—and had all sorts of people rushing over with him to have a look at that something. Samantha took him by the arm.

"This way," she said. "Hurry."

He didn't have to hear that twice. It also crossed his mind that it was out of character for him to follow along so docilely, but he was, as he would have admitted almost freely, not at his best.

He supposed he should have waited to attempt the textile rescue until dark, giving himself a bit more time to get himself together, but he hadn't felt as if he'd had any choice. The longer that lace languished where it wasn't supposed to be, the more chance of it being found or ruined or stolen. And as long as he knew it existed in another time, he couldn't simply leave it there. The truth was, the problem was of his making and honor demanded he be the one to see to the solving of it.

Besides, who else would he have sent? Oliver and Peter had no experience with traveling through time—if they even truly believed that such a thing was possible—and he couldn't ask anyone else in his family to take his place. No, the responsibility was his. He regretted that he had to drag Samantha into it, but, again, he hadn't had any choice. He was convinced, given the ease of their recent journey, that he never would have gotten through the gate without her.

The crowds were as they had been the time before, only this time he drew an entirely different kind of attention. Obviously clothes did make the man. Whether attention was better than anonymity, he couldn't have said. There was nothing to be done about it. He would just have to get through as best he could and hope they weren't robbed. He wasn't sure he had the energy to fend off some twentysomething bent on mayhem.

Samantha led him along a path he knew he never would have managed on his own in his current condition. He followed her, trying to focus on his surroundings. If he'd only had one more night to rest and recover, he would have been fine—

Samantha stopped next to a building. Derrick heard a faint *gardyloo* but couldn't even bring himself to look up and see if it might affect him. He wasn't at all surprised to find it had. He looked down to see sewage dripping down his left arm, but he was past caring. All he wanted to do was sit down until the world stopped spinning so violently.

"It's here," Samantha breathed. "And my phone as well."

He looked at her in surprise. "You're kidding."

"Completely broken, but it's there." She shoved the lace into her bag, then leaned over and collected the pieces of her phone.

"Is it all there?"

"I have no idea," she said. "I think I have all we have time to get."

He would have argued, but when he stepped forward to bend over and look at the ground, he saved himself from bashing his head against a wooden post only because Samantha was fortunately stronger than she looked. She pushed him back upright, then held on to his arm.

"You stink," she said.

"Yes, I imagine—"

"Let's go."

He didn't fight her, mostly because he couldn't fight her. It was truly appalling how terrible he felt, but half the battle was won and there was no turning back.

"Hold on to me," he said thickly.

"Are you going to fall?"

"No, I just don't want . . ." He had to take a deep breath. "Don't want to lose you back here. Hold on."

She took hold of his arm, which he supposed earned them a few looks that he wasn't paying attention to. He focused on the path in front of him, was grateful that the London of Elizabeth's time was a very busy place, then plowed doggedly on. He attempted a supercilious look directed toward those who got in his way, but he was too ill to judge how that might have come off.

"We're attracting a crowd," Samantha said quickly. "Hey, stop that—"

Derrick looked at her and found that she was being assaulted by some hunched-over crone. He pulled her behind him and looked down at what he realized was not a granny but a man, wizened, cackling. He would have made a fine witch for the Scottish play. Derrick suppressed the urge to share that opinion and turned to push Samantha on ahead of him.

They hadn't made it twenty steps before he found himself mobbed. It took him a moment or two to realize that they weren't calling the city guards to come arrest him for traveling through time without permission, they were acting like fans. He frowned, then attempted to make sense of what they were shouting at him.

"Richard Drummond!"

He was not at his best, admittedly, but he was almost certain he was being mistaken for one of the greatest Shakespearean actors of that generation. He couldn't even find the words to deny the moniker, not that it apparently would have made any difference to his misguided groupies.

He tried to keep Samantha next to him, but she kept being pulled away. He finally grabbed hold of her and laced his fingers with hers. He supposed it wouldn't serve him to be rude, so he nodded and smiled and worked his way back to where they needed to go. And then, when he thought he could manage it, he made his move.

"The queen!" he bellowed. "Over there!"

The crowd turned to look and he pulled Samantha into the ring of mushrooms with him. He was more relieved than he wanted to admit to find himself not facing a crowd of adoring fans but a very wide-eyed Oliver Phillips. It was all he could do to keep himself from pitching over into Oliver's arms. Actually given that Oliver's hands were quite suddenly on his shoulders—rather painfully on the right—he wasn't entirely sure he hadn't already done some pitching.

"Let's go," he said, feeling increasingly dizzy. He had the feeling that weakness hadn't come from his little journey through time. "Hurry."

"Car's on the way. Miss Drummond, if you could possibly—"

"Of course."

Derrick felt Samantha put her arm around his waist. Oliver took his other side, his right side, and that almost sent him into oblivion from the pain.

"Sorry," he managed. "Don't mean to bleed on you."

"I think you should stop wasting energy talking," Samantha suggested.

He agreed, but he didn't have the energy to say so.

He knew he had at some point gotten into a car—hopefully one belonging to Cameron—then out of that car—hopefully stopping somewhere he would want to stop. He had a vague thought pass through what was left of his wee small brain that it would be a shame to bleed all over the reception area of the Ritz, but that was driven out by Oliver's loud disgust over the ridiculous lengths method actors were willing to go to. Samantha's agreement was, he thought, perhaps a bit too enthusiastic to be considered polite, especially since it was his method acting they were disparaging, but it was getting him through the hotel lobby unquestioned, so he wasn't going to argue.

He had no idea how they got him upstairs and down the hallway to their suite. Samantha opened the door and helped Oliver get him inside.

"A little help, my laird," Oliver said, his voice fading into the ether.

So Cameron was there. Derrick wasn't all that surprised. His cousin was always concerned about the state of his vassals.

"Was he wounded again?" came the voice from very far away.

"No," Samantha said, sounding as if she were across town. "I think he probably should have stayed in bed another day or two."

"Stubborn fool."

Well, that was offensive, but Derrick couldn't latch on to the words to say as much. In fact, he was having trouble holding on to anything. He did manage to look at the floor, but that was probably only because his head was too heavy to hold up any longer.

His last conscious thought was that, considering the velocity with which he was going to encounter it, that carpet, lovely as it was, was going to leave a mark on his face.

He suspected he would be too unconscious to care.

He woke to the sun streaming in through the window, which meant it had to be late afternoon. Again. He was starving, which he supposed meant that perhaps more than just a couple of hours had passed. He lay perfectly still, taking inventory of his body to see how it might betray him currently.

To his surprise, he felt almost human. *Good* was stretching things, but *functional* was not. He turned his head to find Samantha Drummond sitting in her usual spot in the chair pulled up reasonably close to the bed, her legs hung over the side, her fingers poking around on his computer.

"I'm going to have to change that password."

She didn't look at him. "As well as delete a few things."

He frowned. "What few things?"

"Half a dozen romance novels, an equal number of mysteries, and a very interesting book on medieval healing practices." She looked at him then. "You might want to hang on to that last one."

He supposed he might. "Have you been using my credit card?" he asked sternly.

"Everyone thought I should. Was I wrong not to put my foot down and refuse?"

He studied her for a moment or two. "You're different."

"Using a strange man's credit card while he's unconscious and drooling will do that for a girl."

"I never drool."

"I don't imagine you know what you've been doing," she said, sounding far more smug than she should have.

He shifted uncomfortably but a thrill of fever didn't go through him. Progress had been made, thankfully, but perhaps not quite as much as he would have hoped for. He started to move, but Samantha set his computer down on the table and jumped up.

"Here, let me help you."

He wasn't used to being the one in the bed, as it were, and it took all his reserves of politeness not to growl at her when she put a few pillows behind his head and helped him sit up just the slightest bit.

"Thank you," he said briskly.

"Bet that was hard."

He managed not to glare at her, but that was only because his discomfort at needing help was tempered by a quite proper sense of gratitude.

"I'm not at my best," he allowed. "I apologize."

"Don't worry about it. I'm about ten minutes away from chucking the remote at you and telling you to get your own damned soup."

He blinked, then smiled. "That sounds like something Sunny would say."

"It was something Sunny said," she said. "Apropos, don't you think?"

"Very." He didn't dare move his head too much, so he continued to look at her. "Have you checked the lace?"

"Yes. Would you like to do the same?"

He held out his hand and had a snort as his reward.

"Not on your life," she said in a tone that brooked no argument. "Lord Robert brought gloves, if you think you can get one on. And then, and *only* then, will you touch this lace."

"You historians are bossy."

She pursed her lips but said nothing in reply to that.

He accepted a glove, fumbled with it, then had help in becoming properly attired for the examination of priceless artifacts. He looked the lace over, then shook his head as he handed it back to her.

"Why he doesn't keep it in a vault, I don't know."

"Because then he can't walk past it every day and look at

something someone was wearing four hundred years ago," she said. "I don't blame him at all."

He slid her a look. "The historian speaks."

"Temporarily," she agreed.

"How's the Victorian piece?"

"Not fabulous," she said. "You can have a look at it and form your own opinion."

He took it, then couldn't help but watch how she handled the lace. He had to admit he wasn't at all surprised at the care she took. Obviously she had been very well trained, but there was something in the way she folded it that spoke of more than simple training. Whatever else Samantha Drummond was, she was a lover of old things.

He completely understood.

"Well?" she asked, looking at him.

He glanced at the embroidery, then shook his head—gingerly. "I wouldn't waste my time with it."

"Not worth enough money?"

"No, actually, it isn't. What do you think?"

"My mother wouldn't bother, either," she said with a faint smile. "I was just testing your snob meter."

He started to deny that he had one, then decided there was no point. He was extremely choosey about what deals he agreed to broker, but it was never the amount of money involved. Well, almost never. He looked at her.

"What do you think?"

"Your meter is performing beautifully," she said. "I guess the drooling hasn't damaged it."

"Are you trying to humiliate me?" he asked crossly.

She smiled. "Nah, just a little payback. Lord Robert said you would enjoy it, so, again, since he's an earl and I'm just a peasant, I thought I should take his advice."

"Did he have any other astute suggestions?" Derrick asked politely.

"He said to throw the remote at you, not hand it over, and to use your credit card a lot. I don't think I can throw the remote at you."

"But you've used my credit card quite a bit, is that it?"

"Again, it's the earl/peasant thing. I didn't dare argue." She smiled briefly. "And I'm not serious. I'll pay you back for the ebooks."

"Of course you won't."

"And the other cashmere sweater."

"Not that, either."

"And the dress. It was unfortunately quite expensive, but I couldn't get Emily to take it back."

He knew he should have pulled up his bank account and shown her just how little a dent she possibly could have made in it, but he wasn't sure he had the strength. The best he could do was shake his head.

"I'll make payments," he lied. "If you did want to do something in return, you could order lunch."

"If you like."

"And stay and watch a movie with me."

She looked more shocked than he would have expected her to. It wasn't as if it was a date. He'd been drooling in front of her for heaven only knew how long. He wasn't sure he could date a woman who had seen him in that condition.

"What sort of movie?"

"Anything, and I mean anything, that doesn't involve period costumes."

She smiled. "I'll see what I can find." She handed him his tablet, then rose and walked toward his door. "Any preference for an early dinner?"

"Anything that doesn't involve broth."

She smiled, then left him to himself.

He managed to get himself in a sitting position, then swung his feet to the floor. Getting to the loo and back to bed wasn't nearly as taxing as he'd feared it might be. No puking, no fainting, no needing to call for aid with his trousers in an embarrassing location. He sat down on the edge of the bed and looked at the lace sitting there, tucked safely in its plastic covering and topped by that truly worthless piece of Victorian embroidery, and shook his head. So much trouble for something a noblewoman of the sixteenth century wouldn't have thought twice about losing.

But Samantha understood Lord Epworth perfectly. The man had scores of treasures, but that piece of lace was something special to him. He never would have hidden it away in a vault.

Derrick wondered how Samantha Drummond could possibly have known that. Perhaps she was more attuned to the historically minded collector than she let on.

T_{wo} hours later, he was pretending to watch a modern-day romance starring two of the most vapid actors he'd ever been forced to observe whilst actually thinking about a few things that puzzled him.

First was a question about why Samantha Drummond wanted to turn her back on everything she'd worked for to that point. He wasn't unaccustomed to taking on different personae when it suited his purposes, so he could understand it on a certain level. After all, he'd abandoned Scotland in his teens to embrace a career that his parents most definitely hadn't approved of. That hadn't worked out very well for him, but since that was something he never thought on when he could help it, he let that recollection slide right by.

Perhaps she hadn't had a choice about her profession, though that gave him pause as well. Had her parents looked at their own vocations, flipped a coin, then whomever had won had chosen Samantha's life's work for her? If that was the case, he certainly couldn't blame her for wanting to leave it all behind right along with her parents. It was a pity, though. She was, from what little he'd seen, good at what she did.

The second was how in the world a woman reached the age of twenty-six without having told her parents it was time she left the nest. He couldn't say he'd exchanged many words with Gavin past curses, so he didn't even have a conversation there to aid him in solving the mystery. Perhaps as the last child she'd felt responsible for their happiness. Perhaps she was a spineless waif of a thing who couldn't bring herself to tell *him* to go to hell, much less her parents.

Or perhaps she was simply too kind for her own good.

He looked at her sitting in her accustomed spot—in the chair, not next to him on the bed, as it happened—somehow not surprised to find she was blinking rapidly.

"You," he said distinctly, "are a theatrical pushover."

She laughed a little. "I know it was garbage, but it was a romance. How can you not like a little romance?"

"Because it's rotten stuff. Sickly sweet. Bad for the teeth and tum."

"Cynic."

"Probably."

She looked at him then. "But you're willing to go to great lengths for things not created in the twentieth century. How is that not romantic?"

He waved her on to the telly before he had to answer, though he smiled a little as he did so, because there was just something about the woman that inspired it. Which led him to the last thing that made him want to scratch his head.

She could have made tracks for more interesting locales at any moment, yet she'd chosen to stay and nursemaid him. Guilt over having left lace where it didn't belong? A nefarious desire to watch him at his worst?

Or from the goodness of her heart?

"How about a spy flick now?" she asked cheerfully.

"I won't last through it," he warned.

"Are you too tired, or would it be too boring?" she asked. "You, with all your supersecret gear and getaway cars."

"Too boring," he agreed. "Been there, done that."

"Nod off then, Sherlock, and let me watch another chick flick."

He didn't think he was going to have any choice but to oblige her, though he definitely was going to have to solve at least a couple Samantha Drummond mysteries before he let her go back into the wide world to do her art. There were also a few details about the lace to wrap up, but he would see to those in the morning. At the moment, all he wanted to do was close his eyes and ignore what he was sure was going to be a three-hankie tale of love lost and won back.

That would also help him ignore the woman who was obviously going to enjoy it thoroughly.

Mystery that she was.

Chapter 15

Samantha flinched at the sound in the other room, then dismissed it. Derrick was still asleep, Oliver had promised her earlier that morning to be within yelling distance—she hadn't asked how he was going to manage that—and she had the suite locked up tighter than Fort Knox. Maybe Derrick had fallen off his bed. She supposed she should have been concerned, but Sunny had been there just an hour ago and pronounced him fully on the mend. Samantha was convinced he was virtually indestructible, so she'd left him to his snoozing and gone inside her room to contemplate her future.

She wasn't sure what sort of future she had stretching out in front of her, but her options seemed to be fairly limited. She supposed she might be able to get her plane ticket out of the Cookes' house, but then again, maybe not. If she couldn't, she had the money to buy a new one, but it would seriously dent her savings. All her cash was still taped to the underside of the nightstand, cash she had intended to last her for most of the summer. If she had to borrow anything from her parents, that would set her up for a fairly lengthy amount of indentured servitude in her mother's current exhibit. Then again, since it was what she was accustomed to, she didn't think it would be all that painful.

What would be painful, though, was giving up even the small amounts of freedom she'd enjoyed. She couldn't say being on the lam, as it were, had been terribly comfortable, but at least she'd been on her own—for the most part. The part she hadn't liked had been being on her own in, ah . . .

She could hardly say the words to herself, but there was no denying that the place she'd quickly visited two days earlier hadn't felt all that, well, modern. While Derrick seemed to have lots of interesting friends, he surely wouldn't have gone to the trouble of staging such an elaborate ruse to leave her thinking she'd been four hundred years in the past. What purpose would it have served? She could safely say that the man's overwhelming desire over the past few days had been to get his lace. She couldn't imagine he was making that up.

Which left her pretty much where she was, sitting in an obscenely expensive suite at a ridiculously exclusive hotel, trying to get over the shakes she'd had periodically since she'd stepped back through that circle of mushrooms, then helped Oliver get Derrick into the back of that chauffeur-driven car.

She'd gotten rid of them the day before when she'd spent the evening watching movies in Derrick's room. Maybe it had been the distraction. Maybe it had been feeling like she'd been a part of something more interesting than the endless cataloging of Victorian artifacts and the chewing out of low-level museum staff. Maybe it had been feeling safe—and that in spite of the fact that the one who could have protected her most easily had been unconscious and, yes, drooling.

She supposed what she had currently were less the shakes than they were simply restlessness over what to do at present. She supposed there was no reason for her to stay any longer, but she hadn't wanted to simply ditch Derrick before she could—

Well, she had no idea what she intended to do. Thank him for the all-expense-paid trips to Elizabethan England? Apologize again for racking up stuff on his credit card? Ask him for his address so she would know where to send the checks to start paying off that debt?

And since she hadn't been able to face any of that, she had instead done the unthinkable and arranged a still life on the table in front of her. She had taken out her sketch pad and a pencil.

And she was too terrified to use either.

"Interesting subject."

She tipped her chair over backward in her surprise. In fact, she tipped it so far, that she went with it. She wasn't sure if she was more hurt or embarrassed, but the haste with which she was trying to get herself back on her feet left her little time to think about it. She had help, which surprised her. Derrick kept his hand on her arm until he apparently thought she wasn't going to fling herself anywhere else, then he let go of her and leaned over to pick up her chair. He held on to it for a moment or two, apparently trying to catch his breath, then looked at her.

"We're quite a pair," he managed.

"You startled me," she said. She looked at him critically. "At least your eyes aren't crossed any longer."

"A fact for which I am enormously grateful." He moved to lean against the dresser. "What are you up to there?"

She took a deep breath. "Nothing yet."

"I pulled you out of your happy place, perhaps."

"Nope," she said with a shrug. "I didn't have any inspiration. Actually, I don't have any talent, I'm afraid."

He regarded her steadily. "And who told you that?"

"No one had to," she said with a light, careless laugh. "I have two good eyes."

"Maybe you should silence your inner critic before he destroys all your pleasure in something you might be very good at."

She struggled to mask her surprise. "Aren't you supportive today," she said.

"I'm not fond of critics," he said mildly. "And if you're willing to turn your back on everything you've done to this point in favor of art, it's likely very important to you."

She let her mouth fall open as it wanted so desperately to. "How did you know I was turning my back on things?"

"You introduced yourself as an artist, not an historian. If that's the case, it's fairly logical to assume you don't want to be associated with your past." He tilted his head slightly. "Is that about right?"

"Who *are* you?"

"A student of the species," he said wryly. He shoved his

hands in his pockets, only wincing slightly. "Am I right or have I completely misread you? Well, past that initial misreading, of course."

She shrugged helplessly. "Honestly, at this point I don't have any idea who I am or what I want to do. I don't even know what to do with the rest of the day, much less my life."

"Well, let's deal with today," he suggested, "and go make an old man very happy. The rest will sort itself with enough time."

She couldn't say she had that much faith in the ability of time to right things, but she was willing to at least go listen to his plans. She made herself comfortable on the sofa, then watched him rub his shoulder gingerly after he'd sat down as well.

"Hurt?"

"Healing," he clarified, "which is less painful than it is annoying. But I'm grateful." He sat back and looked at her. "So, now we have to decide what we're going to do."

"We?" she echoed.

"We," he said. "Until the general word is out that we have the lace back in our possession, I don't think you're safe."

"And just how am I going to fix that?" She was appalled to find that her mouth was so dry, she could hardly swallow.

"*We* are going to fix that with a couple of well-thought-out phone calls to the less savory types, then a trip north to deliver the lace back to Lord Epworth." He looked at her seriously. "The main problem I see is the lads who are following you—all four of them. I don't know who hired them, or why there would be two pairs, but I have to assume it has to do with the lace."

"That seems reasonable," she agreed faintly.

"We can hope. I think the best way to proceed is to have Oliver deliver that Victorian rubbish for you and see who comes to observe that little handoff—"

"But that's too dangerous for him," she said quickly. "I couldn't ask him to do that."

Derrick shook his head. "You're not; he's offering. Insisting, actually." He smiled. "Oliver has a rather interesting background. This is the sort of thing he lives for, so I don't like to disappoint him when these kinds of deliveries crop up. He'll be just fine, mostly because he won't be alone."

She didn't want to ask who would be going with him. She could only assume that person wouldn't be Derrick.

"And immediately after he lets us know the package is off," Derrick continued, "you'll give Lydia a little text and let her know your new friend from Scotland Yard saw to that delivery but only after he found something odd inside the wrapping. Because he's such a stellar soul, he promised he would return that something odd to its owner. As for you, your plans for the summer have changed. You're sorry, but that's how it goes."

"I'm a bit of a flake, apparently."

He shrugged. "Oliver trotting through a less desirable part of London is one thing," he said. "You going back to Newcastle and spending even three minutes in Lydia Cooke's house to explain things is quite another."

"Then what about the lace?"

"We'll head to Castle Hammond and hand it back to His Lordship."

She looked at him, surprised. "You're not going to call the cops about this?"

"I think that this might be better if we keep it just in the family, if you know what I mean."

"No press conference?"

He smiled briefly. "No press conference. Word getting back to the Cookes will probably be publicity enough." He considered for a moment, then shifted to face her a bit more. "I have the feeling that once Lydia hears the lace is in the tender care of Scotland Yard, you'll be off the radar. And I suspect—and I've been thinking about this for a bit, so it's less a guess than it is something I'm fairly certain about—I suspect that when the Cookes understand the situation, they'll feign ignorance of the whole thing. I wouldn't be surprised, though, if they send someone to check to see if our little scrap of textile has been returned to Castle Hammond. Case closed."

She supposed so, but she almost didn't dare hope that she would be free of the whole situation so easily. Then again, if those thugs were after the lace and everyone knew she didn't have it any longer, maybe freedom was more attainable than she dared hope.

She looked at Derrick. "And the Cookes? What will happen to them?"

"I'm not entirely sure, actually," he said. "They don't have a history of theft, as far as we can tell."

"How far can you tell?" she asked.

He hesitated, then smiled faintly. "We have access to a few databases with interesting facts."

"Hacker," she chided.

"And that's nothing I'll ever admit to," he said promptly. "I don't know if they've been pinching little stuff all along and this is their first attempt at something big, or if this is the first thing they've ever attempted to steal."

"How are you going to tell?"

He sighed deeply. "Well, the circles I run in are rather small. Word tends to get round fairly quickly about thefts and thieves. I haven't heard anything about the Cookes to this point, but that may change."

"And you don't think the cops should know?"

He shifted, looking slightly uncomfortable. "Well, that's the thing, isn't it? If I let the Cookes go unpunished and they poach something else, where does that leave me? Yet on the other hand, I have a man with an impeccable reputation who would shudder at the thought of the bobbies tramping through his private sanctuary."

"Which is why he called you in the first place, I supposed."

"I am discreet," he agreed. "It's part of our charm."

And keeping an old man from being stressed was likely the other part. She studied him for a moment or two.

"Do you know anyone in Scotland Yard?"

"Someone," he said enigmatically.

"Does he have a secure phone line?"

"Assuredly, and the lovely ability to keep a few things to himself," Derrick agreed. "We'll see what happens over the next couple of months."

She shook her head. "I don't know how I got mixed up in all this."

"Well, the first item of business is to get you out of it," Derrick said. "Oliver's on his way, I've texted your contact, and that should be done this afternoon. I think we can safely head north in the morning and take care of everything else." He considered. "I assume you left gear in Newcastle?"

She nodded. "Money, plane ticket, and lots of polyester."

"How much money?"

"Two hundred and sixty-seven pounds." She paused. "And twenty pence."

"I think we can replace that." He smiled, then his smile faded. "Thank you, Samantha. You have put up with far more than should have been required."

She had no idea what to say about that, so she decided that saying nothing was the best plan.

"I'll also get you a new plane ticket."

She looked at him in surprise. "That's very generous, but you don't have to."

"Least I can do." He paused. "Unless you'd rather stay in England for the summer."

She caught her breath at the sudden longing for exactly that. The thought of roaming over moors, sketching lakes, wandering along the endless miles of coast . . .

It took her a moment or two before she trusted herself to speak. "Oh," she managed, "I don't think I could." That killed her, right there. She had to take a deep breath to get the rest out. "Got to get home, and all that. Things to do."

"What sorts of things?"

She looked at him, sitting there on an obscenely expensive reproduction sofa, and wished things were different. She wished she were different. She wished that for once, she had the time and means to do what she wanted to instead of what her parents wanted her to do. She wished she had saved every penny she had ever earned instead of just seventy-five percent of them. That extra twenty-five surely would have been enough to let her stay in England for the summer.

But eventually the piper would have to be paid. She could either blow her money on what would amount to only a couple of months of freedom, or she could get back home, buckle down, and carve out a future for herself. Dull, but responsible. And given what she'd just been through, responsible seemed so . . . responsible.

It took her another moment or two before she could speak. She looked at Derrick.

"I know it was just for a short time," she managed, "but when one travels to Elizabethan England, nothing's quite the same afterward."

He smiled seriously. "Nay, it isn't."

"I don't think I can go home again," she admitted, "but I think I probably should."

"I would offer you a job as resident expert on Elizabethan textiles, but that isn't really what you want, is it?"

"Nope," she said without hesitation, ignoring what that cost her to sound so convinced. "Don't want anything to do with anything that isn't art. I'm officially out of the historian arena."

Or she would be, just as soon as she went home and saved up enough money to never have to identify another lace pattern.

"I honestly can't blame you." He paused. "But perhaps before you go, you could come with me to Castle Hammond. His Lordship might even give us the private tour once he stops weeping."

"Attached to his antiquities, is he?"

"Very."

She considered, then hesitated. "I should probably text Gavin."

"Tell him you're coming with me to have a private tour of Lord Epworth's collection. We'll hear his head exploding from here."

She laughed a little in spite of herself. "All right." She paused, then looked at him. "Think the embroidery is stolen, too?"

"Given who the recipient is, I would say yes. But whoever is willing to pay for it deserves what they get for buying rubbish. We'll let Oliver deliver it, then I'll snoop a bit on my end and see what turns up."

"Is that legal?"

"You probably shouldn't ask."

"What if the Cookes are famous international jewel thieves and this was just a trial run?"

He smiled, apparently amused. "Then we'll let the bobbies handle it, I suppose."

"Unless it's one of your clients getting stolen from."

"Well," he admitted, "yes."

"Do you have a gun?"

"You probably don't want to know."

"I'm not sure I would be surprised," she said. "I've seen you with a sword."

"It helps to be handy with quite a few things."

Apparently so. She approved the messages he sent both to

the Cookes and her brother, then left him to his conversation with Oliver.

She ordered a late lunch because she had become unfortunately quite familiar with the room service menu. She accepted compliments on her last movie role from the room service girl on the other end of the phone, then hung up and looked at Derrick.

"They think I'm a famous actress."

"So they do."

"They think you're my famous actress self's equally famous boyfriend."

"The burden of celebrity," he said with a light sigh. "We do what we can, I suppose."

She laughed a little in spite of herself, then looked at him and felt her smile fade. "Thank you for the adventure."

"Hmmm," he agreed. "Calling you names, chasing you all over the island, dragging you to places you didn't want to go. Thrilling, no doubt."

"It beats being stuck in a musty old museum."

"Well, if you're going to put it that way, then you're welcome."

She had the most unreasonable wish that it could go on a bit longer. She found herself rather more interested than she should have been in Derrick Cameron. She wondered what his favorite treasure had been, how in the world he had ever gotten involved in the whole antiquities business, how long he intended to keep up the craziness.

She was also tempted to tell him that out of all the colors she'd seen his eyes, she liked green the best.

But that was crazy. She had things to do, her life to get back to. Her trip to England, no matter how brief, had allowed her to test her wings. To her surprise, they were sturdier than she would have thought. But that testing was over for the moment. She would happily accompany Derrick up to York and deliver the lace, but then she was going to have to turn and look life squarely in the eye and get on with it.

She could only hope she might make something of it that would be worthy of a sketchbook.

Chapter 16

Derrick walked up the steps to the castle, wondering how many staff he would have to go through before he encountered the earl himself. At least he was coming in the front door this time instead of picking a lock on one of the side doors, disarming the alarm system, then breaking into Epworth's inner sanctum. This was, he had to admit, much more pleasant.

He glanced at Samantha walking next to him and suppressed a smile. She definitely needed to get out more. He wasn't sure she was going to be able to wipe the look of astonishment off her face anytime soon.

"Weren't you here recently?" he asked politely.

"I was," she managed, still gaping at the house in front of her. "Not that you'd know."

"Why do you say that?"

"Because it was Oliver who followed me." She looked at him then. "I can't imagine you own green shoes."

He started to speak, then laughed a little. "You're very observant."

"Occupational hazard." She looked up at the palatial country house in front of them. "And last time I didn't get in the house. Just the gardens."

"Well, if we have time, we'll do both. I'm sure Lord Epworth will be so pleased, he'll give us access to anything we want."

She took a deep breath, then looked at him. He was slightly surprised to find she wasn't so much gobsmacked as she was uneasy.

"What is it?" he asked.

"Are you sure he won't throw me in jail?"

"You are directly responsible for rescuing his lace from under a planter," Derrick said easily. "We'll just spare him the details of where that planter was or how the lace got under it in the first place. You're safe."

She looked up at him. "You don't really believe in time travel, do you?"

He smiled and paused in front of the door. "We're here. Let's see if they let us in."

"I think it was all just a big delusion," she said. "Maybe those mushrooms were giving off hallucinatory vapors we didn't notice."

"Believe that, if it makes you feel better," he said cheerfully, then lifted his hand to knock. Before he could, the door was opened and Lord Epworth's social secretary stood there.

"Oh, Mr. Cameron," he said, looking as nervous as if he fully expected the axe to fall on his neck at any moment. "I hope you have news. His Lordship is beside himself."

"Not to worry, Mr. Stevens," Derrick said. "I think we have very good news indeed." He gestured toward Samantha. "This is Miss Samantha Drummond. She is someone I believe His Lordship will be very happy to meet."

Stevens's look of unease didn't abate much, but perhaps at the moment any movement away from a nervous breakdown was a good thing. Derrick ushered Samantha inside before him, then walked into the hall and tried not to sigh. It wasn't a sign of envy because he had his own spot to land when he finally managed it and it suited him perfectly. He also wasn't unacquainted with places of grandeur and splendor. But the house they were in was truly exceptional. He might have actually indulged in a bit of envy if he hadn't known what it cost Cameron in worry to keep his own castle out of the hands of the tax man. He didn't envy

Lord Epworth that worry multiplied by the number of rooms and the prime location.

"Let me see to your things," Stevens said, motioning for staff to come collect Samantha's wee suitcase and both their backpacks. "If you'll follow me?"

Derrick surrendered their gear without worry, then nodded and walked with Samantha behind Lord Epworth's secretary.

"This is amazing," Samantha said, staring up at the ceiling.

"It is," he agreed.

"And that was a pretty good client voice you just used."

He smiled in spite of himself. "I only trot it out on special occasions."

She looked at him. "I hope he'll be happy."

"I think he'll be thrilled."

They were led into the earl's private study, or rather, Lord Epworth himself opened the door at the knock and welcomed them inside. He didn't look quite as uneasy as his secretary, but close.

He insisted on introductions before business, which almost made Derrick smile. Good manners, in his experience, generally won out over interest in possessions among those whose company he didn't mind keeping.

They were invited to join the earl in front of a fireplace that was somehow unsettling for its emptiness. Derrick shook off the impression with difficulty. After all, things were going his way. He'd recovered the missing lace. The embroidery had been delivered without difficulty and neither he nor Oliver had seen any thugs on the trip north. He was planning to return to London, get Samantha on a plane, then do a little snooping of his own into the activities of the Cookes. What could possibly be wrong?

Well, he was getting ready to send Samantha Drummond out of his life, but that surely shouldn't have bothered him any.

He listened to her make small talk with Lord Epworth about his roses. She was obviously used to flattering crusty old keepers of special collections because she charmed him without an effort. Derrick supposed that had little to do with her change in wardrobe, though sending her polyester with Emily for deposit at the local charity shop had surely been liberating. Perhaps it was that brush with Elizabethan England that had changed her.

Or perhaps it was just that instead of looking at her as a thief, he was looking at her as a woman.

"Historic textiles?" Lord Epworth asked, his ears perking up. "What a fascinating subject." He paused, then frowned. "There is a woman from the States who specializes, I believe, in Victorian antiquities—"

"Louise McKinnon?"

He smiled. "Yes, that is whom I'm thinking of. I have one of her books on Victorian silver that I found fascinating." He looked at her closely. "A relative?"

"My mother."

"Of course, I should have realized the connection. Are you an aficionado of all things Victorian as well?"

Samantha shook her head. "I prefer things of an earlier vintage, actually, and I'm not overly fond of silver."

"I have a very large collection of textiles you might be interested in, then," Lord Epworth said. "Perhaps you'll indulge an old man his pride in his treasures and come have a look when we're finished with our business here."

"I would love to," Samantha said. "I understand you have a very large collection of remarkable things."

Derrick could see Lord Epworth's distress, but he knew the man fairly well and knew what to look for. The old man smiled, though that perhaps cost him quite a bit.

"Well, it's less than it was, but I have great hopes that Mr. Cameron has some news for me that will eventually remedy that."

Derrick had spent a good part of the train ride north trying to convince Samantha to be the one to hand over the lace, but she had consistently refused. He hadn't been willing to argue with her, so he had finally agreed to do the deed himself if she would keep the lace safe in her messenger bag once they reached the castle. He looked at her, then accepted the lace that had been wrapped carefully and placed inside archival plastic. He handed it over without comment.

Lord Epworth took it, closed his eyes briefly, then looked at him. "Is it whole?"

"Yes, Your Lordship."

Lord Epworth bowed his head. He finally took a deep breath and looked up. "How?"

Derrick nodded toward Samantha. "She had it slipped to her without her knowledge, discovered what she had, then had the good sense to hide it until we could safely retrieve it and return it to you."

Lord Epworth reached for Samantha's hands and held them briefly. "I don't know how to thank you—"

"Oh, I think Derrick is being too kind—"

"No, I'm sure he isn't—"

"Well—"

Derrick listened to them fall over each other verbally for several moments whilst Lord Epworth was in raptures over his recovered treasure and Samantha was trying not to take any credit for its return. He himself simply sat back and let them have at it.

"And you were house-sitting for this couple," Lord Epworth said finally, in disbelief. "Do you care to identify them?"

Samantha looked Derrick's way. "Do I?"

Derrick leaned forward. "An investigation won't be forthcoming, so perhaps it's best to simply suggest you don't have any more house parties with actors for another few weeks."

There was a reason the man still had his house and all his property. It took him less than a minute to mentally run down his guest lists and apparently narrow it down to the appropriate suspects. He looked at Samantha.

"And you were working for this couple that we won't name."

"My brother Gavin knows them," she said helplessly. "I don't think he has any idea who they really are. I certainly didn't have any reason to be suspicious of them."

"Well," Lord Epworth said, "you certainly can't go back there now. Let's go put the lace where it belongs, then we'll discuss a few things." He rose. "Come with me, friends, and we'll examine my new security system."

Derrick smiled to himself as he walked behind Lord Epworth and Samantha down the long hallways toward the earl's sanctuary. He paused with Samantha for a moment whilst the earl stepped aside and spoke briefly with his secretary, then smiled to himself as Lord Epworth offered Samantha his arm and escorted her the rest of the way.

Derrick had been there in that inner sanctum more than once, but still he felt the pull of things that hadn't been created in the current century. He looked at Samantha to see if she would put her foot down and announce that she wanted nothing to do with anything of a vintage nature.

She was pulling on curator gloves right along with His Lordship.

Derrick declined a pair, content to simply watch the other two enter the fray.

In time, he found a chair and helped himself to it. His shoulder was substantially better thanks to Sunny's miraculous concoctions of herbs, but he was more tired than he cared to be. It was actually rather lovely to simply close his eyes and know that he wasn't responsible for the safety of either himself or anyone he cared about, however temporarily.

Not that he cared about Samantha Drummond, of course. If he were to choose a woman to be fond of, he certainly wouldn't have chosen her. He wasn't moved by her ability to charm and delight an old man who loved antiquities. He definitely wasn't ready to become fond of her because of her laugh that sounded as if she honestly hadn't used it all that often and wasn't quite sure how it might come across. He was not interested in a woman who couldn't seem to stop fingering cashmere, or who had spent more time than necessary promising him she would repay him, and who had simply looked at him, mute, when he'd assured her for the dozenth time that repayment wasn't necessary.

He wondered what her life had been like as a slave to her mother.

He knew he shouldn't have been wondering, but since the odds of seeing her again were virtually zero, perhaps he was safe.

He realized that at some point he had dozed only because he woke with a stiff neck. Lord Epworth and Samantha were still going strong, discussing the intricacies of Elizabethan lace making. He remained still, not wanting to disturb them whilst they were having such a wonderful time.

They had apparently put the missing lace back in its place of honor, but examining the other pieces to their satisfaction took a bit of time. Derrick watched as gloves were finally stripped off and final niceties engaged in.

"You'll stay for supper, of course," Lord Epworth said. "And I'll have my housekeeper make up a pair of rooms for you. I have appointments this afternoon, but perhaps you can amuse yourself on the grounds until supper. Ah, Derrick, you've rejoined us."

Derrick heaved himself to his feet, swayed slightly, then caught himself. "Forgive me, Your Lordship," he said politely. "It has been a longish week."

The earl offered Samantha his arm. "Let's return to my office briefly and see to matters of business, then I'll set you free for the afternoon."

Derrick frowned thoughtfully as he followed them. Perhaps he was less functional than he thought or Lord Epworth more grateful than usual, because it was always Stevens who took care of the more pedestrian matters of payment. Besides, he usually billed his clients after the fact, not at the moment.

Eventually he sat down with Samantha across a desk from the earl, then realized Lord Epworth had no intentions of talking to him. He had the feeling he knew what was coming, so he simply sat back and watched, trying not to smile.

"Now, of course Derrick has his very reasonable fee," Lord Epworth said, "which I have willingly paid several times in the past. You see, my dear, he has a very good eye for precious things."

"Does he?" Samantha asked. "I haven't known him very long, but he does seem to be very good at what he does."

"He is. Now, there is, of course, the reward attached to the finding of the lace," Lord Epworth said, "which is separate from the nominal fee charged by Cameron Antiquities, Ltd."

Nominal was, of course, understating things badly, because their fees never had been and never would be cheap. Cameron always said that half the respect they earned came from the staggering sums they charged, and Derrick had never disagreed. Lord Epworth was perhaps being fair by paying him for having tracked down the lace, though in all honesty, it had been Samantha to keep it safe. The money should have likely gone straight to her. Then again, if the man was going to pay her a reward that he was obviously inventing on the spot, so be it. Derrick had no intentions of spoiling it for either of them.

Lord Epworth reached for a piece of paper, examined it carefully, signed it, then folded it and placed it in an envelope. He held that envelope out, waiting steadily until Samantha took it.

"What's this?" she asked in surprise.

"Your reward, my dear. Of course I wasn't sure if you would have had time to set up any sort of account here so if you'll be so good as to provide me with your bank details, I'll have my secretary see to the transfer of funds. This is just to let you know what will be wired within the hour."

Samantha was looking at the man as if she had never heard of bank details before. "But—"

"I hope it will suit," Lord Epworth said, looking quite pleased with himself. "Just a small token of my gratitude, of course."

"Ah," Samantha managed, "I would have to call my parents—"

"Why trouble them when we have Derrick sitting right there?" Lord Epworth looked at him. "Shall I time you?"

Derrick smiled. "My lord, your faith in my abilities is, as always, humbling."

Lord Epworth laughed, sounding thoroughly delighted. "My boy, I'm afraid the extent of your abilities continues to unnerve me, but in this case I'm happy to see you use them for the benefit of this delightful girl sitting next to you. Samantha, whilst Derrick is about his work, perhaps you would care to join me at the window. I'll point out the more notable features of the garden. Perhaps you would enjoy a stroll there this afternoon?"

Derrick smiled to himself as His Lordship checked his watch, then sent him a pointed glance. The game was afoot.

It took him ten minutes only because he kept being distracted by the lovely sight of one of his favorite gentlemen being so kind to a woman who was being just as kind in return. He borrowed a piece of paper, wrote down what Epworth's secretary would need, then accepted compliments on his ability to do things with his phone Lord Epworth didn't want details on.

"Now," His Lordship said with a happy smile, "perhaps you two would care to wander through the gardens or amuse yourself in the house. I've assigned a member of my staff to attend you, should you require anything. We'll meet again for supper, shall we?"

Derrick agreed that they would, took Samantha by the elbow, walked with her toward the door. She was clutching her envelope as if she feared it might take flight if she didn't hold on to it tightly enough. He let her proceed in front of him, then paused and looked at Lord Epworth.

"Very generous, my lord."

Lord Epworth patted him on the shoulder. "It is my favorite piece of lace."

Derrick hesitated, then cast caution to the wind. "You could put my fee in her account, you know."

"Oh, I fully intend to." Lord Epworth smiled. "You, my boy, have a tender heart and too much money, so I thought you wouldn't mind." He nodded toward Samantha. "She's quite lovely. I'm not sure how she'll manage to stay in the country, but I don't think she wants to leave." He shook his head. "Those Cooke people. Very poor form, what?"

"Extremely."

"But all's well now that the lace is where it belongs, yes?"

Derrick had no trouble understanding what he was getting at. "It was recovered very discreetly, my lord. Perhaps we should leave it at that."

Lord Epworth nodded, shook his hand, then waited until Derrick had left the office before he shut the door. Derrick joined Samantha in the hallway and looked at her.

"Well?"

"I don't dare open this here," she said, looking stunned.

"Perhaps not, but we might have some privacy in the garden." He looked at her. "Curious?"

"Queasy."

"Well, I'm sure it's just a token," Derrick warned. "He does still have to keep the lights on."

She shook her head. "I couldn't even keep his porch light on with what I have, so anything at this point is a bonus."

"Then let's go see what your bonus is," he said, though he had to admit he was almost unable to keep himself from shaking his head. In disgust at her parents, as it happened.

The woman beside him wasn't a spendthrift. He'd watched her over the course of several days and made note of her habits. He'd been bored on the train that morning, so he had, to her horror, looked up her parents' salaries. They made ample to see to their own needs and pay her a generous salary as well, but she'd finally admitted, once he'd threatened to hack into her bank account, that they paid her in room and board. No wonder she'd worn such dowdy clothes. She'd probably been relegated to her mother's castoffs. And now that he'd seen what her account contained, he was even more irritated with her parents. It was inexcusable.

He walked with her out into the garden, thanked their escort and promised to call the mobile number on the card if they needed assistance, then waited until Samantha had chosen a bench near a fountain to sit down on. He joined her, then looked at her. The sun was finding all the red in her hair again, turning it into something not at all what it looked like inside. She was currently staring at the roses on the far side of the fountain with such longing, he half wondered if she'd ever seen any before.

He half wondered several things about her, actually, beginning and ending with what might come of it if they were to begin again.

Nothing would come of it, he reminded himself firmly. She was a Yank and had a life waiting for her. He was a Scot and already had his life awaiting him. It wasn't his fault if her life included returning to the semi-slavery of working for her mother. Maybe Lord Epworth's money would give her a bit of a fresh start.

He rubbed his hands together. "Open the letter, woman, and let's examine the booty."

She smiled faintly. "You are part pirate, aren't you?"

"I understand their fascination with shiny things," he said dryly, "probably more thoroughly than I should."

She held the envelope in her hands and looked at it as if she wasn't at all sure what to do with it.

"Want me to open it for you?"

She held it out without hesitation.

"I wasn't serious," he said quickly. "You open it. They're your funds."

She took a deep breath, then with trembling hands carefully broke the seal. He watched her unfold the paper, freeze, then drop it. He picked it up and handed it back to her.

"Well?" he asked.

She laughed a little in a particularly unhinged way. "Fifty thousand pounds. He's transferring fifty thousand pounds into my account."

He whistled softly. "He's *very* grateful. What are the details?"

"I hadn't dared look at those." She scanned the page, then

her mouth fell open. "He gave me your fee—but he can't do that."

"*I* didn't find the lace; you did," Derrick said seriously. "Of course you should have it."

She looked at him quickly. "But I couldn't take it."

"Well, don't look at me," he said, holding up his hands in surrender. "I'm not about to pull it out of your account."

"But you need to eat, too."

He didn't suppose the moment had come to tell her that he had a cool £50 million sitting partly in Switzerland and partly in other places, and that was just his fallback savings. He had triple that in other investments. The sensation of having someone worry about how he would feed himself was so novel, he thought he might like to enjoy it a bit.

"You can buy me breakfast tomorrow."

"I can't—"

"Buy me breakfast?"

"I can't take your money!" She clapped her hand over her mouth, then looked at him, wide-eyed. "Sorry. I'm not usually a shouter."

"I think, Miss Drummond, that if anyone had cause to shout, at the moment, it's you." He smiled. "Think you can sketch some roses now?"

"I think I can have a nervous breakdown now." She looked at him and her eyes were full of tears. "I can't take this."

He didn't think his shoulder would hold up to putting his arm around her, so he settled for patting her back. "Samantha, you'll offend him if you don't take it. Truly."

"But maybe he wasn't thinking clearly."

"You'll *really* offend him if you tell him that." He pointed at the symbol drawn next to the ledger entry that gave her Cameron Antiquities's fee. "That wasn't drawn by a man not in his right mind."

"It's a smiley face."

"It's a smirky face. There's a difference. I think he suspects I may have caused you grief."

"You're paying handsomely for the privilege."

"Happily," he said, quite happily. "Now, hand me a page from your sketchbook and a pencil, if you would, and let's see who draws the better rose." He shot her a look. "Unless you're afraid."

She wasn't smiling. "I'm always afraid."

He felt his smile fade. "And that, Samantha Drummond, is something you should rethink. You outlasted thugs, braved Elizabethan England, and kept me from dying—"

"Sunny kept you from dying."

"You kept me from drowning in drool," he said dryly. "And you also held my nose while she poured her foul brew down my throat. Just think about that. I could have bitten your fingers off."

"You were supposed to be unconscious."

"That damned stuff she makes could leave a corpse sitting up in protest," he grumbled, then he shot her a smile. "Don't be afraid anymore. You have buckets of money in the bank and your whole life ahead of you. What have you to be afraid of?"

She took a deep breath. "I am afraid," she said slowly, "that I won't be good at what I really want to do."

It was amazing, he thought, how it was possible to be sitting in a lovely garden on a not-uncomfortable bench and feel as if one had just been kicked in the stomach by an enthusiastic young stallion. Goat, horse, yob: he wasn't sure what species had almost knocked him off his perch. He supposed it didn't matter. All he knew was that he understood how she felt. He had faced that fear with all the bravado of a young man and . . .

Well, not even a matched set of wild horses would induce him to discuss the details.

"I am not the one to give advice," he said grimly, "but I don't think art has to be perfect. We could try something easier than roses. Look, there are a few topiaries over there. I think I might manage the one that looks like a hedge."

"That *is* a hedge."

"Fancy that."

She looked at him. "You're nuts."

"Quite probably," he agreed. "Let's go examine the fauna more closely and see what we can manage of it."

She blinked rapidly a time or two, then nodded. She put the paper back into the envelope and the envelope back into her bag. Derrick supposed he wouldn't need to thank the earl, but he likely would drop him a note later, because he had decent manners in spite of himself. The man had been very generous. He could have called it good at half that and simply counted it as Derrick's fee.

It was, he had to admit, somewhat reassuring to know there was still some good to be found in the world.

Chapter 17

Samantha waited until the car had driven away before she looked at Derrick. He was standing next to her at the station, holding on to her suitcase. He smiled.

"Well, Miss Heiress, what are you going to do now?"

She wasn't sure why she felt so uncomfortable. She'd had a lovely day the day before, full of so many unexpected things. She wasn't sure what she'd been more surprised by: money she honestly didn't deserve or the camera Derrick had popped into York to purchase for her while she'd been ostensibly taking a nap in her room.

In case the scenery goes by too fast to sketch it had been his only comment, delivered with a small smile.

All of which left her where she was at present: at the train station with money in the bank and her life stretching out before her, and finding it ridiculous that she was disappointed that that life wasn't going to include the man standing there in front of her.

She didn't particularly like him, as it happened. Sure, he was tall, dark, and unfortunately quite handsome, but he was also bossy and able to hack into her accounts without exerting himself. She was just sure if she had anything to do with him it would spell a serious lack of privacy and autonomy for her.

Then again, she didn't have much with her parents, either, so maybe it wouldn't have been as much trouble as she feared.

"Samantha?"

She blinked, then realized she'd been staring at him without speaking. "Ah, what I'm going to do. Well, I'd planned on being at the airport tomorrow."

"Your first-class ticket is open-ended. You could stay, if you liked."

She hesitated. "I'm not sure I could. My visa is, well, I don't know what it is. I think it's a work visa."

"We can change that."

She laughed a little, feeling slightly breathless. "You're handy."

"You have no idea."

"Actually, I think I do."

"Then let's go fix a couple of things."

She took a deep breath, then nodded and walked with him until they found an empty bench inside the station. She noticed for the first time that Derrick hadn't just sat down like a normal guy. He glanced around, considered, then sat, but not in a way that drew attention to himself. She sat down next to him, then looked around casually, just to see if she could see what he saw.

She saw security cameras, a couple of people she suspected were station security, and . . . well, not much else. She frowned.

"I don't see any bad guys."

"Neither do I," he said, "though I hadn't really expected to." He lifted his eyebrows briefly. "No reason for them, is there?"

She shook her head, though she was more uneasy than she supposed she should have been. She had obviously just been through too much over the past week and her nerves were shot. The thought of going home, though, and having to discuss the whole thing with her parents was enough to get on that last nerve she still had.

Derrick leaned back against the bench and looked at her. "Now, before we work on visa issues, what is it you want to do?"

"Well, my parents—"

"No," he said firmly, "you. What is it *you* want to do?"

She frowned at him. "I think you're trying to breed an insurrection."

"I think you just found yourself with a great deal of money and a new camera. You're in England, which isn't as lovely as Scotland, but you'll have to make do unless you venture north and see its wonders for yourself. You have the summer stretching out in front of you. What would *you* like to do?"

She hardly knew how to even begin to think about that. She looked out over the station, not seeing it, and tried to imagine what she would do if she could.

"I think I would like to see the Lake District," she said, turning her head to look at him.

"A haven for artistic types, or so I understand."

She smiled faintly. "Is that so?"

"Miss Potter would say so. I think she drew the occasional doodle for her books. And I believe that she invented the phrase *all of the sudden*, to her publisher's horror, no doubt."

Samantha smiled. "Then that's where I'll go, for all those reasons. But I should call my parents first."

"Shoot them an email instead." He handed her his tablet. "Less room for discussion that way."

She looked at him quickly. "Password?"

"I believe, Miss Drummond, that you already know it."

"I would have assumed you would have changed it already."

He looked at her seriously. "I trusted that you wouldn't reveal it."

"That's a lot of trust."

He shrugged. "I don't give it easily, believe me."

She did. She also had quite a bit of experience with his computer, so she had no trouble writing an email to her parents telling them simply that she'd had a change of plans and would call them when she'd replaced her phone.

"You're using my machine as if you've done so before," Derrick grumbled at one point.

She smiled, because it was true, finished off her note, then handed him back his computer. "All yours."

"My turn, then," he said. "Let's deal with your tourist issues first." He glanced upward, adjusted the angle of his screen, then got to work.

"I'm not sure I want to know how you can do this."

"I'm not sure you do, either," he said absently.

"Aren't you afraid someone will hack *you*?"

"One of my partners does nothing all day but try. I pay him bonuses when he succeeds, though I'm not sure why. Very annoying." He frowned briefly, then his expression lightened. "Visa done. Let's look at a place to stay. What do you think of Ambleside?"

"Is it pretty?"

"So sweet you'll be looking for lemons to counter the taste left in your mouth."

"Not a fan of England, are you?"

He smiled briefly. "Actually, I'm quite fond of the Lake District, but nay, I'm a Scot through and through. I'm only in London because I must be. I'd rather be north of the border, thank you just the same."

She suspected she might share that opinion, if she had the chance. "I don't care. You choose."

He scrolled thoughtfully through places to stay, then apparently decided on something. She fumbled in her bag for her debit card, but he shook his head.

"It's on me."

"But you don't need to—"

"It's on me," he repeated firmly.

She frowned. "You're very bossy."

He looked at her briefly. "Could you consider it chivalry?"

"I'm not sure I've ever encountered it before. Is this what it looks like?"

He laughed a little. "Well, I didn't say I was any good at it." He turned off his computer and put it back in his backpack. "Let's go get you a ticket."

"I can—"

"But you won't."

She blew her hair out of her eyes. "You're impossible."

He heaved himself to his feet and reached for her suitcase. "My finest quality. Let's go."

She trailed along after him for a bit but realized that he wasn't going to put up with that for very long. She ended up standing next to him as he bought her a ticket, then walking with him as he got her to the right train track.

She wondered if she should make a list of the most uncomfortable situations she'd ever been in because at the moment, the comfort of rating her discomfort on some sort of list of things that made her uncomfortable might be the only thing that saved her. She supposed that standing next to a gorgeous man while trying to decide how to say good-bye fit neatly between her having insisted on wearing pantyhose to the first day of fourth grade—she had spent the whole day pulling them up and showing off her panties—and her first date as a junior in high school when she'd sent Ashton Marshall home with a bloody nose after he'd tried to kiss her and ended up leaving his retainer attached to her braces. Orthodontics, stockings, and guys, nightmares all.

She looked up at Derrick as the train pulled to a stop in front of him.

"I don't know how to thank you," she began.

He shook his head. "No, I need to thank you. You were a tremendously good sport about many things."

"I think I benefitted most," she said. She smiled. "The earl did give me your fee, after all, which I need to give back to you—"

He shook his head and reached for her suitcase. He put it up into the train, then put his arm around her and hugged her quickly.

"Up you go, lass." He smiled. "Enjoy your sketching."

She stepped up onto the landing, looked at him one last time, then took her suitcase and went to look for somewhere to sit. She sat on the far side of the train where she wouldn't have to look at him, because she just couldn't look at him again. She stared out into the crowd and found it reassuringly free of anyone she recognized. She was, for the first time in her life, completely alone.

She was surprised at how much that bothered her.

The scenery on the trip west was more varied than she would have expected. She supposed out of all the things that had surprised her, that was the most startling. She could have spent a lifetime in England and never lacked for different things to draw.

She stared out the window and tried to make a mental list,

now that she was back on her own and had all the time in the world to make every list she could stomach. She supposed the first one she should make was of all the final details that had been sewn up over the last twenty-four hours.

Derrick had offered to get her stuff from the Cookes, but she had begged him not to bother. Lydia could keep those yards of polyester fabric and acrylic knitted items. It made her a little nervous to leave her plane ticket behind, but since Derrick had so kindly provided her with another that was waiting for her at a travel agency in London when she decided to claim it, she supposed it was no great loss. She was free of thugs, free of commitments, and free to do anything she wanted to. Unfortunately, all that freedom left her with nothing to do but face the question that left her the most unsettled.

What in the world was she going to do with the rest of her life?

At least she could count on not being stalked by bad guys, working for crooks, or having to rely—at least for the meantime—on her parents. There was something to be said for being a woman of independent means. The first thing she was going to do was find a stationery store and buy a card so she could write Lord Epworth a thank-you. She might even doodle on the inside to truly show how deeply she'd been moved by his generosity.

She looked around her casually, on the pretext of checking out the scenery, and scoped out the people around her for anyone who looked suspicious. Just for something to do and because it made her feel sleuth-like. She could hardly claim to have Derrick-level skills, but she didn't see anyone who looked like they shouldn't have been on a train at that time of the morning. No thugs, no textile thieves, no good-looking Scots in disguise.

She settled back against her seat and supposed she had nothing to do but get on with her grand plans. She had the money to stay in England for the summer and live a life of leisure, though she imagined she would be staying on the cheap as often as possible. No sense in not hoarding what Lord Epworth had given her. But sketchbooks were reasonable and the scenery was free, so perhaps she would end up going home with a little something in her pocket.

By the time she'd taken a taxi up the way from the station in Windermere to her hotel in Ambleside, a hotel that wasn't all that little and definitely wouldn't be found on any budget lodging site, she was feeling fabulous. She had her life under her control in a way she had only imagined it might someday be as she'd first gotten off that train in Newcastle. She was going to step forward boldly, seizing the future by the lapels and demanding that it give her everything she asked for.

Which was obviously why she spent half an hour in her room, pacing and wondering what in the hell she was doing.

Being on her own was perhaps going to be slightly more unnerving than she'd suspected it would be.

She went into the bathroom, repaired her face with things Emily had thoughtfully provided her from a counter that Samantha never would have in her wildest dreams approached for even a sample, brushed and rebraided her hair, then took her good sense in hand. It was still early. She could go for a walk, soak up some local sights and smells, then go back to her room and make a serious list. But not before she'd had lunch and forced herself to stay outside for at least a couple of hours.

She realized later that it hadn't been as hard as she'd feared. The shops were quaint, the weather good, and the surroundings extremely lovely. And the longer she walked, the more she decided that she was definitely better off without any overseas entanglements. She would spend the summer polishing up her artistic skills—and praying she had some—then she would go back home and put her foot down with her parents. Maybe by then she would have figured out a way to survive on something besides the charity and generosity of an old man who hadn't been required to do anything for her.

The world was full of very good people.

It was also full of things that made her nervous.

She discovered that as she returned to her hotel after a lovely meal. She started to put her card key into her door only to find there was no need. It swung in without help. The hair on the back of her neck stood up and it was only good breeding—well, that and a lack of breath—that kept her from screaming her head off.

Damn. She shouldn't have read all those mysteries on Derrick's computer. She *definitely* shouldn't have downloaded that creepy episode from *The Twilight Zone* simply as an act of rebellion against her parents who had insisted she limit herself to period pieces.

She reached inside and flicked on the light. She looked inside the room, then let out her breath slowly. No one was hiding behind the door. No one was sitting on her bed, waiting for her. No one was hiding behind the curtains. Her room looked as it should have.

Maybe she'd forgotten to lock the door.

She told herself she was imagining things. She continued to tell herself she was imagining things as she checked the bathroom, the wardrobe, under the bed, and out on the little balcony. There wasn't anyone in the room.

But there was someone standing across the street.

He wasn't looking up at her, but just the way he was standing was so utterly sinister, she could hardly stand the sight. She jumped back, drew the curtain, then sat down on the bed and reminded herself that there was no need to have a nervous breakdown. She had nothing anyone would want. The lace was back where it belonged. Surely not even retribution was worth following her all the way to Ambleside.

She unpacked her suitcase, checking every piece of clothing, looking in every nook and cranny for a stowaway of some kind. There was nothing she hadn't expected except a pair of pearl earrings and a lovely necklace to match, but since there was a note from Emily attached, she didn't think those were thugworthy. She replaced everything with shaking hands.

She paused, then looked at her bag. She hadn't emptied it, but there was nothing else inside it that shouldn't have been there. She felt around inside it just to make sure. No, it was just full of her usual stuff. She sat on the edge of the bed and suppressed the urge to wring her hands.

She was half tempted to open the balcony door and bellow for the guy across the street to move on to greener pastures, but something about letting sleeping dogs lie echoed in the back of her mind.

She considered, then considered a bit longer. She didn't want to call the concierge because it was entirely possible that she had forgotten to pull her door to. There was nothing missing in her room, so there wouldn't be anything for the police to find worth their time to investigate. Lots of people stood on streets. Maybe the guy across the street was waiting for his wife to come pick him up so they could go out to a late lunch.

She looked around the room, then found a chair and propped it up under the doorknob. Then she double bolted the door with the security lock. She wished she'd thought to ask Derrick for his phone number, but what in the world could he have done? He was probably all the way back to London already.

Actually, for all she knew, he'd decided he needed a vacation and flown to Paris.

She was on her own.

Which she supposed wouldn't be so bad during the daytime. Thugs didn't break into rooms during the daytime, not while people were there. For all she knew, it had been the maids—

She blinked, then she smiled. It had obviously been the maids. Why else would someone have been able to get into her room? They had a master key and had no doubt come in to freshen things up. Nothing else made sense. She didn't have anything on her that anyone would want, with the exception of the clothes Emily—or, Derrick, rather—had bought her.

She let out her breath slowly and didn't mind that it wasn't all that steady. She was safe. She had jumped to conclusions and freaked herself out. She was perfectly safe and nothing was going to happen to her.

Though she was going to figure out first thing in the morning where to go get a phone. Just in case.

She took a deep breath, then looked around the room for something to use for a still life while she had plenty of daylight.

Chapter 18

Derrick looked out the window and watched the scenery slide by. He could have wished for a speedier journey, he supposed, but there was only so much a man could demand of the British rail system. It was definitely faster—and less stressful—than driving. Unfortunately, it gave him far too much time to think.

He imagined Samantha was enjoying the scenery. She had been stunned by the camera, still a little gobsmacked by her newfound wealth, and rather pleased with her rendition of Lord Epworth's hedge. Her life, at least, was definitely looking up. He wasn't sure what his life looked like, but he didn't think it was pretty.

He knew he should have checked his email or texted Peter to inquire about discreet business enquiries or called Sunny to thank her for saving his arm, but all he could do was stare out the window and wonder why it was his life was just not quite so interesting when it was missing a certain textile historian who would rather have been an artist.

No, interesting wasn't the word.

Sweet was the word.

His phone cheeped at him. He sighed, then pulled it out of his pocket to check the text.

Call me.

He frowned. Oliver tended to send short, pointed messages. The only reason he ever wanted to actually pick up the phone and engage in conversation was if there was something disastrous on the horizon. Derrick sighed, then grabbed his pack and made for the end of the car where he might have a modicum of privacy. He dialed Oliver, who picked up on half a ring.

"Hey, mate, you know those two lads?"

"Ah," Derrick said, finding it difficult for some reason to switch gears back to spy mode, "which two lads?"

"The pair we saw in London."

Derrick frowned. "Bald one and skinny one?"

"That'd be them."

"Haven't seen them. Have you?"

Oliver made thinking noises. "I haven't, but I got to wondering why they looked familiar."

Derrick felt something slide down his spine and it wasn't a tingle of pleasure. "Did you? Fascinating."

"Isn't it," Oliver said. "You know, it's funny they should be following our Yank."

"I almost hate to ask why."

"I did a little snooping into their habits."

Derrick was unsurprised. It was, after all, what they all did best. "And what did you find?"

"Well, this is the interesting part. They don't deal in cloth."

Derrick leaned back against the wall. "What do they deal in?"

"Jewels."

"Odd," Derrick conceded. "Maybe they were off on another assignment."

"Possibly, but strange that they should be following our girl for a scrap of lace. It's not like they would have been able to tell the difference between real lace and a Nottingham knockoff, what?"

Damnation, he never should have let her go off on her own. "I don't suppose you've seen them recently, have you?"

"I was going to ask you the same thing."

"I haven't," Derrick managed, "but I haven't been looking all that hard."

"They weren't around when I delivered that embroidery yesterday. Peter didn't see them, either. The other two lads were there, the ones shadowing us down by the Globe, but they left soon enough. The jewel thieves . . . don't know where they are."

"Hell," Derrick said, blowing out his breath. "I sent her off hours ago."

"And you can't call her?" Oliver asked, sounding surprised.

"Her mobile is destroyed."

"And you didn't buy her a new one?"

"Is she too feeble to get to a Tesco?" he asked impatiently. "I assumed she would manage. I did actually book her a hotel." He dragged his hand through his hair. "I'll call the desk and get her. Perhaps she can at least stay put until I get there." He could hardly believe where his thoughts were taking him. "She can't be carrying something else."

"Stranger things have happened."

"I'm finished with strange things."

Oliver was silent for a moment or two. "Think she knows?"

"What?" Derrick demanded. "That she's carrying something else? Impossible."

"If you say so."

"The woman is beyond innocent and she's no thief. Where are you?"

"In London, on the way to your garage."

"You don't have a key to the Vanquish."

"Don't need a key, mate."

Derrick rolled his eyes. "One of these days . . ."

"So says you always. Can you get yourself to Leeds? I'll have Rufus pick you up at the station."

"Why is Rufus anywhere near Leeds?"

"I had a feeling he should be."

Derrick rubbed his free hand over his face. "I'm about five minutes from Doncaster and it'll take me another half hour's train time to get back up there. I'll get there as quickly as Her Maj's rails will allow."

"Where're we headed?"

"Ambleside."

"I'll find you."

Derrick imagined he would. "Thank you."

Oliver made some noise of dismissal, though Derrick wasn't

entirely sure there wasn't some bit of censure as well for a boss who couldn't keep his mind on his business.

Nay, Oliver wouldn't. It was his own conscience damning him. He'd kept an eye out for potential ne'er-do-wells, true, but not as close a one as he should have. He'd been convinced that they had been after the lace. More the fool he, obviously.

He considered rail lines and schedules and routes, then found the number for Samantha's hotel. He waited to ring them until the next station in spite of what that cost him because he simply didn't want to be overheard. He hopped off the train, then dialed as he was walking to catch one going the other way. He spoke briefly to the concierge and found that Miss Drummond wasn't answering her phone and they weren't at liberty to tell him anything more.

It was almost three. If it took him half an hour to get to Leeds, then another three hours to get to the Lake District . . .

He could only hope Samantha would have the good sense to look over her shoulder.

Or lock her door.

Rufus was waiting for him at the station and did his best to break every speed limit on his way north and west. Derrick had nothing to do but curse, which he did, just to keep himself awake. Rufus seemed content to make do with the Beeb on the radio, which Derrick supposed he might have appreciated at another time.

If he had let her walk into danger . . .

"Almost there."

Derrick looked at Rufus. "I should have been more careful."

Rufus glanced at him. "Derrick, my lad, she's an adult. She won't do anything foolish."

"The woman is a girl who I'm sure thinks everything bad that can possibly happen to a person is limited by what's found in a Nancy Drew novel."

Rufus smiled. "You booked her a decent hotel, didn't you?"

"Of course."

"With decent security?"

"I don't think it matters," Derrick said grimly. "We aren't dealing with nice people here."

"I'm not sure we ever deal with nice people, Derrick."

"Aye, but that's you and me and the lads," Derrick said. "This is a brainless Yank we're talking about."

Rufus shot him a look. "Brainless?"

Derrick rubbed his hands over his face. "Very well, she isn't brainless. Her marks at university were embarrassingly high—I checked a couple of hours ago because I had to do something—which left her parents not needing to pay a bloody cent for anything she did and if I ever see the pair of them, I'll have something to say about not having taken that money not spent and setting it aside for her use, but that is perhaps not a useful thought at the moment."

"Perhaps not."

Derrick pursed his lips. "The point is, I don't think she could protect herself from a pensioner poaching her pocket money, much less a lad with more serious business on his mind." He shook his head. "I should have taught her something before I turned her loose."

"And how were you to know?"

"Because I am supposed to know," Derrick said. He didn't add that part of the reason he'd put her on that damned train so quickly was because he hadn't wanted to have to look at her fresh-faced self a moment longer.

He would have kissed her otherwise.

"I want a Scottish lass."

The words hung out there in the car, innocent and unassuming, for far too long.

"Well," Rufus said finally, "that seems reasonable."

Derrick looked at him. "I don't want to get involved with her."

"Never said you had to, did I?"

"But it will be my fault if she's harmed."

Rufus glanced at him. "Then you'd best rescue her, hadn't you?"

Derrick didn't say anything, because there was nothing to say. He had allowed a defenseless woman to go off into the wilds of England alone because he'd been so unsettled by her that he hadn't provided her with the rudimentary security he would have provided for a perfect stranger in similar circumstances.

He hoped she didn't pay a steep price for that neglect.

He called Oliver. He was put on speakerphone, which allowed him to quickly determine exactly the rpm rate at which his beloved Vanquish was traveling.

"What gear?" he demanded. "Fourth or fifth?"

"I'm not sure."

"You ruddy bastard."

Oliver only laughed, which led Derrick to believe he was going far faster than he should have been.

"I don't imagine we have equipment," Derrick said, not daring to hope that might be case.

"Usual setup," Oliver said. "All on our very own supersecret frequency."

"You're chatty."

"Mate, I'm doing a hundred, not a sheep in sight, and Peter's sitting here sweeping for cameras and bobbies. What's not to love?"

"My car wrapped around a . . ." Derrick shook his head. He couldn't think of anything dire enough. "Be careful with yourselves."

"Touching, Derrick, truly. We're less than an hour out, but I'll have to slow down soon. We'll be there by dark. Cheers."

That was too long, but there was nothing to be done about it. He wasn't going to be there any sooner himself.

He only hoped that wouldn't be too late.

Rufus dropped him two blocks away from Samantha's hotel. He stepped into the shadows and felt Peter's particular tap on his shoulder. He took the earbud, put it into his ear, taped the mic along his cheek and switched on.

"Got you," Oliver said very quietly from a location yet to be determined. "Timing spectacular. One right in front of me here, one going up the side of the building. Best get in there soon."

"Handle the street," Derrick said. "We'll take care of the other." He looked at Peter. "You take the roof. I'll get inside."

Peter only nodded and slipped away. Derrick walked quickly down the street and into the hotel. He staggered into the lobby and over to the desk, keeping his hand over the mic taped to his cheek so he didn't give himself away.

"Angus MacDonald," he gasped. "Key—"

"Of course, Mr. MacDonald," the clerk said. "Your assistant called and arranged—"

"Migraine," Derrick rasped. "Key, directions."

"Up the lift, second floor—"

Derrick took the key. "Stairs," he said thickly.

"Over to your left, but do you need help?"

Derrick shook his head, manufactured a sick smile, and put his hand over his eyes to shield them from the light as he stumbled over to the stairwell. He did his best impression of a very sick man on the first two flights, then paused, as if he simply couldn't go on. He waited until he heard Peter's voice in his ear.

"Camera off," Peter said. "Sometimes this is just too easy."

"Tell me you didn't just hack into their system."

Peter laughed a little. "No. Had to have something to do whilst waiting for you. Off you go, lad."

Derrick took the stairs to the third floor three at a time, then strode down the hallway.

"One in through the window," Oliver said. "Hurry."

Derrick had Samantha's door open before he heard her squeaking. He realized she was wielding a chair the split second before she brought it down on his head. He rolled, came up, then smashed their intruder in the face as the man came through the balcony doors. Something broke as the man fell. Derrick felt fairly confident that hadn't been any of Samantha's bones, so perhaps that was all he could ask for.

"Get the light," Derrick said to her.

She was standing near the door, her hand on the light switch. Derrick looked at the unconscious thug on the floor, then nudged him with his foot. That one would be out for a bit longer, thankfully. He turned, strode over to Samantha, and pulled her into his arms.

"Are you unhurt?" he asked quickly.

"Just terrified," she said, her teeth chattering. "Are you some sort of superhero or what?"

"An idiot, rather," he said grimly. He heard Oliver click in.

"Safe?"

"Aye. How about on the street?"

"Friend number one is going to have one bleedin' lovely headache come morning. What shall I do with him?"

"Leave him loose," Derrick said. "I'm curious what they'll do next."

"Whatever you say, boss. What of yours?"

"I thought we'd put him in the linen closet and let him wake up on his own."

"And then where are you off to?"

"I think Miss Drummond and I need a strategy session. We'll disappear for a bit. Peter?"

"Here, boss."

"Cameras still off?"

"Till you say differently."

Derrick looked at Samantha, who had pulled away from him and was looking at him as if she'd never seen him before. Then she apparently caught sight of the mic on his cheek and her expression lightened.

"I thought you were talking to ghosts."

He shook his head and attempted a smile. "Just the lads. How fast can you pack?"

"I never unpacked."

"Excellent. Let's go."

She was very pale. "Fancy toys you have there."

"It helps with the cloak and dagger," he agreed. "How's your acting?"

"The genes of Richard Olivier Drummond flow in my veins," she said. "What do you need?"

"I, Angus MacDonald, have a crushing migraine and wandered onto the wrong floor. You were—"

"Feeling a great disturbance in the hallway—"

"And realized you'd met me—"

"At a conference of pharmaceutical salesmen—"

"Aye, that. You volunteered to dose me up with sweet painkillers, then drive me up the way to my aunt's where you're sure I'll sleep better."

"It's amazing I'll be able to carry my suitcase and you at the same time," she said, some of her color returning.

"You're that kind of Good Samaritan. But first let's put our bad guy in the closet. Peter, any suggestions on where to go?"

"Down the hallway, last door on the left. I'm outside the door if you want help."

Derrick was happy to accept help, even happier to carry their thug down the hallway and stash him in the linen closet. He watched Peter disappear through whatever window he'd jimmied open, then walked back to Samantha's room to find her standing in the middle of it, hugging herself and looking unnerved.

He couldn't blame her.

"I'm not sure I want to know what that was all about," she managed.

"But you might need to," he said quietly. "We'll talk in the car."

"Are we driving?"

"I'm sick of the train."

"Whatever you say."

He looked up at her. "Had dinner?"

"Lunch. I didn't dare go back out."

He winced. "That's my fault. We'll find something on our way."

She looked at him gravely. "Did I hurt you?"

"With that wee chair?" he asked easily. "Never."

"I'm glad I missed," she said. "That's a Sussex armchair. A reproduction, but still pricey to replace."

"Bloody hell, woman, furniture?" he asked in mock horror. "Trying to annoy the parents?"

"How did you know?"

"I had parents, as well," he said dryly. He held up his hand when he heard Oliver click in.

"Rufus is downstairs waiting for you. He'll ferry you to your car, then come pick me up."

"Right." Derrick stood up and took Samantha's suitcase. At least Emily'd had the good sense to buy her something with wheels that was fairly small. "Let's go whilst we can," he said to Samantha. "Our ride is downstairs. Peter?"

"Cameras still off. Empty hallway footage on a loop."

"Thank you." Derrick looked at Samantha. "The cameras will be off until we make the stairwell. You'll have to pretend to help me from there." He paused. "Are you okay?"

She nodded quickly. "Fine."

"Then let's go." He locked the window, righted the chair, then picked up her suitcase and opened the door for her. He had to admit, though, that he went out into the hallway first. Chivalry had to take a backseat to safety now and again. He paused at the top of the steps. "Pete?"

"Camera on," Peter said. "You're live."

Derrick made it down the stairs, barely, fairly sure he would owe Samantha a day at a spa in return for her services, then waited as someone hurried over and took her suitcase for her. He listened to her invent a remarkably believable tale based on their predetermined story, then found himself helped on both sides as he staggered out to the waiting car.

Which was, as it happened, something that looked as if it stood to fall apart any moment.

He piled into the back with Samantha and kept his hands over his face until they pulled away.

"All clear," Peter said in his ear. "Nice performance. That's a wrap for me. Cheers, lads."

Derrick scowled at Rufus. "Is that the best you could do?"

"You don't think I want my car on security camera, do you?" Rufus said, in mock surprise. He looked in the rearview mirror. "Good evening, Miss Drummond. All safe now."

"Thank you," Samantha said faintly.

"Have your keys, Derrick?"

"Aye, just drop us where you can. I'm assuming Oliver parked somewhere discreet."

Oliver's snort in his ear was rather too loud, no doubt on purpose. "Rufus, don't you leave us here, damn you. I'm not walking back to London. Is that where you want us, Derrick?"

Derrick considered. "I'm wondering what you might discover if you shadowed this pair we're leaving behind for a bit."

"I'll keep you apprised, shall I?"

"Please."

"Safe home," Oliver said. "Cheers."

Derrick pulled his earpiece out, untaped his microphone, then tucked both into a jacket pocket. He sighed, then looked at Samantha. She was studying him carefully.

"Standard fare," he said with a weary smile.

"Interesting fare."

She didn't know the half of it, but he wasn't about to enlighten her. Rufus dropped him off at his car without fuss. He got his gear and Samantha's stowed, then opened the door for her.

"Is this yours?" she asked in astonishment.

He shrugged. "It's just a car."

"It's an Aston Martin Vanquish," she said reverently. "It's not just a car."

He smiled. "And I think you just earned yourself a turn at the wheel at some point in the future."

She put her hand on the roof. "Is this Lord Robert's?"

"Does it matter?"

"No, but I want to know whose seats I might potentially spill something on."

"Do you think I'm actually going to let either of us eat in this thing?" he said with mock sternness.

"It's his."

"It's mine," Derrick said, not actually meaning to divulge that, but finding that he still had some pride to defend.

"I thought as much," she said smugly.

He felt his mouth fall open, then he looked at her narrowly. "You're cannier than I gave you credit for being."

"Thanks for the rescue. This is much better than being driven off in a pumpkin."

And with that, she helped herself to his fine leather seats and pulled the door shut from under his hand. He sighed, then walked around the car and opened his own door. He slid in under the wheel, then wondered what Oliver had done to deface his pride and joy. He jerked the Tahitian Love Nest palm-tree-shaped air freshener off his rearview mirror, tossed it out the door with a curse, then shut the door and turned the car on.

He couldn't help it. He sighed happily.

So did Samantha.

He looked at her. "I thought your interests were limited to textiles."

"Oh, no," she said. "Issues of *Road and Track* were always hidden cunningly under stacks of *Textile History*. I had to pay for it with a money order and hit the mail first to protect my anonymity, but my parents were clueless."

"I had no idea how devious you were."

"Drive on, Roster, and I'll tell you more. That near brush with death has made me feel very chatty."

He smiled, then looked at her before he put his car in gear. "You did well."

She didn't laugh so much as make a sound of uneasiness that she was apparently trying to pass off as humor. "I thought I was going to die."

"It's my fault. I should have been more careful."

"Of course it's not your fault. How would you have known? And what could you have known? Those guys were just barking up the wrong tree."

He wasn't at all sure they were, but that was the part of the puzzle he just couldn't quite figure out. He checked his surroundings one last time for anything untoward, then got out onto the road.

"We'll know more tomorrow," he said slowly. "Rufus and the lads will do their bit."

"Who *are* you guys?"

"It's complicated."

"But you're the good guys."

That was a statement, not a question, which he appreciated. He smiled briefly, then concentrated on the road.

"One could hope. And now that we have an endless drive in front of us tonight, put on your chatty self and tell me what you sketched today and where you went."

"It was more of a journey of self-discovery," she admitted. "Because I don't like being alone."

And neither, he realized, did he. He reached over, took her hand, squeezed it gently, then forced himself to concentrate on where he was going.

Because if he wrapped his bloody car around a tree because he'd been fussing over a woman, Oliver would never let him live it down.

Chapter 19

Samantha looked at the clock on the dash and realized she'd been asleep for well over three hours. She had managed to talk until about three, but that had been it for her. She looked to her right to see how Derrick was doing. He looked tired, but coherent.

"Do you ever sleep?"

He smiled but didn't look at her. "I was planning on a very long nap later this morning. How was yours?"

"Not long enough. Where are we going?"

He glanced at her then. "You're fairly trusting, aren't you? To hop in a car with a strange man and allow him to drive you who knows where?"

"Lord Epworth trusts you, you rescued me from a thug earlier in the evening and other various thugs earlier in the week, and you drive a Vanquish. How bad can you possibly be?"

"And I let you drink tea in my car."

"See? You're a prince."

He only smiled and concentrated on the road.

"Where are we going?"

"You'll see. I've tried to time it properly, but I don't know how successful I've been." He shook his head. "I'm more tired than I should be."

She understood, and she'd been the one sleeping all the way to Scotland. She took the opportunity to sit in absolute luxury and put off thinking for a bit longer. She didn't want to think about the night before. She didn't want to know why Derrick and his friends acted more like superspies than treasure hunters— well, she actually wanted to know that very badly, but she could wait for that as well. She just wanted to feel safe for a bit longer until she couldn't ignore reality anymore.

They drove through a village at dawn. It was a charming place that looked as if it had been frozen in time during some happy, prosperous period where everything was good.

Derrick continued on through the village, then turned after a bit onto a long, well-maintained gravel road that wound through forests and fields. The trees were full of shadows and mists and things that were gloriously mysterious and portentous. She had no trouble believing that a medieval peasant would have been terrified to find out what lurked in those forests.

"Close your eyes."

She did, mostly because she had the feeling it would be worth the effort.

"All right."

She opened her eyes, then gasped. There on a rise sat a medieval castle. Well, perhaps there were a few additions here and there, but on the whole, it looked as if it had been ripped out of the thirteenth century and plunked down in the twenty-first. She looked at Derrick.

"We didn't hit one of those mushroom rings, did we?"

"Nay, it's just Cameron Hall, home to the Camerons for centuries." He looked at her. "Not a bad pile of rocks, is it?"

"It's stunning. Is it Lord Robert's?"

"Aye. He's very attached to it. Centuries of Cameron pride and all that."

"And how are you related, and all that?"

He laughed a little. "My grandfather and old Alistair Cameron—he was Lord Robert's, ah, well, his, um—"

She listened to him stumble over his genealogy and found that very odd. "You must be very tired."

"Hmmm," he agreed. "Anyway, Cameron has the title now and my grandfather was the second son, so there you have it. And with every child Cameron and Sunny spawn, I'm more and more comfortable about my distance from the title and responsibility."

"Really?" she asked. "You don't want to be laird?"

"No desire at all."

"Why not?"

"I'd have to wear a suit and tie more than once a year at a funeral."

She smiled. "Considering I'm not sure I'll ever wear another pair of pantyhose, I think I might understand." She looked at the castle and felt herself grow increasingly nervous. "Will they let us in?"

"Might even give us breakfast if we promise to wash up."

She looked at him quickly but saw that he was teasing. "You could have left me at a hotel, you know. I haven't really been invited—"

"You're my guest," he said simply. "Don't fash yourself over it, Samantha. There are plenty of guest rooms so you won't have to sleep on the floor. The only thing that would make your stay more pleasant was if Cameron and Sunny were here. They're marvelous hosts and don't stand on ceremony. I'm not sure Cameron even knows where his shoes are once he's past the front door. I *know* Sunny doesn't."

She had no choice but to believe him, so she decided for once to do just that. She'd spent her life trying to decipher the subtext beneath what her parents were saying. Maybe it was time to just take someone at his word.

He put his car in a garage and the world didn't end, then fetched all their gear and tsk-tsked her when she tried to take her suitcase. She gave in and let him ply his chivalry on her.

She walked with him around the corner of the keep and waited until he'd gotten his key near the front door. It opened before he could manage to get it into the lock and a petite woman who looked like an older version of Emily stood there.

"Ah, Derrick, *mon cher*," she said, leaning up to kiss both his cheeks, "Oliver called to let me know you were coming, but I expected you much sooner than this."

"I thought the keep was best seen by sunrise, so we dawdled." He stepped aside. "Madame Gies, this is Samantha Drummond. Samantha, Madame Gies. She's Emily's grandmother."

"Ah, you know my sweet Emily?" Madame Gies said, reaching out and drawing Samantha inside. "And you look weary, poor lamb." She looked at Derrick. "Food or sleep, pet?"

"Sleep first, if you don't mind."

"Very sensible," she said, "for I imagine you've been driving all night. Come along then, children, and let me see you settled."

Samantha had the impression of an enormous great hall with a fireplace befitting that hall, stone floors, comfortable but very lovely furniture, and then a long staircase that she climbed only because she knew there was the hope of a bed at the top. She soon stood in the middle of a bedroom that looked as if it had been furnished in the Middle Ages and simply blinked stupidly as Derrick brought in her suitcase and set it down on the bench at the foot of the bed. It had curtains that could have been drawn, though she imagined she wouldn't get that far.

"Loo over there, love," Madame Gies said, "and water and juice on the dresser there. Derrick, your room is as it always is. Cleaner than you left it, if I might say so."

Samantha watched him kiss Emily's grandmother on the cheek. "You indulge me too much."

"I'm going to start throwing out clothes if you don't learn to pick them up off the floor." Madame Gies looked at Samantha and smiled. "I'm not serious. He's very tidy."

Samantha wanted to tell her that she wasn't sure Derrick really cared what opinion she had of him, but the woman left before she could. She looked at Derrick, though it took her a moment or two to focus on him. He was yawning uncontrollably, so perhaps he hadn't noticed. He finally shook his head sharply, then walked over to her and pulled her into his arms as if he'd been doing it without thinking for . . . well, forever.

He kissed the top of her head, then pulled away and put his hands on her shoulders. "You're safe here."

"Thank you," she managed.

"I'll see you for lunch. Hopefully."

She nodded and watched him go, pulling the door shut behind him.

She considered, then locked the door.

It had been that kind of week so far.

It was after noon before she'd managed to get herself up, into the shower, and dressed. She dried her hair, braided it, and took her courage in hand to venture out of the guest room. She walked down the stairs, then paused at the bottom of them because she wasn't quite sure what to do next.

A man leapt up from one of the couches set there in front of the fire and walked over to her, smiling broadly.

"Ewan Cameron," he said, holding out his hand toward her. "Cousin to the laird, but unfortunately too far from the title for that to matter. You're Samantha."

"Well, yes, I am," Samantha managed.

"I don't know anything about you, but I'm sure we can remedy that—"

"When hell freezes over," a voice said from the vicinity of the doorway.

Samantha looked over to find it was Derrick who had come inside and banged the door shut behind himself.

"Good hell, Ewan, give it a rest, would you? The poor girl's been traumatized enough already."

"Aye, obviously by your sour self." Ewan wrinkled his nose. "Go shower. Samantha and I will spend the time getting to know each other."

Samantha frowned at Derrick. "What happened to you?"

"Went for a run," he said, looking as if he'd done just that. "Clears my head."

"And fouls the air around you," Ewan said.

Samantha looked at Ewan. "Do you run?"

"Very slowly and only when chased," he said with a wink. "I'll tell you all about it while my cousin goes and grooms. It won't take him long. We can only hope he does more than just brush his teeth."

"Shut up, Ewan."

Ewan suggested something quite a bit viler for Derrick to do. Samantha felt her mouth fall open, but Ewan only reached for her hand.

"Take your time, cousin," Ewan said, tugging her along with

him toward the fireplace. "Sam and I will be getting to know each other better."

"Don't call her that."

Samantha glanced at Ewan, then turned with him to study Derrick, who looked suddenly very uncomfortable.

"Well," he said, "you might not like it."

"Perhaps not coming from you," Ewan said, "but from someone she's fond of? We'll be examining that—"

"Ewan, will you just shut up?" Derrick asked wearily. "Samantha, please feel free to find a chair and break it over his head. You'll do us all a very great favor. I'll be right back down."

Samantha watched him trot up the stairs, then looked at his cousin.

"Is that standard fare?"

Ewan laughed a little and offered her his arm. "Let's go sit by the fire. Castles are cold, even in the summer. And yes, that's standard fare. Derrick takes himself too seriously. I feel it's incumbent upon me to help him stop that."

"I don't know him well enough to know," Samantha murmured. "He seems driven."

"That's one way of putting it." Ewan offered her the seat closest to the fire, then sat down with her. "I'm not as obnoxious as I seem. Just trying to do my part for the betterment of the species."

Fortunately for him, he didn't have as much time for betterment as he no doubt wanted and fortunately for her, Derrick arrived in jeans and a T-shirt, not shorts and his shirt flipped over his shoulder.

Dory Mollineux, his V-neck sweaters, and his Top-Siders would have all wept with envy.

"Let's talk over lunch," Derrick said. "I'm starving and I'm sure you are as well."

"You know, I am, actually," Ewan said, rising with a smile. "Thank you for thinking of me."

Derrick looked at her. "Help me not kill him."

Ewan put his hand over his heart. "I'm here to run security for you and this is the thanks I get?"

"I'm sure you've already eaten," Derrick said shortly. "Go secure."

Ewan looked at her and made her a little bow. "He has spoken and I must obey. I'll try to sit next to you at dinner."

Samantha watched him go, then looked at Derrick. "Is he always like that?"

"Sometimes he's much worse. Let's go throw ourselves on the mercy of Madame Gies, then we'll see where we are."

Samantha was certain she wouldn't stay awake through lunch, but she managed it in spite of herself. And once she thought she might like to have another nap, Derrick looked at her.

"We need to figure a few things out," he said seriously.

"Like what?"

He thanked Madame Gies for lunch, then took Samantha's hand and led her from the kitchen. He stopped at the bottom of the stairs.

"We need to talk about those two lads, the one who broke into your hotel room and the other who was waiting outside—"

"What?" she squeaked.

He shook his head. "They're too far away to be a bother. But they *are* the ones who were following you from York. Well, from Newcastle, actually."

"I think I need to sit down."

"We'll go invade Cameron's study. Come on."

She let him pull her up the stairs because that was better than asking him to carry her, which she was very tempted to do. He led her into something that belonged in a castle, which she supposed was appropriate, and put her within collapsing range of a couch, which she appreciated. Then he sat down on the couch with her and looked at her seriously.

"I don't think those two were after the lace."

"What were they after?"

"Something you still have."

"But I don't have anything," she managed. "Just what Emily bought me—or, you, rather—and my messenger bag. There's nothing left in that."

"Well, they think there's something left somewhere. Gems, apparently, given that jewels are what they deal in."

She felt her mouth fall open. "I'm being chased by jewel thieves? You can't be serious."

He shrugged. "You don't have the lace anymore, yet your room was broken into last night while you were in it."

"And while I wasn't."

He went very still. "What?"

"When I came back from a walk, I found my door open." She took a deep breath. "I thought it was just the maid."

"What had you carried with you on your outing?"

"My bag." She looked at him. "It's in my room. I usually never go anywhere without it, but I didn't think I needed to be that careful here." She considered. "Should I go get it?"

"If you don't mind."

She thought perhaps the trip would help her calm her racing heart, but it didn't do a thing for her. She was still trying to catch her breath as she sat back down next to Derrick and handed him her purse.

"Have at it."

"Anything personal in there?"

"Well, of course there's personal stuff," she said with a snort, then realized what he was getting at. "No feminine protection items, if that's what you're talking about."

"Thank heavens. May I?"

"Feel free."

He pulled things out of her bag and laid them out: wallet, envelope from Lord Epworth, sunglasses, key to her room—

"Oops," she said.

"They'll manage to get another," he said. He frowned at the very normal and ordinary items there, then took her bag and upended it.

A handkerchief came out of one of her unzipped hidden pockets after a fair bit of shaking. Samantha blinked in surprise.

"What in the world is that?"

He peered at it, then reached out and picked it up. It was tied up like a little hobo bundle, which he then gingerly untied. He peeled back the corners, then looked at the small linen packet it revealed. He looked at her.

"What do you think?"

"Too small to be a bomb."

He smiled briefly, then set it down on the table. He pulled out a pocketknife.

"Are you supposed to have one of those?" she asked.

"Don't tell."

She would have smiled, but she was actually slightly unnerved to find that she had again been used as a courier without her knowledge.

Derrick carefully slit open one end of the small linen package, tipped it, then jumped a little as a handful of gems spilled out into his hand.

She squeaked.

Derrick poured the gems onto the coffee table and simply stared at them. He looked at her.

"What do you think?"

She took the handkerchief the little packet had been wrapped in and looked at it. "Sixteenth-century bobbin lace. It's new."

"It's not very clean."

"I mean, it's not vintage," she said. She looked at him. "We're looking at a piece of Elizabethan lace that hasn't been around for four hundred years. It's new."

He blinked. "You think it was planted on you when we were fetching the lace?"

"I don't know what else to think." She shrugged helplessly. "It's not like I've dumped out my bag since then. I was too busy stuffing things into it." She spread the lace out carefully. She could hardly believe she was examining yet another piece of Elizabethan textile, much less one that was antique, but not antique. She sighed. "It's not clean, no, but it's also not showing any age spots. And yes, it's worn a little on this edge here and it's been repaired here, but on the whole, it's in very good condition." She looked at him. "New."

"I'll be damned." He shook his head. "I wonder why?"

"It doesn't make any sense," she said. "There's no way those guys last night could possibly have known I had that. Is there?"

He looked into the empty hearth for a moment or two, then reached for her purse and looked at it. He finally turned it inside out. He looked at her. "Do you mind if get a little more friendly?"

"With my bag?"

"That, too."

She blinked, then smiled. "You're crazy. And yes, go ahead."

He looked in the pockets, then ran his fingers over the lining. And he stopped.

He reached for his knife, then looked at her. "Mind?"

"No," she said, feeling a little breathless.

He unpicked stitches she wouldn't have noticed if she hadn't been looking for them. She felt her mouth fall open as he pulled out a small plastic bag of gems.

"Well, this is interesting."

"Damn that Lydia Cooke."

He laughed a little. "That's a pretty big assumption."

"That bag never leaves my person," she said. "The only time I've been without it is in Newcastle." She looked at him. "Jet lag, you know."

"Understandable." He set the bag down on the coffee table next to the other loose gems. "Notice anything interesting?"

She looked at both collections, then frowned. "Well, apart from the fact that I'm seeing double is the fact that I'm seeing double."

He lifted his eyebrows briefly. "I'd have to dig out a jeweler's loupe, but I imagine those are quite similar sets of stones."

"What?" she said in surprise.

He started to answer, but his phone beeped at him. Samantha watched him read a text, then put his phone away.

"Oliver and Peter are here. We'll set up in Cameron's office downstairs. Lots of comfy chairs and secure lines for Internet surfing. I'll build a fire and we'll do a bit of researching."

"What are we going to do with the loose stones?"

"Oh, I'll just shove them in a pocket."

"Better check for holes first."

He looked at her and smiled. "You know, you're fairly funny for a textile historian."

"Did you expect me to only be able to talk about bobbins and patterns?"

He shook his head, then took the linen, the handkerchief, and the small plastic bag full of gems and shoved it all in her bag he'd turned back outside out. He scooped up the loose gems, then stood and put them in his pocket. She gaped at him.

"You just shoved a fortune in gems in your pocket."

"A fortune, do you think?"

"Well, the lace alone is very valuable—"

"Which is why it's in your purse." He put his pocketknife into a different pocket, then held out his hand for her. "Let's go."

"You're crazy."

He pulled her to her feet. "Sometimes I worry that I am."

She let him lead her out of the study and partway down the stairs before she had to say something.

"You can't just leave those stones loose."

He smiled. "You can't help yourself, can you?"

She sighed. "I really don't want to be an historian any longer."

"But you can't seem to keep away from it."

"It keeps finding me," she said defensively. "It isn't as if I *asked* someone to plant priceless gems on me."

"Twice, apparently."

She looked up at him. "Are you trying to be helpful here?"

He smiled. When he smiled, she wanted to run. Admittedly, the man was just too handsome for her peace of mind, but that had been easier to ignore when she didn't like him. But when he smiled at her as if he actually thought she wasn't completely intolerable, it was very bad.

"Detour through the kitchen for a container," he said, pulling her that way once they'd reached the bottom of the stairs. "So, does it really bother you to be pulled back into something you don't want to do?"

"A little."

"You're very good at it, if that makes it any easier."

She sighed, then looked up at him. "This is the last thing I investigate."

"Ah, an investigative historian." He shot her a smile. "Sexy."

She felt her mouth fall open. "What happened to you? You're so . . . happy."

He laughed a little. "We are looking at a large fortune in Elizabethan gems and you have a piece of new but old lace and no one to claim it. What's not to be happy about?"

She supposed he had a point.

She just hoped he didn't pay a very steep price for that giddiness. She hoped *she* didn't pay a price for the same. She had gone to Ambleside, sure that her adventures with thugs were over. Now, though, she had been drawn back into the thick of things, against her will and better judgment.

Though she had to admit, if she was going to be thrown into craziness, she couldn't think of anyone better to be there with than the man walking next to her, humming something that sounded remarkably like a battle dirge.

Chapter 20

Derrick walked into Cameron's downstairs office to the usual confusion that accompanied a collection of his lads setting up shop.

He had to shake his head briefly over the possessive term. They were his, he supposed, given that they worked for the company he now owned. They were loyal and seemed to enjoy their work, but whether that was because of the company or him, he couldn't say.

How they had all come to be involved in that company was, he had to admit, perhaps slightly random. Oliver had rescued him and Cameron both one night along a deserted side street in London. Cameron had invited him to come in for an interview. Oliver's unflinching expression during the hearing of a private investigator's report of his entire life had earned him both a job and trust. Peter had come a bit later, a lad with a particular set of skills and a willingness to use them.

Their expertise in antiques, his and theirs, had come by working for Cameron for so long. It could be safely said that Robert Cameron had an uncanny knack for rooting out things that were staggeringly valuable. The lads enjoyed that part, but

Derrick was sure it was the spy bit that they loved the most. He trusted them implicitly.

But they did tend to make a bit of a mess with their cables and cords and high-tech intrusion sweeping devices.

Oliver looked at Peter from where he had opened his laptop right in the middle of Cameron's desk, his preferred place to roost. "Clear?"

"Still working on it," Peter said, his head bent over his own laptop.

Samantha leaned closer to him. "Why are you bothering out here in the wilds of Scotland?" she asked.

"Thugs are everywhere," Peter said absently.

"Cynic," Oliver stated.

Peter only grunted and continued with his work.

"Where's Rufus?" Derrick asked politely.

"On the way to London, leading our thugs on a merry chase," Oliver said. "He's a couple of hours out still."

Derrick frowned. "Then how did you get here?"

"Rented a car, mate," Oliver said. "You didn't expect us to take the train, did you?"

He wouldn't have been surprised, but then again, he'd been quite surprised several times over the past few days so perhaps he wasn't one to judge. It had been one of those weeks.

"But," Samantha said slowly, "won't bad guys trace you from your credit card?"

Oliver lifted an eyebrow. "We're ghosts, miss. That, and Peter had to have something to do on the drive north."

She looked at Derrick with a frown. "What does he mean?"

Derrick shrugged. "Paperwork problems. Happens all the time."

"You hacked into a rental car company's system to erase paperwork?" Samantha asked uneasily.

"Not to worry," Peter said, still peering at his screen. "Car'll be back in Inverness with a bow on the bonnet by tomorrow night. They'll never know."

Samantha frowned thoughtfully, then leaned closer to him. "Is this what you do?" she asked. "This kind of thing? For tracking down antiques?"

"We're a full-service operation," Oliver said.

"Except for cleaning," Peter said. "We don't pick up cleaning."

Derrick pursed his lips. "I think before we go any further, introductions are in order. Samantha, that's Oliver, who doesn't know when to shut up, and Peter, who is very shy around girls. You've already met Rufus, who isn't here. Lads, this is Miss Samantha Drummond, who didn't steal a very valuable piece of Elizabethan lace but unbeknownst to her seems to have picked up another freeloader."

"Do we get to see?" Oliver asked. "Just curious."

Derrick looked at Samantha. "Why don't you show them what you found in the lining of your purse."

Bless the girl, she didn't hesitate. She simply walked over to the desk and deposited the bag of stones next to Oliver's computer. Oliver looked at Peter.

"Clear *yet*?"

"Done," Peter said, setting aside his laptop. "What've you got there?" He walked over to peer at the pile on the desk, then let out a low whistle. He pulled a jeweler's loupe out of a pocket and set it alongside Oliver.

Derrick stood back and watched the pair do the other thing they did best, which was to appreciate things that cost vats of money.

Oliver sat back, considered, then looked at him. "Not modern."

Derrick only lifted an eyebrow and said nothing.

Oliver frowned and went back to his study. Derrick waited for a bit, then finally cleared his throat.

"Five," he suggested.

"Bollocks," Oliver said with a snort. "Ten or none."

Derrick waited until Peter had finished his perusal, then looked at his chief hacker. "Well?"

"Twenty," Peter said firmly. "Not a penny less."

"Twenty what?" Samantha asked.

Peter glanced at her only as quickly as good manners dictated. He was, for all his swaggering, all thumbs when it came to the opposite sex. "Twenty million quid," he said. He shot Derrick a look. "Just a guess."

"What do you think, boss?" Oliver said.

"I haven't had a chance to look," Derrick said. He looked at Samantha. "Want to go first?"

"Oh," she said, hesitating, "I don't know anything about gems."

"Derrick will give you the lecture," Oliver said. "Boring

unsuspecting lassies is what he does best, but boring them with lectures about the various methods of cutting gems over the centuries is what he likes the most."

Derrick rolled his eyes. "I have no preference."

Oliver tsk-tsked him. "Shouldn't lie. It's bad for you." He shifted. "Here, Miss Drummond—"

"Samantha."

Oliver smiled. "Samantha. You take my chair while you're looking. And Derrick can indeed give you a lecture that would leave you begging him to stop, but perhaps today I'll give you the quicker one. It's all about the cut. Well, quality helps as well, but the cut's the thing. These would be worth more if they'd been in an original setting—and that setting had been either perfectly preserved or repaired flawlessly—but they're worth plenty as is."

Derrick had his own look after Samantha had finished, then looked at Peter.

"Fifty."

"Well, you *are* the expert," Peter said seriously.

Samantha shook her head. "Fifty million *pounds*?"

Derrick shrugged. "There are a lot of them and that's just a guess. It isn't so much what they're worth as what someone would be willing to pay for them. There is that certain *je ne sais quoi* that comes with owning something from the past, so unless we were to find the right sort of lad or lassie to pull out the bank draft, I might be grossly overestimating the value." He shrugged. "I'd have to think about a buyer or two in order to be more accurate." He scooped the stones back up into the bag, then nodded toward the fire. "Let's go poke around online for a bit. Oliver, do you have another tablet handy for Samantha?"

"Always. Samantha, let me set you up."

Derrick left her in good hands, though he had to admit there was something about how happy Oliver looked to be helping her that set his teeth on edge. It didn't help that Oliver waggled his eyebrows at him as he was seeing Samantha seated.

Derrick left the office before he did something stupid.

Elizabethan gems. Why wasn't he surprised?

He ran up the stairs, collected his computer, then trotted back down to the office. Samantha was already engrossed in what she was doing. Oliver looked up when he closed the door behind him.

"What do you want me to do?"

"Think you can track down those Ambleside lads and find out where else they've been?"

"Might be able to."

"Any word from Rufus?"

"Still the same. He sent me the plate number. I'll see where that leads."

Derrick nodded, then looked at Peter. "And you?"

"I'm snooping."

"Care to divulge where?"

"Stolen property lists."

Well, that might have been interesting, but Derrick suspected what they were looking at wouldn't find itself listed on any stolen property—

He stopped in midstep. Maybe that wasn't quite true. He had to wonder what might turn up if he looked for the theft of a substantial number of gems, say, in a different century. He had his doubts such a thing might appear on any easily found list, but the miscreant—if he'd been caught—might show up in some popular jail or other.

He went to sit across from Samantha. "How are you?"

She didn't look up. "Reading email."

She was starting to sound like one of the lads. "Anything interesting?"

"My parents told me to come home immediately."

"Did Gavin tattle on you?"

She looked up then. "He did, actually. He said I was over here without supervision. I'm guessing Lydia told him I quit."

"I'll supervise you," Derrick said. "You can tell them I said as much." And whilst she was doing that, he would check Gavin's email account to find out exactly what Lydia had told him.

"And just who are you, O Responsible One?" she asked politely.

"A pirate," Peter said.

"Rabble-rouser," Oliver suggested.

Derrick shot them both a pointed look. "A respectable businessman dealing in the acquisition of exclusive antiquities. Tell them you're helping me with a research project. Or you could just tell them to go to hell."

She laughed uneasily. "I'll think about it and email them later. I'll definitely be rude to my brother now, though."

"He would deserve it, the annoying git," Peter said, then he looked up quickly. "Sorry."

Samantha only smiled and went back to her emailing. Derrick watched her thoughtfully for a moment or two. He had to admit that she had changed. The clothes were different, obviously, but it was something more than that. She was sitting in the midst of a roomful of pirates and she looked comfortable. Happy, even.

It was amazing what a little time traveling could do for a woman.

He put his head down and concentrated on his own business, because it was safer that way and would probably save Oliver's life. If he had to look at that smirk one more time, he was going to wipe it off rather abruptly.

He decided it made sense to start with the gems not sewn into Samantha's bag. Those, at least, he thought he could safely say had come from the sixteenth century. It would have been helpful to have ascertained the date whilst he and Samantha had been visiting the last time, but since he hadn't, he would just have to guess. People had looked when he'd shouted that the queen was coming, so that put it definitely pre-1603.

He searched for an hour before he sighed and looked off into the fire. He had a headache and was no closer to where he wanted to be than he had been before he'd started.

He was tired, more tired than he cared to be. He didn't particularly want a nap, but he definitely needed a change of scenery.

"Derrick?"

He looked at Samantha quickly. It was, he was fairly sure, the first time she had called him by his given name. Oliver cleared his throat, because he obviously had something stuck there. Derrick sent him a look that warned him that that thing might be his fist very soon if he didn't shut up, had a single lifting of a single eyebrow as his reward, then looked back at Samantha.

"What?"

"Do you think," she began slowly, "that we could find a list of inhabitants of the Tower?" She looked at him knowingly. "Just for curiosity's sake."

He considered, then looked back at his screen and sent her an email. He watched out of the corner of his eye as she blinked, then pulled it up.

You're brilliant.

She smiled, but she didn't look at him.

He attacked the problem with renewed vigor. It took him another hour to find what he was looking for. When he did, he had to simply sit there and stare into the fire until the information settled into his brain in a way he could process it.

Sir Richard Drummond had been incarcerated in the Tower in 1602.

He looked at Samantha. "Feel like a drive?"

"What?" she asked in surprise.

"I need to think."

"That means trouble," Peter said, scratching his cheek.

Derrick scowled at him. "What are you doing?"

"Hacking your email."

"How's it going?"

"You write very boring ones."

Derrick blew out his breath. "Fix that, would you?"

"Working on it."

Derrick considered, then looked at Oliver. "Will you look for something for me?"

Oliver looked at him. "Of course. What?"

"Sir Richard Drummond. He was tossed in the Tower in 1602. I'm curious as to why and what happened to him."

Oliver sent him a look he had difficulty interpreting, though he had the feeling Oliver was putting together pieces that might not have been particularly apparent to anyone else. Oliver glanced at Samantha.

"A relation?"

"I hadn't considered that," Derrick said, wondering why he hadn't. He looked at Samantha. "Are you related to a Richard Drummond?"

"The Shakespearean actor?"

"The sixteenth-century version," Derrick clarified.

"I have no idea."

"I think you'll know soon." He rose and set his computer aside, then took hers and did the same. "We'll be back in a couple of hours, lads. I have my phone."

Oliver looked at him. "Are you sure?"

"We're driving to the coast and back," Derrick said with a smile. "I think we'll manage."

"Taking the Vanquish?"

"Aye."

"Damn," Oliver grumbled. "There goes my chippy run."

"Stay out of my car," Derrick warned. "And stop hanging things from the mirror."

Oliver only smirked and bent to his work. Derrick ushered Samantha out of Cameron's office, bid good-bye to Madame Gies, then walked with Samantha out to the garage.

"We'll need jackets," he said.

"I'll run back in," she said.

"No, you stay. I'll fetch you something." He went back inside, grabbed a jacket for himself and something else that looked like it might have belonged to Sunny, then went back out into the garage. Samantha was considering the horsepower there and frowning thoughtfully. "Well?" he asked.

"Do you Camerons drive anything but low-slung sports cars and Range Rovers?"

He laughed a little. "We're not a very imaginative bunch, but we like to go fast and not bottom out, respectively. I think we'll take the sports car today, though."

She looked at him seriously. "In case we need to make a quick getaway?"

"It never hurts to be prepared."

She wrapped her arms around herself. "I'm surprised by how unnerved I am."

"Not to worry," he said. "Ewan will follow us at a discreet distance and you don't want to know what he keeps within easy reach."

"I don't think I do." She shook her head. "You live an interesting life."

"And you have a small fortune in gems back inside."

"They're hardly mine. Do you think I shouldn't have left everything there?"

"The lads wouldn't think to paw through your purse, though I think we can guarantee that by the time we're back, Oliver will have made a list of stones, weighed and identified by carat and color, and be well on his way to suggesting potential buyers for them."

"But," she said, aghast, "they're stolen."

"One set is."

"The other set has to be, too."

He smiled. "Probably. But it'll keep him busy and out of my email that Peter's hacked into." He paused, then handed her the keys. "All yours."

She looked so horribly torn, he almost laughed. She clutched his keys as if she didn't intend to give them back.

"I have to go get my bag. It has my license in it."

"I think I'll let you get that," he said wryly. "If I start fetching your purse, I'll never be allowed to forget it."

She went back inside.

She was still carrying his keys.

He leaned against Cameron's Range Rover and considered the state of his life. He was trying not to think about it too hard or attach too much significance to it, but the truth was, he was getting ready to take a woman he hardly knew to his most private sanctuary. He had, as it happened, never taken a woman there. Sunny had been there, of course, along with Madame Gies and Emily, but they were family. But a woman he wasn't related to in some form or fashion?

Never.

He supposed if he'd had any sense, he would have let Samantha loose with his keys and simply gone inside and banged his head against the wall. He didn't dare hope for the return of good sense. He was simply hoping he might dislodge something useful.

She came back out in the garage, looked for him, then smiled when she saw him.

He was in trouble.

Had he ever thought her plain? He was certain he hadn't, not really. Perhaps she would never be as stunning as those society shrews he occasionally dated, but the truth was, he couldn't stand that brittle fakeness.

Samantha stopped short and looked at him in surprise. "What?"

He shook his head and smiled faintly. "Nothing. Just thinking."

"About Richard Drummond?"

He shook his head. "Not at all."

"Worried I'll wreck your car?"

"Only if you don't have a license and have never driven before."

"I got to drive my mother's minivan when I behaved really well."

He laughed, because he didn't doubt it was true. He nodded for her to open the door, then he let her into the driver's side. She sat down, took a deep breath, then looked up at him and smiled.

It was all he could do not to lean over and kiss her.

He stepped back. "I'll get the garage."

"Thanks. I'll try not to run over you on the way out."

He could only hope. He was somewhat reassured to have her make it outside without clipping anything. He closed the garage door, then got in and looked at her. "Ready?"

"I've never driven on the left."

"Best figure it out quickly, then."

"I can't believe you're letting me drive your car." She looked at him. "Do you realize how much this thing costs?"

"Possibly."

She didn't move. "My dad has a Ferrari."

"How many times did you steal it at night and then try to reverse the odometer by putting it up on blocks after you got home?"

She smiled. "That's a movie. And fourteen, if you're curious. The stealing, not the rolling back. I blamed it all on my mother. She's a wild woman at heart."

He reached out and tucked a loose strand of her hair into her braid before he thought better of it. "There are depths of deviousness to you I never suspected."

"You thought I was a lace thief."

"I can be an idiot from time to time."

"Does that include letting me drive?"

"Your father has a Ferrari."

She started to nod, then froze. She looked at him narrowly. "Did you know that already?"

He smiled. "Might have."

"And did you suspect I'd driven it?"

"I didn't know," he said, "but the thought did cross my mind."

"Why?"

"Because you look so much happier in jeans and cashmere than in polyester."

"My mother bought all my clothes."

"Now, *that* is something I felt safe in assuming," he said with another smile. "I have the feeling you may be avoiding that in the future."

"I might be." She chewed on her words for a moment or two. "I think I'm close to having an epiphany."

He smiled. "Will swearing be involved?"

"Maybe."

"Did you email your parents yet?"

She held on to the wheel with both hands, then looked at him. "I have to have my epiphany first, I think."

"A trip in the car might help."

Her expression was very serious. "Thank you, Derrick."

"You're welcome, Samantha."

"For more than this."

He nodded down the hill before he said or did anything he might regret, such as tell her she was undeniably lovely in her unguarded way. He didn't want to think about how he might be tempted to show her just how appealing she was.

"Let's go, lass. Do you like the shore?"

"Yes."

His phone beeped at him. He pulled up the text message.

Hey, why don't I get to drive that?

"Trouble?" Samantha asked.

"Ewan, whingeing."

"And all is right with the world, is that it?"

He smiled approvingly. He liked her more all the time. He leaned his head back against the seat and considered closing his eyes. But then he would have missed the opportunity to look at a woman who had turned out to be not at all what he'd thought her to be at first.

"Would you have let me drive if you hadn't known about my illicit nocturnal activities?"

"Aye."

"Thank you."

"To the end of the drive," he clarified.

She smiled and didn't spray Ewan's car with gravel when she pulled away from the castle, which Derrick was certain he greatly appreciated.

He supposed he would have to return to reality soon enough, but for the moment, he was content to ride with a woman who was laughing as she drove away from his boyhood home.

Life was good.

Chapter 21

Samantha was very grateful she wasn't learning how to drive in Derrick Cameron's very expensive sports car.

She was also grateful her father had been willing to believe that his wife had been running off with his Ferrari late at night after he'd put on his nightcap and was safely tucked up in bed. The first time she'd done it, she'd been sure she would be caught, then grounded for the rest of her life. Then again, since most of her life had felt like a grounding anyway, the risk had been worth it.

She hadn't gotten caught, to her knowledge. Perhaps her father had known and figured there was nothing worse he could do to her than was already being done by the circumstances she had found herself in.

"Thinking?"

She glanced briefly at Derrick. It was still a little odd to be sitting on the wrong side of the car, but that had taken less time to get used to than driving on the wrong side of the road. Fortunately, they hadn't had to go back through the village to get to the road that led toward the shore. There was something to be said about driving an obscenely expensive car on an open road.

"No," she managed. "I'm fine."

"I'll trade you, if you like."

"Are you kidding?" she asked. "Not a chance. I have the keys."

"I think your epiphany is rapidly approaching."

She looked at him quickly.

"Eyes on the road."

She did as he suggested and managed to avoid drifting into a pasture. "I can pull over, if you're getting nervous."

"I want you to tell me to go to hell."

She laughed a little, uneasily. "I've done that before."

"Aye, but not with much conviction. I want you to try it again."

She blinked, then she smiled. "Why?"

"Because I don't want you to get pushed around anymore."

"I don't get pushed around."

"Then pull over right now and let me drive."

She had to take a deep breath. "No."

"And?"

She refused to look at him. "You're letting me drive your Vanquish. I'm not going to tell you to go to hell. Maybe later, if you hack into my email."

"All right," he said, sounding as if he were smiling. "Just keep going. The road winds around to the right. I'll tell you where to turn once we hit the village."

"I hope you're using *hit* in a metaphorical sense."

He laughed a little. "Aye, I was. Carry on, lass."

She had to admit she liked it when he called her that. Very Scottish. Very charming.

Very dangerous.

She was actually quite grateful when he stopped talking and she could concentrate on the road. It was one thing to be out in the open with nothing to look out for but the occasional cluster of sheep, it was another thing entirely to head through a village— and a village with very tight walls, at that.

She only had to back up once to let a lorry go past her, and she managed not to scrape Derrick's car on any of the stone. She couldn't deny, though, that she breathed a sigh of relief when he told her to turn to her left. The road narrowed, if possible, through another handful of houses, then seemed to leave the village behind. There were a couple more houses that sat on very large pieces of land. And then houses disappeared, but the road didn't disappear along with them. She was actually a little surprised at how well maintained it was. The weather on the coast had to have been a constant strain on it, but it was smooth and pothole-free.

And then she realized that the road was ending.

And at the end of that road was a cottage.

It was something out of a period movie, two-story, white-washed, weathered, sitting on a bluff that overlooked a cove. The sand was fine by the water, then the beach became progressively rockier the farther up the bluff it went.

She slowed to a stop, then turned the car off. It was beyond her to do anything but put her hands on the wheel and gape.

"What do you think?"

"I think," she managed, "that I've gone back in time hundreds of years." She stared a bit longer, then realized what should have probably bothered her from the start. "We must be trespassing. Should we go?"

He shook his head. "We're fine."

"Who owns this?"

He looked out at the sea for a moment or two, then at her. "I do."

She sat back and sighed. "I shouldn't hate you for this, but I'm almost beside myself with envy."

He smiled. "Let's go look inside. You might feel differently then."

"I don't know how that's possible," she said, reaching for the door.

"Wait."

She stopped. "Why?"

"Because I'll get the door."

Well, if he was going to put it that way, she supposed she would let him have his way. She handed him his keys, then watched him get out of the car and walk around behind it. She wished, with a wishing that left her slightly more unhappy than it should have, that she had met him in a different spot, or under different circumstances, or in a different location—

No, not a different location. She had known the moment she looked out the window as the plane had approached Heathrow that she was going to love England. Her journeys through the countryside had left her with a longing to wander over hill and dale. But being in Scotland had taken that longing to an entirely new level. She wasn't sure she'd caught her breath since the moment she'd first seen Cameron Hall. She had exaggerated her antipathy for Derrick's owning of the cottage in front of her, but she hadn't exaggerated the envy. How fortunate he was to have such a place to come to.

Obviously he would want the right sort of girl to share that with. He probably had some lovely, native Scottish girl in mind.

She couldn't help but wish that was different as well.

The door opened and a hand appeared. She took it, then realized she was still buckled. Derrick leaned in, unbuckled her seat belt, then helped her out of the car.

And into his arms.

"Oh, sorry," she said, pulling away.

"Hmmm," was all he said. He shut the door, pocketed his keys, then offered her his arm. "I'll give you the tour, if you want."

"I want." What she wanted was a bonk on the head to get rid of her ridiculously and completely unreasonable thoughts, but maybe she could trip on a rock or something and take care of that.

She put her hand under his elbow, then felt him draw her hand into a comfortable place and tuck his arm against his side. He walked with her down a well-maintained path and stopped in front of the front door. He unlocked it, pushed it open, then flicked on the lights. He glanced around for a minute or two, then stepped back and waved her on.

"After you."

She fully expected to see the place done in vintage English Country House, complete with overstuffed chairs upholstered in tartans, threadbare carpets on the floors, and a farmhouse table.

But the house was empty.

She looked at Derrick in surprise. "No furniture?"

"It's a long story."

"I'm always interested in a long story."

He stepped in behind her and shut the door. "Let's take the tour, then I'll tell you. If you're still interested."

She nodded, then spent a happy half hour following him from room to room. At least the switch-plate covers had been left behind. Everything else, including the toilets and sinks, had been stripped. She stood finally in the kitchen and looked at a place on the wall where something had been in times past.

"Your stove is gone."

"It is."

"Along with everything else."

"Aye."

She turned and looked at him. "All right, I'm biting. What happened?"

He leaned back against the wall. "We may wish we had chairs sooner rather than later. The tale is tedious."

"Long and tedious; just my kind of story. And you're stalling."

He smiled briefly, then shoved his hands into his jeans pockets. "I was out driving one day and I ended up in the village."

"In the Vanquish?"

He shook his head. "Range Rover."

"Yours is the beat-up one on the end of the garage, I take it?" she asked.

"Less conspicuous," he agreed, then seemed to find forming words a bit more trouble than he was willing to take.

She waited for a moment or two, then decided to rescue him. "You were out driving one day, you wound up in this village, and . . . ?"

He shrugged. "I was having a pint with the lads at the pub and heard that there was a house on the edge of the sea that was rumored to be rather old and rather lovely. Being the compulsive looker at old things that I am, I decided I would have a wee look at it."

"What happened then?"

"I waited for it to fall available and—" He shrugged again. "You know. Things happened."

She leaned against the wall next to him. "What sorts of things?"

He sighed and looked at her. "Do you really want the entire tale?"

"Am I really going to want a chair?"

He smiled. "We'll go sit on a rock. There are a couple out in front that won't leave us limping for the rest of the day."

And then he took her hand, as easily as if he'd been doing it forever and had stopped thinking about it. She tried not to read anything into it. After all, he was who he was and she was who she was and she had a fascinating . . . well, she had a something waiting for her somewhere where he wasn't going to be. She was sure of it.

She followed him through the front garden, then down the path a bit until he stopped by two rocks that were indeed rather flat and didn't look terribly uncomfortable. She sat down on one, waited for him to sit on the other, then turned and looked at him. "All right, spill it."

He shifted uncomfortably. "I don't want to give the impression that I took advantage of anyone having financial difficulties—"

"Oh, a Scrooge," she said, rubbing her hands together. "Tell me more."

He sighed. "Very well, then. I heard—"

"Down at the pub?"

"Aye, on about the third round which I wasn't drinking, that this reputedly lovely old house was owned by a widow. Given that I make a living convincing people who don't want to sell things that it was actually their idea to beg me to take their treasures off their hands, I thought I would ply my dastardly trade on this poor unsuspecting woman."

She watched him closely, because she couldn't quite believe that he would use those skills in such a nefarious way. Priceless treasures were one thing. An old woman's house was quite another.

"And?" she prodded, when he looked as though he might clam up again.

"She sold," he said simply.

"And?"

He shifted again. "And I allowed her to live here for the rest of her life."

"Allowed?" she asked. "Or insisted?"

"Bloody hell, woman, are you going to tell the story for me?"

She looked at him, then smiled. "How long did she live?"

"Another five years."

"How much rent did you charge her?"

He pursed his lips, but said nothing.

"None, of course," she supplied for him. "Did you pay her utilities?"

He scowled at her.

"Opened an account for her at the local Tesco?"

"There is no local Tesco."

"You're avoiding the subject."

"I suddenly don't think I want to discuss this subject anymore."

She laughed a little, because there was something about the thought of his having done nice things for someone he didn't know just out of the goodness of his heart that made her think well of him. "I imagine you don't, but that's okay because I think I can guess all the answers already. Did you go to the funeral?"

"Yes."

"Find anything left in the house after it was all over or did the kids clean you out?"

He dragged his hand through his hair. "You, Miss Drummond, are a cynic."

"Gavin's my brother."

"He's an estate vulture."

"He learned it at his mother's knee, though he'd never admit it. He vowed when he left home that he would never again in his life put on another pair of curator's gloves. Now look at him."

"I try not to." He shot her a look. "Sorry."

"I have no illusions."

He nodded, then turned his head to look out over the sea. She looked at him for a moment or two, then looked out over the ocean as well. So he had rescued an old granny living on the edge of the sea. She didn't imagine the woman's expenses had been much, but that really wasn't the point.

"That was kind of you," she said, finally.

"I wanted her house."

She closed her eyes against the breeze. "How much did you pay the kids off after the fact?"

His brief laugh was pained. "I hate to think of what *you* learned at your mother's knee. And it was just enough to placate them. My lawyer did the rest. Those fancy London solicitors can be fairly intimidating."

"Did you visit her?"

"Occasionally."

She imagined he had and more than occasionally. And she imagined that he had paid off her relatives a fairly substantial sum, just for the good karma. He was, she was coming to find, just that sort of man.

"It's cold," she said finally.

"It's Scotland."

"It's summer."

He smiled, but he didn't look at her. "So it is." He moved over on his rock, then held open his arm. "It's warmer over here."

"I think it's warmer over here."

He looked at her in faint surprise, then smiled just as faintly. "Are you telling me to go to hell?"

"Now that you've commandeered the keys, sure."

He shooed her over a bit, then joined her on her rock. He put his arm around her shoulders. "I grossly misjudged you, Samantha. I apologize."

"How were you to know?"

"Because I always know," he said seriously. "But in this case, I was lazy and didn't bother to check anything about you. I would have proceeded differently otherwise."

She shook her head. "I wasn't particularly nice to you, either."

"You slandered my German ruthlessly."

"Your German sucks, buddy."

He laughed and squeezed her shoulders. "I'm afraid it does. I'll choose French next time I'm trying out a pickup line on you in a moldy old castle." He looked at her. "What do you think of this?"

"It's glorious."

"It's remote."

"That's part of its charm. Is there shopping nearby?"

He looked at her carefully. "Not much."

"Then it sounds perfect. Why don't you have any furniture?"

He sighed. "No time and I hate to look for that sort of rubbish."

She was going to suggest he unbend far enough for at least a stove and a couple of chairs, but his phone chirped at him. He looked at the text, then frowned.

"Excuse me a minute," he said absently. He dialed, listened, then frowned. "Say that again, sorry?"

Samantha could hear only snatches of the other end of the conversation and Derrick didn't really have all that much to say. She shifted a little so she could watch him, though she couldn't help but notice that while he didn't have his arm around her, he still had his hand on her back.

Honestly, she really needed to date more. The man was going to make her absolutely crazy and she had no experience to counteract it.

"That's interesting," Derrick said. "Hold on." He looked at Samantha. "Richard Drummond is your father's great-grandfather however many—how many, Oliver?—aye, thirteen generations removed."

"That's interesting."

"He died in the Tower."

"Terrible."

"Before he managed to marry and have children."

Fascinating was almost out of her mouth before she realized what he'd said. She looked at him in surprise. "Then how can he be my ancestor?"

"That's a very good question."

She jumped up, then started to pat herself. "Am I fading?"

"That only happens in movies."

She pointed a finger at him. "Don't sit there and look so calm. This is my ancestor we're talking about! How did he get in the Tower in the first place?"

He looked up at her seriously. "He was accused of stealing jewels. Unset gems. Four dozen of them."

She swayed. She realized she wasn't feeling all that great when the world stopped spinning and she found herself sitting on Derrick's lap. He was still talking around her into his phone, which she found slightly annoying, though at least she could hear the other end of the conversation. That might have been because Derrick was holding on to her and talking on speaker.

"Interesting that we have four dozens gems right here, isn't it?" Oliver was saying.

"I think it's worse than that," Derrick said with a sigh. "I think it's time for an employee meeting."

"Oooh, did I win something?"

"Aye, Annoying Git of the Month," Derrick said sourly. "How's Peter?"

"Snoring."

"Rufus?"

"Safely in London. Cameron did us the very great favor of sending a couple of his boys off to tail our Ambleside lads. We'll see what that turns up. Ewan says you're all clear where you are. Coming home?"

"I need to buy a round down at the pub, but we'll be there shortly afterward." He paused. "Based on what you've told me, we may have a new twist here to the case."

"I can hardly wait to hear it."

"I imagine you won't be surprised."

"Should I start looking for alternatives to modern communications?"

Derrick sighed. "Definitely."

"Finally," Oliver said, sounding pleased. "Been waiting to try out some new gear."

"One could hope. We'll be home soon."

Samantha felt him put his phone into his jacket pocket. She considered moving from where she was sitting with her head on his shoulder, then reconsidered. It was cold, but the sunshine was lovely and the sound of the sea soothing.

"Do you think," she said finally, "that those are the same stones only in two different time periods?"

"I'm not sure there's another answer," he said.

"They make me queasy to look at them." She lifted her head then to look at him. "The second set."

"Me, too," he agreed. "You have to wonder, though, why someone would find you in a crowd and plant them on you. Don't you?"

"Dumb luck?"

He sighed.

"All right, not dumb luck. What are we going to do about it?"

He seemed to consider his words carefully. "I'm not sure *we* are going to do anything—"

She sat up and looked at him in surprise. "What are you talking about?"

He looked up at her seriously. "What I'm talking about is your staying safely behind in the twenty-first century whilst I—"

"Go to hell," she said crisply.

He blinked. "You mean to Elizabethan England?"

"No, hell." She stood up and glared down at him. "As in, you. You go to hell."

He continued to stare at her for a moment or two, then he smiled. He rose, hugged her briefly, then took her hand and towed her toward his car. "Let's go back to the castle and plan."

"I'm coming with you."

"Nay, you're not."

She dug in her heels. "Don't make me go without you."

He stopped short and looked at her in surprise. "Would you?"

"I might." She lifted an eyebrow and waited.

"I'll think about it."

"I don't want to drive back to the castle, though. I have thinking to do."

"Whatever you say."

"If you're buying a round, you shouldn't drink."

"I never do."

"Well, now that we've gotten that all straight, I suppose you can carry on."

He looked at her, laughed, then led her over to his car. He opened the door for her, then leaned over and buckled her in. She wasn't altogether certain he hadn't planned to do something else, like kiss her, but he seemed to think that imprudent. He only smiled again, then shut her in.

She stared out over the sea and shook her head. Her father had claimed he came from a long line of exceptionally gifted actors, but she'd never been interested enough in tracing her roots to find out who those actors might have been.

A jewel thief?

Her father would be appalled.

And if she survived getting that jewel thief back into circulation, she supposed she would just keep it all to herself. Because any father who would overlook the fact that she'd poached his pride and joy more than once, deserved perhaps, despite his flaws, to have his illusions of illustrious ancestral thespians preserved.

Chapter 22

Derrick looked at the collection of souls in Cameron's office and wasn't altogether sure where to begin.

The truth was, the truth was very hard to swallow. His first brush with anything of a paranormalish nature had come when he'd first seen Robert Cameron nine years ago in hospital, lying in a bed with tubes sticking out of almost every orifice. It had taken Cameron quite a bit of time to recover from the knife wound in his back and the way his head had been half bashed in by something no one seemed to care to name. Derrick had wondered what that something had been and how a man could acquire those sorts of wounds in the present day without someone having alerted the police, but as with the wounds themselves, the manner of their earning had been something no one had seemed particularly interested in discussing.

He'd subsequently worked for Cameron for eight years as something more than an employee and something not quite as trusted as family—though perhaps the last wasn't true. Cameron had trusted him with all kinds of things, but there had definitely been a line drawn at the divulging of too many personal details. Of course Derrick had had questions about Cameron's past. He had pretended not to think anything of it when he'd gone to various cousins and paid them to forget any even slightly imagined aspirations to the chieftainship of their little clan. He hadn't mentioned the fact that not only Cameron's Gaelic but his excellent French had an accent to it that Derrick hadn't been quite able to place.

But after Sunshine Phillips had arrived on the scene and all kinds of things had happened, Derrick had finally confronted Cameron about things he'd been mulling over for several years.

Such as the fact that Robert Francis Cameron mac Cameron had been born in the year 1346 and apparently somehow traveled through time to take up his place again as laird of the clan Cameron in the present day.

Of course, knowing that had led to knowing things about other Scots in the area, most notably James MacLeod, Jamie's brother Patrick, and their cousin Ian. Derrick wasn't sure he wanted to think about how many times and places he'd traveled with Jamie. No one would have believed him. He wasn't sure sometimes that he believed it himself, not when he was safely in the present day, knocking back a Lilt or watching football on the telly.

He wondered how the others in the room would react. Samantha wouldn't be surprised, of course, because she had already seen more than was polite of the past. Oliver had come face-to-face with things that he didn't seem to care to talk about. Peter had heard stories but never experienced anything for himself. Derrick looked over to see the true loose cannon in the room. Ewan was only leaning against a wall, watching him with a smile that held absolutely no hint of a smirk. Whatever that one knew, Derrick hardly dared speculate on. The truth that connected them all was that they knew Robert Cameron.

And that made all kinds of thinking possible.

"Are you going to pace whilst you lecture us," Oliver said solemnly, "or have a seat?"

Derrick had already seen Samantha seated comfortably by the fire. He supposed there was no reason not to be comfortable himself. He sat, sighed, then looked at the others in the room. He started to speak, then decided that perhaps a visual might be more useful. He put all the exhibits on the coffee table. Two bags of stones, linen tube with one end slit open, and the hand-kerchief made from bobbin lace.

Oliver looked at him. "And?"

"And it makes me ill to look at those gems," Peter said, looking away.

Derrick took the second set, the ones that had been sewn into Samantha's bag, and put them into her purse. He left the others on the table, then looked at his partners, for that was what they would be in this.

"These are, I think, the gems that Richard Drummond is accused of stealing."

Ewan came to sit down. He didn't look terribly surprised, but since his usual expression was one of deliberate and usually inappropriate levity, Derrick supposed lack of surprise was an improvement.

"Then how is it you have them?" Ewan asked politely. "Twice, as it happens."

Derrick supposed there was no point in not being honest. "One set was sewn into Samantha's bag. We're assuming that was done by Lydia Cooke." He paused. "The others, those loose stones there, were wrapped in that cloth, then planted on Samantha in a crowd near the Globe. When we'd gone back to Elizabethan England to fetch Epworth's lace."

Oliver only blinked. Peter looked as if he thought he should smile, but he seemingly couldn't manage it.

"Interesting," Ewan said. "Why Samantha?"

"Good question."

Peter looked up from his contemplation of the floor. "Ollie said there was some dark doings with that Drummond bloke. Just hearsay, no trial. Killed him anyway."

"He died from exposure," Oliver corrected.

"Aye, exposure to an axe on the green," Peter said with a snort. He shot Samantha a look. "Sorry, miss."

Samantha waved away his apology. Derrick thought she looked remarkably well for someone who thought her existence was going to end at any moment. She rubbed her arms, as if she were suddenly rather cold.

"If Richard Drummond didn't take the gems," she asked, "then who did?"

"Probably the same one who saw him put in the Tower for the crime," Ewan offered.

"Then who put those gems in my purse?"

Derrick rubbed his hands together because he was apparently feeling the same chill Samantha was. "That's a mystery we are going to have to solve. But I think the solving of it is going to require a little heart-to-heart with Sir Richard Drummond."

"Oy," Oliver said. He didn't look surprised, but he rarely looked surprised by anything. "How do you propose to do that?"

Derrick swept them all with a look. "We're going to break him out of the sixteenth-century version of the Tower of London and ask him."

There was silence for the space of approximately five seconds.

And then, instead of those men he trusted with his very life—even Ewan, it had to be said—looking at him as if he'd lost his mind and was destined for a Bedlam that didn't exist any longer, they simply looked at each other briefly, then got down to business.

"I'll print out the Tower schematic," Oliver said.

"I'll make a list of possible gear," Peter said.

"Will I have to wear tights?"

Derrick shot Ewan a look for the last one. "You aren't coming."

"Are you daft?" Ewan asked, looking genuinely astonished. "I'm the only one who can act. Well, unless—"

"Shut up, Ewan," Derrick warned.

"Then just what in the hell is it you *want* me to do?" he demanded.

"Create believable personas for us to get us in and out of the city without getting us thrown in jail. And find us a safe place to land in 1602 for twenty-four hours."

Ewan looked as if he was preparing to throw a monumental tantrum. He seemed to reconsider, though, then merely nodded briskly.

Derrick watched his lads—well, and Ewan—doing the third thing they did best, which was to prepare a site for an . . . well, *assault* probably wasn't a good word. *Visit* was probably a better term for it. Whatever anyone wanted to call it, Peter and Oliver were masters at it. Ewan was more suited to charming people out of their priceless treasures, but he could also be quite useful when it came to planning exit strategies. Derrick couldn't say he would be particularly interested in having Ewan along for the ride, but he wouldn't be unhappy to have his advice beforehand.

He looked at Samantha, who was simply watching him, silent and grave. He smiled.

"What is it?"

She shook her head. "Just watching. They're impressive."

He nodded. "They are."

"And your cousin has interesting toys." She nodded toward the architectural printer in the corner. "Good for plans, I suppose."

"And large games of naughts and crosses."

She smiled. "I imagine so." Her smile faded a bit. "What can I do?"

He knew what he needed but almost hesitated to ask. He rubbed his hands together. "I'm not an expert in Elizabethan textiles, but . . ."

She sighed. "I can put off my leap into artistic endeavors for another few days and play historian if you like."

"Then let's invade Cameron's sanctuary. He has all kinds of books up there on all kinds of obscure things. I'm sure he has a book on costumery."

"I don't suppose he has any costumes lying around."

"I think I might manage to find a few in London." That was badly understating what his apartment was full of, but there was no point in telling her things that didn't make any difference at the moment. He wasn't even quite sure what he had that would have served a woman, so obviously things would have to be acquired on short notice. The sooner he knew what they needed, the better.

He left the lads to their work and walked with Samantha up the stairs to Cameron's private study.

Three hours and a lovely supper later, he was sitting on the couch with his bare feet on Cameron's coffee table, trying to stay awake. He honestly wasn't sure he'd managed it entirely. He rubbed the grit out of his eyes and looked to his right. Samantha was sitting in a chair facing at right angles to his. She had lost her shoes somewhere as well, but she apparently didn't feel comfortable enough to put her feet on the furniture.

The sea had done what he'd wanted to but never dared, namely pulled several strands of hair out of her braid. She kept tucking those strands behind her ears. He would have asked her to stop, but then she would have looked at him as if he'd been daft.

He wondered what she would have done if he'd simply leaned over and kissed her.

Likely punched him in the nose.

So to avoid having to explain that, he simply sat lounging on Cameron's sofa and watched her read. She was engrossed, that was obvious. She was also making notes, which he supposed shouldn't have surprised him.

She glanced at him, then did a double take and smiled. "Nice nap?"

"I couldn't help it," he said with a yawn. "Too many nights chasing after a very pretty textile thief."

She blinked. "Me?"

He smiled, deciding that if she had to ask, perhaps it was best not to wax rhapsodic about her charms lest he indeed give into his first impulse, which was to pull her over to sit next to him and show her just how pretty he thought she was. He sat up and attempted to change the subject.

"Find anything interesting?"

"It depends on the date. What did you guess, 1602?"

"I'm thinking so," he said. "Someone was talking about Hamlet when we were last there. The first quarto was registered in late July of that year, if memory serves, so I think we can almost guarantee it was being performed."

Her mouth fell open. "How do you know *that*?"

He put his feet on the floor and leaned forward to rub his face with his hands. He shook off the aftereffects of what had indeed been a very nice nap, then looked as casual as possible.

"I was a bit of a theater buff growing up."

She closed her book. "Did you grow up here at the castle?"

He started to tell her that those were details she probably didn't need, but realized hard on the heels of that that he actually did want to tell her a few things. Perhaps it went with the absolute madness of taking her to the shore. To his house that he'd bought with his own money.

"Never mind," she said with a smile. "Didn't mean to pry."

He looked at her in surprise, then winced. "Sorry. I don't have a very good poker face."

"No, actually, you don't. How you talk anyone out of their antiques is a mystery to me."

He smiled. "I'm actually very good at that sort of thing. Just not about discussing what bothers me."

"You don't have to tell me anything, really. Not if it bothers you."

He studied her for a moment or two. "Do you want to know?"

"I find, actually, that I do." She looked at him seriously. "How weird is that?"

"Thank you," he said dryly.

She smiled ruefully. "I'm sorry." She hesitated, tapping her pencil against her notebook for a moment or two, then looked at him. "I don't date much."

"So you don't know the usual dance, is that it?"

She shook her head slowly.

He considered. "Would you like to come sit here next to me?"

She considered as well, then nodded. "I think I would."

"Then please do."

She left her books on the table, then walked around it to sit down next to him. She looked up at him. "What now?"

"We could hold hands."

"Will you divulge details if we do?"

"I would anyway, but it might make me feel better whilst I'm about it."

She smiled. "You aren't serious."

He lifted one shoulder in a half shrug. "I think it would, but I don't want to force you to do something you don't want to do."

"Hmmm," she said. "Holding hands with a very handsome man in a castle that I think is mostly original, in front of a fire big enough to roast a good part of an entire cow, while I listen to him tell me his secrets? I think I like it."

He smiled in spite of himself. "You didn't mention the Vanquish."

She shrugged. "It's what you drive, not who you are."

He closed his eyes, because it was either that or get himself in all kinds of trouble. He held out his hand, was rather too relieved for his peace of mind when she put hers into it, then propped his feet back up on Cameron's table. He held

Samantha's hand in both his, suppressed the urge to flee—the woman was going to drive him crazy long before he managed to get a handle on what, if anything, he felt for her—then took a deep breath.

"I didn't grow up here precisely," he said. "My parents had a house on the estate, because my father was the second cousin twice removed of the laird, Alistair. My mother wasn't fond of being here but my father never would have moved away. He loathed Scotland, as it happened, but I think he always assumed that one day he would take the title for himself."

"Really?" she asked, sounding surprised.

"Well, Alistair had no children, so I suppose it was a logical assumption."

"Hmmm," she said thoughtfully. "But you said Lord Robert was Alistair's heir."

So he had, he supposed. "It's complicated."

"Hmmm," was all she said. "So, if your father disliked Scotland so much, why did he want the title?"

Derrick shrugged. "The power of it, I suppose, or the prestige. The Cameron fortune was fairly substantial at the time. I wouldn't begin to speculate what the current laird has done with it. He has a gift for making money and finding old things."

She laughed a little. "You know, I keep thinking he's on the verge of drawing a sword—" She shut her mouth with a snap, stared into the fire, then looked up at him. "But that's impossible. I mean, he was born in this century, right?"

He looked at her then, but he just simply couldn't bring himself to answer.

Her mouth fell open. She gaped at him for a minute or two, then shut her mouth with a snap. "I'll think about that later. I have seen some pretty crazy things over here, but . . . well, back to you and yours. Your father wanted to stay and your mother didn't. What happened?"

"They stayed, my mother complained endlessly, and my father repaid her with disdain." He listened to the words come out of his mouth and wondered how he could be so nonchalant about details that had grieved him for so much of his youth. "They were killed in a car accident when I was twelve."

Her hand in his flinched. "Oh, Derrick, I'm sorry."

He shook his head. "It was a blessing in disguise, actually. We came to the keep to be watched over by my grandfather—"

"We?"

He looked at her. "I have an older brother, older by a year. I suppose we were a bit more like twins, though I'll always maintain he's much uglier than I am."

She smiled. "You're funny. Go on. What then?"

"Nothing much that was interesting. I raised all manner of hell, Connor was the angel that received all the accolades, and we each moved on with our lives."

"Where is he now?"

Derrick shrugged. "A few years ago he was acting somewhere. Likely in some local church converted into a leisure center, plying his dastardly trade on those with no taste." Actually, his brother was in Stratford, making a rather large name for himself, but Derrick didn't like to think about that too often.

She was stroking his thumb with hers. He honestly doubted she realized she was doing it.

"And you?"

He looked at her, then. "This will cost you."

"I'll think about it."

"Nay, woman, this will cost you."

"You know, you're too bossy."

He had to admit that was true, but she was getting better at telling him to shove off, as it were, with each of his attempts at ordering her about. He smiled faintly. "I left home early, raised hell other places, then decided that I preferred life north of the border. So, I live in London only because my business is there, but I come home as often as possible." He shifted to look at her. "Your turn."

"Oh," she demurred, "my life is very boring."

"Spill the details."

"Stop bossing me."

"I'm not sure I can," he said solemnly. "I'm very good at it."

"Yeah, well, I'm sick of it."

"We could take turns." He looked around him for paper and pen to use in scratching out a schedule, but the sad fact was, he was too reliant on screens. Heaven help him if the power grid ever went down. He pulled his phone out of his pocket, then smiled at her. "I'll take mine now."

"It'll cost you later," she muttered.

"I'll consider paying, if it's my day to be bossed."

She took a deep breath and stopped stroking his hand. He supposed that was his cue to take over. He stroked the back of her hand with his fingers, wondering if she had any idea how cold her hands were. He almost told her she didn't need to tell him anything, but she was already saying as much.

"I don't have to do this."

He shook his head. "You don't."

She sighed. "It really is a very boring story. Gavin, you know. I also have a sister, Sophronia, which you probably already know, too."

"I might."

She looked at him narrowly. "What else do you know?"

"Nothing interesting. You tell me the interesting parts."

"There's nothing much to tell, but I'll humor you anyway. Gavin left home as soon as he could manage it. He's actually smarter than he looks, though his ACTs were abysmal. Sophronia is an actress, which my father didn't approve of."

"Typical."

She smiled. "His ego is enormous, I will admit, though he's very good. I think he saw Sophie as a threat, so he was never eager to have her home again. All that was left was just me and somehow I turned into the last best hope for a child they could mold."

"And you let them?"

"What else was I going to do?" she asked. "My parents . . . well, my father's a self-absorbed egomaniac and my mother's manic. Even talking to them is like talking to a hurricane. By the time I realized what I was dealing with, I couldn't get out of it. I know it sounds crazy to live under the thumb of someone—two someones, actually—but I couldn't tell them to, well, you know."

"You seem to have no problem with me," he observed.

She looked at her hand in his for so long in silence, he wondered if he'd said the wrong thing. She finally looked at him. Her eyes were full of tears.

"I don't think you'll hold it against me if I do."

He almost teared up himself, hard-hearted sod that he was. He brought her hand to his mouth and kissed it.

"Haven't so far," he admitted as gruffly as he could manage.

"Will that change?"

He closed his eyes briefly, squeezed her hand, and got to his feet. "Don't think it will," he managed. "Let's go for a walk."

"Isn't it dark?"

"Sunny's garden has lights if we want to use them, but I think the moon's full. Now, where are my bloody shoes?"

"By the door."

He looked down at her, then pulled her up with him. "Let's go before we both get too maudlin."

He found his shoes, found hers for her, then took her by the hand and led her down the stairs. He caught sight of Ewan crossing the great hall toward him and held up his hand with an expression on his face that had Ewan shutting his mouth before he could spew out anything stupid.

"Later," Ewan suggested.

"Excellent plan," Derrick agreed.

He fetched two jackets—he realized as he put one on Samantha that both were his—considered turning the lights on but realized it wasn't necessary, then walked with Samantha out into the back garden. The roses were only just beginning to bud, which was the only thing he regretted. He would have been happy with something beautiful for her to concentrate on.

They walked in silence for a bit, then wound up on a bench set against the stone of the castle. He held her hand in his, because he was growing far too accustomed to it for his own good, then looked at her.

"I don't think you have to go back," he said slowly. "Not if you don't want to."

She shook her head. "I'm not sure how I would manage to stay here."

"I might be able to help you find a job."

"Textile research?"

Something more personal was almost out of his mouth before his brain slipped into gear. He shrugged. "Perhaps. Perhaps something else."

"I could sell the drawing I made of your view while you were sleeping."

He blinked. "You drew?"

"I told my inner critic to go to hell before I started."

He laughed a little. "Let's go have a look then. I know a gallery owner in London."

"So do I. He's a jerk."

"Aye, but he owes me a favor or two. It won't induce him to buy anything, but it would at least get you in the door."

"I certainly wouldn't get there myself."

He looked at her seriously. "Samantha, my brother wouldn't take my call, even if I could unbend far enough to make it. This might be difficult to believe, but Gavin has mentioned you in passing and he was complimentary."

"What did he say?" she asked.

"He said he had a baby sister who was brilliant and gifted and there were times he almost felt bad for leaving her behind to deal with his parents."

"You're right," she said quietly. "I find that hard to believe."

"Well, it was after I'd reduced him to tears over salt cellars," Derrick admitted, "so perhaps his defenses were down."

She stood up, pulled him to his feet, then put her arms around his neck and hugged him quickly. She kissed his cheek, then pulled away and backed up. "Let's go back inside."

"Do that again."

She shot him a look. "I don't think it's your day to be bossy."

"I'm absolutely convinced it's my day to be bossy. Come back here."

She walked back toward him, then stopped when she was scarce a handsbreadth away. She looked up at him seriously. "I'm not good at games."

He jammed his hands in his jeans pockets because that seemed the safest course of action. "I don't play games."

"Don't hurt me."

"I'll try not to."

She studied his face, then reached up and put her hand against his cheek. "Less than a week ago you were ready to toss me in jail and now you want me to hug you?"

"I'd actually prefer that you kiss me, but I'm willing to settle for what I can get."

"Why?" she asked seriously.

"Because I like you," he said, suppressing the urge to shift.

She looked at him for several more excruciatingly long minutes, then she leaned up on her toes, put her arms around his neck and hugged him. He cast caution to the wind and put his arms around her as well, holding her less tightly than he would have liked to. No point in terrifying the lass unnecessarily. He closed his eyes at the feel of her lips against his cheek.

Damn it, out of all the things he'd expected, this was the last.

But he released her when she pulled back, smiled pleasantly, then reached for her hand, because pulling her back into his arms and discussing feelings he shouldn't have been having for her was an extraordinarily bad idea.

"Let's go, Miss da Vinci," he said politely. "I'd like to see what you did."

Chapter 23

Samantha stood in a minuscule apartment in the heart of London and felt as if she were trapped in a dream. So many things she hadn't expected in a country that seemed a world away from what she was used to.

The morning had started off with a lovely breakfast at Cameron Hall provided by Madame Gies who was every bit as good at cooking as Emily was at apparently everything she touched. Samantha had been grateful for that and a good night's sleep, as well as another very lovely ride in a screaming sports car to Inverness.

She stood just inside the front door of Derrick's two-story flat and wondered if it had been the ride in the car that had started the surreality, or it if had been getting to the airport to find a private plane waiting to take them back to London that had done it. It was hard to say.

Peter had indeed gotten rid of their rental car, Ewan had been tasked with getting Derrick's car back to London—which she supposed served the dual purpose of Derrick not having to drive it himself and Ewan staying out of Derrick's hair—and she had traveled in yet more luxury south. She loved to fly almost as much as she loved to drive very fast, so the only thing about the trip she hadn't enjoyed had been the length of it. Far too short.

Peter and Oliver had bid them farewell after they'd landed and gone to headquarters to investigate the supply of necessary toys and she had gone with Derrick to his flat to see what sort of costumes could be drummed up. They were intending to meet later in the day to finalize arrangements, then be on their way.

She hadn't been entirely surprised to find all kinds of research waiting for them under Derrick's fax machine when they'd walked into his flat, most of it having to do with Sir Richard Drummond and his activities in 1602. That was apparently courtesy of the laird of the clan MacLeod, James. Derrick had left the sheets of paper where they were, told her to make herself at home, then put in an earphone and begun a spirited discussion with someone—perhaps either Oliver or Peter, or both—about technical details for the upcoming trip. She had decided that she would take him at his word and make herself at home.

Because I like you.

She shook her head at the words and started along the hallway that was just big enough for the stairs on the left and a little corridor on the right. She'd already been in the sitting room, which was crammed full of books on everything from history to fiction. She wasn't surprised to find that Derrick's interests ranged from mystery to classic science fiction and fantasy, but then again, he'd collected his fair share of esoteric nonfiction and literary things her mother would have approved of. A man of varied tastes, obviously.

The furnishings in that room were simple, comfortable, and not cheap, though the only antique in the room was a Victorian console table that was suffering the indignity of bearing stacks of papers and paperbacks. Maybe Derrick had enough of the past just associating with his cousin whose birthdate was not a topic for discussion.

She reached the end of the hallway and found she was in the kitchen. It was lovely, actually, and obviously either new or newly remodeled. There were a few green things in the fridge, but nothing substantial. The food in the cupboards stopped just short of survival rations. Obviously, Derrick didn't eat at home all that often.

The only thing left on the ground floor was a bathroom and

a closet under the stairs that was loaded with black bags no doubt containing things she wouldn't want to investigate in case she broke them. She walked back down the hallway thoughtfully, then went back into the front room to see if there might be anything useful in any of his bookcases. She picked out a book on Elizabethan dance patterns and wandered out into the hallway with it. She made it up half a flight of stairs before she simply sat down and started to read.

"And how do you propose we carry those?" Derrick asked, coming down the stairs.

Samantha listened to him talk, but there was no mocking in his tone, no *that's the stupidest thing I've ever heard* in the way he asked his question. He was apparently very good at getting what he needed to know without being insulting. It was so different from what she was used to with her parents, she could only listen in awe.

He put his hand on her head on his way by, a light touch that made her look up and smile. He smiled in return, then trotted down the rest of the stairs.

"Nay, it's genius, but where do we stash it?"

She had considered posing as a noblewoman, but the thought made her uneasy. Who knew what Derrick and his partners in crime would want to strap to the underside of her skirts? Then again, if she were a servant, they would probably make her *carry* lots of things, so she was half tempted to just go as a boy.

She listened to Derrick pace to the kitchen, in and out of the salon, then stop at the bottom of the stairs. He listened for several minutes, frowning periodically, then he shook his head.

"I'm not sure, even after all the alternatives we've come up with, that we can pass as Tower guards," he said slowly. "Nay, I've no better idea, short of scaling the walls." He paused. "I suppose we could try that, if we had something to collect the used darts in—what? Samantha's purse? Are you *mad*?"

Samantha was happy to suggest that perhaps whoever was on the other end was absolutely nuts, but she didn't have a chance. Derrick looked at her and lifted his eyebrows. She made a writing motion, he nodded, then took the stairs three a time. He came back down, handed her a notebook and a pen, then disappeared into his salon again. Samantha made a note or two, then lost interest. She got up and trudged up the stairs.

Upstairs there was a bedroom with a bathroom in it, a small sitting area that looked out over a garden, then another bedroom. She walked in, then actually heard herself gasp.

It wasn't so much a bedroom as it was a prop room. She wondered what a thief would have thought if he'd broken into Derrick's house. That he'd set himself up to rob a theater, no doubt. She stood just inside the door until she heard Derrick come back up the stairs. He paused and put his hand over his ear.

"What's wrong?" he asked.

"Can I go in?"

He looked at her in surprise. "Of course. As if at home, remember?"

Well, if that's how he felt, she wasn't going to argue. She walked in, then perched on the edge of a very comfortable couch. In fact, it looked less like a prop room and more like a very fancy green room with dozens of costumes stuffed inside it. There was a table with a lighted mirror pushed up against one wall, racks of costumes, rows of hats, and a stand with an impressive collection of wigs. She left her book and half-started notes on the couch, then wandered around to see what was there. It was interesting to just look for the sake of looking, but she wondered if she might stumble on something they might need for their trip.

To Elizabethan England. During the summer of 1602.

She took a deep breath, shoved aside the improbability of that thought, and started rummaging.

It didn't take long to find the mother lode.

She had been looking through boxes full of organized things, makeup and prosthetic noses, facial hair and adhesives. Interesting, but not particularly useful. She had set things aside and continued to dig until she'd worked her way around to the stack behind the table. It was the bottom box that when she opened it left her frozen.

She didn't dare take anything out, because she had a box just like it at her house. It was something she'd packed up the night before she'd come to England, a box that held her old life, the life she had never wanted to have anything to do with again.

Derrick obviously had the same sort of instinct.

"Sam—"

She looked up to find him standing in the doorway. He obviously saw what she had found. His stillness quickly became her stillness as well. She understood that, really. Sometimes there were things about one's past that one would prefer to box up and not face again.

Derrick didn't look away from her, but he spoke to whomever was on the other end of the line.

"Ring you back." He clicked his phone off, then simply stared at her, mute.

She cleared her throat. "May I?"

"No."

She paused. "Please?"

He didn't move. "Can I stop you?"

"Yes."

He dithered. She watched him do it and had to work very hard not to smile. It was so out of character for the very decisive man standing there, she could hardly reconcile it with his usual method of carrying out his life.

He swore suddenly, then turned and stomped down the stairs. Answer enough, she supposed. She was perfectly still until she heard him banging around in the kitchen downstairs. Lunch was apparently on its way, though she had no idea what he was going to find to fix. He claimed to be a terrible cook. She supposed she would find out just how bad very soon.

She spent an hour looking through his past, then carefully placing it all back the way she'd found it.

"Sam, lunch!"

She didn't want to smile, but she couldn't help herself. No one ever called her that except her great-aunt Mary, who loved her, and Gavin when he was annoyed with her. Somehow, coming from a man she had just come to like a great deal more than was good for her, it was very lovely.

She walked downstairs and into his minuscule kitchen. He had pasta, salad, and a fierce frown waiting for her. She sat down when he held out her chair for her, then waited until he sat, said grace with a particularly thick Scottish accent, and picked up his fork as if he was seriously considering using it—on her. She tasted, complimented, then pretended nothing had happened.

Derrick cursed, then plowed through his meal with his usual single-mindedness.

"Well?" he demanded after she'd given him half her dinner and there was nothing left for him to eat.

"LAMDA?" she said casually. "As in the London Academy of Music and Dramatic Art?"

He grunted.

"Your reviews were good."

He looked at her in surprise, then scowled at bit more. "Good?" he echoed.

"Amazing."

"If we're going to be honest," he said, "then, yes."

She laughed. She couldn't help it. No wonder the man was so good at changing who he was. He'd obviously had years of practice and gotten, yes, rave reviews while doing it.

She got up and started to clear the table. She was happy to have company to rinse while she washed.

"I'm unclear," she said at one point, "as to why you don't act any longer."

He leaned back against the counter and looked at her. "It's complicated."

"Life is."

He looked heavenward briefly, then back off at something in the kitchen, not where she was. "I'd done one season with the Royal Shakespeare Company, as you know. I was set to do *Hamlet* that next year in a different production when—" He stopped, then took a deep breath. "That's the part that's complicated." He looked at her. "I was blacklisted."

She frowned. "Just because you were good?"

"Because my costar wanted someone else for the part and she got him, even though he wasn't better than I was. In fact, he'd spent quite a few years being not better than I was, which made my getting that particular part all the more painful for him."

"Who was that?"

He looked at her silently.

She considered, then felt her mouth fall open. "Your brother?"

"Aye, damn him to hell."

She shook her head, because she was fairly sure she hadn't just heard what she'd just heard. "Did he study acting as well?"

"We were in the same class."

"How did you pay for it?"

"We had a small inheritance. I didn't need to use mine."

She smiled in spite of herself. "Scholarship?"

"Aye."

She wondered if he realized that when he was rather more emotional than usual, as he was at present, he tended to slip into the native accent, as it were. She wouldn't have been at all surprised to have listened to him curse in Gaelic.

"Why didn't you say anything to the director? Or . . ." She shrugged helplessly. "Wasn't there someone to appeal to?"

"What was I going to say?" he asked. "That someone had spread lies about me and spent so long doing it that no one would have doubted his character or integrity?"

She leaned against the counter, hard. "Your brother again?"

"Aye." Derrick took a deep breath, then blew it out. "Whilst I had been concentrating on my *art*, he'd been ingratiating himself with anyone with a bit of power. I shudder to think the lengths he went to. And when Ophelia accused me of things I don't care to discuss and my own brother agreed with her—with a great show of sadness and regret, admittedly—there was nothing to be done. The director was complicit, but I had no proof. I was no one and the director was very powerful. My career was over, no matter which direction I went in."

She considered for a moment or two, then looked at him. "Would you ever act again?"

"I would rather stick hot pins in my eyes."

Well, she could understand that very well. It was a bit like what she felt about historical textiles.

"I'm so sorry," she said very quietly. "What did you do then?"

"I went home to Scotland a couple of months before Cameron found himself in hospital," he said without emotion. "Alistair gave me the task of watching over him and there I've been for all these years."

"Does Lord Robert know about your past?"

Derrick shrugged. "I wouldn't be surprised, though I've never said anything and he's never asked me about it. He's curious by nature, but discreet."

"Who was the director?"

He looked at her steadily. "Edmund Cooke, husband and lace thief. And no, I haven't been lying in wait all these years to have revenge on him. I honestly couldn't care less. If he winds up before a magistrate, it won't be because I put him there."

"And Ophelia?"

"Some damned Yank—"

He stopped speaking. She did too, because his tone was so cold and bitter. She knew she shouldn't have taken it personally, but with the way he'd said it . . .

She took the towel away from him and dried her hands. "Well, I'd better go keep looking through costumes."

"Samantha."

"Thanks for lunch—"

He caught her hand. She didn't want to let him keep hold of her, but she also didn't want him to let her go. He turned her around, then pulled her into his arms.

"I didn't mean to say it that way."

"I think you did."

"Your place of birth is immaterial."

"But I'm sure you want a nice Scottish—"

And that was as far as she got, because he kissed her.

She could safely say that Derrick Cameron was good at several things, but he was best at kissing a girl so she knew she'd been kissed.

He finally let her up for air, which she needed rather badly.

"Is this my day to boss you, or your day to boss me?" she asked when she'd caught her breath enough to speak.

"I can't remember. You take a turn."

"Kiss me again, then."

He did, quite thoroughly, until he suddenly stopped. She looked up into his very green eyes and watched him study her for a moment or two. Perhaps he had suddenly realized that she had spent more time punching dates in the nose than receiving their advances. So to speak. He leaned back against the counter, but kept his hands linked behind her back. She suspected that was his invitation for her to continue to stand in his embrace, so she did.

"Let's talk numbers," he said seriously.

"Let's not."

"I'd say there's a zero in there somewhere."

"Are you talking about men I've kissed or men I've punched?"

He looked at her, then bent his head and laughed. She wasn't sure if he was making fun of her or if that laugh was tinged with the hysteria of a man who had just realized the woman he'd been kissing in his kitchen was a . . . well, not as experienced as he might have originally thought, but since it was her turn to call the shots, she decided she would. Call the shots, that was. She pulled away from him and walked away.

"I'm going to go look for sleeves," she said archly. "You stay here and continue to giggle where I don't have to listen."

She stomped off, completely uncaring if he followed her or not.

Well, actually, she did care, so there was something very nice about looking over her shoulder and finding he was following her up the stairs. His hands were clasped behind his back. Maybe he didn't want them off doing something they shouldn't.

He stopped her at the door to his green room. "Would you mind if I kissed you again?"

"Are you asking this time?"

"I asked before," he pointed out.

"I think there were several times you didn't."

He slipped his hand under her hair, then bent his head. "Now that you mention it, I suppose that's true."

She was actually rather grateful to have a doorframe behind her. It gave her a handy place to lean.

"I don't date much," she said, when she could.

"Good."

"I mean, I haven't dated much," she clarified. "A cotillion dance. A few university things. A miserable movie with Theodore Mollineux."

"He won't be bothering you again."

She knew she was too old to feel a little weak in the knees at the sensation of standing in a very handsome man's arms, but there it was.

"And just what are you going to do about it?" she asked politely.

"I haven't decided yet. Something commensurate with his gargantuan ego, no doubt. But he will find you singularly unavailable to receive his annoying attentions."

She felt her smile fade. "Why?"

He looked at her seriously. "Because I like you."

"Enough to kiss me?"

"That, too."

"Enough to date me?"

He nodded.

"Why?" she asked, feeling pained.

The look he gave her almost left her a believer.

"Are you serious?" he asked, sounding slightly incredulous. She nodded.

"I'll make you a list," he said. "And whilst I'm about that task, you might decide if you're interested in dating me."

"Let me boss you around a bit more, then I'll decide."

He smiled, a very small, affectionate smile that finished her off as nothing else could have.

"Very well," he agreed, "but until you've come to your decision about me, perhaps we should get back to work—"

He stopped, but that was because she'd caught him by the front of his shirt and pulled him back to her. She put her arms around his neck, pulled his head down, and did her best to kiss him as thoroughly as she knew how. It wasn't a very good job, she supposed, but perhaps practice would make perfect.

He pulled away sooner than she would have liked, but that was because his phone was ringing. He pulled it out of his pocket, cursing as he did so. "They're going to drive me mad." He shot her a quick smile. "Why don't you go look for sleeves and I'll satisfy the rabble? I think they'll be here in an hour or so."

She frowned. "You don't sound happy about that."

"I'm not," he said frankly. "It will get in the way of my master plan of spending the afternoon doing other things besides looking for Elizabethan gear."

She blushed. He smiled, leaned over and kissed the tip of her nose, then turned her toward the room.

"Sleeves."

She tried, really she did. The timing was lousy, she had an ancestor—a would-be ancestor—who was languishing in the Tower of London, and she was almost dating the man who had every intention of springing him from the pokey.

It was insane.

So was the number of times Derrick dropped down onto the couch next to her, put his finger to his lips, and kissed her very quietly while he was involved in conversations with his partners. She wasn't sure how many times he pleaded a bad connection, tossed his phone, then laughed a little before he pulled her into his arms and kissed her earnestly, though she thought it might have been several. She could say with a fair amount of confidence that his couch was very comfortable but that she wasn't making as much progress in what she was supposed to be doing as she should have.

"Where're you going?" she asked as he got up from where he'd been sitting next to her on the couch, not looking for costumes.

"To take a cold shower."

"Are you kidding me?"

He shot her a look. "No, I'm not. The lads will be here in twenty minutes. Do *not* answer the door. I don't want you getting carried off by thugs. I'll be back in ten."

She sat there surrounded by velvet gowns, detachable sleeves, a ruff that perhaps shouldn't have been in harm's way, and a mobcap or two and considered.

She smiled.

She looked up in time to see Derrick poke his head in the door. He smiled at her but said nothing.

"What?" she asked finally.

"Nothing. Just looking."

"Looking at costumes isn't going to do any good."

"I wasn't looking at costumes."

She shooed him away. "You're embarrassing me."

He looked at her for a moment or two, then walked over to her and pulled her up off the couch and to her feet. He put his arms around her.

"You know, don't you," he began matter-of-factly, "that if I keep this up, I won't be able to concentrate on what I'm supposed to be doing."

"What, you don't want to snog all the way through Elizabethan England?"

"Well," he began thoughtfully, "what I want and what's sensible can sometimes be two different things."

"I agree."

"You don't have to sound so cheerful about it."

She hugged him quickly, then turned him around and gave him a push. "Beat it. I won't let anyone in."

He went but shook his head as he did so. She fanned herself

with a stray farthingale, then tried to concentrate on what she was supposed to be doing.

It was difficult.

She finally resorted to sitting on the steps and waiting. Derrick appeared, looked at her, then took a deep breath before he opened the door at the knock. She watched as Oliver and Peter tumbled in the front door, laden with black bags that looked very suspicious. They were followed by Rufus, and then by Lord Robert himself. She got up when she saw him. He started when he saw her do it, then held out his hand to her.

"Please," he said with a smile, "call me Cameron—which you haven't done yet—and don't stand on ceremony. I'm just here as one of the lads."

She was fully prepared to doubt that, but it turned out that nothing could have been truer. She hovered on the edge of the group as they sorted through things poured out onto a large square coffee table in the front room. Derrick was quite obviously the one they all assumed was in charge. While suggestions were made, it was, in the end, his decision they went with.

She jumped a little when she realized Lord Robert was leaning against the wall alongside her. She looked at him.

"Yes, my lord?" she asked politely.

"Cameron," he said with an amused smile. "Or is that impossible?"

"I don't think I could ever call you Cameron," she said. "My lord."

"You'll have to work on that, but perhaps later." He nodded toward the men discussing their upcoming adventure. "What do you think?"

"I think Elizabethan England is a dangerous place."

"And I think you're very sensible. You needn't go along, you know."

"He might need me." She heard the words come out of her mouth, then found she couldn't take them back. "Derrick, I mean. Though I'm not sure how."

"You might be surprised." He seemed to be choosing his words carefully. "Will you be surprised by other things?"

She looked at him and considered who she thought he might be. She had borrowed Derrick's tablet on the flight down and made good use of a genealogy program she'd signed him up for on a trial basis. She had noted the Camerons through the ages, made mental notes of the death dates, then formulated her opinion. She looked at the man standing next to her.

"Do you have a middle name, my lord?"

He seemed to be fighting his smile. "Did Derrick tell you I did?"

"Derrick said he wasn't at liberty to divulge any of your secrets, though I believe he told me that when he had his bare feet up on the coffee table in your study."

"As long as that was all that was bare, I won't kill him for it," Cameron said mildly, seeming to be rather satisfied with something. Perhaps that Derrick could keep his mouth shut. "I might have more than one name attached to my poor self, 'tis true." He lifted an eyebrow. "Do you care to guess?"

"Francis."

He only smiled. "Don't call me Francis."

"I never would," she said. "My laird."

He shook his head wryly. "Somehow, Mistress Samantha, I think you'll survive this adventure quite well. Even if it does find itself in Elizabethan England."

"Did Derrick tell you I don't want to be an historian any longer?"

He shook his head. "He keeps secrets very well. I just have a decent nose for rebellion in the clan, as it were. Your mother's preferred era is Victorian, yet your study was not. Perhaps I'm reading too much into it."

Or perhaps not. Samantha looked at him, medieval laird, modern-day laird, and thought that perhaps Derrick had been very fortunate in his luck of the familial draw. She would have commented on that, but Derrick's phone rang and he held up his hand suddenly.

"It's Jamie. He may have something else useful for us."

Samantha had read Jamie's notes because she'd been the one to organize them in order and summarize them for the boss. She listened to him start a conversation in rapid-fire Gaelic and smiled to herself at the English words thrown in when Gaelic wouldn't do.

"Do you know Jamie?" Cameron asked.

She shook her head.

"He's laird of the clan MacLeod down the way from my hall."

"Has he been laird once," she asked, in Gaelic, "or twice?"

Cameron laughed a little, then made her a slight bow. "You, Mistress Drummond," he said, also in Gaelic, "are a match for that lad over there."

"Thank you, my laird. But don't tell him I understand him, would you? I think I might like to keep a few secrets of my own."

"I imagine you would. And you might ask him about a few of his, namely to do with where he and that rascal Jamie go on blokes' weekends away."

She frowned, then it dawned on her what he was getting at. "You aren't serious."

"Jamie is the original adventurer," Cameron said with a shrug, "to the endless despair of his wife, who I understand will kill him if he dares take any of their children with him on his jaunts to places and times not his own. Derrick has been his partner in crime for a year now. I haven't dared ask him too much about his adventures." He smiled. "I'd best go see what madness they're combining."

Samantha watched him walk away and realized why it was that he and Sunny hadn't been all that surprised by Derrick's shoulder wound. Maybe that wasn't the first one Derrick had earned on his little weekenders through time.

She leaned heavily against the wall, because she was too restless to sit but too unsettled to stand. She could hardly believe she was listening to the men in front of her plan an assault on the . . . well, on the Tower of London.

But it was her life they were saving, so she couldn't bring herself to tell them to stop. Not that they would have, perhaps. Derrick was determined.

She shook her head. The Tower of London.

They were absolutely insane.

Chapter 24

Derrick fidgeted as he rode through predawn, the *very* predawn London of the twenty-first century. It wasn't in his nature to fidget, so he took a deep, slow breath, then forced himself to look on the current assignment as nothing more than that: an assignment.

The plan was simple. He needed to get Richard Drummond safely out of the Tower jail and get himself and his companions safely back home. Unfortunately, the more he looked at the reality of what had to happen, the more the plan seemed to complicate itself. And one of the most complicated aspects of it was finding out the identity of that unknown quantity who had planted those gems on Samantha.

He didn't suppose that person would be looking for her, but then again, perhaps he would be. It had been suggested the night before that it made sense to have her back in approximately the same place so they could use her—and this was what made him extremely nervous—as bait. He had immediately and vociferously balked at that suggestion, but Samantha had merely looked at him, silent and determined, then turned back to the lads to figure out what she could carry for defense and not land in jail herself.

In the end, he had agreed to her coming along only because Jamie had called him and provided him with a safe place to use as a base, a place where Jamie assured him Samantha would be the safest of them all whilst he and the lads went about their business.

That decision made, he'd sent Samantha up to sleep in his bed, then camped in the salon with his lads. At that point, he had supposed there was safety in numbers.

Samantha had spent the day before with a professional historical costumer Cameron had drummed up for him, having a realistic and very elegant Elizabethan mini-wardrobe created for her. Thankfully he'd already had most of what Samantha and Jamie had decided he would need—the very useful laird of the clan MacLeod apparently having nothing better to do with his time than look up little details he promised would make the man and woman—and his presence had only been required first thing to take a few measurements. He had lingered in the shop with Oliver, trying not to frighten the seamstresses. Oliver had, unsurprisingly, found a pile of scraps and had a nap of unseemly length.

They'd regrouped at his flat for a supper he hadn't cooked, checked their gear once more, then tried to catch a handful of hours of sleep before setting off on their journey.

The immediate plan was to get back to the right time, then get through predawn London to Sir Thomas Mauntell's house. The Globe wasn't in exactly a posh part of town back in the day; he could only hope they didn't get either mugged or murdered before they managed to get across the Thames and at least out of the bear-baiting environment. Money was, as always, something of an issue, though he had been very grateful for the courier that had arrived at his flat the day before with a pouch from Jamie. It had contained a handful of coins, enough hopefully to see them through their trip. Jamie tended to be slightly more pragmatic about money and, it had to be said, romance than he was about more exotic things, so Derrick had been surprised he'd bothered, but he hadn't questioned the generosity. He would have to agree to journeying to one of the less-palatable destinations Jamie had on his list very soon as repayment.

But once the details had been planned and seen to as thoroughly as possible, Derrick had been plagued by what he still couldn't figure and that was who had planted those gems on Samantha, and why.

"Three minutes to launch," Peter said. He looked over his shoulder from where he sat in the front seat. "Think our gear will work?"

Derrick shrugged. "It's battery powered. Why not?"

Peter looked hopeful. Actually, he looked rather ill, but Derrick couldn't blame him. He glanced casually at Oliver sitting next to him, but Oliver was in superspy mode, silent and deadly looking.

"Check," Peter said, fiddling with his watch. "Four twenty-nine and three seconds."

Derrick looked at his watch, knew Oliver was doing the same, then hoped that the fairly long-range earbuds and mics they all had taped to themselves under their shirts for use later wouldn't find unexpected static in a different time period. It was a self-contained system they had previously tested extensively in the most rural spot in Scotland they'd been able to find, but he had no idea why it had never occurred to him to ask Jamie to help him see what it would do in the past.

But if it didn't work, they would do what they always did, which was improvise. He looked at Samantha. She glanced at him, then smiled.

"At least I'm not the servant this time."

"I'm not sure that's an improvement," he said, "but you do look very lovely."

"And the cloak's handy for hiding all kinds of things."

He didn't want to ask her what Oliver had talked her into carrying. The only thing that made him feel better was that Oliver had spent an hour with her in the salon after dinner the evening before, teaching her how to use those things. Derrick was fairly sure he might regret her having learned any of it at some point, particularly if she decided to use any of her skills on him.

"And here we are," Rufus said pleasantly. "Give me a wee page when you need me to pick you up."

"Where'll you be?" Derrick asked politely.

" 'Pray I'm not in the loo,' " Peter and Oliver quoted in unison.

They'd been saying that in unison for as long as Derrick could remember, though Rufus had never actually said those words. It was just their good luck charm of sorts. It was actually rather reassuring.

Derrick leaned up and put his hand briefly on Rufus's shoulder. "Thank you."

"No worries, lad."

They piled out of the car and huddled together on the sidewalk. Samantha was shivering.

"So, what now?" she asked. "High fives all around, or do we just jump right in?"

Derrick rubbed his hands together. "I say we just jump in. Let's find the appropriate spot."

"Do we have to hold hands," Oliver said quietly, "or just step in together and hope for the best?"

Derrick knew it was a serious question. He looked at Oliver and Peter in turn. "This is the way it works. You step into the gate, thinking about where you need to go as you do so, then the gate opens to that spot."

"Does it always work?" Samantha asked.

Derrick supposed there was no point in not being entirely frank. "Most of the time."

"And when it doesn't?" Oliver looked at him. "What then?"

"We'd better hold hands," Derrick said. "At least we'll wind up in the same place that way."

Peter only swallowed. Mostly.

Derrick nodded in a businesslike fashion, then took Samantha's hand and walked with her over to where the mushroom ring found itself. He supposed he should have been relieved to have found it still there, but he imagined the gate would work just as well without its defining marker. Then again, gates seemed to spawn that sort of ring around themselves.

"What do we do on the other side?" Samantha asked.

"Hope no one sees us," he said grimly. "Let's go."

He had to admit that the one thing about time traveling that made him slightly queasy was the traveling itself. There was something about those gates that shifted in a way that left him with a vague sort of headache he didn't care for. It never lasted more than a few minutes, fortunately, but he could have done without it. James MacLeod had the constitution of an ox, for he only ever emerged on the other side of anything with a fierce grin and boundless enthusiasm.

"I'm only touching you, Phillips, because I don't want to get lost," Peter said distinctly.

Oliver snarled a curse at him, which seemed particularly appropriate for the moment. Derrick took hold of Samantha and Oliver, then looked at his companions.

"Cheers."

Samantha laughed. He supposed he couldn't blame her. It seemed the most sensible reaction possible at the moment.

He walked through the gate, towing his companions along with him, then stumbled out into somewhere that was definitely not modern London.

"Smells like a bleedin' sewer," Peter gasped.

"Launch successful," Oliver said briskly. "Let's get this done."

Derrick couldn't have agreed more. He took Samantha's hand in his, then got them safely beyond the gate and on their way.

"Derrick?"

He shook his head. There was just something about the way Samantha said his name that left him feeling as if he'd just sat down in front of a merry fire.

"Aye, love?"

"Tell me again where we're going and how Jamie knew about it. I'm not sure I had a genealogy chart available last night to write it all down."

What he was sure of was that she needed something to take her mind off what they were doing at present. He looked at the lads. "We'll make for the river, hire a boat to ferry us across—and hope the wherryman is still half asleep—then disembark and walk quickly to Mauntell's house. Stick close behind us."

"And keep a weather eye out for prostitutes and contents of chamber pots," Oliver said blandly. "Don't think I didn't do my research."

"I never doubted it," Derrick said. At least the Thames was within throwing distance. With any luck, they might manage to get there without fending off any ne'er-do-wells. He glanced briefly at Samantha. "I'll tell you how Jamie got his information, though it's a bit of a story."

"I have plenty of time."

He smiled at her briefly. "So you do. It's a bit convoluted, but this is how it works. One of Cameron's ventures is a trust for the preservation of structures of note owned—or on the verge of being lost, quite often—by those who don't want to sell to the National Trust. It's the Cameron/Artane Trust for Historical Preservation, by name."

"What's Artane?"

"A great whacking castle on the north coast," Oliver muttered from behind them. "Derrick, the girl needs a proper tour after this is done."

Derrick nodded in agreement, then continued. "I suppose the players aren't particularly important to name, but apparently an elderly relative of one of the owners seems to spend an inordinate amount of time taking little trips."

Her expression wasn't visible in the darkness. "To where?"

"Oh," Derrick said with a shrug, "here."

She caught her breath. "Elizabethan London? You can't be serious."

"I think she's a big fan of the Bard."

"Well," she said, sounding stunned. "It's an old woman?"

"Oh, I don't think I would use *old* as a description of her," Derrick said with a smile. "She is, from all reports, quite young at heart. I've never met her, though I've heard quite a bit about her adventures."

"Maybe she could clear up that Shakespeare/Marlowe debate once and for all," Samantha said faintly.

"It would certainly do the world a great service," he agreed. "So, as it happens, Jamie's brother-in-law Zachary's wife is related in an extremely roundabout way to this seasoned woman. Zachary introduced her to Jamie and thanks to her efforts, Jamie has spent several years collecting details about our current location."

"I can't believe we're having this conversation."

"I can't believe I wore good shoes," Peter said from behind them.

Derrick had to agree with both statements. Again, if he hadn't lived through several trips with Jamie to times and locales not his own himself, he would have thought the very idea absolute bollocks.

He promised Samantha more details later because he was starting to get a little uncomfortable. The moon had already set—which boded well for their assault—but it made the current walk dodgier than it might have been otherwise. It took longer than he was happy with to find a boat with a captain who was both awake and sober, but he finally selected a likely-looking lad, promised him a handsome fee after they reached the far side, then made sure that his rapier and the daggers Oliver and Peter were carrying were plainly visible. He laced his English with a thick French accent and made conversation about the mother-in-law he and Samantha were escaping as they rowed across the river. The French weren't any more popular in London than anyone else, but there was no possible way to pass for a native, so he had considered it the least objectionable of the available choices.

They disembarked without landing in the drink, he paid the man and watched him take a practiced nibble at the coin, then counted himself fortunate that that part of the journey had been accomplished with such little fuss. One thing down, a dozen more to go.

He took a moment or two to get his bearings, then nodded up away from the river. "This shouldn't take long."

And that was the last thing he said for quite some time. They spent at least half an hour tromping through a rapidly awakening London and attracting all kinds of stares he'd hoped to avoid.

"Not exactly technologically savvy here, are they?" Oliver murmured from behind him, finally.

"Not exactly," Derrick said grimly.

Streetlamps would have made things easier, but then they would have been more exposed. Then again, by the time the sky was lightening and the city was fully awake, he was completely lost. He wondered if perhaps he'd been rash in thinking he could memorize an Elizabethan street map and have it possibly resemble what he was looking at from the ground.

"Bobbies at twelve o'clock," Oliver said, just loudly enough to be heard.

Derrick swore silently. He continued on, but was forced to face the fact that he had quite likely plunged them all into something they wouldn't be able to escape from.

And then, a miracle.

A woman stepped from the back gate of some grand place as if she'd simply come out for a breath of fresh air. She looked at them, paused, then turned toward the guards. She shooed them on their way with a cheerful story about how fortunate it was to find guests coming right to one's back gate instead of having to go search for them through all of London. The guards frowned, then continued on their way.

Derrick could hardly believe their good fortune, but he wasn't about to argue. He found himself herded with his little group inside a high wall and the iron gate shut behind them. The courtyard was reassuringly free of anything but a garden, a fountain, and stables. Not a guard in sight.

The old woman looked at them, then lifted her hood back from her face.

Samantha gasped. "Granny Mary?"

"Who else?" The woman stepped forward and hugged Samantha tightly. "You know, Sam, it's one thing to run into a favorite great-niece in the local Starbucks, it's something entirely different to find her traipsing about London at an unearthly hour of the morning. I'll need details."

"It's, um, complicated."

"If it means you're out from under your mother's thumb, then you should do complicated more often." She pulled Samantha over to stand next to her and linked arms with her. "Who are these handsome young men you've brought along as an escort?"

Derrick tried to pick his jaw up off his chest, but it was difficult. He could only stand there and gape.

Samantha gestured toward them. "Derrick Cameron, Oliver Phillips, Peter Wright. We're here on an, ah, adventure."

"I'll just bet you are, cupcake." Mary shook hands all around, then looked at Derrick. "You're Robert Cameron's cousin, aren't you? In charge of the treasure-hunting business presently?"

"Ah—"

"I've heard about you," Mary said, nodding knowingly. "And about your lads there, as well. I'm Samantha's great-aunt, by the way."

Derrick watched Samantha turn to look at her great-aunt. "But how do you know Derrick?"

"Well, first because I know his cousin, Robert. He's in business with Gideon who's funding the other half of a preservation group. Very high-end, fancy properties in need of some TLC."

"Who's Gideon?" Samantha asked blankly.

Mary looked at her in surprise, then laughed. "Good heavens, girl, you need to get out more. Gideon is Megan's husband, Lord Blythewood. Have you never wondered about your cousins?"

Samantha shrugged helplessly. "I knew Megan had married an Englishman and so had Jennifer, but it's not like I got an invitation to the wedding or anything. I'd thought about trying to get in contact with them, of course, but you know how Mother is about handing out phone numbers."

"Yes, I do," Mary said crisply. "I imagine she was afraid they would corrupt you by filling your head with unwholesome things like thoughts of independence and insurrection."

Samantha smiled faintly. "Probably so. Well, that and you know the girls and I aren't exactly close."

"Well, you're a damn sight farther away from Jennifer than you might think, but we'll discuss that later, when we have some privacy." She nodded toward Derrick. "That lad there might be able to give you a few details about your cousins and their doings, perhaps. I don't suppose he's told you what *he's* been doing with his free time lately."

Derrick found himself being regarded closely by two women with inquiring minds. He held up his hands slowly.

"It wasn't my fault."

"Ha," Mary said. "I know exactly what you've been up to over the past year, my boy, you and that rogue laird from down the way. I suppose that's fortunate or you would be hopelessly lost here."

"We *were* hopelessly lost," Samantha said.

"I wasn't," Oliver said mildly.

Derrick shot him a look, then turned back to Mary. "We were looking for a safe place to, ah, roost whilst we're about some business. James MacLeod gave me a suggestion."

"And does Laird James's place have a name?"

"I was hoping for the house of Thomas Mauntell," Derrick ventured.

Mary smiled in a particularly self-satisfied way. "Of course you were, because I'm the one who suggested it to him."

"You know James MacLeod?" Samantha said.

"We're Facebook friends," Mary said with a shrug, "and I read his wife Elizabeth's books. I've been to their castle several times. And Derrick, you were less lost than you thought. You're at Mauntell's back gate. Let's get you inside, get you fed and settled, then you'll tell me what you need. Thomas is having a masquerade ball this evening. I imagine many interesting people will be here."

"Granny Mary, how in the world do you know this man?" Samantha asked, sounding slightly faint.

"Oh, he was one of William's patrons early on. We met at a party several years ago and hit it off." She leaned in a little. "Actually, I cleaned his clock in cards and that tickled him for some reason. He thinks I'm a rich, eccentric noblewoman from France. He puts me up when I'm in town and I dote on his children. Well, that and I make him biscuits and gravy like my grandmother used to make. Dulls the pain of all the money he continues to lose to me."

Derrick felt a little faint, but perhaps that was just the smell. "Thank you, Miss—"

"You can call me Granny in private, lad, but in public I'd stick to Lady Mary."

Samantha smiled. "Lady Mary?"

"My girl, when you're sojourning in a time not your own, it's best to go in style."

"But, Granny, shouldn't you be home?" Samantha asked, sounding pained. "Knitting? Conducting meetings of the Ladies' Aid Society? Pruning your roses?"

"Some people go to Florida," Mary said with a shrug. "Some don't. Besides, if I'd had to listen to that blasted Fiona McDonald wax rhapsodic about the virtues of acrylic yarn by the pound any longer, I would have throttled her. Let's get in out of the damp, shall we?"

Derrick heartily agreed, especially if a fire was perhaps going to be involved soon. He didn't imagine Samantha would feel it, but he was dressed fashionably in tights and breeches. If he couldn't put on jeans, he would settle for being warm.

He was invited to follow the two women and found himself slightly more grateful than he probably should have been that in spite of himself they had landed where they were supposed to. He could hardly bear to hope the rest of the trip would go as easily.

He jumped a little when he realized Mary was looking at him over her shoulder.

"You know, you look a little like Sir Richard Drummond," she mused. "He's in the Tower."

"Yes," Derrick managed. "We know."

"I'll just bet you do." She lifted her eyebrows briefly, then led Samantha into the house.

He followed, glancing over his shoulder to make sure Oliver and Peter were still managing not to look as gobsmacked as he imagined they were feeling. Peter was pale and Oliver absolutely expressionless. Business as usual, thankfully.

Mary ushered them inside with great ceremony and continued to lead them through the kitchens and into the house. Derrick was slightly surprised to find Sir Thomas up and about, but perhaps the man had things to be doing.

"Ah, Thomas," Mary said with a first-rate French accent that Derrick would imagine she hadn't come by in the twenty-first century. "These are friends of mine from the continent, Derrick of Beaumont and his wife, Samantha."

Derrick trotted out his best courtly manners, ones he also hadn't polished in the twenty-first century. "Sir Thomas," he said, inclining his head. "We appreciate your hospitality."

Sir Thomas looked at him thoughtfully. "Lady Mary said yesterday that she thought you might be passing through London, so you are not unexpected. Your manor is near Beauvois?"

"It is," Derrick agreed, because he wasn't about to blow Mary's story for him. "A mutual friend did me the favor of alerting Lady Mary to my plans."

"In trade, are you?" Sir Thomas asked.

"Nothing to equal your business," Derrick said, because Jamie had done his homework for him and he knew just exactly how much trade Thomas Mauntell did every year, importing expensive textiles and other high-end luxuries.

And then he realized what else Mary had said, something that hadn't registered at the time.

Samantha was going to be posing as his wife?

"Our good Derrick has a keen eye for antiquities," Mary said, drawing Samantha's arm through hers, "which keeps his lady in pretty clothes and several maids to attend her."

Thomas looked behind them, then frowned. "Yet you have come so far with so slim a retinue?"

Or words to that effect. Derrick wondered if it might be time to plead a headache or pinch Samantha so she would swoon and he could carry her off without having to say anything else.

"They were robbed," Mary said, "and their serving girls and groom driven off. Not much for the remaining lads to do but loiter in the stables."

"How terrible," Sir Thomas said, clucking his tongue. "Mayhap other servants can be acquired for you, if you like. I'll have one of my maids show you to your chamber now. We have ample room outside for your servants."

"Thank you," Derrick said, knowing he would hear about that last bit in great detail at some point in the future. He thanked Mary for her help, thanked Lord Thomas profusely for his hospitality, then followed after the maidservant who showed them a surprisingly large room on the second floor. It had a brick chimney, which he had expected, and a large canopied bed.

He let Samantha distract the girl whilst he pulled Oliver and Peter aside.

"I think we'll attempt a tour of the Tower perhaps near noon," he said quietly.

"Whatever you say," Oliver said with a shiver.

"After getting lost this morning, I'm not taking any chances that things may have changed without some historian having made adequate note of it," Derrick said grimly. "Keep yourselves safe, lads. Try not to brawl."

The lads left in the company of the maidservant who spoke no French, which was handy given that Oliver and Peter apparently spoke no English. The girl was suitably smitten with their full sets of teeth and skin free from pockmarks, so Derrick supposed they would get along well enough. He closed the door, then turned, leaned back against it, and looked at Samantha.

"Well?"

"I'm terrified," she said, sounding as if her throat were very dry.

"Your great-aunt has paved the way for us," he offered.

"That's what I'm terrified about," she whispered fiercely. "She's out of her mind!"

He locked the door, then crossed the room and pulled her into his arms. He smiled at her. "She is formidable."

"Did you have any idea she would be here?"

"None," he said, "though I'm grateful for it."

"Did you know she was my great-aunt?" she asked suspiciously.

He bent his head and kissed her softly. "No. You, Miss Drummond, are a complete mystery to me."

"Liar. I bet you checked my ACTs and my college grades."

He laughed a little. "Had to have something to do to keep from biting my nails on the way to Ambleside, but I promise that's the only thing I investigated. Your email and your family tree are perfectly safe. You do realize, though, that you're related to several souls of various, ah, vintages."

"I'm not sure I want to know."

"Jamie will happily discuss your genealogy with you when we get home," he said cheerfully. "Now, Mistress Samantha, would you rather have a predawn nap or something to eat?"

"I don't think I can do either," she said uneasily. "The dress is too big to lie down in and too tight to eat in. How long are we going to be here again?"

"Hopefully not too long," he said. "I think I'll try the Tower tour later with the lads, then we'll see where the evening takes us. If there's a party here, I might be able to ask a few prying questions without having it come back to haunt us. I can't imagine that our good Sir Richard went to the Tower quietly. Surely someone will be willing to gossip about it."

She shivered. "Will you think less of me if I confessed that I just lied? I'm terrified, but not for Granny Mary."

He pulled her as close as he was able and wrapped his arms around her the best he could.

"Not to worry, Sam," he said quietly. "We'll be in and out of here as quickly as possible."

"Have you done anything worse than this? With Jamie, I mean?"

He smiled. "Would it make you feel better if I said yes?"

"Only if it was much worse than this and you got out alive."

"I think I can guarantee a happy ending. Would you care to hear a couple of infamous episodes?"

"Please." She pulled back far enough to look up at him. "I can try to sit, if you want. But maybe not too close to the fire. This fabric was hideously expensive."

He found a window seat made just for sitting and listening to tall tales, then joined her there and prepared to delight and astonish with things where he had truly feared might spell the end of his illustrious career as a time traveler.

He could only hope that their current adventure wouldn't be the one he wouldn't be alive to tell about when it was safely behind him.

Chapter 25

Samantha paced in the bedroom she'd been given, partly because she was nervous and partly because she simply couldn't sit down. The next time she traveled through time to help rescue an ancestor upon whom her very existence depended, she was going to see if she could do so in a place where the clothes were more comfortable.

She had no idea how long Derrick had already been gone, but it seemed like at least an hour had passed since he'd trotted off toward the Tower, Oliver and Peter in tow. At least he had money, thanks to Granny Mary's ability to clean clocks at the gaming table, and he had two shadows at his heels, ones she certainly wouldn't have tangled with. She'd already had a lesson from Oliver in self-defense; she suspected he'd only shown her the mild stuff.

She jumped half a foot at the knock on the door. She'd already been attended by two different maids, but sent them on their way while pleading a headache. She walked across the wooden floor, then opened the door carefully. The relief that rushed through her at seeing her grandmother's sister there was almost more than she could take.

Mary came in and shut the door behind her. "You look like you could use a drink."

"I don't drink."

"Neither do I, generally, so I called for some tea. At least that way the water's boiled. I'm not even sure I trust the wine."

Samantha waited while tea was set up, then listened to her aunt dismiss the servants with what she could only assume, having grown up with her father, was a first-rate local accent. Mary arranged herself at the table, then looked up.

"Come sit, girlie, if you can."

"I think I could *be* the tea table with this shelf I'm wearing around my hips," Samantha muttered. "Who thought up this ridiculous-looking getup anyway?"

"Oh, I imagine you could give a fairly decent lecture on that, couldn't you?" Mary asked, her eyes twinkling. "Make good use of that stool, sweetie, and let's take our minds off things for a bit. That Derrick Cameron is one good-looking kid."

Samantha had to agree, but she was too busy trying to sit to say as much. She got herself arranged, managed to get something down her parched throat without wearing it down the front of her dress, then looked at her great-aunt.

"Does anyone else in the family know you do this?"

Mary leaned back against the wall and propped her feet up on a stool she dragged over with the toe of her shoe. "Helen, of course, but she's been on several jaunts with me to oversee the births of Jennifer's children."

Samantha looked at her in surprise. "My cousin Jennifer?"

"Who married Nicholas, Earl of Wyckham, in . . . well, sometime in the early thirteenth century. Can't quite bring the exact date to mind at present."

Samantha felt her mouth fall open. "So, that's where you've been going? I thought you were volunteering with the Peace Corps!"

Mary smiled. "Not yet. Perhaps when I'm older and don't have the energy for this any longer."

Samantha suppressed the urge to snort. Mary MacLeod McKinnon was every day of seventy-five. Heaven help them all if she ever decided time traveling wasn't enough excitement for her.

"Derrick's very handsome," Mary noted. "But then again, he is a Cameron. Good genes."

Samantha knew her great-aunt was trying to distract her, which she appreciated. She found herself torn between blushing and feeling quite ill. There was actually no reason to blush because there was nothing between her and him, but there was every reason to feel very nervous because he was off taking the tour of the Tower of London.

"We're not a couple," she managed.

"Uh-huh," Mary said. "That's not what it looked like to me. So, how did you manage to run into him? And you can relax, Sam. He'll be fine. Jamie says he's extremely bright and sly as a fox. He'll manage to get himself in and out of the Tower on a tour without giving anything away. He's dressed appropriately and he's very handsome. The only thing I would worry about is every female in the area hitting on him, but since you're not a couple, that's not a worry. Now, details."

Samantha tried to take a deep breath, but there was no hope of that thanks to her corset. She supposed she could breathe later, maybe when they'd gotten back to their proper place in time.

"Gavin found me a job over here for the summer—"

"As well he should have," Mary said with a snort. "Useless ass."

Samantha had to smile. There was a reason Mary was one of her favorite people.

"He did manage to get me over here to England, so I can't say too many bad things about him. He got me a house-sitting gig with a couple in Newcastle."

"And?"

"Well, it turns out the people I was house-sitting for are textile thieves," Samantha admitted. "They wanted me to deliver something for them in London, which I agreed to because I had no idea what they were up to. Inside that package, though, was a piece of Elizabethan lace that they had stolen from a client of Derrick's."

"How much of that did he know?"

"Most of it, actually. He followed me from Newcastle to

London, rescued me from Elizabethan England, then we sort of came to an understanding about the fact that I wasn't a thief."

"And you're here to rescue Richard Drummond from the Tower," Mary said.

"Don't you think that's a good idea?"

Mary laughed a little. "I do, actually. He's insufferable in person, but a very fine actor. I'm not sure how he got mixed up in anything worthy of being tossed in jail, but I suppose your Derrick will figure that out."

Samantha studied her great-aunt. "You don't know?"

Mary started to speak, then sighed. "I know he's been accused of stealing gems, but that's only because someone mentioned it at supper last night. Jamie texted me a couple of days ago at home and told me what Derrick thought was going on. Once we nailed down a few details, I hopped on a plane to London, then snuck back here to wait for you."

"But, Granny," Samantha said weakly, "the jet lag . . ."

"One of the benefits of being old," Mary said with a smile. "Don't need much sleep. So, here we are, happily trying to sit in on these crazy Elizabethan fashions, waiting for your boyfriend to get back from his casing of the Tower of London."

"He isn't my boyfriend," Samantha protested.

"Well, cupcake, he'd obviously like to be." She nodded. "I have two good eyes and years of experience looking at this kind of thing." She made herself a bit more comfortable. "I'm assuming you have come along not just to keep him company."

Samantha tried to swallow, then had to have help by means of some more tea. "Well, the thing is, the jewels the Richard Drummond of the current day is accused of stealing somehow got slipped into my bag the last time Derrick and I were here retrieving some lace that I had left hiding in the past. He's not happy about it, but I came along partly to act as bait. We figure whoever planted them on me might try to get them back if they knew I was here."

Mary looked for the first time slightly unsettled. "There's some danger involved in that, Sam, I don't mind telling you so. People get away with all kinds of things here if they know the right higher-ups."

"I'm going to try to stay out of the way of those types." She took as deep a breath as her corset would allow. "I don't suppose you've heard anything about anyone missing some gems, have you?"

"I can certainly ask around," Mary said. "I wish I'd known sooner, but Jamie didn't say anything."

"I don't think there was anything to know," Samantha said with a shrug. "It makes you wonder, though, doesn't it, who would have that many jewels swiped from him and not want to publicize it so he could get them back."

"Oh, I don't know," Mary said thoughtfully. "Richard's stonewalling them in the Tower, or so I hear, so no joy there. Maybe the owners are just trying to do a little sleuthing in private. Or perhaps Mauntell knows something."

"Is it possible to find out?"

Mary pushed her stool aside and got to her feet with more energy than Samantha had at the moment. "I'll go ask a few questions."

"But can you really trust anyone here?"

"You underestimate the power of my biscuits and gravy."

Samantha would have smiled, but she was just too nervous to. "What if Lord Mauntell's involved?"

"How many gems?"

"Forty-eight."

"How much does Derrick think they're worth in modern pounds?"

"About fifty million pounds."

That Mary didn't look shocked left Samantha feeling slightly shocked.

"Granny, that's a lot of money."

"Honey, that's because they're antiques. People always pay more for old stuff. But back here, they're just ordinary rocks. I'm not saying they aren't valuable, but they're going to be worth a fraction of that right now."

"Do people have that much money?"

Mary laughed a little. "Arundel's rumored to owe about a half a million smackers to dozens of tradespeople."

"Well, that doesn't mean he has it in the bank," Samantha pointed out.

"The poor saps who made his clothes certainly don't," Mary agreed. She shook her head. "But for a minor lord, losing that many gems could indeed be quite a hit to his treasury. I'll go do some careful snooping." She started toward the door, then paused and looked over her shoulder. "There's a masquerade tonight, you know, followed by supper. Dancing as well. Who knows who we'll find there?"

Samantha could hardly bear to think about it. She promised her great-aunt she would try to rest, then watched Mary leave. She picked up her tea, then almost dropped the cup when the door opened suddenly.

She closed her eyes briefly. It was just Derrick. Unpierced, unshackled, unarrested. Perhaps that was good enough for the afternoon.

She tried to get up, but her dress was just too formidable. Derrick laughed a little and walked over to pull her up to her feet. She put her arms around his neck and hugged him tightly.

"Remind me to bring you to Elizabethan England more often," he said cheerfully.

She pushed away from him and tried to scowl. She was sure that was ruined by how hard she was shaking.

"Well?"

He reached for her hands and chafed them. "You're cold."

"I'm terrified."

He saw her seated back on her stool, then sat down across the little tea table from her and helped himself to something to drink. "It was, if you can believe it, almost the same as touring the Tower in our day. Gawkers, purists, and sellers of goods outside the gates. We didn't see anything interesting, but I will tell you that the yobs in this town are everywhere."

She smiled a little. "Then *Romeo and Juliet* wasn't just fiction?"

He rolled his eyes. "I've never seen so many teens and twenty-somethings with nothing better to do than roam in packs and vex innocent nursemaids."

"Did you brawl?" she asked casually.

"It was only good sense that kept me from it," he said dryly. He drained his tea, then smiled. "How about a nap?"

"You go ahead," she said with a snort. "The picnic table I'm wearing and I will just sit here and keep from getting wrinkled."

He laughed a little. "I have to admit some of the fashions of the day leave me baffled, but there it is. Isn't that thing detachable?"

"Not a chance," she said with a sigh.

"Not to worry, then. I'll stay awake with you."

She pursed her lips. "Of course you won't. Go lie down. I'll just go lean against the wall and see if I can fall asleep without breaking my neck in the process."

"If I could, I would text Emily to have flannel pajamas waiting for you when we get home," he said with a smile. "Let me get you settled as comfortably as possible, then if you don't mind, I might close my eyes for a couple of minutes."

She didn't mind and she was happy to have help getting herself reasonably close to the tapestry-lined wall where she could at least lean her head back without too much trouble. She had a kiss on her hand for her trouble, then watched Derrick walk comfortably across the floor and with equal ease throw himself onto the bed. He was asleep within sixty seconds. She knew, because she had counted.

If only their mystery could be solved as quickly.

It had to have been pushing at least ten when she found herself standing next to Derrick, torn between admiring and wanting to go throw up.

Well, maybe *stood next to* was an inaccurate representation of where she was. She stood as close to Derrick as possible, but what was possible with her enormous skirts wasn't much.

"This is fun," she murmured. "What's next?"

"I'm afraid that would be supper," he said, looking almost as green as she felt.

"Hey, you're supposed to be good at this."

"I am *accustomed* to this," he corrected. "*Good* is still up for debate. I think, though, if we can get through supper, we'll manage to get to dance together."

"That does sound like fun," she said brightly.

He shot her a brief smile. "I think so. I also think if we can hang on that long with this crowd, I'll slip out sometime after the moon has set and do what needs to be done." He nodded at the small purse dangling from her wrist. "There are things in there to get you through till the morning."

"Chocolate?"

"I should think you would be hoping for pharmaceutical

aids, but yes, just chocolate. Something sharp. Another thing or two." He looked at her seriously. "Stay here and wait for me."

"Because of the fabric of time?"

"That, too, though that doesn't seem to stop your aunt Mary." He shook his head. "Why Jamie hasn't unfriended her for her illicit activities, I don't know."

"I think they go to plays together when they're here at the same time. She knows Shakespeare personally. I think she actually has seats." She shivered. "I'm not even sure I can talk about this."

"I don't think Granny wants you to," he murmured. "Here she comes with a purpose."

Samantha couldn't deny that. Granny Mary's eyes were alight with something. Samantha had already heard about her great-aunt having acted in the Scottish play during her first trip to Elizabeth's time. She could hardly wait to see what other tidbits the woman intended to favor them with at present. Mary stopped in front of them, then leaned in close.

"Bingo."

"Bingo?" Samantha whispered. Heavens, not another thing she'd introduced to Elizabethan England that shouldn't have been there. "Are you playing it?"

"No, I have a lead in the case." She looked at Derrick. "Get to know Walter Cooke. Lord Walter Cooke, rather. Minor baron. Not particularly wealthy, but he's on edge about something and his son is a putz." She smiled. "There you go, lad. Run with it."

Derrick opened his mouth—no doubt to thank her—then shut his mouth abruptly. Samantha understood. The man coming to a stop in front of them looked vaguely familiar, but she couldn't quite place him. Perhaps he reminded her of someone she'd seen in a magazine, or on TV, or . . . or in a photograph.

He looked remarkably like Edmund Cooke, actually.

Sir Thomas appeared as if by magic and introduced them to Lord Walter Cooke. Mary shot her a knowing look that Samantha had no trouble interpreting. Derrick apparently needed nothing but his nose for old things to launch him into a friendly dialogue with the man in front of them. Samantha just nodded and pretended that she spoke only minimal English. It was just as well. She might have blurted out something unhelpful otherwise.

Her very powers of tongue biting were taxed to the limit

when Lord Walter's son stumbled over to them as if he'd seen a ghost. She didn't like to judge anyone too quickly, but she could safely say that that one gave her the creeps. He was short, greasy, and smarmy. Only good breeding—and, it had to be said, an intense desire to get back to her own time alive—kept her from punching him when he bent to kiss the back of her hand and slobbered on it instead. Derrick removed her hand from Junior's and tucked it under his arm, then proceeded to make polite conversation with father and son.

The younger Cooke, Francis, apparently didn't have much patience for the rigors of polite society because he turned away from Derrick in the middle of a sentence and looked at her in astonishment. "You seem so familiar," he said.

She looked at him blankly, because that's what she was supposed to do. Derrick assured him that wasn't possible because there wasn't a woman in London who was half as lovely as his *wife*.

Samantha watched Francis Cooke watch her while he was listening to Derrick and had the overwhelming urge to run go take a shower. He just seemed as if he were trying to tell her . . . something. She wasn't used to getting hit on, so—

She felt her heart stop.

Well, it didn't stop, actually, but it definitely paused. He was looking at her as if he had lost her and he was absolutely thrilled to have found her again.

"Of course," he said, turning to look at Derrick closely, "it isn't as if one would want to keep one's lady wife anywhere near Blackfriars or even the Globe, *n'est-ce pas*?"

Samantha put her hand over her ribs partly because she felt as if he'd just punched her and partly because that's where the second set of gems, the ones that had been planted on her in Elizabethan England, were currently residing, secured to her skin with athletic tape. She was a duct-tape kind of gal, never leaving home without at least a yard of it folded up in her purse. She'd saved more than one actor's trousers with that useful means of securing a seam. She supposed Derrick had stock in whatever company produced athletic tape in the UK. She also supposed she was babbling inside her head. It helped drown out the thought she was having that was so far-fetched, she could hardly think it.

It wasn't possible that Francis Cooke had planted those gems on her, was it?

Dinner was announced. She walked through the gallery with Derrick, losing the younger Cooke in the process. She sat where indicated, considered supper, then wondered if there might be antibiotics in her purse, just in case. She had no idea what she was going to find on her plate, but she didn't hold out much hope that it would be safe to eat, much less tasty.

She realized a handful of hours after that, that dinner was perhaps the least interesting of all the things she was going to have to worry about that night. When she and Derrick went back to their room, servants followed, apparently fully expecting that they would be sleeping in the same bed. She supposed they were only lucky that Lord Walter and Sir Thomas weren't joining them.

"Oh, these are strange and wondrous fasteners," the maid breathed.

"French," Samantha said with a shrug, hoping that said everything that needed to be said.

She had to admit, though, that she was grateful Granny Mary had provided her with a heavy robe. It might have been summer, but it was cold. Or perhaps that was her nerves again, rearing their ugly heads. Whatever the case, she was happy to go stand by the fire and watch Derrick dismiss the maid, telling her he could see to his lady's needs for the rest of the night.

He shut the door, then leaned back against it. He was minus his boots and doublet, which left him standing there in a tunic, shorts, and hose. He smiled.

"Long day."

"Very."

He pushed away from the door and came to take her hand. He saw her seated in front of the fire, then sat on the stool that had been her only option earlier in the day.

"Jewels?"

"I'm still wearing them."

He rested his elbows on his knees, then reached out and took her hands. He simply ran his thumbs over the backs of them for several minutes in silence. She would have thought he had fallen asleep if it hadn't been for that endless motion. He finally looked up at her.

"What did you think of Francis?"

"He has beady eyes and he drooled on the back of my hand."

"It was all I could do not to flatten him, believe me."

"My hero," she said with a smile.

He smiled wearily, then rubbed one of his hands over his face. "I think I need a couple of hours."

"I'll wait up."

He shook his head. "Nay, lass, you won't." He rose. "Let's go to bed."

"Ah—"

"Trust me."

Well, she couldn't say that she didn't, which meant she supposed she did. She watched him bank the fire as if he'd done it several times before—probably in different centuries—then gulped when he took her by the hand and pulled her across the room. He pulled back the covers, frowned, then remade the bed.

"We'll try on top instead," he said.

"Bedbugs?"

"Actually, no, but I like to be able to make a quick getaway when necessary."

He took the bolster and laid it down the center of the bed, then left her standing where she was and went around the other side. He stretched out, then looked up at her.

"Well?"

She smiled a little, then lay down on the other side. She propped her head up on her fist and peeked over at him.

"Have an alarm?"

"No, but I have a good idea."

"I can't wait to hear it."

He laughed a little, leaned up on an elbow, then leaned over and kissed her. He pulled back, started to speak, then shook his head and kissed her again. He kissed her for quite a while, truth be told.

"You'll never get to sleep if I don't stop," he announced at one point.

She laughed a little. "Project much, Lord Derrick?"

"In this case, probably," he admitted with a brief laugh. He kissed her once more, then looked at his watch. "If we go to sleep now, we'll have a lovely two hours before I need to go."

She reached for his hand and held it, hard. "Please be careful."

He leaned forward and kissed her softly. "I have many reasons to want to be, not the least of which is right here in front of me."

She could only look at him, mute, because she had absolutely no idea how to respond. She couldn't say anything, because she would have said too much. All she could do was close her eyes and nod.

She woke to darkness. Derrick's hand wasn't around hers any longer and she couldn't hear anyone breathing but herself. She would have fumbled for the bedside lamp but she realized immediately that there was no bedside lamp. She got up, noted for posterity's sake that even wooden floors could be very cold in the middle of the night, then made her way over to the fire. She brought it back to life, then lit a candle in the fire and set it on the table.

Her little reticule was sitting there, but she was fairly sure that wasn't where she'd left it. She frowned thoughtfully, then worked it open and peered inside it.

There was indeed chocolate—a Kit Kat, as it happened— wrapped in paper that went right into the fire the moment she'd finished her breakfast. There was a pocketknife, a very small syringe fully loaded with something that was identified as *knock-out drug for thug*, and a piece of paper. She left the knife and needle inside, then pulled out the piece of paper and unfolded it. She looked first at the title.

All the Things I Like About Samantha Drummond.

She would have smiled, but she couldn't quite bring herself to. Derrick Cameron, the man she was perilously close to being inordinately fond of was quite probably at the moment floating down the river toward the Tower of London where he intended to break in and rescue her ancestor.

Potentially for no other reason than it meant her life.

She took a deep breath and began to read.

Chapter 26

There was nothing like a little breaking and entering to really bring the bloom to a lad's cheeks.

Derrick had to admit he would have preferred to have had another chance to run their current operation more than just in their heads, but there wasn't time. At least whatever massive meltdown Peter and Oliver were planning on having, they were apparently planning on having later. They were nothing short of terrifying all dressed in black with masks over their faces, looking like something straight from one of Shakespeare's worst nightmares.

He supposed the main advantage they had was that they'd had the historical record to consult before attempting their assault. He knew exactly where Richard Drummond was being housed and only had to worry about getting there with a minimum of fuss.

He couldn't deny that it was the potential for a general-alarm-type fuss that concerned him, but what was there to be done? He wasn't superstitious by nature, but he'd had enough of James MacLeod's don't-unravel-the-threads-of-times lectures to know that leaving Sir Richard in the Tower where he couldn't woo and win some future ancestor of Samantha's father was going to have unpleasant repercussions through the family tree.

Besides, he wanted to know who had put Richard Drummond in the Tower. Knowing that might give them some clue as to who had planted those gems on Samantha.

They had paddled along the edge of the Thames in the pitch black and glided to a stop several yards short of the Traitor's Gate. He supposed he should have felt bad about swiping some poor lad's boat, but he would compensate him handsomely thanks to Mary McKinnon's jackpot she'd insisted he make free with.

Peter looked at him expectantly. Derrick nodded, because there was no reason to put off the operation. Peter donned a snorkel, gave him a thumbs-up, then eased over the side of the boat into the water. Derrick had insisted that Peter pump himself full of a variety of Sunny's herbs the day before and he would make sure the lad ingested vast quantities of her nastiest brew when they returned home. Swimming in the Thames was perhaps never a good idea, but in Elizabethan England it could be downright perilous.

There was suddenly a little pop and the outer gate swung open. Derrick paddled into the receiving area, as it were, leaving Oliver the task of silencing any guards there who might find their clandestine activities requiring an announcement. Four men fell senseless, fortunately not into the water. He was actually quite relieved to see Peter crawl out of the water and up the steps, poor lad. The second gate swung open soundlessly. He and Oliver stepped out of the boat, leaving it for Peter to guard, and slipped up the steps.

And from there, it was almost too easy.

They made their way to Sir Richard's cell with no less effort than he'd supposed they would need to make. He'd considered it very carefully beforehand and decided it was better to leave guards unconscious than slide by them and take the chance that they would raise the alarm. He intended to be in and out in less than six minutes, assuming Sir Richard was in any shape to run with them. They had contingencies, of course, if they found things not quite the way they expected them, but those alternate plans lasted no more than half an hour. The drugs would definitely have worn off by then.

He honestly didn't particularly care for guns though he certainly was proficient with several types. At the moment, though, he had absolutely no compunction about firing tranquilizer darts into each and every guard in his path. Oliver came along behind and collected the spent shots, continually looking over his shoulder for lads potentially following them.

He lowered Sir Richard's guard to the floor in the shadows, then stood guard as Oliver picked the lock to the cell. He was fully prepared to find more guards inside, but that wasn't quite what he found.

He found Francis Cooke sitting nervously in a chair, unfettered and obviously waiting for someone.

Once Francis saw them, he started to hyperventilate. Derrick supposed he should have expected that given that he and Oliver were dressed all in black with just their eyes showing.

"Drummond's over here in the corner," Oliver said. "Unconscious, damn him to hell."

Derrick holstered his gun and folded his arms over his chest as he looked at Francis. "And you?" he asked mildly. "What are you doing here?"

Francis was apparently not so terrified that he couldn't speak. "I'm waiting for Lord Derrick," he said. "I overheard him saying he planned to rescue Sir Richard." He took a deep breath. "I'm going back with him to that other place."

Derrick found himself rather glad that he was wearing a mask that covered his face. This was, he could safely say, not at all what he'd expected. "Other place?"

"F-F-Faery," Francis said, fighting to keep his teeth from chattering. "That secret world beyond L-L-London. By the Globe. Through that ring of mushrooms."

Perfect. How was it possible that out of all the souls who could have traipsed through time, it had to have been the fool in front of him to manage it? Derrick drew himself up.

"And what were you doing on that side of the Thames?" he demanded harshly.

"Gambling," Francis squeaked.

"And drinking?"

He shook his head vigorously. "I never drink. And I say that such is a blessing, for I never would have believed what I saw otherwise."

"And what did you see?"

"A world like my own, only everyone was dressed poorly, as if they were servants." He lifted his chin. "I saw it with my own eyes. It wasn't a vision."

"How many times did you see this vision?" Derrick asked sternly. "And pray you answer the question properly."

"Just once!" Francis exclaimed. He paused, then apparently decided honesty was the best policy. "I waited there many times before I saw the woman come through the selfsame portal, followed by Lord Derrick. I tried to follow them back to their world, but couldn't."

"You put the gems in the woman's bag the next time you saw her, didn't you?" Derrick said sharply. "You waited for her and shoved your stolen treasure—"

"They weren't stolen!" Francis interrupted. "They should have been mine long before now—" He froze. "How did you know?"

Derrick reached up and pulled his mask off his head.

Francis gasped. "You!" He leapt up and backward so quickly, he stumbled over his chair and landed heavily against the wall. He stood there, his chest heaving. "How did you get in here, Lord Derrick? And why are you dressed as a demon?"

"That doesn't matter," Derrick said. "What does matter is why you put the gems in my lady's bag."

"So I could find her again in that other world and collect them," Francis said. "And that I not be discovered with the gems on my person." His eyes shifted. "Too many here are watching me."

Derrick ignored that and nodded toward Richard. "And him?"

"Someone must be blamed."

"Awfully unsporting to blame an innocent man."

"He's an insufferable prig." Francis pointed at Derrick. "Take me to your wife and let me get my inheritance back."

Derrick lifted an eyebrow. "No."

Francis pulled a pistol out, froze, then fell over rather ungracefully and quite heavily onto his face. Derrick looked at Oliver who only shrugged and put away his dart gun.

"Clock's ticking, mate. And I'm hearing rumblings outside. We'd best be on our way."

"Damn it," Derrick muttered. He looked at Oliver. "I'll tie

him up and collect the dart. Leave a note on that table explaining what happened, would you?"

"Sure, boss."

It was done in less than half a minute, then Derrick pulled Richard to his feet and heaved him over his shoulder. It about knocked him to his knees, which made him think that perhaps the first thing he should do when Drummond awoke was tell him to lay off the desserts. Oliver tucked the page into Francis's shirt.

"What's it say?" Derrick gasped.

"I was naughty and tried to steal my father's jewels."

Derrick smiled briefly, then carried Richard Drummond out of the cell. Oliver locked it up behind them, then they made their way quickly back down the passageway.

Getting Drummond into the boat was a bit of a trick, but they all seemed to have plenty of adrenaline for the task. Peter shoved the boat away from the steps, then leapt inside it. Derrick rowed, because there was absolutely no way in hell he was going to simply sit there without losing his sanity.

He didn't relax until they had tied up where they'd begun their adventure. Oliver took his turn hauling Richard Drummond out of the boat and heaving him over his shoulder. Derrick flipped a young lad, who had obviously been sent to keep watch, a gold sovereign, watched the kid's eyes roll back in his head, then hoped the poor boy would have it when he woke.

Peter looked at Derrick. "Almost done." He sounded almost awed by the prospect.

"Aye," Derrick said, "perhaps after you've dried off and aren't in danger of catching whatever you've been swimming in." He looked at Peter, then Oliver. "Thank you both."

Oliver was smiling pleasantly. "Anytime."

"Careful what you wish for." Derrick looked at Peter. "And you, my lad?"

"I'm still digesting."

Derrick smiled. He imagined that was the case. He was glad to have the worst of it over with, though he wasn't entirely sure there wasn't more to come. He certainly hadn't intended to find Richard Drummond unconscious, but he was definitely out cold. He was alive, though, which was perhaps all they could hope for.

Getting to Sir Thomas's was much less taxing than it had been the first time. They managed to get Sir Richard inside the gate, then he carried him over to the stables. They had approximately thirty seconds to change out of their gear, stuff it in rucksacks and be back in Elizabethan clothing before Derrick heard voices. Peter was not exactly dressed for company under his cloak, but perhaps no one would notice.

"Hope you have a good story," Oliver said grimly.

"Thinking of one right now," Derrick promised him, then he took a deep breath before he staggered out of the stall and into the courtyard. He leaned over with his hands on his thighs and pretended to suck in hearty breaths. Honestly, at the moment, that wasn't much of a stretch. Mary and Thomas came to a skidding halt in front of him.

Mary should have been in the theater, that was all he could say about it. She had apparently dragged Sir Thomas out of bed because she'd been sure she'd heard a great commotion in the courtyard.

"Oh," she said, putting her hand over her heart, "what have we here? Lord Derrick, and looking very out of breath indeed! What fresh hell has befallen us, good sir?"

Derrick heaved himself upright and looked at Sir Thomas. "A miracle."

Thomas was apparently not much of a morning person. Then again, considering the lateness of the party the night before, the poor man was running on probably three hours' sleep.

"A miracle?" he echoed, rubbing his eyes.

"Come and see," Derrick said, gesturing toward the stables.

He let Mary lead the way and tagged along behind to keep Sir Thomas from escaping. Mary stopped at the open stall and looked inside, then gasped.

"'Tis Sir Richard Drummond!"

Thomas goggled. Derrick had never seen anyone do it with quite such commitment before. The man grasped for the door of the stall and continued to gape at the man lying there in the hay.

"But . . . how is this possible?"

"*How* is less important than *why*," Mary said. "You must obviously see to this man's needs."

"But he's a thief," Thomas protested. "He was just in the Tower yesterday—"

"Shall you ruin the life of the greatest actor of all time?" Mary asked sternly.

"That'd be Burbage," Sir Thomas said, looking slightly green.

"And this man has you to thank for everything he has," Mary said firmly. "You must render aid."

Derrick found himself the recipient of Sir Thomas's interest. The man was looking at him as if he were directly responsible for his distress. Which he supposed he was.

"He was in the Tower," Sir Thomas said in a low voice. "How did he come to be in your care?"

Derrick tried to look appropriately stunned. "My lads and I were off for a pleasant stroll," he said, "when we suddenly found ourselves near the Tower."

"You were lost, of course," Mauntell said.

"But of course," Derrick said smoothly. "And then, a miracle! This man fell into our arms, as if from heaven. Obviously, there are strange and mysterious forces at work here. Supernatural forces, no doubt."

"No doubt," Sir Thomas said weakly.

"We carried him here, of course, because what else would a gentleman do?"

"What indeed?"

"Imagine our surprise when we realized whom we had in our care."

"I'm imagining," Mauntell said. He took a deep breath, then nodded. "He'll need proper care. Can your men carry him inside? The servants won't be awake yet. We'll nurse him back to health."

"Ah, but look at him, Thomas," Mary said gravely. "He looks as if they haven't fed him in a fortnight."

Derrick had a different opinion on Sir Richard's meal schedule, but he supposed the current moment wasn't the one in which to voice it. He volunteered to carry Sir Richard inside not because he particularly wanted to but because he particularly wanted Oliver and Peter to make sure no one had dropped anything in their haste to change clothes. Well, that and he thought Peter might want to get dressed. He heaved Richard over his shoulder, exchanged a look with his lads, then turned and carried the man out of the stables and across the courtyard.

Getting him upstairs to a bedroom was a bit of a trick, but he managed it. He flopped him onto the bed, then stood back, his chest heaving. No more gym time that week, that was for certain. He turned and found his arms full of, well, wife.

Odd how lovely that sounded.

She hugged him quickly, then stepped back. He was the recipient of a look from Sir Thomas he couldn't quite identify, but he imagined it had to do with how fortunate he was to have such a woman.

He stood to the side with Samantha as Sir Thomas and Mary had a look at the patient.

"He's had quite a blow to the head," Mary said with a frown. "Shall I call for a surgeon?"

"Only if you intend to cut off his head, but then where would that leave you?" Mary said with a smile. "What he needs is rest. Probably several days here in one of your most lovely chambers, being waited on constantly by your prettiest maidservant."

Thomas blew out his breath. "He's insufferable."

"But continually nipping at Burbage's heels," Mary pointed out. "And insufferable as he might be, he acknowledges your patronage every chance he has."

"That's because I keep paying off his bloody gambling debts," Thomas said, then he clamped his lips shut. "My apologies, Lady Mary."

She waved aside his words. "Not to worry, my friend. You are too kind to him, but that is known generally as well. There is the problem of this coming afternoon, though."

Thomas looked at her in alarm. "What is to be done?"

"Something," Mary said firmly. "His career will be over if he doesn't appear on stage."

"But he's been in the Tower—"

"On false charges," Mary finished for him. "Come, Thomas, and be reasonable. You know he hasn't the wit or the stomach to steal Cooke's treasure. He has ample for his needs, especially since his greatest need is the adulation of his audience."

"There is that," Thomas agreed slowly.

"Do you truly believe he would trade that for a paltry handful of gems?" She laughed softly. "No, my friend, you know him too well for that. He was delivered into your hands by a power we likely couldn't begin to understand and surely shouldn't question. Take the gift, nurse him to health, and be prepared to be showered with purchases of your goods by grateful lovers of his work."

"That still doesn't solve the problem of this afternoon."

Derrick cleared his throat. "What's this afternoon?"

They turned and looked at him as one. Mary tilted her head to the side and considered. Thomas stroked his chin, then looked at her.

"There's a resemblance," he noted.

"They could be brothers," Mary agreed.

"Indistinguishable, truly."

Derrick felt his mouth fall open. "What," he managed, "are you suggesting?"

"*Hamlet,*" Mary said crisply. "Sir Richard is starring, but he obviously won't be there today. You must, Lord Derrick, take his place and save his reputation."

"But . . . but . . ."

The other two simply watched him in silence.

Something rushed through him. He wasn't quite sure if it was terror or adrenaline.

To play Hamlet at the Globe?

Mary waved him away. "Go clear your head, good sir," she said, shooting him a look that brooked no disagreement. "I'll arrange the rest. Sir Thomas, if I might ask a favor of you. There is someone I think needs to be sent for as quickly as possible."

Derrick felt himself being pulled from the room and realized it was Samantha doing the pulling. She continued to pull until she'd gotten him outside in the courtyard. To his surprise, the sky was lightening, though he certainly couldn't remember that much time having passed. He looked at her in surprise.

"Am I in shock?"

"Probably." She took his hand she'd been holding and kept it in both her own. "How are you?"

He dragged his free hand through his hair. "I'm not sure."

"Really?"

He looked at her helplessly. "Common sense dictates that we pack up and leave immediately, whilst there's still time and the cover of darkness. Or what's left of the darkness."

"But?"

"But if we go and your ancestor doesn't perform, who knows what repercussions there might be?"

She blinked, then she laughed softly. "Someone wants to tread some boards, methinks."

He pursed his lips. "You are a cynic."

She put her arms around him, then smiled up at him. "I don't think you have any choice," she said. "Like Granny said, his career will be ruined if he's not on stage this afternoon. By the way, how did it go in the Tower?"

"Too easy," he admitted. "But we found Francis Cooke waiting for us in Sir Richard's cell. He knows about the time gate and was the one to slip the gems in your bag."

"Where is he now?"

"Tied up with a note pinned to his shirt."

She looked at him in surprise. "Really? What if he blabs?"

Derrick took a deep breath. "He knows my name, but hopefully there's not another Derrick Cameron lingering in London at present. As for anything else?" He shrugged. "No one will believe him. They'll probably lock him up in Bedlam."

"Do they have it now?"

"I imagine Francis will find out. He might find out other things when it's discovered that he was stealing from his father."

She nodded, then rested her head against his shoulder. "It's very pretty out here this time of the morning."

"Are you trying to distract me?"

She sighed and tightened her arms around him. "You going to be okay?"

"Do you really want the answer?"

She lifted her head to look at him, then froze. "Company at twelve o'clock."

He looked over toward the house, then pulled Samantha behind him. He supposed that was overkill, but it had been that sort of day so far already.

Sir Thomas stopped a handful of paces away, Lord Walter Cooke in tow. Thomas cleared his throat.

"Lady Mary asked me to send for him," Thomas said.

"And I came quickly," Lord Walter said, looking as if he didn't dare hope for anything. "Do you have tidings?"

Derrick found a linen envelope pressed into his hand. He

stepped forward, inclined his head, then held out the packet without comment.

Lord Walter felt it, apparently realized what he was holding, then looked quickly at Derrick in surprise. "How?"

Derrick fumbled behind him for Samantha's hand, then pulled her forward to stand next to him. "I'm sorry to tell you this, my lord, but your son stole the gems."

The man closed his eyes briefly. "He has threatened to many times. How do you know?"

"Through a set of strange and mysterious circumstances I dare not tell, though you can thank my wife for their safe return."

Lord Walter considered. "Where is my son now?"

"I can't say," Derrick said, hoping that sounded more like he couldn't say than he wouldn't say.

The man closed his eyes briefly, then nodded. He stepped forward, took Samantha's hand, and bent low over it. "I don't know how to thank you," he said quietly. "Your bravery—"

"Lord Derrick is too kind," Samantha said. "It was his bravery that brought us all to this place at the right time. He is the one who deserves your thanks."

Thanks were extended all around. That and a dozen gems that were extracted from the linen, carefully tied up in what even he could see was an exquisite handkerchief, and handed to Samantha.

"A small token."

"Oh, I couldn't—we couldn't—I mean—"

"I believe it is because of you that a miracle was wrought. My family will be forever grateful." He nodded briskly. "I will see that Richard Drummond's name is cleared, now that I have the proof."

"Thank you, my lord," Samantha said gravely.

Derrick watched him and Sir Thomas return back to his house before he heaved a sigh of relief. "Tell Granny good-bye, Sam, and let's get out of here."

"Not so fast, my lad."

Derrick looked at Samantha's great-aunt, who was wearing a look of calculation he didn't care for in the least. "I've had a change of heart," he said firmly.

"What you have, my dear Derrick, is a sticky wicket. How much do you know about Richard?"

"More than I want to—"

"But perhaps not as much as you should. Let me enlighten you further. He's a Scot, which you may or may not know. His uncle is the laird John, who is also Samantha's great-uncle the appropriate number of times removed. Richard disagreed with his uncle about the course his life should take, then ran away to London to seek his fortune. He worked first to lose his accent, then to learn his trade. He is, I can safely say, one of the great actors of his generation." She paused and looked at him seriously. "But you could fill his shoes, I think. It's uncanny how much you resemble him. Good Scottish genes, I suppose."

Derrick considered, then looked at Samantha. "We saw him in Newcastle, didn't we?"

"As a ghost?" she asked in surprise. She thought about it for a moment, then nodded. "I think so." She laced her fingers with his. "It makes you wonder why he was there, doesn't it? For all we know it was to get us on the path that led us back here."

He rubbed his hands over his face and suppressed a groan. "Hot pins." He looked at her. "Red hot."

She smiled. "We'll be watching from the floor."

He shook his head. "I can't believe I'm agreeing to this."

"I think you already agreed to it. Besides, you'll have rave reviews. Think how green your brother will be."

He laughed a little, because there was nothing else to do. He looked at Samantha's great-aunt. "Well, Madame Torturer, can you get me backstage?"

"Already seen to."

That's what he was afraid of.

"Go on, Sam, and put him to bed for a couple of hours," Mary said. "I'll see the gossip spread properly about Sir Richard's miraculous liberation from the Tower, then we'll get Derrick to the theater." She rubbed her hands together enthusiastically. "I love a good play."

Derrick watched her go, then looked at Samantha. "And you? What do you love?"

She leaned up and kissed him quickly. "Tell you later. You look like you need a nap."

"What I need is a stiff drink."

She laughed and pulled him back toward the house. He went, because she was surprisingly strong and because he was exhausted. He nodded to Oliver and Peter on his way, then allowed Samantha to get him all the way to their bedroom and put him to bed. She took off his boots, then leaned over and kissed him softly. He frowned as she straightened.

"That's it?"

"That's it, sport. You need your beauty rest."

But she did do him the favor of lying down on the other side of the bolster.

"Set your alarm and I'll check it," she said.

He sighed, then did as she bid, because he had the feeling there was no getting out of what he was scheduled to do in a few hours. He put his arm around her and the bolster both, then propped his head up on his hand where he could watch her.

"I think I like you," she said with a sleepy smile. "Break a leg later this afternoon."

"Will you come?"

"Wouldn't miss it."

He lay down, closed his eyes, and tried to sleep, though he had the feeling he wouldn't come close to managing it.

The Globe.

Hamlet.

He could almost not bear to think about it.

Chapter 27

Samantha stood on the floor of the Globe, at the back where she could lean against the wall and have drinks spilled down the back of her simple lower-class-gal dress, and contemplated the quirks of Fate.

For all the time she had spent in the theater, she had to admit that she had spent very little of that time in front of the stage. She had mostly stayed behind the curtains, fixing costumes, reassuring her father that he was the most amazing thing to hit the stage since Sir Laurence himself. That she should find herself standing in the cheap seats, in the original Globe, waiting for a production of *Hamlet* in which she knew the star . . . well, it was memorable. She might have to make a list.

First on that list would be waking up to find herself alone in bed with the bolster. She'd sat up quickly, fearing that she'd been left behind, only to find Derrick sitting in front of the fire. He'd been as motionless as a statue, staring out the window as if he contemplated dire things. She'd crawled out of bed—again being quite grateful they hadn't had to come to Elizabethan England in the winter—and gone to kneel in front of him.

He'd studied her for so long that she wondered if he'd forgotten who she was. Then he'd simply smiled that charming, half-crooked smile she had come to love and leaned over and kissed her very softly.

She'd known he would survive.

She had called her maid to help her dress, then insisted that they leave Lord Derrick alone, no reasons given. She'd seen him fed, watered, then ferried off to the theater.

Second on her list would be cleaning up evidence of their stay with help from Granny Mary. She had given Lord Walter's gift back to her great-aunt and asked that she find a particularly unique yet believable way to get them back to him. She had been given a rucksack of things Granny hadn't let her sort through, things she was sure James MacLeod wouldn't have approved of. But when it came to that feisty, amazing woman who was seventy-five years young, there was just no arguing with some things.

She'd rolled her dress up far enough to have it fit in Oliver's pack and set off for the theater with Derrick's lads in just ordinary middle-class women's wear. Sir Thomas had been faintly horrified, but seemingly been willing to accept Mary's excuse that Samantha just wanted to mingle with the common people whilst in London.

The lines to get into the Globe had been appallingly long, but she'd waited, then taken up her current spot at the back of the crowd. She supposed she would have been able to see more if they'd bought seats a level up instead of standing on the floor, but Oliver had insisted it was better where they were.

In case they needed to make a hasty getaway, of course.

If she were going to be honest with herself, that wasn't what worried her. It was one thing for Derrick to have the guts to get up on stage. It was still that one thing for him to have the sheer audacity to get up on a stage that found itself in Elizabethan England.

But it was another thing entirely to hope he remembered lines from a play he'd auditioned for over a decade ago.

"Not to worry."

She looked at Oliver who stood on her left. "Worry?" she said, her mouth horribly dry. "Why would I worry?"

Oliver smiled faintly. "He has a photographic memory. Leaves the rest of us at a disadvantage."

Peter snorted. "And you can pick any lock ever created. Nothing is safe."

Samantha looked at him and smiled. "And you could probably bring down the world's banking system with a few clicks."

"Well," Peter said modestly, "probably."

She took a deep breath, then took another handful of them. All right, if Derrick knew his lines, that was at least one thing she didn't have to worry about. And she had read his college reviews. If he was only half as good presently as he had been in the past, well . . .

The guards suddenly took their place on stage and she realized the time for fretting was over.

The play was the thing.

She forced herself to remember not to lock her knees and made a conscious effort not to wring her hands. She thought perhaps she didn't breathe at all during the scene with the guards and ghost, and she was certain she hadn't swallowed as the bulk of the court took their place and Claudius started pontificating. She closed her eyes, because she just couldn't watch.

"A little more than kin, and less than kind."

She opened her eyes and found Derrick there, on stage, at the original Globe.

And she realized in that moment that that was where he belonged.

Well, not in 1602, but on stage. It was hard to deny his beauty, but that was just the start of it. As the play wound on, as far as she was concerned, he *was* Hamlet. If there had ever been anyone born to keep his head while everyone around him was losing their minds and trying to make him look like the crazy one, it was Derrick Cameron.

She wasn't even sure she had noticed whether or not they'd taken an intermission. She was fairly sure she hadn't taken a decent breath until the final scene when Hamlet was fighting with Laertes. The swordplay was terribly real and she couldn't help but notice the maniacal grin on Laertes's face as he and Derrick sparred.

And then Hamlet fell.

And the rest was silence.

Well, it was for the space of approximately five seconds before the crowd erupted in thunderous cheers and clapping.

She looked first at Oliver, who was making a tremendous noise, then at Peter, who was watching her.

"He's good," was his only comment.

She supposed that was the understatement of the year.

And then Oliver swore. "Bedamned guards. Pete, get her to the gate. I'll fetch Derrick."

Samantha wasn't sure that was such a great idea, but Peter was apparently utterly uninterested in her input. She wasn't sure how he managed it, but he got them both out of that crazy crowd. He ran with her, keeping hold of her hand until he found a place for them to stand near the ring of mushrooms. She heard all kinds of commotion coming from inside the Globe, which alarmed her greatly. She looked at Peter.

"Is he okay?"

He held up a finger. "Out yet?" He frowned, then looked at her. "They're working on it. Oliver says to go ahead."

"No."

He hesitated, then nodded. "As you will." He paused. "I think he's having a hard time getting past his adoring fans."

She didn't doubt it. She waited with Peter for what felt somewhat like an eternity, then finally saw Derrick and Oliver trotting toward them with a purpose. She hardly had time to say anything before Derrick had grabbed her by the hand and hauled her with him toward the gate. They clasped hands, the four of them, then stepped inside the circle.

A woman screamed.

Samantha looked over her shoulder and saw the Eye, then the Globe behind them. The cluster of people they'd simply appeared in the midst of were backing away, as suspicious as medieval Londoners.

"Magic show!" Derrick called loudly.

"Paging Rufus," Peter said.

"Walk quickly," Oliver suggested.

Samantha supposed there was wisdom in that, though at least a couple of teenagers were calling for more tricks. She clasped hands with Derrick and they hurried for the street. She was enormously grateful when that sleek black Mercedes appeared by magic at just the right spot at the curb. She didn't even hesitate; she simply flung herself into the backseat, not complaining when Derrick piled in on top of her and she almost gave herself a black eye against the door.

"Sorry," he gasped. "Oliver, *move*. And shut the door."

The car pulled away before Oliver managed that, but apparently the three crazies she was with weren't unaccustomed to taking off with the doors open. Samantha managed to get herself upright, then switch seats with Derrick so his head wasn't crushed against the roof. He buckled her in, buckled himself in, then sat back with a sigh.

"Clear?" he asked.

"Fully," Peter said. "Thanks, Rufus."

"My pleasure, and no, I wasn't in the loo, you little—"

Oliver laughed and peeled off his headset. "Now, *that* was a proper adventure." He looked around her at Derrick. "Where do we go next?"

"Go ask James MacLeod," Derrick wheezed.

"Where to, Master Derrick?" Rufus asked.

Samantha found Derrick looking at her. She held up her hands. "I don't care."

"I do," Peter said pointedly. "I want a decent shower."

"What the hell," Derrick managed. "The Ritz, Rufus, if you please."

Samantha found her hand taken. She looked at him and realized he was watching her closely. She simply returned his look, thinking that perhaps he might enjoy what he was fishing for if he had to wait a bit longer for it.

"Well?" he asked, finally.

"Brilliant."

"Tolerable."

"How're those hot pins looking?"

He laughed a little. "Don't ask me right now. I might give an answer I'd regret later."

She squeezed his hand, hard. "I'll give you a full review when we've eaten something I recognize."

"I'll do better than that," Oliver said. "I recorded the entire thing."

Derrick laughed a little. "You didn't."

"Had to stay awake somehow, mate."

Samantha laughed at Derrick's curse, then leaned her head

back against the seat and closed her eyes. She had started a list earlier that morning, but realized she hadn't finished it. She wasn't quite sure what it would contain, but she knew what the last entry would be.

All's well that ends well.

Or maybe all good things ended at the Ritz. She didn't know, but she was happy to have the chance to decide.

She stood in the bathroom the next morning, looking at herself in the mirror. Did it show, that place she'd been? She didn't feel any different physically, but she was definitely different mentally. She had stood in the midst of history and watched it roll on around her.

She was changed.

She considered braiding her hair, then put the brush down and walked out of the bathroom. No braid, no polyester, no quarter.

Derrick was sitting on the couch simply staring off into space. He looked at her immediately, then blinked in surprise.

"No braid?"

"Elizabethan England."

He stood up, then walked over to pull her into his arms. He looked down at her seriously. "My turn today."

"Is it?"

He bent his head and kissed her, so apparently it was.

"You know," she managed a few minutes later, "you've got to stop that. It's distracting you from stuff I'm sure you should be doing, like deciding what to have for breakfast."

He smiled, kissed her once more, then put his arm around her and led her over to the couch. "Order whatever you like. I'll trust you."

"Well, it can't be any worse than what we ate on our little trip to the past."

"Please," he said with a shiver. "Let's not think about it."

"And I think that was the good stuff." She looked over the menu, ordered something hearty for him and less hearty for herself, then set the phone aside and looked at him. "Well?"

He took a deep breath, then reached over and handed her a manila envelope.

"What's this?"

"Something Cameron sent over this morning. Faxes from Jamie."

"Did we change history—" She stopped, then smiled. "No, I don't imagine we did. Are these reviews?"

"I can't bring myself to look."

"If it makes you feel any better, you were astonishing."

He blew out his breath. "I shouldn't care."

She reached for his hand. "You know, it's a little frightening to think about failing at something you love. But you didn't fail. You were riveting."

"You just like me."

"Yes, and I told you how absolutely amazing you were at least a dozen times last night."

"I thought that was just to impress the lads."

She smiled, because she didn't believe that for a minute. "Where are they, by the way?"

"Off doing what they do. Wreaking havoc, making hay, causing a ruckus. Fetching reviews from Cameron and delivering them to me here with a smirk."

She smiled and reached for the envelope. She pulled faxed copies of photocopies of what looked to be originals of some kind of seventeenth-century *Variety* magazine. She found what she was looking for, then handed it to him.

"You left women swooning and men wishing they could wield a sword like you."

He smiled briefly, read, then slid the pages back into the envelope.

"Nice."

She laughed a little. "That's all you can say?"

"It's what I did, not who I am."

She smiled. "I said that first."

"Well, aye, lass, I think you did." He leaned toward her, then stopped. "If I start that up again, we'll never get out of here."

"Are we going somewhere?" she asked.

"I thought we might take a little trip north to Stratford. You should see Anne Hathaway's house whilst we're there. Not to be missed."

"Is there an ulterior motive to this trip?"

"Come along and find out." He nodded toward her room. "What'd Granny give you?"

"I didn't want to look yet, because I was afraid of what Jamie would think. But I'll go get it."

She retrieved the pack from the dresser and carried it back in to find that Derrick had her bag sitting on the table. He looked up.

"Cameron brought this as well from its hiding place in his safe. I'm curious as to what it contains."

"Which first?"

"Gems."

She watched him pull the clear zippered bag out of her purse and lay it on the table. He opened the bag, spilled the gems out, then blinked in surprise. "There are forty-eight."

She took a deep breath. "I know."

He considered, then looked at her quite seriously. "I'm not sure, Miss Drummond, that I have told you adequately just how I feel about you."

She shifted uncomfortably. "Do I want to hear it?"

He took her face in his hands, then kissed her, a whisper of a kiss she barely felt. He pulled back and looked at her. "If I tell you now, I'll unman myself by a display of unseemly emotion."

"Then you aren't furious with me for having Granny give the others back to Lord Walter in 1602?"

"Nay, lass," he said quietly, "precisely the opposite."

"Would you have been disappointed if I'd kept them?"

He looked at her, then smiled. "Do you want me the hopefully decent man to answer that or me the pirate to answer that?"

She laughed, then kissed him that time, because she thought she just might love both incarnations. "I already know the answer."

He smiled. "You made the right choice, one I'm not sure I would have had the courage to make. I'm impressed. I'm assuming that both the linen and the handkerchief are still in the past?"

"I thought it wise."

"Jamie will be impressed." He nodded at her pack. "What'd Granny give you?"

"We need gloves."

"What's wrong with our grubby hands?"

She shot him a look. "Your archival preservation technique needs some work, but I'll let that slide just this once. Just try to keep this stuff out of the butter during breakfast."

Her pack produced a length of lace that would have made a very lovely bridal veil. It made Lord Epworth's piece of lace look like a placemat. Samantha shook her head.

"I'm not sure she should have sent this home with us."

"Us? She sent it home with *you*."

She looked at him frankly. "Share and share alike."

He shook his head, but he was smiling. "There's breakfast at the door. Let's eat, then we'll be on our way."

"By train?"

"Heavens no, lass. We're taking the Vanquish. If I happen to see my brother, I want him to know I'm driving something that runs."

She watched him go open the door, then shepherd and eject the staff members who had brought them something to eat. She ate, she supposed, though she spent more of her time looking at Derrick than she did putting away breakfast.

He looked at her with a piece of toast halfway to his mouth. "What?"

She shook her head and smiled. "Nothing. Just seeing if there's a difference."

He put the toast down. "Think there is?"

She leaned forward, put her arms around him, then kissed his cheek before she let him go and got up to go brush her hair one more time. "I always thought you were amazing," she threw over her shoulder.

"Hey, come back here and tell me that again."

She only looked back, smiled, and continued on.

She had to admit, an hour later as they were driving past the outskirts of London, that the Vanquish was a wonderful way to get around. She didn't sleep, but she certainly spent her share of time staring aimlessly out the window. The scenery was all kinds of charming, but so was the driver, so she had to admit she felt a little torn. She held his hand much of the time, or shifted a little in her seat so she could study his profile. And she wondered about him, what his life was like when he wasn't working, what he wanted.

But she didn't have the guts to ask him any of it.

"Thank you for the list," she said finally. "Of things you like. Well, you know."

"About you?" He smiled. "You read it?"

"I did."

He smiled and continued on. She supposed that the moment to ask him what he wanted out of life was just not the present one, so she settled for simply enjoying the ride, the company, and the scenery.

Derrick's phone cheeping at her made her jump. He turned it on, then handed it to her. "That's probably Oliver."

She looked at the text. "It is. He says the bald guy and the skinny guy are lurking around the theater."

"Would you ask him if someone could please come babysit my car so no random thug keys it?"

She did, then learned that Ewan had gone north with them and would happily keep an eye on Derrick's car. She looked at Derrick. "Are you worried?"

"About those thugs?" he asked in surprise. "Well, I'm not sure we can shoot tranquilizer darts into them in this day and age, but no, I'm not worried."

"Whom do you think they're working for?"

He shook his head. "You know, this is what I still can't understand. You were given embroidery and lace by Lydia Cooke herself. No one else could have planted it on you. I thought this pair was after that, but that proved to be untrue, as events have shown. They're unabashedly interested in jewels and probably in the jewels Lydia Cooke obviously sewed into your bag. But why send the jewels off with you if she was sending those two thugs off after you to retrieve them?"

"Unless they weren't working for her."

"But if they weren't working for her, then how could they possibly have known what you had sewn into your bag?"

She felt her mouth fall open. "Now, that's creepy."

He lifted his eyebrows briefly. "Agreed. So, I suppose the question now is, who would be interested in those jewels and might suspect that Lydia was trying to—well, let's limit her to at least moving them to a different location. Who would know? Who would care?"

She felt something slide down her spine and it certainly wasn't Derrick's hand. "Edmund Cooke."

"That's what I was thinking."

"I thought they were happily married."

"I'd say that might be assuming too much, but we'll see."

"What are we going to do?"

"*I* am going to crash his rehearsal and chat with him in public. *You* are going to sit in the car with Ewan and his collection of things he shouldn't own." He shot her a look. "Today is my turn, remember?"

She shrugged. "Whatever you say."

He shot her a skeptical look, then turned back to the road. She considered, then decided that perhaps the occasional romance novel Granny Mary had slipped her might come in handy. She looked at Derrick.

"Hold hands?"

He looked at her in surprise, but didn't argue. And he left her hand on his leg when he shifted, which was handy, giving her ample opportunity to trace lazy circles on his jeans.

He took her hand and put it back in her lap. "Stop that."

She reached up and slipped her hand along the back of his neck. He rolled his eyes.

"No."

"Yes."

"This will not get you what you want, Samantha."

"Won't it?"

He glanced at her, then laughed miserably. "Who *are* you?"

"Someone who survived Elizabethan cuisine and stood through an entire performance of *Hamlet* that seemed to last about ten minutes, that's who. Now, don't you think I'd be safer right next to you?"

He opened his mouth, no doubt to argue, then sighed. "Very well," he muttered. "But stop touching me before I run off the road."

She folded her hands primly in her lap and smiled. "All right."

He shook his head with a sigh, then concentrated on getting them to where they needed to be. Eventually, he pulled his earphone and mic from off the dash, put them where they were meant to go, then started up the usual drill.

"Peter, how does the area look? Excellent. Ewan, which car park? Aye, that's close enough. We'll watch for you—nay, I'll not run over you, you ass. Oliver, thugs under wraps?" He was silent for a moment or two. "We'll make for the theater. I'm assuming quarry is there." He waited, nodded, then looked at her. "I don't like this."

"You'd like it less if your car got stolen with me in it."

"I suppose you have a point there." He looked at her briefly. "You know that thing you were doing before?"

"The *give me what I want because you can't help yourself* thing?"

He nodded. "Do that again later."

She smiled, because he was so utterly charming, she could hardly keep her hands to herself.

Fifteen minutes later, she was walking with him along the river, past houseboats, and down to what she assumed was the rehearsal theater for Edmund's latest.

"How are we going to get in?"

"I thought I'd pretend I was my brother."

"Well, there is that."

He got them inside the building with no trouble and inside the theater with only a puzzled frown as their reward. They made it halfway down the aisle before things took a turn she couldn't say she'd expected, though Derrick didn't seem terribly surprised by at least part of it.

"Edmund straight ahead," he murmured. "And, oh, look, there's Lydia doing her best harpy imitation."

"No, I think that's your brother staggering around up there on stage." She watched him for another moment or two, then shook her head. "He's terrible."

"Aye, he is." He nodded toward the wings. "I think *that* one there is Lydia Cooke."

"Could be."

"I'm not sure this can get any dodgier," he said grimly. "I imagine you know what I'm thinking about now where you're concerned."

She looked around, then froze as she watched a couple get up from where they'd been sitting several seats away from the aisle where she was currently standing. Obviously they'd been watching the rehearsal as honored guests.

"Um, Derrick?"

"What?"

"It just got worse."

"How's that, love?"

She pointed. "See those people over there?"

He looked, then froze. "Tell me they aren't who I think they are."

"Oh, they are," she said. She had to take a deep breath. "Those are my parents."

He swore.

She was fairly sure she had, too.

Chapter 28

D errick cursed, thoroughly and at length. He was actually quite happy to have a live mic taped to his cheek, because that made interrogating possible miscreants all that much easier.

"All right," he breathed, "which one of you saw Samantha's parents and didn't bother to tell me?"

"Not I, said the fly," Oliver intoned solemnly.

"Not I, said the fish," Peter added cheerfully.

"I'm going to kill you both," Derrick whispered furiously. "Slowly, painfully, and happily. And if you don't think I'm going to, think again."

"We're keeping an eye on the thugs backstage," Oliver said. "What else do you want from us?"

Derrick supposed it was better not to say. He thanked them briskly, then turned to the most immediate of the problems facing him presently. That would be Edmund Cooke himself, who was looking as if he'd just seen a ghost. His mouth was working, but only babbling sounds of misery came out.

"Edmund," Derrick said pleasantly. "It's been a bit, hasn't it?"

"Derrick Cameron," Edmund managed finally. "What are you doing here?"

Derrick pulled Samantha behind him, just in case, then looked at the man who had ruined his life. "Oh, a bit of this and that."

Edmund licked his lips nervously. "I heard you have a job hunting down little vintage knickknacks."

"Something like that."

"Why are you here, then?" Edmund said with a sick attempt at a smile. "It isn't as though I have any, is it? Vintage things, that is. Or anything of value, really—"

"You damn well do!" shrieked a voice from the darkness.

Derrick considered stepping in, then decided the smartest thing he could do was step back and let Lydia have at her husband. At least that way he would see for whom the jewel thieves were working, if they were actually working for someone and not operating on their own.

Only Lydia didn't leap for her husband, she leapt for Samantha.

"Give me your bag!" she screamed.

A knife flashed in the semidark.

Derrick reached out to disarm Lydia only to have her flinch a little, as if something had hit her in the back. She looked at him, made a feeble stab with the blade, then her eyes rolled back in her head. He caught her wrist to keep the knife away from his chest, then caught the rest of her before she collapsed. He carefully laid Lydia on the ground and made a production of putting the knife well to the side of her.

He also managed to remove the very tiny dart with approximately five minutes of downtime out of her flesh and disentangle it from her sweater before Edmund stumbled over.

Derrick stood up, then put his hand behind his back. He felt Samantha carefully take the dart out of his hand. He assumed she would stick it in something that didn't include either her flesh or his. He looked at Edmund who was hovering over his wife, but not reaching down to see if she was well.

"She fainted," Derrick suggested.

"Is she still breathing?" Edmund asked, sounding as if he very much hoped she wasn't.

Derrick squatted down and felt for her pulse, which was strong and steady. He took the knife, rose, and handed it to Edmund. "I think there are enough witnesses who will testify that she was holding this. You might want to find a place to keep it safe."

"She's crazy," Edmund stated.

Derrick wasn't about to pass judgment, but he was happy to get rid of the knife. He also did the bobbies the favor of taping Lydia's wrists together with the duct tape Samantha handed him. He put Lydia into one of the seats, then taped her there as well. No sense in leaving her free to do more damage. Then he turned back to his business with Edmund.

He pulled out of his pocket the clear bag of gems that belonged to the man in front of him. He watched, mildly interested, to see what Edmund's reaction would be. He'd been turning over a suspicion or two during the trip from London, but he hadn't cared enough to even give voice to them.

Edmund took the bag, then his mouth fell open.

"How—"

"Your wife sewed them into Miss Drummond's purse, they were discovered, and we've been working diligently to get them back to the proper owner."

"But . . . how did you know that owner was me?"

"Because that's what I do," Derrick said coolly. "In that little knickknack business I own."

Edmund looked shattered. He took a deep breath. "I hired, um, unsavory types to, ah, follow Miss Drummond."

Derrick wasn't surprised. He held up his hand to keep Edmund from saying anything else. "Oliver, send those lads on their way. I'm sure Mr. Cooke will be depositing payment into their accounts in the morning. No reason for them to hang about unnecessarily."

Edmund stared at him in surprise. "Who are you talking to?"

"None of your business," Derrick said. He looked at the man who had taken from him what he'd thought he wanted the most. "That's over with. Back to business. Have a look at those stones."

Edmund looked at them, counted them, then looked at Derrick in astonishment. "They're all here. All four dozen—but—" He gasped, then he let out his breath slowly. "They're not separated." He looked around himself frantically. "Lights!" he shouted. "Turn on the bloody houselights!"

"Edmund, Edmund," Derrick said with exaggerated concern. "Don't get so worked up about this."

"You idiot," Edmund snarled, "they're all mixed up."

Derrick frowned. "All mixed up?"

Edmund made a noise of impatience. "The regular stones with the other ones."

"What other ones?"

Edmund shot him a look of disgust. "What, you don't know this? There are thirty-six regular stones, then twelve that are magical."

Derrick would have smiled, but it was obvious to him the man in front of him was absolutely serious. "Magical?"

"Lights!" Edmund bellowed, then he took a deep breath. "One of my ancestors had these stolen from him by his son. He had them given back to him by a . . ." He looked around, then leaned closer. "By a young woman who he was convinced was a fairy. He had tried to give her twelve in gratitude for the return of the rest, but she had them delivered back to him. He was told they were covered in fairy dust, something that was certainly true given that she had sprung up from Faery through a ring in the grass."

"Oh," Derrick said, drawing the word out as long as possible to give himself time to come up with something else to say. "Interesting."

The houselights went on and Edmund rolled his eyes and stomped off to a spot where the lights were actually of some use, then started to poke at his inheritance.

Derrick leaned his head back. "Fairy dust?"

"I told Granny they were fairly dusty," Samantha said with a snort.

"Fairly dusty, fairy dusted—what's the difference?"

"Apparently a family legend," Samantha said. "And that didn't take him long, did it?"

Derrick had to agree that it hadn't. Edmund had the gems divided into two hands. He came to a stop in front of Derrick and looked at him.

"I owe you a debt I cannot repay," he said, sounding as if the words were being pulled out of him by Victorian dental pliers. "I'd like to give you one of these."

"Four," Samantha said promptly.

Edmund gaped at her. Derrick had to admit he did the same thing. But Samantha Drummond was on fire. She looked at Edmund Cooke coolly.

"We'll have four, because there were four of us involved in getting you your inheritance back. And we'll have four from the fairy dust collection." She picked up the plastic bag and held it open. "Put the regular ones in here."

He did, looking at her as if he feared she would hurt him if he didn't comply.

She zipped up the bag, then handed it back to him. "Now, pick four from the other hand."

"That's a lot of money," he managed.

"I'm sure the original fairy would consider counting the cost to be terribly gauche. You cost Derrick his career because of your cowardice. Make it up to him right now."

Derrick could only stand there and marvel at her. Had he ever wished she would just stand up for herself a bit more?

He had the feeling he might live to regret that wish.

Edmund looked, then gingerly flicked the four smallest stones away from the rest of them. Derrick supposed he would have only been surprised by anything else. Edmund looked at those four for several moments in silence, then held them out.

"Thank you."

Derrick accepted them only because Samantha elbowed him so hard in the ribs.

"It might pay your rent for a few months," Edmund added.

Derrick winced at that because Oliver's snort had almost deafened him. He saw the police coming in the side door and supposed he would be in for it now. He sighed and shoved the gems into his pocket.

"Derrick," Samantha warned.

He fished them out and handed them to her, then watched her shove all four into one of her jeans pockets.

"How is this different?" he asked with a frown.

"I checked my pockets for holes this morning." She looked over to her left. "Looks like Lydia's coming out of her little nap."

Derrick wasn't sure he cared what she had to say, so he took Samantha's hand and pulled her back out of Lydia's sights. It was interesting, however, to listen to Lydia rage with decreasing coherence at her husband. Samantha leaned close to him.

"I believe she just called me a Girl Guide. Is that sort of like a Girl Scout?"

"Hmmm," he agreed. "And isn't that interesting that she intended to sell the lace then decamp for France?"

"And that she stole the gems just out of spite," Samantha said. "I don't think she likes Edmund very much."

"In that," Derrick said frankly, "I would have to say Lydia Cooke and I fully agree." He looked at her. "What next? Bobbies or your parents?"

"I'm not sure which will be worse."

"The police will be, so let's have at your parents first. Besides, they might surprise us."

Or, perhaps not. He had known about them by reputation, of course, and by what they'd done to Samantha, but he was still surprised by how utterly annoying and condescending they were.

"Mother," Samantha said weakly, turning to look at her parents. "Father. What are you doing here?"

"We came to fetch you, of course," Louise McKinnon said crisply. "And of course your father just had to take a detour to see this rehearsal."

"I've been corresponding with Edmund since we knew you were going to stay with them," Samantha's father said with diction so crisp, he made his wife sound as if she'd had marbles in her mouth, "so I felt I should pay him a visit here." He looked down his nose at Derrick. "And who, may I ask, are you?"

Derrick looked over his shoulder to see Connor striding up the aisle. He nodded toward him. "His younger brother."

The amount of theatrical arse-kissing that then ensued made him realize that perhaps he'd gotten the better deal after all. He lasted approximately three minutes before he pulled his phone out of his ear, took Samantha by the elbow, and left the theater.

He gave the police a statement and all his pertinent information, listened to Samantha do the same, then found a bench outside the theater and sat down with her.

"We probably shouldn't hold hands," he said with a sigh.

"Probably not."

That set less well with him than he'd thought it might. He considered, then shot a text to his favorite detective inspector, letting him know the barest of details about what had happened

and asking him to have a look at the case, which would definitely keep his lads and Samantha out of it. Then he texted
Oliver.

?

Waiting on you.

I'm waiting on the parents.

Hahahahahaha.

Derrick pursed his lips and showed the conversation to
Samantha, who only looked rather green. He continued to glance
over at the door to the theater. And before he could truly digest
the madness of the day, people poured out the front door and the
press magically appeared.

"Amazing," Samantha murmured. "Feels like home."

Derrick grunted. He imagined her father attracted press as
well, whether they wanted to come or not.

He didn't move, though, even when Edmund moved close
enough that Derrick could hear him clearly. Well, he would
have heard him clearly across a stadium, but perhaps that was
beside the point.

"That man there, Derrick Cameron, has restored to me my
family's legacy. And I have a confession to make. I made a mistake many years ago and gave a part that should have gone to
him to another." He bowed his head. "I'm grieved to this day
and can only hope he'll forgive me."

"Slick," Samantha said under her breath.

Derrick looked at the crowd gathered around Edmund, then
sighed. "I'm not all that, am I?"

"Oh, I think you left people in tears four hundred years ago.
I was one of them."

He smiled. "I don't think even my brother can top that."

"Do you really care what your brother does or doesn't do?"
she asked searchingly.

He shook his head. "I don't." He looked up. "Your parents."

She muttered a very unladylike expletive with surprisingly
good diction.

He smiled at her, amused, then stood up and prepared to
greet the family again. And he ignored the fact that his brother
had come with them and was impatiently waiting to be acknowledged.

"Come along, Samantha," Louise said imperiously. "We're

going to go visit Gavin's gallery in London, then we'll decide on a brief tour of the more important sites in the UK before we go home. Your father has rehearsals."

Derrick held out his hand. Louise looked at it, then looked at him suspiciously.

"Who are you?"

He was fairly sure she'd heard him introduce himself to her husband, but perhaps she wanted to be acknowledged.

"My younger brother," Connor said loudly, before Derrick could say anything.

Louise looked at Connor and frowned. "Is he?" She looked at her husband. "Is he?"

"They certainly look quite a bit alike."

Derrick found himself on the receiving end of paternal scrutiny.

"I see," Richard Drummond said, stroking his chin thoughtfully. "Edmund made some noises about his having cost you a role."

"It was a long time ago," Derrick said with a shrug. "Water under the bridge."

"Degree?"

"Acting, from LAMDA," Samantha said. "Scholarship. Insanely good reviews."

Her father looked at her as if he weren't altogether happy that she knew that, then turned back to Derrick. "Your brother acts. Why don't you?"

"Because he can't," Connor spat.

Derrick looked at his brother and wondered for the first time why he had spared a moment's thought over him. He was a petty, jealous, little man who had never had any friends but those who didn't know him well. The rest lasted until they wearied of having him tear them down to make himself feel better.

He looked at Samantha's parents. "I am going back to London myself. If you would like, I would be happy to take Samantha so you could speak a bit longer with Edmund. I can't imagine he'll want to let you get away before he's able to tell you how flattering it is to have a couple of your reputation and stature visit his production."

Samantha's mother puffed up. Her father puffed as well, though not quite as much. He looked at Derrick.

"I suppose," he said slowly.

"I'll deliver her safely to Gavin's. Your son and I have done business together in the past and he knows me." *Just don't call him for a character reference.*

"Very well," Richard said slowly. "We have an appointment with him at seven."

"Seven it is," Derrick said cheerfully. He looked at Samantha. "Miss Drummond?"

Samantha would have said good-bye to her parents, but they had already decamped for a spot in front of the press. She walked with him away from the crowd. She perhaps would have spoken, but apparently she realized at the same time he did that they were not alone. Connor was following them like an Elizabethan London stench.

"Don't tell me you're still dogsbodying for Robert the Usurper," Connor sneered. "Can't find a better job?"

Derrick sighed. Sometimes there was just no talking to people.

"And how desperate is that girl there—"

Derrick stopped and looked at him. "Shut your mouth right there, Connor," he said coldly, and in Gaelic. "If you say one more thing, I promise you, you'll regret it."

"You wouldn't dare."

"Oh, he would," Samantha said cheerfully, also in Gaelic. "And if you don't want him to kick your arse six ways to Sunday, I'd suggest you, well, I don't want to be impolite." She took Derrick's arm. "Come on, Derrick. You can drive the car this time."

"What car?" Connor shouted after them. "Some rental Ford?"

"Just keep walking," Samantha said firmly. "Don't look back."

"I want to hurt him," Derrick said distinctly.

"No, you don't. You want to spend many years out of jail driving your car and sitting in front of your house and enjoying the money from the sale of your gem."

"A fairy breathed on it and made it magical. I can't sell it now."

She looked up at him, laughed, then pulled him along.

"And why didn't you tell me you spoke Gaelic?"

"A girl needs her secrets. Walk faster. Your brother is following."

He didn't imagine he would make it all the way to the car park without some sort of confrontation. It made him feel slightly better to have Oliver almost run over his brother as he jaywalked across the street. And if Oliver had left his hand on the horn a bit longer than necessary to alert everyone in the area to the indignity, Derrick wasn't going to complain. He stopped in front of the passenger's side of the car and waited until he heard his brother come huffing and puffing up. Connor looked down his nose.

"This isn't yours."

Derrick clicked the lock, opened the door, then saw Samantha inside. He closed the door, walked around the back of the car and got in under the wheel. He started it up, let the engine idle for a moment or two, then backed out of the stall without looking at his brother.

"He looks like he'd like to throw up," Samantha remarked.

"Did you take a picture with my phone?"

"I thought I should."

"Did he see you?"

"Well, of course. What good would it have been otherwise?"

He paused, leaned over and kissed her, then smiled into her eyes. "You are a wonder."

"And you have a forgiving heart."

"Well, that's debatable. Will you text Oliver for me and see what he's up to?"

She did, then laughed a little now and then. "He says he's on his way home, assumes you've tidied up the scene of the crime, and wonders if the reservation at the Ritz is still good or if he should stop at Marks and Spencer for something prepackaged."

"Tell him thank you, that we have a few fairied gems to split up, and no, I'm not paying for his dinner. I'll call him when we hit London. He loves art galleries and Peter could do terrible things to your brother's computer system."

"Sounds promising." She laughed a bit more, then set his phone down and looked at him. "Do you want to come with me to Gavin's?"

"I wouldn't miss it. I need to go fetch something out of the flat."

"What?"

"Your drawing of the sea."

"Where is it?"

"In my bedroom, lass," he said seriously. "Where I had intended to look at it every day."

She was silent for so long, he had to look at her. A single tear rolled down her cheek. "I can draw you another," she whispered.

He only reached for her hand.

And he held it the rest of the way back to the city.

The brief foray into Gavin Drummond's gallery was less satisfying than he would have hoped. Gavin was absolutely gobsmacked by Samantha's sketch of the view in front of his house—submitted anonymously for inspection, of course— wanted to know where Derrick had gotten it, and demanded that since he dealt in art and Derrick didn't that he be given the artist's number. He also demanded the piece so he could sell it. Derrick didn't want to let it go, but the chance to give Samantha a start in something she loved was too powerful to refuse.

And just as he knew when a good deal was about to go sour, he knew that she was going to go off with her parents and there wasn't a damned thing he could do about it. He managed to get her off into a corner by herself whilst her parents and brother were otherwise occupied. And once he had her there, all he could do was look at her.

"Aren't you going to tell me not to go?" she asked quietly.

He took a deep breath. "I'm not sure this is my day to boss you."

She looked slightly shattered. "I see."

He reached out and pulled her against him, then held her as fiercely as he dared.

"I want you, Samantha Drummond, to make up your own mind," he whispered against her ear. He had to take several decent breaths before he could pull back only as far as was required to be able to look at her. "And while I'm not an advocate of ruining relationships, I can't take away from you what you need to gain by drawing the line for your parents yourself."

Her mouth fell open.

He realized his was hanging open as well.

"Where did *that* come from?" she asked.

"I have no idea."

"You sound so reasonable and grown up."

He started to defend himself when he realized she was teasing him. "Trust me, it's like a fever. It'll be gone soon enough and I'll be back to my world-weary, unpleasant self."

She threw her arms around his neck and held on to him tightly. She held on to him even though harrumphing had started up over in the direction of her parents. She lasted much longer than he'd expected she would. She sank back to her heels and looked at him.

"I need to go."

He nodded, because he couldn't say anything.

She kissed him, a fleeting kiss he scarce felt, then she turned and walked across the room.

Derrick walked out of the gallery and went home. Because he could do nothing else.

He got up the next day, showered, went downstairs and made himself coffee, then found his keys and walked to the door. Because that's just what he did.

There was an envelope that had come through the mail slot. His first instinct was to call a bomb squad, but he rolled his eyes instead and picked it up. His name was on the front, which was somewhat reassuring. He opened it, then pulled out the single sheaf of paper.

All the Things I Like About Derrick Cameron.

He looked off into his salon, then decided that he should save something for a reward after he managed to get through the day. He returned the page to its spot inside the envelope, shoved the envelope into the back pocket of his jeans, then left his apartment and caught a cab to his office. His phone rang. He looked down, then sighed, but answered anyway.

"Interesting, that a piece of Victorian embroidery turned up here in my office," said a familiar voice.

"Yes, Detective Inspector Avery," Derrick said politely, "I imagine it was."

"Don't suppose you would have any idea where it came from."

"Did it find itself back in the proper hands?"

"Happily, it did."

"Then I would have to say that I can't remember anything about it."

"Why did I know you would say that?"

"Because you know there might be other times when I might say something else entirely and hope springs eternal?"

"I suppose so." Avery cleared his throat. "Stop sweeping for speed cameras on your long drives, Derrick. You're about to bankrupt us."

Derrick smiled, then rang off and continued on his way.

He wandered into his office half an hour later, cursing traffic under his breath and considering cursing other things quite audibly. He paused, then took stock of the situation.

Oliver was passed out in the middle of his rug, looking fairly dead. Peter was staring off into the distance as if he considered things he shouldn't, a glass of some sort of green sludge in one hand. Sunny's doing, no doubt. Rufus was happily buried in the *Financial Times*, but he at least looked up and winked.

"Cousin?"

Derrick looked over to see Cameron standing at his door. "Aye?"

Cameron opened the door fully and nodded for Derrick to come in. Derrick did because Cameron was his laird and he liked to make the odd display of obedience now and again.

"Well?"

"Well, what?" Derrick asked.

"You aren't just going to let her go, are you?"

"Why is everyone so interested in my love life?" Derrick asked crossly.

"Because I like her. She's just the breath of fresh air you need."

"I don't need any fresh air."

"Derrick, my lad, you need a woman who doesn't care about what you own. And Samantha doesn't care. Does she have *any* idea what you have in the bank?"

"Of course not. But she covets my Vanquish."

"I never said she wasn't a bright girl, just not a greedy one. As for anything else, I'm not sure what else you want."

Derrick leaned back against the door. "I want her to have time. I might be the first bloke she's ever kissed."

"And this is a bad thing?"

"What if she's not content?" Derrick asked, though the words were almost more than he could spit out.

Cameron looked at him seriously. "Derrick, I didn't know your mother, but if I might make a comparison, she sounds as if she was every bit like mine." He paused. "There are some people, men and women both, who will never be happy, no matter in what circumstances they find themselves. There is not enough money, no castle grand enough, no life easy enough to content them."

" 'My crown is called content; a crown it is that seldom kings enjoy,' " Derrick said with a sigh.

"Exactly."

"But Sunny's content," Derrick said slowly.

"In Scotland, in London, walking the floor with a lad who thinks naps should be limited to a quarter hour a day," Cameron agreed. "If you want my suggestion, give your Samantha time, but give her a chance."

Derrick sighed.

"I think she might surprise you. Oh, I have something for you."

Derrick accepted the package, opened it, then looked at the mounted colored pencil sketch in his hands.

It was the drawing of Samantha's that he had given to Gavin the night before, the drawing of his shore.

He looked at his cousin. "How much did you pay for this?"

"Five thousand, but that was a special price for me because of our long personal history with Gavin Drummond. He promised me that when he got his hands on more by this artist, the price would go up sharply."

"His head will explode when he learns whose art he's selling."

"I'd suggest keeping it quiet then, until he's well and truly hooked on the commissions this mysterious Scottish artist is bringing him. Apparently he hasn't figured out who *Sam* is, though perhaps he thinks it's the artist's initials and not her name."

Derrick smiled. "She'll be pleased with both things."

"I forced him to allow me to set up an account for her. The money's waiting when she wants it."

"Good of you."

"He's an untrustworthy whoreson, but there you have it." He studied Derrick. "What are you going to do now?"

Derrick considered all the things he could do. He could go back into his office, nudge Oliver awake, and get back to business. He could go home, bury himself in his salon, and read fiction until he was numb.

Or he could take a chance on something that was so spectacularly wonderful, he hardly dared hope that it might be within his grasp. He looked at his cousin.

"I'm going back to the flat to hang up my gift. Thank you."

Cameron smiled. "Then what?"

Derrick got up and walked to the door. He looked back at his cousin briefly.

"I'm going to go make a list for someone I love."

Chapter 29

Samantha stood at the French doors of her room that opened onto a balcony that overlooked the lake in front of her and made a list of things that had happened to her recently. It was, after all, one of the things that she did best. It was in no particular order, just things that came to her as she stared out over scenery that apparently artists had been making tracks to see for decades.

First on the list was that she had insisted that she was simply too old to have to sleep on a cot in her parents' hotel room. If they could afford a room facing the lake, then so could she. She had paid for it with her own money, which had seemed like a reasonable thing to do. She had been there for a week, staring out the window, spending vast amounts of time on various benches, sketching. It had been glorious.

Having her own room had also given her the chance to unpack in privacy. She had been extremely relieved to find there had been nothing added to her suitcase. It was just the clothes Emily had bought for her, clothes Samantha was utterly convinced Derrick would get billed for. She hoped he didn't mind.

Her bag, however, had not been similarly free of interlopers. She supposed she shouldn't have been surprised given the fact that Derrick had a cadre of snoops and procurers of the impossible, but a bright, shiny new cell phone had been in her purse, already loaded with a list of numbers she might like to use in the future. Derrick's had been first, but she assumed that was just because he was first alphabetically. Her phone's wallpaper had been a shot of the sea from his house on the coast. She knew that because she could have drawn that view from memory. She *had* drawn it from memory, as it happened.

It haunted her dreams, actually.

Second on her list was that she had decided that perhaps she could occasionally be a textile historian. If absolutely necessary. If it were required by someone who might, if necessary, call upon her for her services. If that someone was a Scot who might want to decorate his empty house with the odd, historically significant piece of cloth. Or need company on an adventure to perhaps a safer time period, like Regency England or a duller part of Victoria's reign.

Third on that list was the fact that she didn't really want to date anyone. She wanted to just meet a certain someone in a parish church, take her vows, and get on with her life.

A life that she had no intention of living under her parents' thumbs any longer.

Fourth was the fact that there was a rather substantial manila envelope sitting on her bed, an envelope that had been delivered half an hour earlier with only her name scrawled on the front of it.

She contemplated the view in front of her for a bit longer, then decided that there was nothing to be done but actually go and see what was in that envelope and who had sent it. She was fairly sure it wasn't from Lydia Cooke, who was now safely wrapped up in a straightjacket, or her husband, who was still spending as much time in front of cameras as possible, apologizing for his sins, or Connor Cameron, who she imagined was polishing the handlebars of his bicycle—which was likely the only mode of transportation he could afford—and cursing his brother.

She was fairly sure of all those things because her name had been written on that envelope in Derrick's hand.

She sat down on the edge of the bed, opened the envelope,

then spilled everything out onto the coverlet. There was a set of keys, a handful of photographs that looked as if they'd been cut straight from books they should have remained attached to, and what turned out to be a sketchbook bound in leather, but bound in a way that it would lie flat when being used.

She looked at the keys. They were a mystery she would have to solve in a minute. She settled more comfortably on the bed and reached for the pages. They were attached with a binder clip that she removed so she could get a better handle on what they were. On the first, printed in very bold letters, was the following:

A List of Important Sights for Artists Who Have Just Earned a Great Whacking Check Selling Their First Piece.

She set that page aside and saw there in black and white a check for £3,250, made out to her. Next was a letter from Robert Cameron explaining to her that the check had been cut from an account he'd set up in her name. The original funds had come from Gavin who had sold her painting to a very interested buyer. He apologized for having to pay a gallery fee but offered to continue to act as her broker with her brother for as long as she wanted to keep her identity secret. He suggested that perhaps she might want to keep that up until Gavin had sold enough of her art that he would feel an arse if he refused to sell her work simply because she was his sister. Samantha heartily agreed. She set the letter aside.

Next was a list of sights not to be missed, with the aforementioned pilfered pages offered as exhibits and mini-maps. She flipped through them slowly and noticed that they seemed to be leading her in a particular direction. A particularly northerly direction.

That left her a little breathless, actually.

She sat there for a moment or two, then looked at the clock. It was barely ten. It might take her a couple of days to get herself to that final X on the map she realized was the last page, but that wouldn't happen if she didn't get an early start and go find a car to rent.

She made a decision and decided there was no time like the present to implement it. She put everything back in the envelope, pocketed the keys, then quickly packed everything into her suitcase. Then she walked out onto the veranda, locking her room behind her.

Her father was sitting at a table, obviously going over some script or other. She didn't care, honestly. He would be, she had to admit, brilliant in whatever he chose to do. She might even come see him, if she had the time and money to cross the Pond.

He looked up as she approached and actually smiled. "Samantha."

"Father." She sat down in a chair at his little bistro table. "Interesting script?"

"I've read better, but one does what one must when the director is tempting." He set it aside and looked at her. "What about you?"

She was fairly sure that was the first time in her life he had ever asked her what she was up to.

"Someone sent me a list of sights to see. I thought I might like to go see them."

Richard considered her for several minutes in silence. "I had an email from someone earlier this week. Actually, more than one, if memory serves."

"From whom?" she asked in surprise.

"Derrick Cameron."

"Oh," she said faintly. "What did he say?"

"He sent me something from his accountant."

She blinked. "He has an accountant?"

"He definitely needs one." Her father looked at her shrewdly. "You have no idea what he's worth, do you?"

"I don't care."

"Well, he obviously thinks your father might care."

"I can't imagine why."

"I imagine that will occur to you in time. You're an exceptionally bright young woman."

She hoped he would mistake the color crawling up her cheeks for something she'd eaten for breakfast that maybe she shouldn't have. "What else?"

"Oh, just something from his attorney, a few character references from other people, and a couple of reviews from his LAMDA days." He shrugged. "I believe they were get-to-know-you things."

"And what did you send him back?"

"Oh, nothing yet. I'm working on what would be appropriate. I'm not sure I'll have any say in it, actually."

"In what?"

He only smiled.

"Cryptic."

"So it is, and here comes your mother." He looked at her quickly. "Don't you dare cave, Samantha."

She blinked. "Cave?"

He reached out and covered her hand with his. "I'm sorry I didn't help you out of the nest sooner. Consider this penance—ah, Louise, here you are."

"And here *you* are," Louise said, sounding extremely put out. "Really, Samantha, trying to find you this week has been a study in frustration. I have things for you to catalogue for me before I send them off back to the States."

Samantha had a look from her father that she had no trouble interpreting. If the time was ever to be, it had to be then. She stood up, took her mother's hands, then kissed her on both cheeks. Her mother recoiled as if she'd been bitten.

"What are you doing?"

Samantha only smiled, then leaned over to kiss her father's cheek. He smiled up at her.

"Have a lovely drive, Sam."

"I think I will."

"Well, you've certainly had enough practice over the years, haven't you?"

She smiled. "I'll call you when I decide what I'm doing."

"What?" her mother screeched. "What are you talking about, you silly child?"

Samantha turned away, then stopped. She turned back to her mother. "Thank you," she said quietly. "You've given me a love for old things. I think that will serve me well in the future."

Her mother started babbling. Samantha shot her father a meaningful look, then walked away before Vesuvius erupted.

She went back inside her room, grabbed her suitcase, her bag, and Derrick's envelope, then hurried to the front desk. She was somehow unsurprised to find she'd already been checked out and her car was just out the back doors, ready for a hasty getaway. She nodded over it all, then froze and looked at the manager.

"My car?" she echoed.

The manager took her suitcase for her and ushered her out the door. And there, underneath the portico was a 1967 MG, mint condition, wire wheels, and painted a lovely British racing green.

She caught her breath. Then she looked around quickly.

Those Cameron Antiquities, Ltd., lads could be, as Oliver would freely admit, ghosts when the situation warranted.

She looked at the manager. "Who brought this?"

"I don't have any idea," he said, looking faintly unsettled. "It was just here, your room was paid for, and the charge returned to your card." He shrugged. "I don't remember doing any of it." He looked at her. "Do you have any idea?"

"I do," she said with a smile.

He waited, but she didn't think it was prudent to enlighten him. So she plunked her suitcase in the trunk that indeed opened with one of the keys on her ring, then got in under the wheel and simply took a deep breath. The top was down, the day was glorious, and she would have wept if she hadn't been so tempted to laugh.

So she laughed instead.

There was a Garmin taped to a ruin-resistant part of the dash with a note telling her to turn it on. She did and the navigation system began.

Very high-tech, but she supposed she shouldn't have expected anything else.

She pulled away from the hotel, almost convinced she could hear her mother still shrieking. But she wasn't going to stick around and find out for sure.

Three days later, she drove through the village near Derrick's seaside house, then turned along the road she knew led out to the sea. She'd turned off the navigation program an hour ago, because to her surprise, she knew the way.

She pulled up next to a well-used Range Rover, turned the car off, then leaned her head back against the seat and enjoyed the late afternoon sunshine for a moment or two.

She supposed she could have hurried on her way north, but she'd decided not to. She had sketched, entertained deep thoughts, and relished every moment of knowing there was a man in the world who thought enough about her to give her that sort of journey.

She got out of the car, tossed the keys on the driver's seat, then walked around Derrick's lesser beast to see what she might find.

Derrick was sitting on one of their rocks, staring out over the sea. He didn't move, which she had expected. If he hadn't had a bug in her car tracking her every step of the way, she would have been surprised. Because, after all, there had been several things along the way—people in the right places, freshly charged batteries for her phone and navigation system waiting in odd places, flowers magically being delivered by small children while she was sketching—that had given her the idea he was involved in some kind of super-private spy network somewhere.

She sat down on the rock next to him and looked out over the sea for a few minutes before she came up with just the right words.

"So," she said slowly, "is this how it's going to be?"

He looked over at her and smiled. "How is that?"

"You sending me messages and waiting for me to come running?"

He scooted over and patted the spot next to him. "Didn't check your rearview mirror all that often, did you?"

She laughed a little. "I didn't. I was too busy being dazzled by the scenery."

"Lass, you need a security detail."

"I'm beginning to think I had one."

He only smiled.

"How'd you get here first?"

"Aston Martin Vanquish, love. It goes faster than your car by quite a bit. And I had Peter sweeping for bobbies for me, which you did not."

She moved to sit next to him. "Did you loan me that MG on purpose so I couldn't go as fast as you?"

"Nay, I *bought* you that MG because a learner's sticker doesn't look quite as silly on that sort of car as it would on mine."

She froze. "You bought me a car?"

He looked at her seriously. "I thought you might need one to get around in."

"Awfully generous of you."

He shrugged, but it didn't look all that casual. "Again, sparing myself the embarrassment of an L sticker on mine." He continued to look at her gravely. "Self-serving, as always."

She looked out over the sea that rolled in endlessly against the shore. It wasn't that she hadn't seen the sea before. There was just something about that sea when it found itself running up against a Scottish shore that gave it a certain cachet. Or that might have had something to do with the man sitting next to her. She considered the ramifications of that gift she'd just been given—and the keychain that said *I'm Scottish* on the front and *You'd better not kiss me or my husband will kill you* on the back, then looked at Derrick.

"Am I going to be staying long enough to get a UK driver's license?"

"I don't know," he said carefully. "Are you?"

She lifted an eyebrow. "That, good sir, does not sound anything like a proposal of, well, anything. And I want to know why you made me drive all the way up here instead of you coming down to get me."

He took her hand, brought it to his mouth, and kissed it. Then he looked at her seriously. "Because, my dearest Samantha, I wanted you to have a damned long time to think about where you were coming and have an equal number of times to change your mind."

She frowned. "Are you bossing me again?"

"Once I get the ring on your finger, I thought I might try."

"Every other day."

"Well, aye, I suppose I'll be limited to that."

"Still not much of a proposal."

"Then how about this?" He knelt down right there on the uncomfortable pebbles in front of her. "Would you like to take driving lessons and get your UK license?"

She pursed her lips. "Am I going to need it?"

"Our children might be happy if you could drive them to school. Which you won't be doing in that death trap, by the way. I'll buy you something safer tomorrow."

She considered. "We're not sending our kids to boarding school, are we?"

"Hell, no."

"Aren't you getting ahead of yourself?"

He pulled something out of his pocket and held it up. "Would this bridge the gap, do you think?"

She laughed a little. "You just can't bring yourself to ask the question, can you?"

"I checked my pockets for holes."

"Well, there is that."

"As for the other, I'm not afraid."

"Of course you aren't," she said dryly.

He paused, then took a deep breath. Then he looked at her, the single most unsure expression she had ever seen on his face.

"Samantha Josephine Drummond," he said slowly, "will you marry me?"

"How did you know my middle—never mind." There was no point in asking that question. The man knew because he had the ability to hack into things she didn't want to think about. She smiled. "Yes, I will."

He put the ring onto her finger, looked at it for a moment or two, then bent his head and kissed her hand. Then he looked at her. "Thank you," he said quietly.

"Are you kidding?" she said. "I'm getting the good end of the deal. A great car and an empty house."

"It's not entirely empty."

"Are you going to show me?"

"In a minute." He stood up and pulled her up to her feet. "After I've said hello."

It was indeed several minutes later that she was walking into his front door with him, his ring on her finger, and his arm around her shoulders. Once they were inside, she turned and put her arms around him.

"Still looks pretty empty to me."

"You haven't looked over the fireplace." He tilted his head in that direction. "Go have a look."

She hesitated, then released him and walked into the other room. She stopped in front of the fireplace and stared at what was hanging over the mantel.

The picture she had given him.

She looked up at him as he came to stand next to her. "I thought Gavin sold this."

"He did. To Cameron, as it happens."

She smiled. "And he gave it to you?"

"Housewarming gift."

"Very generous."

"He wants you to do something for him."

She felt a little faint. "Can life improve?"

He clasped his hands behind his back. "That depends on what you think of maybe spending a fortnight or two at Stratford starting later this month."

She blinked, then felt her mouth fall open. "I don't know. Do I get good seats?"

He smiled uneasily. "You tell me where you want to sit and I'll see what I can do."

"Are you going to give me details?"

He shook his head. "I thought I would just turn you loose with your sketchbook. You should see Anne Hathaway's house. Not to be missed."

"You said that before."

"You didn't get to go look."

"What are *you* doing at Stratford?"

He took a deep breath. "A brief run of *Hamlet*."

She laughed and threw her arms around his neck. She hugged him tightly, then pulled back and looked at him. "Who's directing?"

"Edmund Cooke."

"Finally," she said. She considered then looked at him. "Are you happy about this?"

He shrugged. "I've worked for worse." He smiled down at her. "You should ask me about the cast."

"Should I?"

"Claudius is an actor of particularly important stature."

She fought her smile. "You're not going to tell me that Sir Richard Drummond is making an appearance."

"He has volunteered to play the ghost," Derrick admitted, "when last he visited me in the flat in London. But nay, it isn't him."

She considered, then felt her mouth fall open. "My father?"

He nodded.

"You're kidding."

"I never kid about future fathers-in-law."

She pulled away, walked around the room, then came to a stop in front of him. "Wow."

He shoved his hands in his pockets and looked at her carefully. "Why *wow*?"

"*Wow* because my father just gave up Hamlet and settled for Claudius," she said. "I don't think he would have done that for Sir Laurence himself."

He didn't move. "And is that a good thing as far as you're concerned?"

She walked over to him and put her arms around his waist. She waited until she felt his arms come around her before she leaned up and kissed him.

"Personally, I couldn't care less," she murmured against his mouth. "I love you because you're just Derrick William Cameron—"

"Who told you my middle name?" he interrupted, smiling.

"The guy who schlepped my luggage inside that delightful bed-and-breakfast on Day Two of the great journey north. He thought I should know."

Derrick smiled. "I think you have a tale or two to tell, but I want to hear more about the other first. You were saying that you loved me . . ."

"Yes, not that I've heard the same from y—"

And that was as far as she got for a bit. She wasn't sure if he was rewarding her for not caring that her father had not only agreed to be in a play with him but had exerted absolutely no influence on the selection of Hamlet himself—which she was sure Derrick would appreciate later—or if he had missed her, or if he just loved her.

"I missed you," he said simply. "And I love you."

She looked at him blearily. "Was I talking out loud?"

He laughed a little. "You were distracted."

"You have that effect on me."

He pulled her close, wrapped his arms around her, and held her tightly.

"Marry me," he whispered against her ear. "Please."

"Yes. When?"

"You decide."

"After *Hamlet*," she said without hesitation. "I don't want to be distracted by you while I'm watching you."

"When I figure out what that means, I'm sure I'll agree," he said dryly. "Your aunt Mary left you a wedding dress back at the keep."

She turned her head and rested her cheek against his

shoulder. "She's got to stop poaching things from the past. She's going to get herself in big trouble."

"It's actually from the present. She jetted over to Paris with Emily earlier in the week. Actually, they brought you samples so you could decide what you wanted."

"My mother will have a fit."

"Probably," he agreed, "but your father thoroughly approves. He signed off on an entire trousseau and not a damned thing in it will be polyester."

She pulled back and looked at him seriously. "I was too nice to them, probably."

He shook his head. "It says a great deal about you, doesn't it? I believe *I Like That You're Kind to People Who Don't Deserve It* was number ten on that list I made you, wasn't it?"

She took a deep breath. "It was. It was number eleven on yours, wasn't it?"

"Wonder why I got bumped like that?" he asked innocently.

"Because number ten had to do with your being lovely to old women who do deserve it." She smiled. "I'm not very original, but it was heartfelt."

"I think you're remarkably original and I love your lists. Let's go buy a round for the lads, then we'll make a list of all the lovely things they say about you. Then we'll go home."

"Home?"

He smiled. "We'll figure that out, too."

She let him take her hand, but she didn't move. He stopped and looked at her in surprise. "What?"

"One condition."

He studied her thoughtfully. "You get two days' bossing to my one?"

"It's about time traveling."

"Nay, I will not take you to Elizabethan England for our honeymoon."

"I think I'm serious," she said, finding that she was very serious indeed. "I don't want to tell you what to do, but—"

He shook his head before she could finish. "I've already hung up my skates, as it were, and Oliver and Peter have already paid a social call to the laird down the way. I don't think he'll lack for company."

She let out the breath she'd been holding. "Thank you."

He slid her a look. "Don't want to change your mind and give me my freedom?"

"Derrick?"

"Aye, love."

"Go to—" She took a deep breath. "You know the rest."

He laughed, pulled her into his arms, then swung her around a couple of times before he set her on her feet, kissed her soundly, then pulled her toward the door. "Let's go, then we'll figure out when to marry, then where we'll live."

"Do you mind?" she asked. "Letting Jamie go on his jaunts without you?"

He ushered her out the door, then pulled it shut and locked it behind them. Then he looked at her and his expression was suddenly serious.

"It is an activity for a single man," he said, "or a laird who can't seem to find any extreme sport mad enough to satisfy his need for massive adrenaline rushes. I think I can safely say that James MacLeod will never find himself in need of a rescue, but he was born in a different time and has a different skill set than most men. And a wife who sighs a lot and knows he'll be home for dinner, eventually. Actually, I think he just does it to provide her with authentic period details for her novels, but I'll deny it if you repeat that."

She smiled. "Then what will you do?"

"I don't know. What will *you* do?"

"Paint your view."

"Paint *our* view."

"Yes," she said happily. "Our view."

He kissed her for her trouble, then took her hand and walked over to her car. He opened the driver's side, helped her in, then walked around and got in on the passenger side. He pulled out his phone, sent a text, then leaned back and smiled.

"Lots of legroom," he said contentedly.

"Who'd you text?"

"Oliver, to come get the Rover."

"Does he have a key?"

"He doesn't need one, unfortunately."

"Interesting skill."

"He can pick any lock invented," Derrick said with a smile. "It might serve him in good stead one of these days. Richard

Drummond, *Sir* Richard Drummond, was certainly grateful for that several hundred years ago."

"No one would believe it," she said. "I can hardly believe it and I was there. I wish I'd had pictures of that bedroom."

"Oliver took some."

"Well, he did have a camera."

"Bragging rights," Derrick agreed.

She would have to get copies, because there were bed hangings that she had wanted to examine more closely but had never had the chance. She sighed. Perhaps she was never going to get history out of her blood, but perhaps now it didn't matter as much.

She backed out of her slot next to the house, turned around, then headed toward the village. She looked down at the ring on her finger briefly—it was rather hard to miss, actually—then at Derrick. He was simply watching her, a small smile on his face.

"What?" she asked.

"Thank you for saying yes."

"Like I would have said no."

He lifted one shoulder in a half shrug. "You might have."

"Come on, didn't you do more research than that?"

He took her hand, kissed it, then put it back on the wheel. "You give me too much credit. That's why I was pacing like a caged animal for the past two hours wondering if you would change your mind at the last minute and drive somewhere else. The fact that you didn't hurry led to my anguish."

She smiled. "Had to keep you guessing somehow."

"Heaven help me."

She laughed a little because she was happy for him, happy for herself, and their lives were stretching out in front of them with treasures to be found and procured. So many good things already in their lives and so many wonderful things to look forward to.

She could hardly wait to make a list.

Epilogue

Derrick paced along the hallway on the bottom level of his flat, from the front door to the kitchen and back again. Nervousness wasn't in his nature, not truly, but then again, this was something big. Very big. Very important to someone he loved very much.

He heard her coming just as he'd touched the door again. He turned and watched as his wife came down the stairs. It should have been less gobsmacking than it was, that sight. He'd been married to her for six months, after all, and should have been accustomed enough to the sight of her.

Fresh-faced Yank that she was, a girl who had to spend a certain amount of time in Scotland every fortnight or she began to wilt.

He wasn't sure he was equal to telling her just how much he loved her.

So he decided he would take matters into his own hands and show her—

He ran into her hand as she stood on the bottom step.

"Not on your life."

He frowned. "I was just going to kiss you."

"No, you weren't just going to kiss me and, no, you can't hug me, either. You'll wrinkle my suit."

"It could be put back on the hanger temporarily."

She blew her hair out of her eyes. "Derrick, really. I'm close to throwing up."

"That's why I'm here to distract you," he said. He smiled pleasantly. "Altruistic, as usual."

"Self-serving, as usual," she said, but she smiled as she said it. "If I get through this evening without puking all over his gallery floor, then we'll talk. Right now, I just need to go get this over with."

"All right," he said with a sigh. He pulled his earbud out of his pocket, taped a mic to his cheek, then leaned forward and carefully kissed her on the cheek before he turned his phone on.

"Got you," Oliver said.

"Here as well," Peter said. "Rufus in front in three."

Derrick looked at Samantha to find she was gaping at him. "What?" he asked in surprise.

"Are you taking the lads with us?"

"Of course. Where's the sport otherwise?"

"Sport," she said, with hardly any sound to her voice. *"Sport?"*

"Samantha, my love, you're about to go to a gallery opening featuring your art. Your brother has knelt in front of you and begged you to give him exclusive rights to sell your paintings and we forced him to reduce his fee to an obscenely low ten percent. I'm in a suit. What more do you want?"

"What are Oliver and Peter planning on doing?" she wheezed.

"Making sure no one fingers anything hanging on the wall and taking copious notes of all the compliments heaped upon your lovely head. What else?"

"Laxatives in Gavin's foie gras?"

"Caught that," Oliver said. "Brilliant idea."

Derrick smiled. "I'm sure they'll be on their best behavior. You look lovely. I imagine Rufus is outside."

She stopped him with her hand on his arm. "Do I really look okay?"

"Lovely," Oliver chimed in.

"Gorgeous," Peter agreed.

"Shut up, the both of you," Derrick suggested. He looked at Samantha. "You're stunning and your carriage awaits. Shall we?"

She took a deep breath, took his arm, then nodded. He locked up behind them, then opened the door for her to get in the back of Cameron's black Mercedes. Rufus congratulated her on her upcoming success, then got them out into traffic with a minimum of fuss.

Derrick held her hand, then shifted so he could look at her. She was still looking a little green, but he supposed that couldn't be helped. He took her hand in both his own, then stroked the back of it because he knew it soothed her. Heaven knew it as the least he could do in return for all the ways she'd run interference for him over the past seven months, though he would have done it anyway simply because he loved her.

They had spent the month they'd been engaged in Stratford in a large manor house with several bedrooms. He'd tried to send Oliver and Peter off to actually do some business, but they'd insisted they needed to lounge about uselessly on the off chance that some theretofore undiscovered ruffian appeared and tried to vex Samantha. Him, they cared much less about. He had apparently been all on his own.

Well, all on his own except for his future father-in-law, who had seemingly been delighted to accept an invitation to take up residence in one of the bedrooms—the one between Derrick's and Samantha's, as it happened—an invitation Derrick couldn't quite remember having extended.

It had been surprisingly pleasant. He had offered Richard the keys to the Vanquish, Richard had complimented him on his performance during rehearsals, and father and daughter had occasionally gone for long walks together. Derrick had happily accepted the occasional invitation to come along. He supposed he shouldn't have been surprised that perhaps it had been Louise McKinnon to be the fly in the soup. Samantha had come to terms with that without fuss, but she had seemingly enjoyed her time with her father who had accepted a sketch of the original Globe—looking particularly authentic, it had to be noted—with a brisk nod and a rough clearing of his throat. Relationship healed.

And when it came to him, Samantha had been ferociously

protective. She had more often than not been the one to poach his earpiece and mic and work out with Oliver and Peter peace and quiet for him to rehearse. It had been a novel sensation, that of being looked after for a change. And she had sat through every one of his performances with tears streaming down her face.

They had married quietly in the village chapel the week after the show closed, with only his family and hers in attendance. Well, he supposed he counted the lads and the MacLeods in his family and she counted Gideon and Megan de Piaget, her great-aunt Mary, and her father in hers.

Cameron had thrown an enormous party for them at the keep, then done them the very great favor of taking his family and camping in Derrick's boyhood home for a few nights, leaving them the castle itself.

Because he was a Cameron himself, after all.

He had thanked his laird very kindly for the concession a couple of days later, then taken his bride and gotten on with their lives.

Well, they'd spent a month backpacking through the Continent, looking at old things and famous art, but perhaps that was beside the point. Samantha wanted to be in Scotland when they weren't in London and he had loved her for it.

And so they had set up shop in his flat until they could find something more suitable, he had gone back to work, and she had gotten to arting—along, of course, with agreeing to dispense her expertise in antique textiles. She had been given her own earphone and mic and proved to be very adept at distracting buyers with discussions of how best to display their new treasure whilst secretaries wrote out eye-watering cheques to Cameron Antiquities, Ltd.

The other half of their life they spent in Scotland in the house by the sea that had slowly accumulated first the necessities, then the comforts. Samantha's flawless Gaelic had helped pave her way into the hearts of the villagers, along with periodic visits by her father, who had apparently over the years taken very seriously his own Scottish roots and the need to keep the mother tongue alive. Derrick supposed what had cemented things for them had been a visit from Samantha's mother who had swept in like a banshee, offended everyone within earshot, then swept back out again, trailing shards of sharp things in her wake. Perhaps pity wasn't such a bad thing after all.

"And here we are," Rufus said brightly. "Ah, and someone to come get the door." He looked at Samantha in the rearview mirror. "Break a leg, ducks."

She smiled sickly and thanked him. Derrick got out first, then held down his hand to help her out. He put his arm around her shoulders very carefully so as not to muss either her suit or her hair, then took her hand and kissed it.

"Surviving?"

"I've been popping those antinausea things Sunny gave me all day and they're just not working." She looked up. "This isn't just morning sickness, this is terror."

"What do you have to be afraid of?" he asked.

She took a deep breath. "I don't want to make a fool of myself."

He shook his head. "Sam, whilst I think your brother is a git of the first water, I must admit that he has an uncanny knack for spotting talent, either in this century or those gone by. Would it ease you any to know I never go after paintings when he's anywhere in the area?"

"You've already told me that," she said, sounding rather ill. "Five times today."

"There was six. He knows talent when he sees it, damn him anyway. He had no idea until yesterday that you were the artist. If he'd thought you had no talent, he wouldn't have insisted on the show in the first place. If learning the artist was his sister had made him uneasy, he would have canceled the show without a second's hesitation."

She looked up at him. "Think so?"

"I know so," Derrick said with feeling. "I've watched him do it before. He once called off a deal as the cheque was being smoothed out in preparation for the signature. He's ruthless."

"And I'm only giving him ten percent?"

"Aye," Derrick said with satisfaction. "Which he agreed to almost without clenching his fists."

He offered her his arm, then led her to the gallery doors that opened to reveal her brother standing there, looking extremely relieved.

"I was almost afraid you wouldn't come," he said.

"Really?" she asked in surprise. "Why not?"

"Better offer," he said sourly, shooting Derrick a glare. He held open the door and allowed her to proceed inside.

Derrick found himself almost running into Gavin's forearm.

"You ruthless . . ." Gavin seemed to be struggling to find just the right insult.

Derrick only smiled, ducked under his arm, and walked into the gallery. He patted Gavin on the shoulder when the man caught up to him, then elbowed him out of the way so he could get to the guest of honor. Derrick exchanged a brief glance with his wife, lifted an eyebrow, then watched her walk onstage, as it were.

She was marvelous.

After a pair of hours spent either trailing discreetly behind her or positioning himself near important people to listen to their praise, he found himself sitting on a bench, flanked by Oliver and Peter.

"What'd we ever do without her?" Peter said with a sigh.

"Don't know," Oliver answered. "She's a right proper lad, isn't she?"

Derrick scowled at them both in turn. "Don't you two have anything better to do than moon over my wife?"

Oliver sat up suddenly. "Oy, that bloke is getting awfully too close, wouldn't you say?"

"That bloke, Oliver my lad, is the Duke of Clarence," Derrick said dryly. "You might want to leave him alone."

"He's still standing a mite too close," Oliver said, rising effortlessly to his feet. "I'll just go be a presence."

Derrick imagined he would. He lost Peter a few minutes afterward only to be soon joined by Cameron himself and Samantha's father, Richard. He looked first at his father-in-law.

"What do you think?"

"I think she's wonderful," Richard said frankly. "And she deserves every bit of success she's having tonight."

Derrick had to agree. He looked at his cousin. "Thank you."

Cameron shrugged, but he was smiling. "I didn't do anything."

"You married your wife who is keeping my wife from sicking up her supper on the Duke of Clarence's well-polished shoes."

Cameron laughed a little. "There is that, I suppose." He

shook his head. "You two are quite a pair. Why do I have the feeling you're not only going to be buying a bigger flat here in London, but one in Stratford as well?"

"One show a year," Derrick said. "Samantha insisted."

"And you stomped your little foot and refused until she insisted, is that it?"

Derrick looked at his cousin coolly. "You're about to lose your good seats, you know."

Cameron only laughed a little. "I want you to feel properly abused over that mighty secret you kept for so long. And nay, you needn't return the favor, though I am curious why you're only doing one a year."

"I don't think I can stand being in the same ten square miles with Connor more often than that."

"He behaved himself this summer," Cameron pointed out.

"Aye, because a ghost or two I know paid him a visit or two," Derrick said with a snort. He looked at Cameron, then shook his head. "How I got mixed up in anything of a paranormal nature, I don't know."

"Has it been worth it?" Cameron asked with a faint smile.

"Of course."

Derrick found himself soon abandoned by his companions. Aye, he would have to make another list and add it to the Cameron-Drummond Book of Lists that Samantha tended religiously. Because his wife was a maker of lists and he liked making lists of the things he loved about her as often as possible.

He stood up when he saw her walking toward him, then sighed lightly as she walked into his embrace.

"Well?" he asked quietly.

"Gavin's chortling. I think that means it was a success."

"He's glaring daggers at me, which tells me it was a huge success." He pulled back only far enough to look at her. "Are you finished with being feted, or shall we stay?"

She paused, then took his hand. "Just one more thing."

He followed her across the gallery, then around a corner to a hallway he hadn't been down before. He frowned at the pictures hanging on the walls because they weren't paintings, they were photographs.

"Is your brother stealing photographers now?" he asked with a half laugh.

"You'll see."

He continued with her to the end of the wall, then jumped a little when she simply pulled a picture off the wall.

"Sam, I'm not sure he'll be able to live with this," he warned.

She took a deep breath, turned, then handed him the framed photograph.

"What's this?" he asked.

"Oh, just something I Photoshopped," she said dismissively. "I'm not a good photographer, but they were images I thought you might like." She looked up at him and smiled. "Just a little thank-you for tonight."

He looked at the photograph and shook his head slowly. There was the Globe—something he would lay money on Oliver having taken in the past—then their house in Scotland, then the sea washing up to both. Roses bloomed between the theater and the house, just as they did in their favorite garden in Stratford. He started to compliment her, then looked more closely. He could have been wrong, perhaps, but he was just certain in front of the Globe was the faint imagine of a man dressed in an Elizabethan doublet and hose. He looked at Samantha.

"Who is that?"

"Sir Richard Drummond." She shrugged. "I had to paint him, because he doesn't photograph very well."

He started to speak, then shook his head. "I won't ask. I am curious, though, why black and white?"

She shrugged. "It felt old."

"Why the roses? Are they from Stratford?"

"Scotland," she said. "From Sunny's garden. Because you took me out there in the moonlight and made me feel beautiful." She smiled up at him. "That's all."

He put his arms around her and held her close for several minutes, finding himself in spite of his usual glibness simply unable to speak.

"I love you," he managed finally.

"I love you," she said, hugging him tightly. "Let's go home."

Two men leaned against the outside wall of the gallery and watched as a handsome couple was picked up in a sleek black Mercedes and ferried off to their home.

"Well, Ambrose," said one, "that was a right proper evening for them both."

"Aye, Hugh, it was," said the other. "All's well that ends well, especially when there are canny Scots behind the scenes."

The first sighed and flexed his fingers. "Heard Drummond's doing *King Lear* tonight."

"Well, the Globe is just around the corner."

"I've brought tomatoes and other overripe fruits appropriate for the moment."

And then Ambrose MacLeod, laird of the clan MacLeod during the marvelous flowering of the Renaissance, smiled, pushed away from the wall, and then followed his compatriot into the cool evening air.

family lineage in the books of
Lynn Kurland

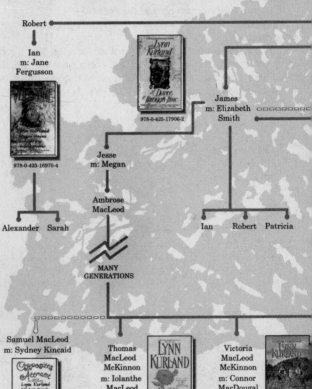

Robert

Ian
m: Jane
Fergusson

978-0-425-16970-4

Jesse
m: Megan

978-0-425-17906-2

James
m: Elizabeth
Smith

Ambrose
MacLeod

Alexander   Sarah

Ian   Robert   Patricia

⟋⟍ MANY
GENERATIONS

Samuel MacLeod
m: Sydney Kincaid

978-0-515-12865-9

Thomas
MacLeod
McKinnon
m: Iolanthe
MacLeod

978-0-425-18197-3

Victoria
MacLeod
McKinnon
m: Connor
MacDougal

978-0-515-14127-6

MACLEOD

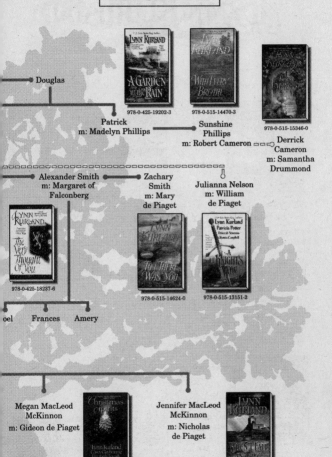

Douglas

Patrick
m: Madelyn Phillips

978-0-425-19202-3

978-0-515-14470-3

Sunshine
Phillips
m: Robert Cameron

978-0-515-15346-0

Derrick
Cameron
m: Samantha
Drummond

Alexander Smith
m: Margaret of
Falconberg

Zachary
Smith
m: Mary
de Piaget

Julianna Nelson
m: William
de Piaget

978-0-425-18237-6

978-0-515-14624-0

978-0-515-13151-2

oel   Frances   Amery

Megan MacLeod
McKinnon
m: Gideon de Piaget

978-0-515-12174-2

Jennifer MacLeod
McKinnon
m: Nicholas
de Piaget

978-0-515-14296-9

PA-8265

family lineage in the books of
Lynn Kurland

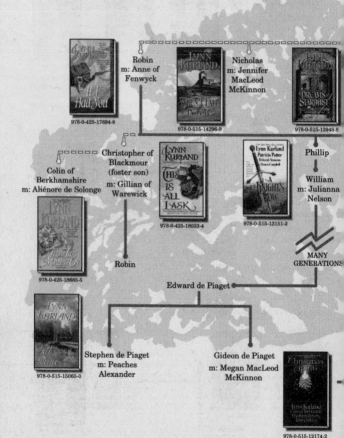

If I Had You
978-0-425-17694-8

Robin
m: Anne of Fenwyck

When I Fall in Love
978-0-515-14296-9

Nicholas
m: Jennifer MacLeod McKinnon

Dreams of Stardust
978-0-515-13948-8

Colin of Berkhamshire
m: Aliénore de Solonge

Christopher of Blackmour (foster son)
m: Gillian of Warewick

This Is All I Ask
978-0-425-18033-4

A Knight's Vow
Lynn Kurland, Patricia Potter, Deborah Simmons & Glynnis Campbell
978-0-515-13151-2

Phillip

William
m: Julianna Nelson

Much Ado in the Moonlight
978-0-425-18685-5

Robin

MANY GENERATIONS

Edward de Piaget

My Heart Stood Still
978-0-515-15065-0

Stephen de Piaget
m: Peaches Alexander

Gideon de Piaget
m: Megan MacLeod McKinnon

Christmas Spirits
Lynn Kurland, Casey Claybourne, Elizabeth Bevarly & Jenny Lykins
978-0-515-12174-2

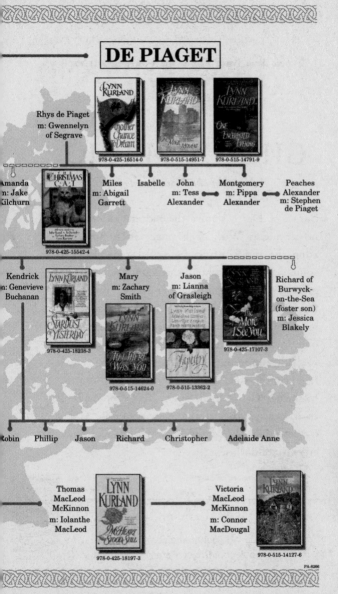

DE PIAGET

Rhys de Piaget
m: Gwennelyn
of Segrave

978-0-425-16514-0 978-0-515-14951-7 978-0-515-14791-9

Amanda
m: Jake
Kilchurn

Miles
m: Abigail
Garrett

Isabelle

John
m: Tess
Alexander

Montgomery
m: Pippa
Alexander

Peaches
Alexander
m: Stephen
de Piaget

978-0-425-15542-4

Kendrick
m: Genevieve
Buchanan

Mary
m: Zachary
Smith

Jason
m: Lianna
of Grasleigh

Richard of
Burwyck-
on-the-Sea
(foster son)
m: Jessica
Blakely

978-0-425-18238-3 978-0-515-14624-0 978-0-515-13362-2 978-0-425-17107-3

Robin Phillip Jason Richard Christopher Adelaide Anne

Thomas
MacLeod
McKinnon
m: Iolanthe
MacLeod

Victoria
MacLeod
McKinnon
m: Connor
MacDougal

978-0-425-18197-3 978-0-515-14127-6

PA-8266

B

From *New York Times* bestselling author

Lynn Kurland

GIFT OF MAGIC

A Novel of the Nine Kindoms

Sarah of Doìre knows the pattern of spells is no accident. With each page, each powerful rune, she and Ruith are being led somewhere, to someone—but by whom, she cannot tell. Sarah's gift of sight only allows her to see the spells themselves, not the person behind them.

A reluctant sorcerer still learning to trust his own magic, Ruithneadh of Ceangail knows he's woefully unprepared for the adversaries they'll face. But he and Sarah must collect and destroy his father Gair's spells soon. Many mages seek their power, and in the wrong hands, Gair's magic would plunge the Nine Kingdoms into an eternity of darkness.

LynnKurland.com
facebook.com/ProjectParanormalBooks
penguin.com

M1137T0712